BLOWING EMBERS

BOOK TWO OF THE EMBERS SERIES

Lauri J Owen

PEARLSONG PRESS
NASHVILLE, TN

Pearlsong Press
P.O. Box 58065
Nashville, TN 37205
1-866-4-A-PEARL
www.pearlsong.com
www.pearlsongpress.com

Trade paperback ISBN: 9781597190596
Ebook ISBN: 9781597190602

Book & Cover Design by Zelda Pudding.
Zodiac/Sun image by Starblue.

Library of Congress Cataloging-in-Publication Data

Owen, Lauri J.
   Blowing embers / Lauri J Owen.
      p. cm.— (The embers series ; bk. 2)
   ISBN 978-1-59719-059-6 (trade pbk. : alk. paper)—ISBN 978-1-59719-060-2 (ebk.)
   1. Wizards—Fiction. 2. Indigenous peoples—Alaska—Fiction. 3. Shapeshifting—Fiction. 4. Alaska—Fiction. I. Title. II. Series.

PS3615.W43B56 2011
813'.6—dc22

2011018695

This one is for my two wonderful manuscript readers,
Lesleigh and Philippa,
without whose tireless work
this series would have been less than a passing thought.

CHAPTER I

SOME SAY DEATH GLIDES IN ON ANGEL-BLACK WINGS, while others say that it kisses away one's last breath like a gentle grandmother. Kiera's reaper, however, hurtled down the frosted field on four razor-clawed feet.

Narrowed eyes sharpened the terrifying vision of more than two thousand pounds of raging bear, leaping as he ran, and larger with every heartbeat.

So much larger.

Again she set her feet and leaned forward, hands up. Her throat squeezed when she swallowed.

"Hold it fast," Lady Agni yelled from the sideline, spurring a snake of annoyance to wind through Kiera's chest.

Adrenalin shook her hands, numbed her lips. Further crisped the details of the horror coming for her: ruddy fur, erect on rippling shoulders. The needle white of bared teeth. The grunt of forced breath each time those massive front feet crushed circles into the snow.

And then he was there.

What must have been fifty thousand pounds of force slammed into her Air shield, shoved her back three yards and to her knees.

The shield held, and fire sung in her veins. "Ahh!" she screamed joyously. Defiantly. Her feet pushed her back up as she leaned forward and fed more air into the space between them, forcing him back.

Undaunted, the bear continued his drive. Twisting like a cornered wolverine, he clawed furiously, used knife blade teeth to tear the unseen barrier between them, but as her air continued to flow the space grew larger, wider, and she knew he was losing. All at once he drew back, away from the shield's edge, and in that split second Kiera wondered if he would accede defeat. A smile began as he threw himself like a supplicant to the ground at her feet, but instead of begging her mercy, open jaws roared his furor. Giant claws blurred, ripped bloody gashes into the black earth dividing them.

Too late Kiera understood, and before she could send a sheet of air deep into the winter's dead soil between them, the knife's-blade claws broke through to her side of the shield. Without pausing he leapt up and back, lifted the shield, and Kiera, off the ground. A vision of trees, mountains, fog, and sky flashed across her eyes, and her breath, and the elemental air that she held *oomph*ed out when her back slammed into the snow.

An enormous naked man landed on top of her, a rare grin lighting his face. For a moment she stared into deep brown eyes set in a god's rugged mien, skin as dark and warm as umber, as the wind blew a tendril of black hair across his jaw.

"Damn it," she wheezed.

Instead of answering, he kissed her mouth.

She pressed her own smile away and shoved him back. "Get your clothes on, you barbarian."

Still grinning, he offered a hand up, and as he dressed she brushed snow and mud off her backside. As her posterior could attest, even in late spring here in the alternate Alaska she'd been swept to late last year—cycle—the mornings bled cold. And the fog clung like a frightened child to the granite tips of the mountains most every day—turn—until late afternoon. Break-up would come soon, she hoped, this month—moon—like it did in the Alaska she'd come from, thawing the rivers and ponds, tempting flowers out of moons of hiding, and forcing the green back into the birches. Just as back home, the sun stayed longer each turn, and soon it would shine for all her waking hours—marks—plus many more. And she yearned for its warmth. For a moment she wondered if other people, those not akin to fire, craved its touch as much as she did, ached as keenly for its loss during the long winter nights.

Cheers and a spattering of applause drew her attention back to the fifty-odd people lining the lane her husband had just traversed, and she felt a twinge of pride for the soldiers, shifters and not, former slaves all, standing, watching the display with pleasure writ large on their faces. In less than a moon of training many had learned how to call strands of the element under which they were born, and to which they were akin, and some had even learned to fashion a shield similar to the one she had used to hold off her bear. She hoped these shields would protect these soldiers, her soldiers, from magical attacks, and today—thisturn—she was trying to learn wheth-er they could hold up against shifter attacks as well. It had seemed to work.

Well, until he'd cheated anyway.

With a sigh, Kiera turned and walked to Lady Agni, the most powerful

Skani mage Kiera knew, and her teacher in the ways of Alaska magic.

"Yes, Lady Agni, I know what I did wrong," she grumbled, but Agni raised a hand.

"Yes, Governor Kiera, you now see the need to anchor the shield, but your true mistake happened after he *gained* the shield."

Kiera opened, then closed her mouth.

"In a true battle, you must not give up just because your first line of defense has been breached." Agni's tone grew grim. "Instead of correcting your mistake, Lady Kiera, you let Lord Laszlo lift your shield, with you anchored to it, and drop you to the ground, where you lay vulnerable to his next attack. And because it was your husband, you simply gave in when he did so, and Governor Kiera, *you must not*. What you do in training is what you will do in battle."

Chagrined, Kiera grimaced, then nodded. "Of course you're right, Lady Agni. On every count." She turned to Laszlo. "How did you know to dig under it?"

He lifted a shoulder. "There is always a way in, *a'kala*."

"A good lesson," Lady Agni admonished mercilessly, and Kiera frowned. But Agni was right. Being a strong mage was fine, but that wouldn't be enough help unless she learned how to think like a soldier. And it was hard not to worry herself sick about mistakes like that, with war a certainty. The only unknown was when, though it would doubtless be soon.

No, she thought; another unknown was how many Governor Vrishka commanded. And how well they fought. And if they had allies.

Kiera wiped a hand across her face, and turned back to the line. "Who wants to go next? I'll attack with fire." Her mood lightened a little when the color fell from the faces closest to her.

THE WARMTH OF THE STABLES radiated above the roofline, beckoning the soldiers in to thaw the frost from their bones. Kiera hurried inside and plopped into a chair tucked next to the brazier. Shoulders shuddered as the radiant warmth began piercing her chill, and she scooted her chair as close as she dared. Despite popular myth, being plump did absolutely nothing to ward off the cold.

Agni had trotted back up to the manse, but many of the men had followed her here to the next training session. Well, some of the *otuks*, the soldiers whose authority lay something below the captain's, had, anyway. They bustled in, letting the chill breeze suck a measure of heat from the room every time they opened the door, and Kiera nearly climbed onto the stove. She finally stood and thrust her hands over the radiating steel, and turned to watch their faces as they stumbled in. Some grinned while they made small talk, and some elbowed and joked with others. Some smiled at her when they caught her eye or as they found their seats, and she marveled at how completely the soldiers now seemed to accept her compared to when she'd first landed here.

Here. Where was that—exactly?

Well, it was called Alaska. Just like the place she'd come from—one of the fifty United States. The place from which an unnatural flame had stolen her by means she did not yet understand. But, well, *here* was where she and her nephew, Alex, had found themselves lost, cast into a country whose terrain, weather, and an odd proclivity for same names rendered it a virtual copy of the Alaska whose flag held the big dipper, but the similarities ended there.

Here in this alternate Alaska, some people commanded elements and were named mage. What elements, and to what degree they could call them, depended on the turn and the time their mothers had finally pushed them into the world. Those were the Skani, the people she most resembled, but even though she, too, could do magic, she refused to name herself one.

Others, the indigenous people, held the ability to shift their shapes, and she had learned that the Alaks, the shifters, could transform themselves at will into bears, or wolves, or coyotes, depending on the tribe to which they belonged. *Oh. And dogs.* A vision of her own near-death spiked an icy chill as she recalled the last time the Shunakah, the giant snow dogs, had graced her eyes.

The door opened again and she lifted her eyes to Laszlo's, who would soon be lessoning the *otuk*s on some aspect of battle strategies. A smile started on his face when he caught her staring, startling a return grin from her, and as he held her eyes a softness filled her chest, wrapping her with the warmth that her feet still craved. *God*, she loved that man. And she knew—could see it every time he looked at her—that he loved her as much, and maybe more than she loved him, if such were possible. That his love was a blessing, a miracle, was an understatement. The love with which he gifted her had healed her heart and filled her world.

All of which would have led to the inevitable happy ending, she was sure, if not for the fact that another city's—deconn's—ruler had taken issue with the fact that she and Laszlo, among others, had overthrown the last governor of Fairbanks, her deconn. Undoubtedly they would soon come to try and overthrow her. Well, too, the fact that Alex's father, one of the Shunakah, desperately wanted his son back might complicate her plans for happiness as well. He'd murdered her sister back in the old Alaska, but had somehow found his way here as well, and had tried to kill her once, and maybe twice. The fact that Alex would be a shifter, too, was a complication she couldn't bear to think much about just yet.

Her smile slipped away and a sigh escaped her before she could catch it. Laszlo drew his brows down and started making his way across the room to her. Feeling chagrined, she summoned a smile and lifted a hand to stop him. She needed to stop worrying and focus on the tasks at hand. They were here to learn warfare, and she needed to let him teach it.

He stopped and tilted his head just slightly. Perhaps evaluating the truth in her smile. The concern she read on his face sparked a wash of tenderness, which she let rise to the surface, and after the briefest of pauses, he nodded and turned back to the front of the room.

Maybe because her body had spent every ounce of adrenalin her fear had invoked, she relaxed perhaps too deeply into the cushion cradling her back and found herself thinking dreamy thoughts. Her eyes, aided by the flickering firelight, gave Laszlo a surreal cast. He seemed to tower above the men seated in front of him, a primordial storyteller, arms akimbo as if to release gems of wisdom to the ignorant masses. His lips spilled jeweled words that rode a soft green ribbon through the inky room, brushing faces and tickling ears, but for her the sounds had abandoned all pretense of meaning.

But not even dreams could blur his heartwrenching beauty. A strong man, a big man, bigger than any she knew, with a face like iron. Many feared him, but she never had. Those hands he held up often held her, too tightly, and peace and pleasure soon followed. Always followed.

When she yawned, she noted his meaningful pause. She met his eyes and smiled her apology, but her traitorous heart couldn't summon any guilt. The truth was that she would never be commanding an army, never, much less designing a grand battle strategy, or deciding how many troops to send where. That was Laszlo's job. Laszlo's and the *otuks*'. And maybe Marco's, their co-ruler's, despite his absence from tonight's lesson, but lately he'd been too busy, uh, spending time with his bride-to-be to find much time for training.

Perhaps as tired as she, the sun had slid behind the mountains by the time Laszlo finished his lecture. Feet still up, Kiera waited in her chair as the men filed out. Too intoxicated by the warmth of the brazier to want to move, she instead waited for him to come sit with her. Soon he did, followed by an Alak she didn't recognize. They both remained standing, but she held her seat, hoping they would either sit or politely ignore her breach in etiquette.

"I was flattered by your rapt attention, *a'kala*," Laszlo told her blandly, and she looked up and into his face, and wondered how annoyed he felt.

"Sorry, sorry. I am just—exhausted. Please forgive me, Laszlo." She sat up, away from the brazier's heat, and tried to look repentant. "Thisturn was so busy—and some turns I still find myself feeling a little weak."

He pressed his lips into a line, and Kiera wished she'd kept that confession to herself. That look meant he'd start coddling her again.

Maybe to avoid further unease, Laszlo switched topics. "*A'kala*, Kiera, I present Kuruk."

Kiera leaned forward to get a better look at the man whom her husband's hulking frame nearly hid, and who bowed deeply when Laszlo spoke his name.

"Please rise, Kuruk," she told him tiredly, and when he did, she forced herself to add, "I am pleased to know you."

Something seemed familiar about his face, but she couldn't quite place it. "We've met before, I think, Kuruk. Where?"

His back stiffened, but he refused to meet her eyes.

Laszlo pretended not to notice. "As of nexturn, *Otuk* Kuruk will serve in the manse."

"Oh, welcome, Kuruk," Kiera said a little more enthusiastically. "You will like working in the manse, I think. Especially now that we have Alak and *nuwyr* representatives meeting every turn, there's always something to do."

"As your *talu*," Laszlo added, an unmistakable glint in his eye.

"My what?"

"The soldier who accompanies you as you go about your tasks."

"*A bodyguard?* Oh for heaven's sake, Laszlo. I'm safe inside the city! And besides, we're together most all day, er, turn, and all night." She sat back and folded her arms. She knew he worried, but this was nothing short of ridiculous.

He wore a mulish face. "No, *a'kala*. Our tasks take us apart. You are still weak, and often preoccupied—" that seemed pretty pointed—"and Kuruk is someone who will not permit himself to be."

Kiera opened her mouth, but looked up at Kuruk, who radiated unease. A sigh slid out instead of the words waiting just behind her tongue, and she swallowed them down. She'd settle this with Laszlo later.

KIERA MADE HER WAY BACK toward the manse alone. She let Laszlo and—what was his name? Kuruk?—go on ahead so she could stop by the greenhouse and see if the latest batch of salmonberry wine was ready. Once processed, makers aged it in wooden barrels for moons, and she was pretty sure that a batch was due for bottling—and salmonberry wine, made from the berries grown inside this very greenhouse, was a taste she'd come to crave.

Lorgda milled around inside, humming softly to himself as he watered plants. The bright feeding lights had been dimmed for the night, and in the near darkness a stranger might not notice the concavity that encompassed the left side of his face, a horrendous injury an unnamed mage—but one she suspected she knew—had inflicted on him while he was still a slave. His face would probably never look serene, but he seemed content here where he could work alone. Things had changed some since Vayu had gone, and Lorgda had come to her privately and asked to have his assignment changed from tending pigs to plants. Although many people wanted this job in the ever-warm greenhouse, choosing him for it had been easy.

The shadows hid her from notice until she shifted—just a soft rustle of her coat, but he noticed, and looked up, alarmed.

"Good eve, Lorgda," she called, and stepped into what light the house offered.

His posture relaxed. He leaned over a plant and plucked a wayward leaf before turning back. "Good eve, Governor. And how might I help you?"

"I came to see how the salmonberry wine was coming."

The light made it hard to see, but Kiera swore a tiny smile flashed across his face. "And you wondered if you might have a bottle before I ship it to the manse."

"Well, yes, since you asked. I'm down to that stuff you serve in the great hall. No offense, Lorgda, but, uh, I prefer the salmonberry."

Lorgda took ten steps toward the back of the greenhouse and disappeared through a doorway. In a handful of minutes, and to Kiera's glee, he emerged carrying a bottle in each hand.

"Oh, thank you, Lorgda!" Kiera beamed, and trotted over to take them. "I can't tell you how much I appreciate it!"

"These are a little early, Governor, but I will get you some better juice in two turns, maybe three. Will these tide you 'til then?"

Kiera grinned. "I'll do my best to make them last."

With her treasures cradled in her arms, she left the greenhouse. Full dark had fallen, so she slowed her pace so as not to trip. One true joy this land had gifted her was salmonberry wine, and she wasn't going to let tired feet stumble while she carried it through the wending stone path back to the manse, and her apartment.

Night made this path tricky. While the sun shone, workers cut and reset stone along the west wall of the manse, which had taken some damage during the brief, but successful, slave rebellion. At night they left their tools, and pieces of stone, lying in wait for the next turn's labor. Concentrating on every step, she failed to hear the telltale sounds until she turned a corner and ran right into someone's back.

Faster than she could blink, the someone turned and flat-palmed her cheek, then shoved her backward. Without arms for balance, Kiera stumbled back, once, twice, comically, and sat down hard on the ground. Her right hand tried to brace for the fall and glass shards from the broken bottle bit into her palm. The crash the bottle made as it flew apart came after.

Stunned, she sat for a moment on the ground, watching the blackness of the spilled wine soak into the snow. A shadow blocked the scant light, then passed, and she looked up.

Two men fought nearly silently now, a big-bodied shifter and a blond Skani, caught in each other's arms as they pummeled every spot their free hands could reach. It was too dark to see their faces, but she didn't waste time wondering who they were. She'd heard that these fights were happening, Skani against Alak, Alak against Skani, and in some cases Skani against Skani. One thing all had in common was that one of the fighters had invariably been a slave and the other was an awyr, one of the middle class of mages. Maybe some of the Alaks were trying to right wrongs, claim vengeance against one who had hurt them, and not that that was right, but other times the violence seemed utterly senseless, just a product of hate and intolerance. Change came slowly, Marco had told her, but this was absurd. What was she supposed to do? Condone it? Pretend not to see it?

No.

One bottle, the one her left hand held, had miraculously survived her fall, so she leaned back and anchored it in the snow next to the wall behind her. Using her one good hand, she braced herself and stood. She bladed her posture, set her feet and, in less time than it took to draw a breath, called air.

"Stop this!" she shouted, and sent a basketball of air ahead of her words.

They flew apart, and then down when it hit them. One, the Skani, jumped up, snarling, and lunged for her. With a gusty sigh, she raised a hand and sent an air-cleaved hardball into his gut.

"Just stop already!" she scolded as he collapsed into the snow, retching, then reached back to grab her wine. "This fighting is just stupid. You should both be ashamed!"

The shifter tackled her and down they both fell.

With a sharp crack, his first punch smashed her eye closed and ripped a screech from her lungs. "You bastard!" she screamed, and slapped him hard, then again, and tried to shove him off. She bucked up and slid out her feet, but instead of finding an anchor, her heels slid lines in the slick snow. His next punch was clumsy—she blocked it easily, then locked her fingers and slammed her fist into his nose.

His hand rose as blood spattered across both their faces, then gushed through open fingers and dripped dark circles onto her dress. Gritting her teeth, she used air to slide the stunned man off and rose to her knees. The first man still lay where he'd fallen, eyes open wide, so she turned to retrieve her wine.

"Damn it," she snarled as she lifted the broken neck off the corpse of her final bottle. She leaned over it, preparing to mourn, but felt a spark of good cheer rise instead. Not much of the wine had spilled, and if she carried it with tender hands, she could save the bulk of what remained.

Lifting it gingerly, she turned to the men and let anger heat her voice. "Listen to me, you imbeciles. You both just attacked a governor of this deconn." Even in the frail light, she saw their faces lift, then blanch. *Good.* "I will not have any more of this fighting! I am charging you two to spread the word. Tell your friends, and everyone else you know that I will punish anyone who's found fighting out here." She took a breath, stared from face to face. "We're about to go to war, you idiots! Everyone in here will be relying on everyone else. That man," she pointed at the man she'd punched with air, "may be the one fighting off magical attacks to save your ass when Vrishka's army attacks, and this one," she pointed at the bloody shifter at her feet, "may be the one who stands between you and certain death when it comes to call in the form of a Shunakah."

Both men stared at the ground, and even in the brittle light she saw the Skani's hands shake when he clasped them in front of him. Although she knew they thought she expected shame, she hoped her words would spark insight. Still, she didn't want them frightened, not of her, so she softened her voice. "Oh, I'm not going to punish you. Not this time." A weary thought struck, and she spoke it without thinking. "Although I should, because now I am never going to get Laszlo to back down from that goddamned bodyguard. Ugh!"

Both men raised faces fraught with both fear and puzzlement, but she waved it off. "Never mind. Go see the healer—" she pointed a finger at one, then the other fighter—"but remember what I told you. The fighting stops, or I will start taking it personally. Do you hear me?"

Both nodded, and she turned back to the manse, her broken bottle held firmly between her hands.

BLOWING EMBERS

A MAN IN RED LIVERY stood just inside the main doors, the one spot, ironically, almost no one ever came through. Instead of grimacing she nodded at him, and hoped he wasn't there in wait for her. It was near dinnertime, and she'd come this way precisely because she hoped to gain the upper walkway and make her way to her apartment without anyone seeing her. She particularly hoped to avoid the main body of the people who would be gathering for dinner in the great hall, where she had insisted the residents of the manse, and rotating group of former slaves, now take evening meals. People had to start getting to know each other, and learning to trust each other. But before descending to her place at the table she needed to change out of her ruined dress and wash her blood-stained face. She still wasn't sure how she'd be able to hide her swollen eye.

Oh—and she had to find a new container to hold the precious liquid inside her broken bottle.

No expression rolled across the liveried man's face as he took in her appearance, but it must have been hard not to gape. "My Lady Governor, a visitor requests an immediate audience."

Kiera raised her eyebrows. "I'm not prepared to receive a visitor. They'll have to wait." But before she could flee up the stairs, a group rushed toward her, coming from the great hall.

Their faces came into focus as they marched closer. Lady Leith, the former governor's wife. Naga, lover of the former governor's son. Marco, also the former governor's son, but her dearest friend and lately her co-ruler as well. Another lady. Oh—it was Allie, Marco's fiancée.

And Chanda.

A sigh erupted, one born from the depths of her embarrassment and colored with no little anger as well. Bloody face. Dress a mess. There would be no hiding the fight she'd been in. And now, to top it off, Chanda.

Chanda. Charming, beautiful Chanda. Pretend slave sympathizer and a man she'd seriously considered bedding. Probable face smasher of at least one slave, and a would-be rapist. Of her.

CHAPTER 2

"**M**Y LADY KIERA," CHANDA SMILED, and kissed her hand as regally as if she didn't have spatters of blood coloring her face, an eye that had nearly swollen shut, and a broken bottle clasped tightly in her other fist. And still it took every ounce of self control she could summon not to peel his hand off hers.

She had expected to feel rage, and maybe fear when she next saw him, but instead simple embarrassment wrapped her tightly inside a shawl of unease. In lieu of reacting—she hoped, anyway—she pasted on her most meaningless smile. "Chanda." His eyes crinkled as he smiled, and she wondered whether his heart held humor at her appearance, or something more malignant. "Have you come home, then?"

"If you can spare me a half mark, I would speak with you, my lady," he evaded.

Marco's face held suppressed mirth, true amusement most likely at her disheveled appearance, and she wanted to slap him. Both Allie and Leith avoided her eyes, but Naga openly gaped, and she found herself wanting to slap them all as well. This night was not going well. And it wasn't going to get any better. Laszlo was going to be really mad when he found Chanda here. And, yeah, he wouldn't be terribly pleased that she'd fought, either.

Kiera heaved a sigh. "I have to change, Chanda, and so how about we talk a little later, okay?"

Chanda took a smooth step back and bowed at the waist. Marco grinned openly over his back, and the five of them turned and marched a path toward the great hall.

"Please don't hold dinner for me," she called to their backs, then mounted the stairs with legs as weary as her heart.

"KEER, KEER," HER YOUNG NEPHEW called as Kiera closed the door to her apartment.

She turned to face him and he stopped, open-mouthed.

"Oh, Kiera, what happened?" Emmy, Alex's nanny, gasped. She stood from her seat at the table and rushed over. Took the bottle from Kiera's hands. "Come sit down. Let me call a healer!"

Wearing a grimace, Kiera let Emmy lead her across the thick blue carpet to one of the couches crouched in the central area of her very blue home. With a flicker of thought, she lit the fireplace and leaned back into the overstuffed, earth-toned cushions, closed the one eye that hadn't swollen shut, and waited for the warmth to reach her.

"Don't call a healer, Emmy. I'm fine."

A clink as Emmy squeezed the bottle in next to others on the far table. "But Kiera, your face!"

Small hands found hers and she peeled open her eye to stare into Alex's, too large with concern, as he plopped down next to her on the couch.

"I'm fine," she told him, too. "I broke up a fight outside the house, is all."

"Did you bleed?" Alex asked her in a very serious voice.

"Nooo," she drew out the sound. "The other guy did. But I do need to clean up." She settled back and let the cushions cradle her back. "In just a minute." She opened her eye again. "Why are you still here? You should be down eating your dinner."

From somewhere behind her, Emmy answered instead. "Alex has something to ask you, Kiera." When he hesitated, Emmy stood and walked over. "Come on now, Alex. Ask her so we can go on down."

"Keer," he began, and squeezed her hand. Oh dear. This was something serious. She suppressed a frown and tried to look attentive.

But his words stole her breath. "Keer, I want to be a soldier." Shoulders lifted as he sat up straighter. His face looked so earnest, and the fear and determination she read in his wide brown eyes, eyes so much like her own, hurt her heart as much as the sounds doubtless issued from the folds of his. She understood this, even if she hadn't expected it. Not so soon. Not at nearly seven cycles old, for God's sake. But what had the last cycle held for him? The loss of his mother at the hands of his father. Being uprooted and forced to live with her, who had been, in truth, someone he hardly knew.

And then, last Christmas, a strange dog—a Shunakah, she now knew— had attacked them both outside their condo in the old Alaska, and had somehow triggered the unnatural flame that had transported them both here. And here—well, here he'd nearly been killed in a battle against an army of Shunakah and watched her nearly die. And again, when they'd overthrown Vayu. She'd almost died then. And now they awaited another war, one that every soul in the city openly feared.

He had to feel helpless. Did she have the heart to deny him the only way he could think of to try to feel safe? And a way that might well help him survive when the attack came?

His eyes watched her face, trying to follow the trickle her thoughts made.

"Let me think about it, Alex," she finally said, and rose from the couch. "Go and have your dinner, and tell Laszlo that I'll be down as soon as I change."

BUT LASZLO SLAMMED OPEN the door a handful of minutes later. Without preface, he stalked to where she stood next to the window and lifted her chin with a hand. With gentle fingers, he touched her swollen eye. He pressed his lips into a thin line and looked into her face.

A smile lifted her lips at the worry he strove so hard to conceal, but it was there, lurking just below the surface. The jaw he clenched, the eyes that narrowed just a fraction.

"I'm fine," she told him, and lifted to tiptoe to kiss his cheek. "Don't go barging off to wreak vengeance, either. I broke up a fight, is all, and if I hadn't been so tired, honestly, I would have seen this coming." She paused to grin. "I left them both chastised and cringing in the snow."

The muscle clamping his jaw relaxed just a little. "Chanda is here," he told her, jumping ahead to the next order of business.

"I know. I saw him downstairs when I came in. He rushed right over, surrounded by Leith and Naga, to ask for an audience."

Brows raised in an otherwise still face. "What did he want?"

"I don't know. I put him off." She paused. "Didn't he ask you for the same? I mean, didn't he ask to talk with you? Or us?"

The corner of Laszlo's lip twisted. "No, *a'kala*. Chanda knows better than to speak with me."

She watched his face, and wondered whether that was because he refused to recognize Laszlo, or because he was as afraid of Laszlo as Laszlo thought he was. Or both. "No. You're right. But whatever it is, I'm sure it isn't good."

"Come sit, *a'kala*."

"No, no. I'm fine. Really. I'd like something to eat." The wet, reasonably cool cloth had taken some of the swelling from her eye, and she'd washed the spatters of blood from her face and changed her dress. "Do you think I look all right to go down?"

He let a smile rise and linger. "No, *a'kala*. I think that you should let

Saman heal your eye. You can eat your dinner here. Please, sit."

The comfy couch beckoned, and she let him lead her back to it. "Alex asked me if he could become a soldier," she told him as she pulled her legs up.

His face showed no surprise as he lifted a fuzzy blanket from the couch's arm and wrapped it around her.

"Did you know?" she asked, suddenly suspicious.

"He did not ask me," he replied blandly.

"But you knew—what? That he would?"

His eyes met hers. "I know that he feels afraid, my heart. It is a frightening time. That he wants to learn to fight does not surprise me."

"He already knows how to fight," she told him as she settled back. "He was in martial arts training, the same stuff I know, for two cycles."

"It has not served him as well as he would like, I think," he told her gently.

"I know," she whispered as he sat down and lifted her feet into his lap. "But it scares me, Laszlo. I mean, I know that he'll just be training, and that no one would ever send a child out to fight, but is this really what he should be doing? I just don't know." She lifted her eyes from the fire and met his. "Do you think I should let him?"

His face was inscrutable, but he appeared to consider her words. "I believe," he finally answered, "that you will make your choice no matter my, or anyone's, thoughts."

It was hard not to sound tired. "Laszlo, I really do want to know what you think about this."

The fire sizzled as it chewed the final log in two. Without answering, Laszlo left the couch and tossed one, then another chunk of spruce into the open maw, then squatted in front of the hearth and settled them into place with his hands. Like her, fire did not burn him. He could even call it—a little, anyway, which no other shifter she knew could do, though all Alaks used earth energy, albeit unconsciously. A puzzle, indeed, and one that she was determined to solve once they had settled all the rest of this madness.

Before she could further prod him, someone knocked at the door. Laszlo rose smoothly and strode across the room. Saman stood outside, and as Laszlo led him over, Kiera wondered crossly who had summoned him.

"My Lady Governor. Oh dear," Saman clucked as he leaned over her to look into her face. "Will you please close both eyes, my lady?"

Warmth spread under his fingers as he brushed her cheekbone. Her breath slid out as the pressure leaked away, and followed a knot she hadn't realized her chest held, out her fingers and feet, leaving an empty stillness behind, and she found her back melting into the cushion's doughy embrace. Another breath, in and out, and sound came whispering back, silky notes stroking the lyre of silence. She opened her eyes—both eyes—and stared into the healer's kind blue ones.

"It was very minor," he assured her, "and I do not see any other damage. Did you take any other blows, my lady? Anything else that pains you?"

Her head felt a little muzzy, like she'd just awakened, and she tried to remember if she'd felt this way last time he'd healed her. She might have that time he healed her after fighting the Shunakah outside the manse, but she'd been pretty heartsick and might not have put the two together. "No," she replied with an absent shake of her head, but her right hand stung when she laid it flat to push herself up, so she lifted it, palm up. A small sound of frustration escaped her as she eyed the punctures.

Saman took her wrist in a gentle hand and pulled it up. His brows compressed as he swept the flats of his fingers across her palm, and when he released her hand, the damaged skin wore the pink of healing.

Her hand continued to heal as she watched it, and when the skin finished knitting itself together, she looked up at Saman's face. "How do you do healing? You do it so well. And so fast."

His smile looked shy. "Oh, thank you, my Lady Governor."

"Just Kiera is fine," she told him as she dropped her legs to the floor. "But please, sit. And tell me what you use, what elements, and how, if you don't mind."

His eyes flicked to Laszlo, then down at the floor before he lifted them to hers.

Kiera smiled her encouragement. "Please, Lord Saman. Sit. I've wanted to ask someone about how healing works for a long time, but I haven't had a chance until now."

The crackle of the fire punctuated the heavy silence. Perhaps to quiet Saman's unease, Laszlo stepped from behind Kiera's couch and dropped down next to her, leaned back and rested an arm behind Kiera. A moment later, Saman sat, a little hesitantly, on the opposite couch and folded his hands in his lap.

"What would you know, my Lady Governor?"

"Well, what elements do you use when you heal?"

He couldn't quite hide his struggle to keep her eyes, and Kiera wondered why in the world he felt so nervous. Was it a social gaffe to ask the healer to sit with her that had his socks in a knot? Or was it that he feared her anger at his answer? Or maybe it was a trade secret?

"Saman, if you would prefer not to discuss this, I would appreciate your recommendation of a book that explains how healing works, maybe one you'd give to a new healer or something. But if you're worried that I have some ulterior motive, I assure you that my interest is completely genuine."

If not for the slight relaxation in his legs, she would have missed the lump of tension leaving his body. She still wondered what he had thought, and if she could figure it out. "No, no, my lady. I will of course tell you whatever you wish to know."

"What elements do you use to work a healing?" she asked for the third time, and hoped her face looked warm. And patient.

The smile that brushed his lips seemed genuine. "Healing, my lady, requires manipulation of all four elements."

Kiera leaned forward. "Do you use the elements inside someone, then, or call more, or both?"

As she'd hoped, Saman warmed to his topic. "Oh, both, my lady. Oftentimes in injuries tissues are crushed, segments torn, and so it's a matter of reinflating, urging parts back open." He used the first two fingers of a hand to gesture as he spoke. "The tears must be closed as the tissues are molded back into shape and reconnected. If the tearing is too grievous, or a section has been too damaged, elements are used to create new sheets, which are grafted to the living tissue."

As excited as Saman, Kiera found herself nodding. "That makes sense. And you use what, earth? Water?"

Saman's smile was a little too bright. "Oh, all elements are needed, my lady."

Ah. "Lord Saman, I know how Lord Vayu felt about using earth and water energy. I assure you that I don't hold the same prejudices. I have used earth, and in fact all of the elements, in my own workings, and I am pretty sure I've done some healing myself," Kiera smiled in what she hoped was a deprecating manner, "though I will admit that I'm not exactly sure how I did it."

Pure excitement on his face, Saman leaned over his legs in a mirror of Kiera's posture. "Truly?"

"When I first called fire, before I knew what I was doing, I managed to heal myself, and Alex, too," she lifted a hand to her neck, "from some fairly significant damage."

"It was a fair healing for a novice," Saman nodded, and his voice held real praise. "I noted it when you came in with the shoulder puncture. What did you use?"

"I think I used earth. Earth and maybe fire. A mix."

Saman nodded again. "That is what my students would use. Earth carried in fire to close the worst wounds. But for complete healing, it requires water as well. Knitted in."

"Pulled, or used from the person?"

"Both, both, my lady."

A frown pressed her lips together, and Kiera sat back. "I'm not very good with water. I don't like it."

Laszlo's voice startled her. "Is healing difficult to learn?"

Saman met Laszlo's gaze. "Learning skilled healing is very difficult, and does not come easy for most, if that is your question. One must manipulate complicated spells, spun and sent quickly, and it requires an enormous input of elemental energy. If the damage is significant, the casting of two or three at nearly the same time. One for breath, one to work the tissue, one for comfort from pain, or to maintain deep sleep. Most mages use many strands, a great quantity of energy, and find it challenging to scale their pulling and spinning so precisely, as well as working that quickly, as time is often a factor."

Kiera sat up. "Would you be willing to teach others to heal? Even rudimentary skills will save lives. We will soon need more healers, Lord Saman, when we go outside the deconn."

Saman stood, and bowed. "I am yours to command, my Lady Governor." His gaze flicked to Laszlo's. "She needs to rest, my lord. I recommend a light dinner and an early night."

That he gave her husband directions for her care raised her hackles more than just a bit. "I can't do that, Lord Saman, but thank you," she told him. "I have to meet with several groups yet tonight, as well as a—" She gestured with a hand, trying to find the right word. "A—guest later this evening."

The men passed a look between them as Kiera pushed the blanket off and stood. "I am fine," she told them both, "so you two can stop with the meaningful looks. Good night, Lord Saman, and thank you."

Saman bowed and retreated swiftly. Emmy entered as he opened the door, a tray in her hands.

"Lay it on the table, Emmy, and then you may leave us," Laszlo told her blandly as he settled back on the couch.

Brows raised as Kiera watched Emmy lay out her dinner and hurry out of the room, but she flashed Kiera a relieved smile as she closed the door. With a small shake of her head, Kiera sat back down and pinched her husband's leg. "How did Saman know to come, Laszlo, and Emmy to bring dinner?"

Although she could tell a smile lurked, it never rose to the surface. Instead, he sounded matter of fact. "I sent for Saman and told Emmy to bring up your dinner before I left the great hall."

Exasperation warred with tenderness in her chest. Yes, he was consistently high-handed with her, especially when it had anything to do with her health or her safety, and yet she understood it and, if she told herself the truth, she wasn't sure she wouldn't do the same. And yet it rubbed. Still, she loved his strength and his stubbornness, the two strands that, if they were elements, would be the twin lifestreams that flowed through his body, and made his heart beat.

She made a face as she rose to plop down at the table. This man, the one who would ride down the Devil to get what he wanted, might at times raise her ire when he pulled the reins from her hands, but because what he did for her he did out of love, because that kind of love was a precious gift, he deserved her understanding. And perhaps her patience as well.

"I'm sorry for worrying you," she told him as she smeared blueberry jam onto a piece of bread. "I'm tired, and I haven't felt well the past few turns." In truth, she hadn't felt completely healthy since—well, since Vayu had nearly killed her, but that secret she held close, and would until this crisis had passed, or until it resolved itself. It seemed reasonable that it would take some time to completely heal from the vast injuries she'd sustained, and if something wasn't healing right, she was sure Saman could fix it. But not now. She needed to do what she could to get them ready for whatever was coming. "It was worse this morning. I think I'm fighting something off. Being sick always puts me a little off kilter." She looked up at his face and tried to read whether he'd bought her story. "I really am sorry."

Without revealing a clue of what he thought, he walked over and pulled out the chair next to her, then sat. With one hand, he pinched an errant strand of her hair, then brushed it out between his fingers, and she felt her shoulders relax.

The pie smelled good, so she spooned some onto her plate. "What do you think Chanda wants?" she asked him, and took a bite. "This is heavenly!" she exclaimed through her full mouth. "You should have some!"

His lips quirked as she fed him a spoonful, and he watched her eyes as he chewed it. "Chanda has been with Vrishka," he began, and the muscles clenched in Kiera's stomach. "I believe that he returned to bring Vrishka's words to us."

She laid down her spoon. "What words would Vrishka send Chanda to tell?"

One shoulder rose as he shrugged. "Terms."

Kiera shook her head to show she didn't follow. "Terms of—what? Surrender?"

"Surrender. A peace accord." He shrugged again. "Both."

She started to stand, but he rested a hand on her forearm. "Laszlo, I have to go find out. Besides, I need to meet with the Skani, uh—" she closed her eyes and searched the elements for a half breath—"in about a half mark. They want to start the brooding parties again, and I promised to listen to their reasons. I'll talk to you and Marco about it nexturn. But I think you should go with me to meet with Chanda."

"Stay," he urged, voice silky, and Kiera felt her lips lift at his unspoken invitation.

"Cheater," she accused softly.

His hand squeezed her arm as he leaned over and brushed a kiss on her cheek, then her mouth. "I have already told Leith that you will meet with her in the morning," his husky voice told her lips.

A sigh escaped her, but her will to flee the contentment wrapping this moment had fled. And his shirt had come open at the top, revealing skin she very much wanted her hands on. Hiding a smile, she moved out her chair and straddled his lap. "You seem to have removed every roadblock, Laszlo," she told him sternly as she slipped her fingers into the gap between the two woolen flaps fronting his shirt. "Except for Alex. Unless, of course, you arranged for him to stay gone for the evening, too?"

"Yes," he whispered as his hungry mouth met hers.

CHAPTER 3

A THROBBING HEADACHE WOKE KIERA to agonizing pain. Through slotted eyes she cast an evil glare at the dawn's defiant fingers, sliding past the heavy curtains to tickle the room's edges. Holding her eyes closed, she slid off the bed and made her way to the bathroom. Somewhere here she'd stashed a packet of pain reliever, although remembering exactly where proved something of a challenge to her freshly woken and tormented head.

Her stomach knotted and turned, so she plopped down on the floor and rested her head against the cold stone of the wall. A picture of her mother flashed through her thoughts—face pinched with pain, she took tens of pain relievers and hid under blankets for an entire turn, and sometimes two, trying to survive one of her migraines. "God," she whispered, "please don't let this be a migraine." Stress. It had to be stress. God knew there was enough of that.

With a final growl her stomach eased a little, and as it did she remembered where she'd stored the pain reliever—in the basket next to the toilet, right next to the sour stomach tincture. She reached it without getting up and tore it open, then poured half of the bitter powder into her mouth. Nearly gagging, she chewed it to bring saliva into her mouth, and forced herself to swallow it down. Within moments precious relief poured through her, and as it did she sighed and leaned back against the wall.

When she felt better—and she was surprised at how good she felt, and so quickly— she used the toilet, then started a bath. Although she hadn't looked when she rose, she knew Laszlo had been gone for no more than a mark since the room still felt warm, and she could take a bath if she hurried since she wouldn't have to wait for the fireplace to heat the room. She would be in time for breakfast.

Breakfast. Blech. Maybe just tea this morning.

A scant mark later, Kiera made her way down to the great hall, by far the largest and most palatial room in the manse, and to the table she'd assigned herself and her family—a square picnic style with benches, like everyone else's, but set under the giant rose window at her request so she could bask in the light as she ate. Unlike during Vayu's time, no dais lifted the members of the governing body above the people. She made everyone eat with everyone else, and Kiera found time every turn to say "good morning" and "good evening" to as many people as possible. Maybe it wasn't a democracy yet, but she planned to make it one.

Marco and Allie had already come down. They sat chattering with Alex, while Emmy smiled indulgently when Alex chimed in. Amba, Laszlo's mother, sat next to the two empty spots where she and Laszlo would sit, and also smiled every time Alex said something. Amba flashed an open-mouthed grin when she saw Kiera, then turned her head and said something to Alex, who looked up, screeched, and ran from his chair to launch himself into her arms.

"Keer! Keer, are you all right?" he asked her shoulder. He leaned back and gave her face a critical onceover. "Your eye is all better thisturn?"

Genuine amusement lifted her lips. "Yes, Alex. I am fine. Saman came and healed my eye last night. Did you sleep well?" she asked as she unhooked him, then took his hand and walked him back to the table. "Did you stay with Gran Amba?"

"Yeah. We played filkin five times," he grinned up at her, "and I won twice."

"Good job, Alex! That's really something, since she doesn't let you win like Emmy does." They both knew she did, so there was no sense in hiding it. "You should be proud!"

Even his voice smiled. "I'm getting better."

"Yes, you are. Now sit down while I go say hello to Leith. Have you seen Laszlo this morning?"

"Not yet," he sung out as he dropped down next to Emmy.

With a shake of her head, Kiera squeezed his shoulder and moved off. She took in the room as she walked its length. Even after moons here, she sometimes found herself intimidated by the manse's eminence. And the three-hundred-foot triple-story great hall would indignify even the proudest. Like most of the—let's face it—palace, the room bled blue. A low, middle-hued blue carpet clutched the entire floor. Delicate blue walls erupted from the edges and curved gently inward as they rose to clench the apex of the concaved ceiling. Winged statues, wings painted blue, punctuated the empty spaces, unobtrusive guards both watching and pointing the way to each of the dozen or so black double doors spaced evenly in alcoves along the side walls.

Leith and her party—which included, among other Skani, Naga and Chanda—sat at a table just outside one of the doors, the one farthest from Kiera's. She and Leith had not yet spoken about what had happened in those last moments of Vayu's—her late husband's—life, but neither had she told anyone else that it was Leith who had killed Vayu, and that it was Leith, and not Vayu, who had plunged the same knife into her sternum to try and silence her as well. It had very nearly worked.

Kiera still hadn't decided what to do about it.

Leith spoke animatedly, even heatedly, but her words died on her lips when she saw Kiera.

"Good morn, Lady Leith." Kiera nodded to each as she looked around the table. "Lady Naga. Lord Chanda." When was she going to speak with him? Maybe later thisturn, after training? She sure wasn't looking forward to it. "Lady Ralg. Lord—" And then it was Kiera's turn for her breath to falter, and her heart sped up to make up for it. She fought to keep her face smooth, her voice steady. "Thesin."

Thesin, one of her would-be initiators into the world of brooding, forcefully if necessary, nodded back, lips tight and eyes icy. There was no love lost here on either side.

With a wrench Kiera forced her gaze back to Leith's and refused to speculate on what they had been talking about. She feared she knew, and that was something she didn't know what to do about, either. She'd have to take this up with Marco, who served as the informal Skani envoy, and pray the three of them could head it off before things got out of hand.

Intrigue. Marco had told her many times that this deconn ran on lies and intrigue, and she was a novice at both.

No one ever said ruling a deconn was easy. Right?

Kiera willed her stomach to unknot and pasted on a polite smile. "You wanted to speak with me about reinstating the brooding parties, I believe, Lady Leith."

Naga answered in a voice so saccharine sweet that Kiera feared she'd need a dentist afterward. "Oh, my Lady Kiera, won't you please reconsider? It is past half this brooding moon and we—" she smiled at the rest of the table—"would like very much to meet, to dance—to use this time to celebrate life."

"It is our custom," Leith broke in coldly, "and we ask you to consider that."

And then back to Naga. Had they rehearsed this? "We know how important respecting customs is to you, my Lady Governor, and all we're asking is that you allow us to do what our mothers and their mothers have done."

While they spoke, Chanda watched her face. She could feel his gaze, and Thesin's.

"And how does the fact that war waits on our doorstep factor into this?" Kiera asked them both, and let a measure of the impatience she felt creep into her voice. "Should we just pretend we don't need the Skani to train as early, and as hard, as the Alaks do? The call to arms could come nexturn," she reminded them, and watched Naga's face fall.

Chanda leaned forward and took Naga's hand between his. "It gives our people a reason, my lady," he told her earnestly. "And this custom is very important to us, so perhaps a compromise is in order?"

A gritty voice spoke from behind her. "What did you have in mind?"

Laszlo laid a hand on her shoulder a moment before he stepped in close enough to touch, and all eyes at the table rose to some point over her shoulder.

The warmth from the close proximity of his body spread across her skin and chased away some of the tension that seemed to live there. She leaned back just a fraction until her shoulder met his chest. This was a man who always had her back. Always watched her, but rarely spoke in public and never interfered unless she needed him. He wasn't shy. That wasn't it at all. He was thoughtful, thoughtful and quiet, though as fierce and mean as the seven hells if someone crossed him.

Or her. As both Chanda and Thesin had done.

And everyone knew these things. Knew Laszlo's nature and what he was capable of, as they had all watched him tear the throat from Vrishka's former army captain, an enormous polar bear shifter, during a tournament just a few moons earlier. And they knew what he had done to the men— Thesin and another—who had tried to force her favors her first night at a brooding party. It wouldn't take a careful look to detect the sharp spike of fear in both Chanda and Thesin, but Chanda took the trophy for fastest recovery, and even managed to offer a polite smile. Ethereally beautiful Naga stared at the table as if afraid to hope, or afraid to look at Laszlo. It was hard to tell which.

Chanda finally broke the silence. "Well, my lord, we propose that the parties resume, but with less wine and early nights." He smiled broadly, perhaps trying his charm on Laszlo. "The Skani understand the need to train."

"No rings," Kiera told them all, but looked longest at Thesin. "No rings, and no one will be forced. It must be voluntary, or I will not recommend that my co-rulers allow it."

Nearly in tandem they nodded, with Thesin the last to agree. If they decided to let these parties resume, she would have to make sure the women knew they didn't have to bed anyone, and she should probably put guards in the room as well—mean guards who would step in if one of the men wouldn't take *no* for an answer.

"And the Alaks may attend as well, as full participants," Laszlo added, surprising everyone, if the looks on the Skanis' faces reflected their true thoughts.

Naga lifted her face and looked up at Laszlo for a long moment, as if remembering—which she might have been since she and Laszlo had been lovers once. A long time, maybe a decade or more, in the past. Kiera couldn't see if he stared back or not, but she must not have found what she was looking for because her gaze dropped back to the table.

Even so, a jealous spike pierced Kiera's middle, and she fought to push it down, or out. He didn't love Naga, she knew he didn't, and it had been a very long time ago.

As if he knew, the hand on Kiera's shoulder squeezed.

All looked at Leith, still the second among the Skani. After a moment, she nodded once.

"We will announce our decision at dinner," Laszlo told them as he drew Kiera away from the table, but paused to tell Chanda, "and at that time we will decide when to meet to hear Vrishka's words."

Without waiting for a response, they walked to their table together, hand in hand.

"How is your morning, my love?" Kiera asked him as they sat down. Servers had already set out the food, and Laszlo spooned some of the hot—well, it looked like pie and smelled like fish, so fish pie?—onto his plate, then offered her a spoonful.

"Oh, no thanks. I'm just going to have tea this morning," she told him, and reached for the steaming pot.

The spoon clanged against the ceramic bowl when he dropped it. "*A'kala*, you need to eat," he told her. "You have lost some body mass, and you need to keep up your strength."

His words made her smile. Back home, no one would tell an already plump woman she needed to eat more. "I'm fine. I promise I'll eat later."

"Are you feeling unwell?" he asked, and although his voice was mild, she knew he was fishing.

"Laszlo, I told you I'm fighting something off. I had a headache this morning, and it's made my stomach a little uneasy. I don't think that's a reason to panic."

His eyes flicked to hers, and the threat of a smile lingered around the edges of his mouth. She let hers come, and blossom into a grin. Every turn she spent with him was a good one. "I love you, Laszlo," she told him, and sipped her tea.

THEY SPLIT UP FOR THE MORNING. Marco and Kiera went to the magical training rooms to practice spellwork with Agni, and Laszlo ran soldiers though their basic exercises. As always, they came together in Kiera and Laszlo's apartment for lunch.

"I think we should let the parties resume, with the conditions Chanda mentioned," Kiera told Laszlo, Marco and Allie as they ate. "And that they let the Alaks attend, as Laszlo said."

"I agree," Marco nodded.

"However," Kiera added, "I still worry that some of the men may still think it's all right to force unwilling women. That has to be addressed. I was thinking that we could put the word out. Have someone read a proclamation or something. And we will also need guards in the room. Someone neutral, who women can go to if they need help."

Laszlo spoke between bites. "Good thoughts, *a'kala*. I also believe both to be necessary." The look he gave Marco was hard, but his voice stayed cool. "Is there a time when you will again join us for training?"

The color rose on Marco's face as he stared at his food. "Yes, brother. I'll come thisturn," he mumbled.

Laszlo nodded and took another bite.

Allie gave Kiera a pleading look, but she couldn't summon any sympathy for Marco. He had been shirking training more turns than he came, and she felt as much annoyance as Laszlo. And not just because Marco needed the training—they all did—but because the Skani watched Marco, and when he didn't come, some of the Skani who did melted away. How could she convince them to take this seriously when Marco obviously didn't? It was maddening.

As a compromise, she changed the subject. "Another thing I want to do is end these stu—er, these titles. Lady. Lord. For heaven's sake." She looked at Marco. "What do you think?"

Kiera suddenly realized that her bodyguard—wasn't his name Kuruk?—hadn't shown up. Hadn't Laszlo said he would start thisturn? She smothered a smile, and decided to keep it to herself. She wasn't going to remind him if he'd forgotten.

Marco was staring at her. "What do you mean, Kiera? Just—just stop naming mages as nobility?"

His outrage fueled her own. "Why, yes, Marco. That is exactly what I mean. If mages want to call themselves something, how about *sunwyr*, or *awyr*, since that's what they are. What I don't like," she laid both hands on the table, " is the sense of entitlement they feel. I can't get any of the *sunwyr* to do a damned thing around here, not even help with the magical tasks, and I'm pretty sure that was their job before. They've lived their entire lives riding on the backs of the rest of the deconn, and maybe if they didn't have titles, they'd start remembering that they're just people, too."

Marco frowned into his cup, but Allie's mouth formed an O, such a comical sight that Kiera almost laughed.

Laszlo did, from the belly, and they all turned to watch him as he warmed to it and let it all out, all nursing various levels of shock at his reaction. He had to set his utensils aside or risk losing them, and he didn't stop until he'd spent his amusement.

His amusement, his laughter, was so genuine that it was hard not to laugh with him, but Kiera forced herself not to, although she couldn't quite press her grin all the way away.

"And Kiera," he told her when he'd calmed himself, apparently continuing their conversation from this morning, "I love you as well, my heart."

Those words, so rarely spoken, both surprised her and brought a brush of tears to stand in her eyes. A small smile said he saw them, and the way that he looked at her told her what they meant to him, and she stared at him for a long moment, pressed this moment away for safekeeping.

When he looked away, she turned to Marco. "Marco, I can see that you don't agree with me," she prodded.

"Well, no, Kiera, I don't." He raised a hand. "Not because I think the mages should be nobility, or that the ones without magic should be forced to do all the work. But Kiera," he pled, "can you imagine what would happen if you told the Skani mages you were stripping away their nobility? Things are tense now, as you know, and this could push relations past the point of negotiation."

"The Skani place very great stock in ceremony," Laszlo interjected, and drank deeply.

Kiera knew that of course Marco had the right of it. "I know you're right," she admitted, echoing her own thoughts. "And I suppose I knew this wouldn't be possible, at least not right now, but I wanted to throw it out as something I'd been thinking about."

"I am pleased," Marco told her, "that you two have reconsidered your position on the brooding parties. That has been a sore point, and this will go far in settling some hard feelings, I think."

"Even with the added conditions?" Kiera asked.

He nodded. "And I think your ideas are good ones, the guards best of all, though you may need to tell them to watch the goings on, since the women are not likely to solicit help. And mix them, both Skani and Alaks. Some may work better with different people."

"Has Chanda spoken to you?" Laszlo asked Marco.

"Not about anything important," Marco admitted glumly. "He seems to be waiting for Kiera."

"Ceremony is important to the Alaks, too." Kiera told Laszlo as she pushed her plate away.

"Oh, most certainly, *a'kala*," Laszlo told her somberly, but she saw the glint in his eye. "Some far more than others."

Marco snorted, which made Kiera laugh. Allie looked from Laszlo to Kiera, then to Marco, brows drawn in apparent confusion. Kiera had to work hard to keep from shaking her head in wonderment. Allie seemed a nice girl, but not terribly bright.

"I will ask Amba to speak to the Alak who wish to attend the parties," Laszlo told them, "and Marco, I want you to speak to the Skani. The Alak are not accustomed to casual sex. Bedding, for Alaks, is most often a promise of something greater. Be certain that they understand that they must be very plain about their intentions with any Alak they wish to bed."

Confusion wrinkled Marco's forehead. "Then why send Alaks to brooding parties where there is little besides casual sex if the risk of misunderstanding is so great?"

Kiera answered. "Because we need to integrate."

Chapter 4

KIERA LAID THE HEAVY SCARLET DRESS ON THE BED and stood back to look at it. The velvet fabric looked rich, both plush and elegant, in the orange firelight her lamps cast. Squarenecked and nearly unembellished except for one thin golden rope that crisscrossed the bodice and wove into the skirt's fabric below, this dress would cling to her chest and upper arms, and billow out at hips and elbows to cover both feet and hands. It was a little fancy, and formal, for a brooding party, where hopeful women more commonly wore the most revealing clothes in their closets, but for the first brooding party under the new rule she wanted to look—well, not regal, exactly, but she wanted the attendees to take her very seriously. Seriously as a ruler. That would be harder to pull off, she thought, if her breasts were practically falling out of her top.

And she meant what she'd told the Skani. That's why she was going, and why she'd asked Laszlo to go. Meant it so much that she sure as hell would—well, not punch— no, she mustn't do that—but she'd definitely intervene if she caught even the smallest indication that any of the men were pressuring any of the women to have sex.

Yes. She understood that for the Skani these parties constituted a celebration of life. They had certainly made sure she knew that; that phrase was almost a mantra, and someone inevitably said it every time they spoke to her about reinstating the parties. Perhaps it had something to do with the low Skani birth rate, or maybe they just really, really got into their sex. Instead of judging them she tried to understand, and even if she couldn't quite manage that, she would do her best to respect their traditions. What she could not—would not—accept, however, was the practice of forcing women. Telling them, as she had been told at her first party, that they had the power to choose with whom they had sex, but that they had to choose someone.

So no rings. Leith had given her rings, rings but no real instructions, and that night two men, Thesin and Gethor, had stripped them from her fingers, and took her choice with them.

Not this time. If the women, or the men for that matter, wanted to decline, or wait until another turn, she wanted them to have the power to say *no*.

Thus the dress. Her rules. They—the Skani—would all know the rules came from her, since they all witnessed her first brooding party, and she wanted them to see her as the woman who not only made those rules, but would carry them out.

What she didn't want to think about was Chanda. She'd told him that they could speak at the party, but she didn't want to hear his words. Like a child wishes a monster gone from the closet, she wanted him to go away. A stone had settled in her stomach the very moment she realized that he carried Vrishka's message, and she knew the words he told her, told them, would start the rip that would tear Fairbanks apart.

A heavy breath escaped her, and she lay back on the bed next to her dress and stared up at the ceiling. Someone had painted hundreds of tiny birds on either side of the dark beam that ran center and lengthwise. Her hand found the velvet fabric, and she ran it back and forth. For a moment she wished she could fly away, then felt ashamed that she had. If she flew, she'd have to take Alex with her, and Emmy wouldn't leave him, so her, too. And Laszlo, of course. And Marco would probably insist on coming, and he'd need Allie. How big would her wings have to be to carry them all away?

A smile started at the thought, but fell. The Skani made up the entirety of the problem, really. Their insistence on retaining their noble status. The unwillingness to help her with anything, or to even speak with the Alaks. They wanted to sleep late, and drink wine. Well, she couldn't begrudge them wine, she supposed. But why wouldn't they help?

And it wasn't like she could just kick them out. First, Marco would never hear it. Second, even if he agreed, she wasn't sure if they would be able to force them out. Third, even if they managed to get all of the *sunwyr* and *awyr* Skani out of Fairbanks, they'd just go join up with Vrishka, which would give him a very distinct magical advantage when the former Fairbanks Skani decided they wanted their deconn back. How many *sunwyr* mages did Vrishka have, anyway?

The Alaks and the *nuwyr*—the Skani who had no magical ability—well, so far they hadn't caused any trouble for anyone. They worked hard, they hadn't killed everyone who'd oppressed them, and they had agreed to stay in Fairbanks, as free women and men, to help Fairbanks survive. And Fairbanks desperately needed them, because without them there was no one to farm, process food, care for animals, cook, and do all the other mundane tasks a city needed to survive.

But trouble nonetheless brewed there, too. She knew some complained bitterly over the fact that the Skani continued to live in the manse while they eked out their lives in tiny homes. Some asked what had really changed, and who could blame them?

Amba kept them calm. Amba, who had led the revolution, who still commanded great respect, and Amba counseled peace and patience, and pointed out that for the first time, perhaps ever, one of them ruled the deconn.

God bless Amba.

"Are you feeling unwell?"

Kiera sat up. "I didn't hear you come in!"

Laszlo sank down on the bed next to her. After the briefest of pauses, he wrapped an arm around her and urged her forward until her face met his chest. She relaxed into him and let her breath out. "No," she mumbled. "I am feeling fine."

"You are worrying."

It was not a question, but she answered it anyway. "Yeah."

His voice poured over her like water, cool and clean, and washed her fears away. A precious respite, even if it only lasted a moment. "Everything will be all right, *a'kala*."

They sat that way for a time, letting firelight kiss the arms that wrapped the two of them together. Kiera knew, somehow, that he truly believed what he told her, and even though she wasn't silly enough to believe it just for that reason, she wanted so very much to believe he was right.

His kiss brushed the top of her head. "Do you still want to go to the party?"

"Yeah," she said as she pulled back. "I thought I'd wear this dress. Do you think it's too much?"

He didn't ask what she meant. Instead, he gave her one of his rare smiles, a rarest of the rare, one set in an open face. "No."

"What are you going to wear? No – wait. Let me guess," she told him as she stood and pulled her dress off and picked up the scarlet. "Black?"

Another smile. "Yes."

They walked to the hall together, arm in arm, and entered the cavernous room the Skani used for brooding parties. A magnificent room, longer than it was wide, and as large as a church, but it managed to avoid intimidating its guests. Thick carpet beckoned entrants to pad its length, and plush navy and blue couches invited the weary to lie back and cast aside their cares. A dance floor lay on the far side of the room, and a band played soft music from a raised platform.

The time was early, but tens of sets of eyes lifted as Kiera and Laszlo entered the room. Kiera had no shawl to check, so they walked past the door attendants and made their way through the room. Every person who met her gaze earned a smile from Kiera, but she knew Laszlo would wear what she thought of as his stone face until they were alone again. Most smiled back, some sincerely and some less so, but a few looked away, or held her gaze assessingly. Instead of holding court in the monarchial chairs Vayu and Leith had used, Kiera chose a set of couches near the back of the room where she could watch the dancers as well as most of the room, and they sank into one.

A server rushed up and offered wine, and they took glasses filled with what looked like crushed rubies. Laszlo lifted his glass, and she tapped it, and they drank. "You look very beautiful," he told her over the rim.

That startled a smile. "Well, thank you. And you, my handsome husband, look good enough to eat."

It took some work to keep his face still, and Kiera grinned at his effort to do so. "Well," she told him in a quiet voice, "it is a brooding party, my love. Don't blame me for thinking the same thing every other woman who sees you will think." She leaned forward and lowered her voice, and slowed the tempo even further. "You're by far the sexiest man in this deconn, Laszlo of the Denaa, and it only takes one look to know that you'd be amazing in bed."

He said nothing, but his eyes held promises she planned to make him keep. Tonight.

Still smiling, she leaned back and took in the room. On two sets of couches along the side wall—and to her surprise—sat about a dozen Alaks, women and men, about half of each. All wore fine clothes, all had obviously primped, and every one of them looked nervous. She knew none of them, but applauded their courage. Whether this would work or not was anyone's guess, but she sure hoped it did.

Even with the near hundred milling and sitting here and there, the room still stood largely empty, yet even so it was clear that the Skani had left gaps between the Alaks and the places they chose to sit. Maybe, just maybe, by the end of the night that would change.

"They are not here yet," Laszlo told her, answering the real question before her eyes could finish perusing the room. "None but Marco."

"Where is Marco?" she asked, brows down.

"He is walking toward us now from the southwest corner."

Kiera made a face. How could someone tell which direction was which indoors?

"He is coming from your left," Laszlo translated patiently.

Sure enough, Marco strode across the carpet toward them, Allie in hand and a wide smile painting his lips. He dropped down on an opposite couch, leaned back and pushed his feet out. After she perched on the edge, Allie stared at the floor with an angry set to her mouth.

"You look lovely," Marco told her, and Kiera looked at him, then at Allie with a half smile. Apparently oblivious to his fiancée's mood, Marco chattered on. "Doesn't everyone look good tonight?" He sat up. "They all seem so happy to be able to attend parties again. And did you see that a group of Alaks came?" He indicated with his head. "I did not think any would, but they're sitting over there."

The likely source of Allie's wrath approached from what Kiera now knew was the west. Bandel, one of Marco's longtime friends, a lovely young woman, blonde and buxom, the latter of which the dress she wore showed off to a very good effect. Had she followed them over?

Allie's glance slid to Bandel, and her mouth further hardened.

"They are here," Laszlo said into the quiet Bandel's presence had startled in Marco.

As nonchalantly as possible, Kiera turned her head toward the door. Sure enough, Chanda had entered, Naga on his arm and Leith in his wake. Even less pleasantly, Thesin followed, and Gethor, the other man Kiera had first met at her brooding party initiation, and two other Skani men Kiera didn't know well.

The thump of her heart startled her, and she swallowed it back down. It wasn't that they scared her, exactly—not Thesin or Gethor or even Chanda. It just seemed as though things were skidding out of control, and here she sat on a plush couch in her nice dress, hoping that here, in this world where men made all the rules, she could convince them to take her seriously. That she could do that something that would allow her—them—to keep hold of the precious victory they'd won. That the slaves would stay free. That Alex would grow up to be a fine man. That she'd get to see it.

A hand squeezed her knee, and she turned to Laszlo.

He stood smoothly and extended a hand. "Dance with me."

"I thought you didn't like dancing," she teased, trying to lighten her own mood.

"I like holding you," he said quietly, an echo of words once spilled in dark times. Those words, wound with the love he had always given her, buoyed her, and she rose and let him lead her to the dance floor.

Neither spoke as they danced. The slow music lulled her, and her heart-beat slowed as they moved together. As she relaxed into Laszlo's strong arms, felt them encase her, the knot of fear in Kiera's chest softened. Not gone; there was no way to banish it, but when the music ended she felt relaxed, and strong, and as they walked off the floor she cast a grateful look into her husband's understanding face.

Kuruk stood next to their now empty couches when they returned to them, back straight, eyes forward, and hands clasped behind his back. Kiera lifted a brow and her face and showed them both to Laszlo, who gazed back impassively. Beyond all doubt, he would never relent on this, but even so, she wanted to argue. For so many reasons, and so very much. But not here, in front of everyone.

And on second thought, she realized as she stared into his handsome face, that might be precisely why he had chosen this moment to bring Kuruk on board. More in admiration for his scheming, she shook her head just a little and smiled her surrender, but hoped he realized this matter was far from settled.

"Greetings, Kuruk," she told him as she took a seat on the couch, since there was no sense in making him pay for Laszlo's stubborn heart. "Enjoy-ing the party?"

His chin moved. Was that a nod?

A fresh glass of wine awaited her. She picked up the flute, took a sip, and set the glass back on the table. Blueberry, just like the last one, and she just didn't want it.

Someone called her name, and she had to turn completely around to see Marco nearly trotting across the floor toward her. Allie was nowhere in sight, and Marco wore the falsest smile she'd ever seen. Her heart sank.

"Would you dance with me?" he asked a little breathlessly as he grabbed her hand. All she had time to do was to cast Laszlo a look before Marco dragged her up and out to the floor.

With two dozen other couples they stood at the edge of the floor, await-ing the band's choice, and fortune smiled for a moment. The band played another larghetto. Either that or this was the "get to know your partner better" mark.

"Where is Allie?" Kiera whispered into Marco's hair.

"Shhh," he answered in a voice so quiet she almost couldn't hear him. "She is mad at me and went to sit with my mother."

Kiera closed her eyes. "Why are you flirting with Bandel?"

His shoulders stiffened. "I was not!" he denied hotly, abandoning all pretense at quiet, then glared at a man who looked over, missed a step and crushed Kiera's toes under his boot.

"Ow!"

He pressed his mouth into a hard line and yanked Kiera close. They danced stiffly, and neither spoke for a minute, then two.

All around them graceful dancers flowed together, one step, another, a gentle turn, brightly clad arms clasped tightly, reminding Kiera of a field of springtime flowers yearning to unfold under the noontide sun.

A fierce whisper drew her attention back to the frustrated man who still squeezed her too tightly. "I do not know what is happening, Kiera, but something is." He paused to look over her shoulder, then made a face. "Bandel won't leave me alone, and that's not all that's got Allie tied up. She won't tell me," he lamented between steps.

"What do you mean 'something is up'? Is it brooding? Don't they do brooding in Barrow?"

His look was pained. "Yes. But I told her I will not lie with another, and I will not, but Bandel will not leave me alone. If Valen was not gone," Kiera shuddered, "I would think he had played one of his games. Someone has said something to Allie, Kiera, and she has more anger for me than I have ever seen in her."

Would Chanda do this?

"I don't know if it is him," Marco answered, reading her thoughts. Or her face. "But be cautious tonight, Kiera. Many pots are being stirred."

As if cued, the music ended at that moment, and Marco led her back to the couches they'd chosen.

People filtered in, in ones and twos, and some in groups. All Skani. Some came to greet Kiera and Laszlo, and some came to Marco first. The dance floor filled, as did the couches. So many people came that even the Alaks had to share. Kiera danced several of the minuets and bourrées with different *awyr* men, none of whom affiliated closely with Leith or her clique. Kiera wondered if their asking was meant as a message to Leith, and to Chanda, but none spoke on the floor, nor did they stay after the dance had ended. A pretty young mage asked Laszlo to dance, but he declined, and no others came calling.

A mark passed, and Chanda did not come to speak with them.

Kiera tried not to watch them, but every time she looked in their direction she found Chanda's gaze on her. Each time he caught her eye he smiled, a warm turn of mouth that seemed to have forgotten all that had passed between them. Not sure what else to do, she returned his smile, and turned back to watch the dancers.

Water gave way to fire as another mark passed. Kiera looked at Marco, then at Laszlo. When she started to stand both reached for her, so she sat back down.

With a little scoot, Marco moved next to her and put an arm around her shoulders. He smiled widely and leaned in. Although he had most definitely drunk too much wine—in fact, he reeked of it—no slur stuttered his words.

"It is a game, Kiera," he muttered from next to her ear, and Laszlo, who stared at the dance floor, made a slight movement of his chin that could have been a nod. "They want you to come over."

The stink was too much, so Kiera leaned away from him. "I thank you, Marco," she said in a conversational voice, "but I have danced enough for now. However, I think that you should go ask one of the Alak ladies to dance, since no one else has been brave enough to."

His eyes darted toward Allie, and chagrin washed across his face before his smile chased it away. "Might as well," he agreed. He stood, and then bowed deeply before he strode away.

Fire gave way to earth, then earth to air.

Couples began filing out, first just a few, and then more. The dance floor seemed empty, the music louder, with fewer people clotting the room. A headache started, but faded after a glass of mediocre wine. Laszlo held her knee in his hand. Marco danced with each of the Alak women, and seemed to enjoy himself. Two other Skani men, ones who had danced with her, asked Alak women to dance, then a handful of Alak women, Bandel included, asked the handsome Alak men to partner them on the dance floor.

"A lovely first party," remarked Chanda from her right side, the one opposite Laszlo. With her heart in her throat, Kiera turned.

The time had just turned to water.

CHAPTER 5

"**D**OES WATER FRIGHTEN YOU?" CHANDA HAD ASKED her once, in the dark of night. The night he proposed, then threatened her safety with Vayu after she refused. The night he tried to force himself on her.

With a shaky breath, Kiera pushed her dark thoughts away. "It is a lovely party," she agreed.

On an opposite couch, Chanda sat and crossed his legs. His lips lifted as he watched her, a gentle smile, but his eyes belied it. If he wanted to play a game, she'd play. And if he wanted the silence filled, he could do it himself.

Her eyes lifted to the dance floor, which had emptied, although people gathered around its edges in twos and threes. Perhaps because of the late mark, the tempo of the band's songs had slowed. As Chanda took her measure the musicians commenced a solemn adagissimo, far too slow a tempo to dance to, but just right for conversation.

Or a funeral.

Kiera blew a breath and summoned a smile.

Chanda sipped his wine.

Determined to wait him out, Kiera let her gaze scan the room. Perhaps a fifth remained of those who had come, and those who stayed watched her, some covertly, but most met her eyes. Marco sat among the Alak women, chatting and laughing, a glass of wine in his hand.

"He seems very relaxed," Chanda noted, a shade dryly.

She considered several answers before deciding on, "I'm happy he is."

Chanda settled back in his seat. "So what's next, Kiera?"

She met his gaze. "What do you mean?"

A shoulder lifted. "Will you move on Barrow? Free their slaves as well?"

His frontal attack took her off guard, and she watched his face, tried to divine his feelings. "Is that what Vrishka is afraid I'll do?"

"Kiera, you are very brave." His tone straddled the line between earnest and patronizing, and she had to fight to keep her face clear. "But you are also reckless. You charge ahead without thinking about the future. You can't deny that. And you have shown over and over that you have no understanding of the greater forces at work here, or the reasons we, the Skani, have chosen to do things in our ways."

Through gritted teeth, she shot back, "Chanda, I don't have to be a Skani—or an Alak, for that matter—to understand that what Vayu—" she said *Vayu*, but she meant *Skani*, and hoped he knew it—"was doing here was wrong."

Chanda raised both hands in a *see what I mean* gesture, but smiled to soften his words. "Kiera, I admire you. Everyone admires you. You are loyal and compassionate as well as brave, and you are truly lovely. But you leapt too soon, and you shook this deconn to its core."

"It wasn't just me, Chanda," she interrupted. "And you know that. This—" she spread her hands—"was something I *helped* to happen. I didn't think it up, I didn't design the plan, and I didn't execute it. I didn't even lead anybody! All I did was offer what help I could give." And wouldn't he be shocked to know who else had helped, someone who apparently played on both sides, but the consideration of that would have to wait. For now. "And the truth is that my part ended up being pretty small, so don't reduce this to some fluke of mine."

He had leaned back while she spoke, a look of patient condescension painting his face. "Perhaps," he conceded, "but that does not matter, because, Kiera, it is already falling apart."

"Oh fuck you, Chanda," she shot back. "We didn't expect this to be easy, and we *will* make this work."

His amused look was almost her undoing, but she closed her eyes for a moment and pulled in a deep breath. How could Laszlo sit there listening to this, and with Chanda so obviously ignoring him, yet keep hold of his temper? "Tell me what Vrishka has to say." She opened her eyes. "Are we going to war or what?"

"Oh, no," Chanda told her with a shake of his head, and Kiera couldn't find it in her heart to believe his blithe words. "He proposes a treaty, of course, and I agreed to bring it to you for consideration."

"*We* will be very happy to consider his offer."

Another amused smile. "Well, to start, and understand that this is his initial—what did you call it, *offer?*— Governor Vrishka wishes you to surrender to his superior armed forces. He will assume rule of Fairbanks, and will designate an emissary to carry out his will."

Her mouth fell open.

"As for the Alaks," he continued, still wearing his small smile, "they will not be forced back into slavery, but the ones left in Fairbanks will agree to remain in the tasks previously assigned them."

"What do you mean *the ones left in Fairbanks?*"

"Governor Vrishka will take the bulk of the Fairbanks army to Barrow, but he will leave a sizeable force here, under his own captain, of course, to ensure the deconn's safety from the various outside threats."

Kiera leaned over her knees and looked into Chanda's face. "How can you work with him, Chanda? How can you say these words to me with a straight face? Regardless of anything else, you told me you have friends in the nadeconn. If he does this, you know he'll keep tearing families apart to take slaves. And no matter what you say, you know he'll put things back the way they were here. Don't deny that, Chanda. Don't you dare."

Chanda's face looked hard, and she couldn't read it. "Kiera, he said he will let the Fairbanks slaves remain free, and that is a large step. Change must come slowly so to avoid tearing things apart."

Not because she would ever consider Vrishka's offer, but because she wanted to know if he was coming with his army to fight if she said *no*, which he might expect her to, she had to know if Chanda was lying. So what would someone feel if they were lying? What emotions would that evoke? Fear. Fear, for sure. Maybe satisfaction? And excitement if he looked forward to it?

Could she do it without touching him?

The lights seemed overbright. After a sharp glance up, Kiera shaded her brows with a hand, closed her eyes, and hoped she looked like she was thinking about his words.

Her sight shot out and into his boot, and the flesh underneath. To her surprise, she felt nothing; it was no different than shooting through the air in search of strands. Up, up she went, into his middle. When her sight snapped back into her, it brought strands of water. Feelings rushed in, raw emotions, but she ignored them until she could anchor a small flow from foot to foot.

Her hand dropped, her eyes lifted, and she let herself feel Chanda.

Anger. A very strong current of anger dominated all else. Fear edged it, encased it on all sides. Flecks of excitement floated in the morass, as well as irritation, or frustration, and something that tasted like shame. As her eyes held his lust leaked through, then grew stronger, became the main flow, and her back straightened. She felt her face flush. Like ink from a frightened octopus her own anger and disgust erupted and bled into the pool of emotions churning inside her until she couldn't tell whose were whose.

A breath, then two, before she closed her eyes again and severed the flow.

But they kept coming. She opened her eyes to find Chanda watching her, his face colored by curiosity, but she could tell he didn't know the cause of her distress.

Fighting panic, she turned her gaze to Laszlo, who sat so still he seemed immobile, not four inches from her left thigh. Aside from the press of his lips, just a shade too tight, he looked calm, nearly serene. But as his eyes met hers black rage, more fury than she had even known a person could feel, flowed into her, covered and consumed the flow from Chanda. So much fury that she choked on it.

Her hands lifted as she tried to make it stop. From someplace else she could hear her breath, fast and short. She jumped to her feet, still fighting panic, and wondered what to do. How to make this stop.

Lightning fast the flow from Laszlo changed. Fear overtook the rage, tore it down, consumed it. His hand found her shoulder, but that only made the flow stronger. Her stomach knotted, pulling her over, and she gasped because his fear and anger were burning a hole in her belly.

Chanda stepped in, reached out a hand, but Kuruk appeared between them as if conjured. "Do not touch her," he growled, voice fierce, and Chanda's hand fell.

With a hand across her stomach, she forced herself to stand straight and looked out at the room, desperate for something, anything, to interfere, to distract her, to help her get hold of herself.

As her gaze met others', their emotions came as if called and dropped like rain into the bucket inside her. She identified them as they passed into her. Interest, excitement. Fear. Some felt anger. Was it at her or Chanda?

Was he right? Were things really falling apart?

Desperate to keep calm, she tried to keep it down, keep it back, but she couldn't make herself listen to the words people were saying to her, Laszlo and Chanda and maybe somebody else. Staring at a wall seemed to work best—the flow lessened then, just a little, but that little she held precious. As she stared, tried to concentrate on the woodwork, the statues, she wondered briefly if calling another element would help, but the thought of sending out her sight sent fear scuttling down her back. Her magic was the only thing keeping these emotions from consuming her, and what would happen to that if her sight left her body?

Damn water. Damn water!

Only after she thought it did she realize she'd said it, was chanting it.

A hand took hers and squeezed, and her breath bled out as the noise dimmed. Fire. Someone was feeding her fire.

Warmth filled her chest, pushing silence ahead of it. She sat down hard, fell back onto the couch and tried to catch her breath. Outside sounds crested, crashed as she stared at the ceiling and concentrated on the sound the air made as it passed her lips. When she felt calmer, she lifted her head and found Marco's face just inches from hers.

"Thank you," she whispered.

He knelt between her and Chanda. "Idiot," he mouthed through a grin, then looked mock disbelieving, the sarcasm large on his face. "Water?"

Both dismayed and embarrassed, she shrugged and sat back. Laszlo took her hand and she looked into his face. "Sorry," she told him. "I'm okay."

Marco plopped down on her other side and dropped an arm on the back of the couch behind her.

"Quite impressive," Chanda told her, and when she turned to him, his face said he meant it. Was that because water was her opposite, that she shouldn't really be able to summon it? His face didn't say, and in truth she didn't care. Behind him, however, stood Leith, and Naga. And several others, including Thesin. None of them looked impressed, least of all Leith.

"I apologize," Kiera told them all, "if I scared you."

"Kiera is a powerful mage," Marco interrupted before she could tell a lie. Well, when she thought one up, though that might take a minute, and even so she knew it'd be thin. It was probably good he had, she grudgingly admitted, then wondered what else he would say. "She is still gaining power," he continued, voice strong, authoritative. He reminded Kiera very much of Vayu when he spoke like that, and his ability to play the monarch was perhaps the best legacy had father had left him. "She is well on her way to becoming Fairbanks' first helfarch. I am certain she did not mean to startle you, but her power grows so quickly at times that it is, at moments, hard to control. I say it is good that we were inside the manse—" where magic-stopping gold had been inlaid throughout, she remembered—"and not outside where someone might have been harmed by the attraction of such power." The smile with which he finished belied his words, however, as did the gaze he cast upon the onlookers. It told them in no uncertain terms that their loss would mean precious, precious little to him.

"Agreed, cousin," Chanda nodded, ignoring the connotation. "Which leads me to the final point Governor Vrishka asked me to make. If I may?"

Marco nodded regally, and Kiera looked between them as anger rose and burned away the last of her embarrassment. Tried not to fume because the voice Chanda used with Marco was nothing like the voice he used with her. So she outranked Laszlo, the former slave, with the Skani because she wasn't an Alak. And Marco, who wasn't yet an adult, outranked her because he was a male.

But despite that her face held her anger—she knew it did—everyone ignored her, which further stirred her anger.

"Because she is so powerful, Governor Vrishka wishes Kiera to remain in Fairbanks as a defender, and you, of course, Marco, for the same reason. If you accept his terms, which Lady Kiera will explain to you, and they are not really of consequence, nothing will really change here. And you will avoid the bloodshed, cousin, the enormous loss of life, that will come if war is declared between the two deconns."

Again, Marco nodded, as if considering Chanda's words, but Kiera knew his heart nearly as well as her own.

Still angry, and tired of these charades, she stood.

"May I enter an opinion?" Leith asked, not at all humbly, and all turned to her. She held Marco's eyes.

"Of course," he told her, and Kiera's stomach knotted. A hundred people stood close enough to hear. All Skani.

"I opine, Lord Marco, that we should accept Vrishka's terms."

Fury shot through Kiera at Leith's betrayal of this deconn, and of her own son. "Do you, Lady Leith?" she said carefully, and turned all the way around to face her. *I will tell him*, she thought, and thought it hard, knowing that Leith would read her thoughts on her face. *Cross me here and I swear I will tell everyone exactly how dearly they should hold your opinion.* "Do you honestly think that Marco, and Laszlo and I of course, should simply surrender this deconn to Vrishka, an unknown ruler, who will do who knows what here?"

A thick silence fell, and watchers looked from Leith to Kiera, and back again. Kiera grudgingly admired that Leith held fast to the serenity on her face, but then she'd had decades of practice with Vayu and all the games they played in this stinking court.

"It was my first thought," Leith prevaricated as she backed down. "But Governor Kiera's point is a good one. But I do suggest that we consider his words."

Kiera forgave her the last, said to save her own face in front of this audience, but she would never forgive her willingness to hand over this city to another tyrant. Never. And now that she knew what Leith was about, and what she would do, she had a decision to make.

"We will retire for the evening and discuss this nexturn." That was Laszlo, and he took Kiera's hand and led her toward the door.

Marco followed them out.

THE LAMPS BURST TO LIGHT as Laszlo opened the door to their apartment. It took less than a thought now, Kiera mused as she closed the door behind them and watched Laszlo cross the floor to the couches. Without a word he poured two glasses of Lorgda's good wine before lifting one in offering to her.

It was an exaggeration, of course, to say she would soon be a helfarch, the most powerful mage known to the Skani. Learning to control her power had been a challenge— and still was, as tonight had made obvious to everyone. Would what she had learned be enough, she wondered, to stand against Vrishka, and whoever else owed him fealty?

And how angry was Laszlo at her?

With a sigh, she walked over and took the glass. With the other hand she bunched up her skirt and perched on the arm of the couch. "Did I blow it?" she asked before sipping the wine, and braced for his answer.

"What secret of Leith's do you hold?" he countered.

She took a long drink, then plunked the glass on the table next to her thigh. "I don't want to tell you," she finally answered, unable to meet his eyes, but raised a hand to stop the protest before he could voice it. When she spoke, she hated that fear and pain colored her voice. "No, Laszlo. It isn't that I don't trust you, or that I meant to keep secrets from you." She let out a sigh. "If it makes you feel any better, I haven't told anybody."

His flute made a sharp sound as he planted it next to hers before dropping down on the couch next to her feet. Almost too quickly, he slipped an arm around her waist and pulled her down and into his lap, where he wrapped both arms around her and pulled her tightly against his chest.

It startled a laugh, a small sound that drifted through the stillness of the room. She turned her face and rested her cheek against his shoulder, and tried to let that quiet fill her. "Please don't be angry with me, Laszlo," she began, but maybe because it had all been too much, and maybe because she finally felt safe enough, tears rose, so she closed her eyes, and her mouth.

His hand lifted her face and pressed his lips to hers. Tender, soft; a kiss of love. But as his tongue met hers, light exploded behind her eyes. All the emotion she'd felt, the anger and the fear and the need, all that she'd thought gone, surged up, coalesced into a molten ball, fire, inside her chest. Sound, smoke escaping the flames, rose and filled her mouth. Spilled into his.

The ball burst, and fingers of flame shot into her throat, flew out to her fingers, and dropped into her groin, where it pooled and pulsed. Urgent, urgent need filled her, and she pushed back and stared into Laszlo's startled face.

Words spilled through her lips as she shifted so she could straddle him, but they seemed far away, and she couldn't care what they were. Her hands found his shirt, tore it open. When she had bared his chest her hands grabbed both his shoulders as she leaned in and bit the muscle above his nipple. Teeth met teeth through the skin. Lost in the moment, perhaps trapped in whatever spell had ensnared them both, he groaned and thrust his iron-hard erection into the juncture between her thighs.

Sparks shot across her eyes. The friction nearly sent her over the edge, but this wasn't what she wanted. She stood on her knees and yanked the belt from his pants, threw it aside, then pulled open his pants. He tried to sit up so she could peel them down. "No," she breathed, used fingers to lift aside the cloth wrapping her bottom, and mounted him.

Wildly she pumped, as fast as she could, lifting up to thrust deep, driving the fire into him, pulling it back inside her, her fingers hawk's claws gripping his upper arms. In twenty heartbeats a frisson pulled her head back, and her breath hissed through gritted teeth as he thrust up, hands deep in the flesh of her hips. He groaned, climaxed, but she didn't slow, kept up the frantic pace, her need unsated. A stuttered time passed, violent, uncontrolled thrusts, rough movements and meaningless sounds, her hands, his, between them, drawing her release, and at last her lips parted, froze in a grimace, as heat exploded in trembling waves.

They collapsed together, breathing hard. Kiera's head fell to his shoulder. Her hand found a welt on his chest, and when she lifted her fingers, sticky blood stained them. She lifted her head, horror a stone in her gut, and opened her mouth to apologize, but he put a finger to her lips, a smile on his own.

"I acted like an animal," she whispered from behind his fingers, her eyes holding his. "I don't know what got into me. I think it was all that water—I needed to get all that out. I—I'm so sorry."

His smile grew until his teeth showed. "No, *a'kala*. Do not be sorry." With gentle hands he eased her head back down to his shoulder. Goosebumps rose on hers as she cooled, so she sent fire to the fireplace, and Laszlo wrapped them in the fuzzy blanket she'd left lying on the couch. The crackle of the fire made the only sound for many minutes.

Laszlo nuzzled her cheek with his chin. "You did nothing wrong tonight, *a'kala*," his voice sounded gentle, sweet, though it slid toward amused when he added, "although perhaps you should speak to Agni before calling to water a second time."

"Leith is the one who stabbed me," she whispered. "Not Vayu."

Laszlo's hands flexed, clamped down on her back, his whole body tensed, but he stopped himself from pushing her back. He exhaled a hard breath, then a second one. Unwilling to go on until he calmed, she waited.

It took fewer than ten heartbeats for his hands to relax.

"Yes," she still whispered, unable to raise her voice. "I know."

His arms wrapped her. His voice sounded rough. "What do you know?"

"I know I should have told you. I know I should have told Marco. I know it was stupid not to."

He exhaled again, but it didn't sound angry. "Why would she act so boldly, Kiera, knowing that you held this secret?"

"I don't think she thought I remembered," she told him, then lifted her face so she could see his. Oh, he was still very angry. He had pressed his lips into a thin line and his eyes looked both cold and frightening.

"What are you thinking?" she asked.

His gaze dropped to hers. His still-palpable rage sent a shiver down her back, but his voice stayed mild, merely curious. "She thought you did not remember because you were near death when she did this?"

"That's what I think," she admitted. "I didn't tell anyone afterward, so she must have thought I didn't remember."

His anger hadn't softened, though he kept it from his voice. "Tell me what happened, Kiera."

Her voice rose and came fast as fear pushed sharp fingers into her gut, but whether worry of what Laszlo would do or dread of reliving her horror sparked it she didn't know. "Not unless you promise not to do anything. At least not right now."

His hands came up so quickly, grabbed her shoulders so fast, that she flinched back hard, and she watched chagrin slide over his face before something else washed it away. In one fluid movement he stood with her in his arms and marched across the floor to the bed.

"Kiera," he said as he laid her down and pulled a blanket across her, "I love you more than I love my own life, or any other's. And I know that your love for me is as great." He sat down next to her and stared into her face. "But you must trust me as well, *a'kala*, trust that *I* will not act as an animal."

Her mouth opened in protest, the horror of his words a wound in her heart, but his face said *listen*, so she held her words, but kept them in her mouth.

"In fairness, I will admit that I am at times the barbarian you call me, but never will I endanger you, Kiera, nor do I take the responsibilities of ruling this deconn so lightly that I would seek my revenge on Leith this night or without due thought. But you must tell me the truth, my heart, and trust that I will use what I know to take care of you, and our people."

"I have never, ever thought you were an animal," Kiera whispered, and felt a tear escape even as she tried to blink it back.

His finger caught it, and he leaned in and brushed a kiss against her mouth. "I know," he said against her lips before he leaned back. "It is my anger that spoke, and I ask that you forgive those words." He gifted her with a small smile. "That Chanda still lives is evidence of the depths of my patience."

That he could make a joke, even such a bad one, roused a tremulous smile, and he kissed her upturned lips. "Can you bear to relive it once more, Kiera?"

Ignoring the knot in her stomach, she nodded, but not because she wanted to talk about what had happened, or even because he'd asked. Not really. She would tell him because if things had been reversed, if it had been him who had withheld a secret this big, she would be angry—hell, furious—he hadn't told her, and she owed the truth to him. And he was right; he deserved her complete trust.

But she still dreaded it. Had pushed that entire turn away and tried to forget it, as silly and selfish as that was. But that didn't mean she had to face it alone a second time. "Will you lay with me?"

Without a word he pulled his shirt over his head, and she scooted over to make room as he slid his pants down his legs.

She loved his skin, such a rich umber, and the heavy, thick lines that drew his body. His strong, strong body, the body her own ached for, took such pleasures from, and in. The one she clung to for comfort and sought above all else when she felt afraid.

She lifted the blanket so he could lie next to her, and when he'd settled, she pressed against his side as close as she could get, laid an arm over him, and rested her head on his chest. His arms wrapped her, bracketed her. A line between her and the rest of the world.

Her eyes closed and she soaked up his warmth.

And still. And still she didn't want to. Not even Laszlo could stand between her and what slunk like a whipped dog along the edges of her thoughts, make what had happened not.

Saying those words would draw back the pictures. Force her to remember how her body had strained for fire, how it felt when the convulsions tore muscle from bone and she sucked water into her lungs, desperate for something, for anything, to fill the chasm that, with each beat of her heart, had siphoned the living particles from every cell. How after a time she'd wished for death as much as she'd once wanted life, and how obscenely clear the light had been that splashed her face from the window above the barrel.

Her mouth felt dry, so she used her tongue wet her lips. "It was after I'd been in that barrel for a long time." A prickly ball filled her chest, the remnants of the fear she'd felt and the pain of remembering it, so she let out a breath, hoping to ease the pressure. She could do this. "I heard voices, but I couldn't really hear what they were saying. He, Vayu, opened the lid and pulled me out of the water." She wiped a hand across her face and let out another breath. "He had a knife. A long knife. He told me—he told me that he was going to kill you, that he wanted me to know that. That it would be painful."

The talking dried her mouth. She swallowed once, then again. Laszlo's arm squeezed her closer. "I was so afraid," she whispered. "But she—she cut him. Stabbed him before he could do it. In the neck. He fell."

Kiera wiped her mouth, stripped away the sticky film that gathered in the corners, and took a moment to breathe. In. Out. In. Out. Her eyes closed, and she didn't try to open them. "She told me that I—I disappointed her, and that it would be me. Who had done this. Killed Vayu. Because she—she couldn't be a—a—the one who killed Vayu. While Marco ruled." Laszlo's face looked so calm when she opened her eyes and stared into it. How she wished she could school her features like that. "What she said didn't make sense. She said you couldn't rule. I didn't know that you—that the slaves—had taken the city. I didn't understand, but then she stabbed me." Her hand squeezed the blanket below her breasts, covered the scar. "And I couldn't breathe. I panicked. I pulled—I pulled everything. I pulled from Leith, and she fell, and I think I blacked out."

His quiet voice sliced into the silence that had fallen but did not tear it. "You were very brave."

"Laszlo, I was pretty much a failure on all counts," she sighed, and tried to push back the shame that stark truth evoked. "He knew, he knew and shielded, and he knew how to hold me, and—"

His chest flexed as he moved. "No, Kiera. Without your help we would have failed that turn." Gentle fingers lifted her face so she could see the pain her words had inflicted, and the depths of his anger, and the way his love for her blunted them both. His teeth showed when he smiled, and erased it all, at least from his face. "Plans always go wrong. If you'll remember, I have said so many times when explaining to the *otuks* how battles are planned."

"Ouch," she said to acknowledge the hit, but smiled to let him know that she knew he was teasing, and that it was okay, a relief, to stop talking about this. "So what should we do about Leith?"

His eyes drifted to the ceiling as he considered. "I do not have an answer, Kiera." After a moment he added, "But I think for now it is better to hold the secret."

"From Marco?"

"From all."

"Why?"

"Because it will create a rift between them, among the Skani, and for a time we need everyone to stand together." He turned to face her, a remnant of his earlier anger lighting his eyes. "But only for now."

"All right," she agreed, and laid her head on his shoulder. A thought struck. "Wait. Let's make a deal," she said, and lifted her head. "I will do as you ask, but in exchange you send Kuruk back to the army."

The fire sizzled, and Kiera looked from it to Laszlo, who scooted up so that he could rest his head against the headboard. "No."

"I don't need a bodyguard." She lifted a hand. "I don't even know him, Laszlo."

"No."

"I don't trust him."

His head turned. "Why?"

"I don't know him. He won't talk."

His laugh startled her. "He fears speaking to you."

"What?"

"I believe he is in love with you."

Her mouth dropped open. "How do you—no. Why, Laszlo? Why in the world would you choose someone you believed to be in love with me to be my bodyguard?"

His voice was very serious. "In the heat of the worst moment, Kiera, when you are forced to choose, who would you save? Alex, or a child you did not know? Love chooses for us, Kiera. And when I am apart from you, I will know that someone who will choose you first stands ready to do so."

It took a minute to digest all that. To believe it. "So you're not jealous?" Even though it made a lot of sense, she wasn't sure that she could do that, or would want to, and she felt frankly surprised that he would.

"You are the most honorable woman I have ever known, Kiera. I have no fear."

Her breath made a ragged sound when it left her lips. "I don't deserve you," she said, and meant it.

He kissed her hair and ran a rough hand down her back. "The honor is mine." A shiver followed his fingers as they slid across the rise of her hip, then lower. "Let me show you."

CHAPTER 6

"KIERA, YOU MUST WAKE." THAT WAS LASZLO, and she opened her eyes to find him standing next to the bed. Dark still crowded the room. And cold. He hadn't even lit the fire, yet here he stood, fully dressed in black leather

Despite the blur of not enough sleep, she knew these facts added up to trouble. She pushed back the blankets and dropped her feet to the floor. "What is it?" Without answering he handed her a dress, and she laid it on the bed and stripped off the warm bed gown.

"I must ride out by second earth," he told her as she dressed. Five a.m., she translated. Good God, it was early. "Vrishka has made his first move."

Her heart thudded as he turned her so he could lace up the ties in the back. "Are we all going? If so, I'm not wearing this."

"No," he said over her shoulder. "I do not believe I will need more than a tou."

"What?"

"A thousand soldiers. You will stay here. And Marco."

Kiera gritted her teeth as she pulled free, then turned to face him. "I love how you've suddenly become the dictator, Laszlo. Do you think maybe we three should talk about this before you go haring off? I don't even know what's going on yet."

His face hardened and his tone warned her that he meant every word. "I will not argue this with you, Kiera."

The ties at her back popped open when she crossed her arms, and one shoulder of the dress slid down her chest, somewhat dimming the effect she'd been going for. Angrily, she shoved the fabric back up and held it there. "You can't keep me tucked in this damned house just because it's dangerous out there, Laszlo."

His lips made one straight line. "I *ask*," he told her, striving for patience, "that you stay because the Alak will follow you if this goes badly, and the

Skani will do Marco's will."

Well, damn it. A breath escaped, and she nodded, then turned so he could finish tying her dress.

After she'd dressed and brushed out her hair, he whisked her down the stairs and into the great hall. Marco had already arrived, and Allie—they must have made up—as well as a few others, including Leith, and Chanda.

Amba, Laszlo's mother, had come, too, and Kiera breathed a sigh of relief. A kind woman, perhaps—at times, at least—but no one crossed Amba, the sole Alak, aside from Laszlo, who held no fear of the Skani despite being a slave for most of her life. Kiera thought maybe Amba confused the Skani nobility. She certainly made them uncomfortable, maybe because now they all knew that she had led the revolution against them that had finally freed the slaves from Skani ownership.

As though time had caught her in a curtsey, a woman knelt in the middle of the half circle the group made. Her thin shoulders shook, and Kiera rushed up and crouched down beside her. "Are you cold?" she asked, and her breath caught when the woman looked up and into her face. She knew this young blonde woman. The Skani slave she'd rescued from a drunken man's grasp that night so many moons ago when she'd visited Mayor Nick's manse. On her way to Fairbanks for the very first time.

"Oh, my lady, thank the goddess," the woman gasped, her breath caught on a sob, and grabbed Kiera's dress. A man stepped forward, one who had been speaking with Chanda, and who wore livery in Nick's gold and purple. He bowed deeply, and Kiera kept her eyes on him as she stood and lifted the young woman to her feet, then wrapped an arm around her waist to keep her up.

"My Lady Governor, I beg an audience," the man told her in a formal tone, one she'd heard others use with Vayu, and Leith.

"Why did you bring this woman?" Kiera demanded, and tried to rein in her anger. Surely this man didn't make the decision to send a frightened young woman traipsing across the deconn in the freezing night without even a damned coat.

Flushing, he bowed again, this time more deeply. "I beg your forgiveness, my Lady Governor," he told her as he stood, and she could tell it took some effort to meet her eyes. "The choice was not my own. She followed me, and when I discovered it, I had come too far to return."

Kiera looked down at the woman whose freezing body pressed against her own. This woman—girl, really, as she couldn't be seventeen—wore a tattered dress, one in which grease or food had stained the front, and which was so threadbare that a good stretch would tear off the sleeves.

Her eyes found Marco's and she made a face she hoped said that she was sorry, but she didn't know who else to ask. "Will you have someone take her to get something warm to wear?" At this mark the hall was as icy as her room since no one had yet lit the braziers. She looked back at the girl and added. "And to eat."

With a nod he motioned to a woman, a servant she hadn't seen, who rushed from an alcove and peeled the woman from Kiera, then dragged her away. The girl looked over her shoulder at Kiera as though afraid to leave her side.

"It's all right," Kiera told her. "Go. And take a bath. That always helps me. And have someone bring you to my apartment later."

Amba snorted for some reason and Kiera turned to find her staring at Chanda, who looked ever so slightly defiant, though his cheeks looked a little too pink in the thin light. What was this about?

A hand fell on her shoulder, and she looked into Laszlo's face. He, too, stared at Chanda, though, unlike Amba, he did not look amused.

Although it was hard to imagine how someone could draw a sexual innuendo out of what she had told the girl, she suspected Chanda had, and hadn't had the grace to keep it off his face. What an idiot he was.

To break the flow she turned to the man in livery, who stood motionless, perhaps hoping that no one would direct the anger flowing through the room at him. Kuruk, her new bodyguard, stood just behind him, though Kiera could not fathom why he thought that prudent.

With a sigh, she began. "Please tell us what you came to say."

The man bowed again. "As I told Lord Governor Laszlo, my Lady Governor, a force of near a hundred men has attacked the villes outlying Talium during the dark of the last two turns. Men have been killed, homes torn down or burned, and children taken. Despite that, my Lord Nickinum does not believe these are the acts of a slaving party, and he begs your assistance in driving them out."

Kiera turned to Laszlo, whose face had gone calm and smooth, a look she knew masked deep anger. *Beware*, she thought, *you bastards*, and felt a snake of satisfaction wind round her middle. They would be very sorry indeed if Laszlo found them.

"This is not Lord Vrishka," Chanda interjected, interrupting her thoughts. "He would not violate the armistice," he insisted, voice urging them to believe him. "He has given a tenturn for consideration, to commence when the terms are relayed, and nine turns remain."

Laszlo's voice rolled through the hall. "Who else then, Chanda?"

A smile lifted Chanda's lips, a look he forced to seem casual. "The Shunakah, perhaps. I do not know."

With a snort, Laszlo turned and strode out of the hall, leaving Kiera to deal with this mess.

Heaving another sigh, she turned back to the poor envoy. "Go get something to eat, then go to the stables north of the manse and find an *otuk* to take your orders from." She turned to Amba. "Will you have Emmy bring Alex to me?" To Marco she said, "Will you meet me in my apartment?" then turned and left the hall herself, Kuruk on her heels and a stone in her belly.

EMMY BROUGHT NOT ONLY ALEX, but breakfast, and a lot of it, which was good since Marco brought Allie and Amba had come, too.

On turns like this one Kiera desperately missed coffee, her one prior addiction, and the sole thing she truly missed from her former home. Instead she tried to satisfy herself with tea, which in truth wasn't too bad, but it lacked that caffeine kick that would have sharpened the fuzzy edges a too-early morning left lingering around the edges of her thoughts. Her stomach felt knotted, and she didn't even try to eat anything. A headache threatened, too, but the powder of Saman's she'd mixed with her tea should soon wipe that away.

"Laszlo is marching out with a thousand soldiers," she told the room between sips. She raised a hand to forestall the objection framing Marco's lips. "I know. I told him the same thing you're about to say, that he thinks he's the dictator and blah blah blah. He wants us to stay because the Alaks will follow me and the Skani you if this is a trap or something goes wrong, and I agreed because he's right, so if you're mad, vent it at me."

Marco shook his head. "It's too early for this," he complained, and slid back to rest his head on the back of the chair. Wearing a little frown, Allie took his hand and rubbed her other across his thigh.

"Kuruk, would you like something to eat?" Kiera asked the silent man who stood just behind her chair at the table. The addition of this ten-person square table had been a good idea, she thought, since the three rulers so often met here and needed a large flat surface for whatever they were working on, with room to spare for food and drink.

When he didn't answer she swiveled around to look at him. His gaze skittered from hers as he shook his head, and she felt a frown press her lips together. "Have you eaten?" she prodded, forcing him to lift his eyes to hers.

"No, my lady." His voice sounded gritty, something like Laszlo's, though not quite as hard. Was he a bear, too?

Even though she couldn't see her, Kiera felt Amba's amusement, knew she was grinning, which wouldn't help matters any.

"Everybody, please forgive my lapse," she said as she turned back to the table and picked up her tea. "This poor soul is Kuruk, whom Laszlo chose to act as my bodyguard when he's away from the manse. Kuruk," she gestured, "this is Alex, and Emmy, his nanny, and this is Amba, Laszlo's mother, whom you may already know, and this is Marco, and Allie, Marco's fiancée."

Nothing. She turned her head to find him staring at the window just past the table. He looked like he wished that he could be anywhere else but here. "Kuruk, I won't bite you," she said sternly, to which Amba snorted. Kiera flapped a hand at her without turning from Kuruk. "As you can see, Kuruk, you're not going to get an inch out of anyone here, but don't take it personally. We're pretty informal, so please try and relax." She smiled. "The truth is that it makes me feel a little uncomfortable with you hovering behind me all the time." She motioned to a chair beside her. "Please sit down. You can guard me just as effectively from right here, and if you eat something, just think how much stronger you'll be for it."

She could see him wavering. "*Sit*," she urged, and patted the chair.

Someone knocked, and Kiera sighed as Kuruk bolted toward the door.

He escorted the young woman from Nick's to Kiera's table. From five feet out the blonde woman, who had bathed and changed into one of the manse's servant's dresses, a vast improvement, dropped into a curtsey.

Kiera stood. "No, no," she said, but had forgotten to let go of her tea, so she plunked it down before walking to the girl. "Don't do that," Kiera said, and tried not to sound chiding, but this bowing and scraping wore on her and thisturn she just didn't feel patient. "We don't do that here," she said again as the woman stood, a confused look on her face, which reminded her of how Emmy had looked at her once.

"What's your name?" Kiera asked as she led the girl to the seat she'd invited Kuruk to sit in, then changed her mind and sat her in another. She flashed Kuruk a look to warn him she wasn't giving up on him yet.

"Dula, my lady," was the woman's quiet reply.

"Have you eaten?" Kiera asked, and started dishing fruit into the plate near the woman's hands when Dula shook her head.

When Dula grabbed a pinch of blackberries Kiera retook her seat, waited until Kuruk looked at her, and pointed to the one next to her. When he looked like he would balk, she told him, "I'm not going to do anything else until you sit down."

With a truculent set to his mouth he slipped into the chair and sat with his back too straight, hands on his thighs.

Satisfied, at least for now, Kiera turned to Alex. "I have decided that you can train to be a soldier," she told him, and watched the smile slide across his face. "Although I do have some stipulations."

His face was a picture of joy, which roused a pang of sadness, but she smothered it. She wasn't going to think about that now. "Oh, thank you, Keer!" he bubbled. Marco, too, grinned, as did Emmy, who adored Alex, but Allie's smile looked at best polite, Kuruk stared straight ahead, and Amba seemed thoughtful.

"Alex, I will allow you to train, but you need to understand that you will not be a soldier for many cycles—" she leaned forward, face as stern as she could make it, wanting to impress the utter sincerity behind her words into his heart—"and you must not think that it's ever okay to join a battle of any kind for any reason or do anything whatsoever that might endanger you without my—*my*, do you hear me, Alex, and not any others'—my explicit permission, which I guarantee will not come for many cycles. If you cannot swear to me that you will do that, I will not allow you to train." When he opened his mouth to answer, she added, "And Alex, if you disobey me in any way, the training will stop, and not just temporarily. Do you understand me?"

Eyes huge, Alex nodded, but then he grinned, his six-cycle-old joy washing away all else. And he had doubtless already forgotten her warning, but she meant to make sure that she reminded him. Often.

And so now for the other part. Turning to Kuruk, she smiled and hoped it didn't look like she was trying to soften him up. Was this how Laszlo felt, she wondered, when he arranged everything just the way he wanted it?

Kuruk's face said that he was suspicious. *Good instincts*, she thought with just a little envy. It seemed like she never caught the schemes until too late, but she was learning.

"I want you to train Alex," she told him in a voice that she hoped brooked no dissent. "Not where the other soldiers train, not for now, but he needs to learn from a soldier, and you're an *otuk*, which means that you're a very good soldier." He opened his mouth, undoubtedly to object, or refuse, but she charged on. "Whatever you would teach a new soldier is fine, swords or hand-to-hand fighting or whatever, but I want this done, Kuruk, and I want you to do it." She leaned closer and spoke quietly. "I don't trust anyone else to do this, Kuruk, and he needs to learn."

Anger, and maybe embarrassment, suffused his face—and she didn't blame him since what else could he do but smother it in here in front of everyone, and to her as the governor—but he held it, softened it, and somehow managed to wipe it away in fewer than five heartbeats. It still shone in his eyes, though, when he'd had a few moments to think up some words and tried to finally speak them, but again Kiera interrupted. "I'll go, too," she told him, and watched the anger drain away. Most of it. "I want to brush up on hand-to-hand, and I will train with Alex." Well, for some of the turn at least, but she'd deal with that later.

That done, she looked to the girl still wolfing fruit a few chairs over. "Dula, I know you do not want to return to Talium. That you came here to escape it." Dula's hand froze, terror suffused her face, but she did not look up. A frown pressed Kiera's mouth, but she forced her voice smooth. "I'm going to ask Emmy to find you something to do. Since you've come, you're staying." Emmy nodded, obviously pleased, and Kiera returned her nod, satisfied.

Marco looked amused when her gaze caught his, and she smiled back. If only everything was this easy to fix.

KIERA ASKED KURUK TO FIND HER a sparring partner, someone skilled at hand-to-hand, and she spent the rest of the morning in the stable practicing *tai kwon do* with one of the soldiers, Balek, a young shifter with annoyingly abundant energy, and whose wicked humor snuck further out the more he relaxed around her. In the stall next to hers Kuruk started Alex with a staff, and drilled him in high blocks and high strikes, then low blocks and low strikes, for the same marks she sparred.

Two things surprised Kiera: Kuruk's patience and Alex's dedication. Frankly, she expected Alex to whine like he did when she made him do something, but even when his arms had to be aching—hell, her body ached after the first mark—he scrunched up his stubborn face and kept going. And when he faltered, or made a mistake, which he did a lot of during the first marks, Kuruk softened Alex's anger with soothing words, and encouraged him when he started to tire. But he was a strict master, too. He offered no false praise and made Alex meet the bar he'd set before he offered a word. Maybe Alex's two cycles of martial arts training helped, and maybe the fear Kiera knew he carried drove him on, but by lunchtime they were both sweat-soaked and satisfied with a morning well spent.

"Do I have to go to school after lunch?" Alex asked as the four sat on the hay in his stall and passed a jug of water around, and Kiera noted that his arms shook when he lifted the jug to his mouth. She would have commented, offered encouragement, but they both knew that would stop when his muscles grew stronger.

Kuruk, who looked as fresh as he had this morning, had leaned his back against the boards lining the stall, though he took the water when Alex offered it. After he'd taken a drink, she raised her eyebrows to him in a silent question. As an *otuk*, he'd know better than she what kind of training schedule a young soldier should have.

Perhaps surprised that she was asking his opinion, he held her eyes for so long that Alex looked from one to the other, trying to puzzle out what secrets passed between them. After another long drink, Kuruk looked at Alex. "He should go to school," he said, then stood and walked out of the stall.

Alex jumped to his feet and chased after Kuruk. "But we'll practice again nexturn, right?" he called as he jogged to catch up.

"Yes, Alex, if Lady Kiera says you may."

"Oh, now there is a bitter answer," Balek teased in a voice loud enough to be heard through the stables, and grinned at Kiera. With a vigor that Kiera envied, he jumped to his feet and offered her a hand. "I imagine that is because he would rather be teaching a pretty lady like you," he told her as he pulled her to her feet, a naughty glint in his eye.

Kiera grimaced so hard her eyes narrowed, and Balek burst out laughing, pleased that his joke was such a success. "I hardly think so," Kiera told him sternly, though she secretly thought it was likely a lot closer to the mark than he imagined.

The hay had pierced her pants, so Kiera dusted off her bottom and used a hand to try and covertly dislodge what remained. "Can you come nexturn, Balek? God knows I need the practice." She lifted her eyes. "And oh, do you have a bath out here?"

The mischievous grin he quickly hid told her he had deliberately misread her words. "I do not think it will hold the three of us," he told her in mock seriousness. "Kuruk will have to wait."

Before Balek's last word was out, Kuruk was there, his broad back a palisade between her and the joker. His words were quiet, and hot, and he said them in their native language. Balek's head dropped as he listened, and he nodded when Kuruk had finished. Without a word to her, without even turning around, Kuruk strode away.

Kiera's eyes followed him as he walked down the hall toward the door, his ramrod back a testament to his anger. When he disappeared through the door at the end of the stable, she lifted her gaze to Balek, the tall young man who had waited for her full attention. "I am sorry, Lady Kiera. I did not mean disrespect." His voice sounded so earnest, so clearly upset, that Kiera couldn't find it in her heart to hold it against him, so she patted his arm before stepping out of the stall.

"What I want," she told them all, "is for Alex to take a bath so he can get to school by the time the other children return from lunch. I am going to head back and take a bath myself before magic lessons. Kuruk," she called, "will you bring Alex up when he's finished so he can change his clothes?"

"Yes, my lady," came Kuruk's reply from someplace she couldn't see.

A VICIOUS WIND RIPPED THE DOOR from Kiera's fingers as she left the stable, and it banged against the wall before she could catch it. Above her, dark clouds wrapped the noontide sky in a funereal shroud. In two steps the wind reached icy fingers into Kiera's coat and tore the hood from her head. "Good God," she complained to the bitter wind, and stumbled back into the stable. After her hood had been tied fast she ventured back out, head down against the gale.

Snow would fall, a lot of it, and the realization made her stomach churn. Laszlo was out there, Laszlo and a thousand of her people. With this wind pushing those clouds, it could well turn into a blizzard, a whiteout, and people died in those with no help whatsoever from enemy soldiers.

As if summoned by her thoughts, a wet splat hit her coat, then another, then a hundred. She made a sound of frustration, but the wind snatched it from her lips and sent it spinning behind her. Head still down, she pushed ahead, back toward the manse.

In thirty steps a white film covered the front of her pants as well as her coat, and the wind drilled lumps of half-frozen water mercilessly inward as if it were determined to bore a hole clear through her thighs. The temperature had dropped like a stone from a window, and wind chill drove it to deadly. The ice on her pants burned like fire would have once felt.

One foot slid and she nearly fell. After she'd regained her balance she lifted her head to gauge how much farther, praying it wasn't far, but all she could see was a curtain of white streamlets whipping toward her. The wind took offense at her upturned face and shoved snow into her eyes, across her cheeks, up her nose, and tried to force a clot between her lips, but she ducked her head and used a hand to wipe the wet before it iced her eyes closed.

A look behind her showed that the stable was lost as well. Fear and frustration warred in her chest. Fear for herself, though not for Alex. Kuruk would surely keep him in, but impotent anger was the greater of the two that she felt for Laszlo, and for the soldiers caught in this storm. It was the worst one she'd seen here, worst by far, and she had no idea if they—the soldiers—had plans for this kind of thing. She really should have paid attention to Laszlo's lessons. Did they carry ropes? Buddy up? And where would they find shelter? Walking around in this would be deadly to anyone, everyone, with time as the only variable. How long until a bear froze to death?

Her own shaking—when had she started shaking?—reminded her that she, too, would soon freeze to death if she didn't find shelter. Which way should she go? How funny would it be—well, not funny, but tragic—if she froze to death just a few hundred feet from the manse? Fifty from the stable?

Her eyes closed as her laugh escaped and rode the wind away. Her? Freeze to death? If she froze to death, it would be from terminal stupidity.

Eyes still closed, her sight shot out of her body. Noontide, the cardinal fire mark, and despite the blizzard, fire flowed everywhere, including, to her great surprise, in the mixed pools driving the storm. Perhaps sensing her dire need, hundreds of strands broke from closest main flows without her call, wrapped her sight in delicious heat, and followed it back into her body of clay.

As fire churned delightfully in her chest, she wondered exactly what she should do with it. Neither Agni nor any author of the dozens of magic books she'd read had provided even the slightest clue about how you might warm yourself in a blizzard, or in any circumstance for that matter. Well, the obvious—and most important—thing was to warm her legs, so she sent coils of yellow fire around her thighs, then down to her boots. The snow popped, spluttered, and steamed off as the fire streams met, merged and blanketed her legs, leaving delicious warmth in their wake. Unfortunately, and before should could stop it, the two iciest spots on the front of her pants and a section on the back of her left thigh caught fire and burned off, leaving her skin bare to the wind.

Chagrined, she decided the next order of business was to clear a path. But which way? It seemed like the manse should be in front of her, but she could have turned—how would she know?—and even a small shift in direction would send her off toward the river, or on a trek to the back gate. Afraid to lose heat while she searched, she squatted down, wrapped her arms around herself, and sent her sight back out. Surely, *surely!* she would be able to find the manse with her sight.

Never had she sought to find a place, or for that matter anything in the physical, with this tool for the elemental dimension. But it had to be possible. Wouldn't the manse bend the flows? Or something?

Up she went, up as she searched for some clue. Streams flowed, mostly fire, large and small and predominantly from the northeast. If the manse stood where she thought it did, it should be southeast of where she knelt, so she drifted that way. Within moments, she found it. A block, a huge rock in the middle of a river. The gold, she remembered. The manse's builders had lined the manse with gold to stop the elements from flowing too heavily inside it, maybe to keep mages from using it on each other there. In any case, and to her very great relief, it lay exactly where she thought it was.

Down she came and found her body shaking hard with cold. How long had it been? Ten seconds? Fifteen? It had to be forty below zero out, but even so that seemed too soon for hypothermia to start. *Oh*, she remembered. *My pants.* Without trying to stand she sent fire to encase her, but kept it a good five feet out to avoid having to return naked to the manse. In the span of five heartbeats glorious warmth restored her temperature as well as her determination, and she stood and looked in the direction of the manse.

Agni would chide her for using gestures, but despite the fire, the cold had rendered her thoughts as sluggish as her limbs, so she raised a hand and pointed ahead of her. "Manifest," she whispered to the wind, and an arm of fire shot from her fingers and blasted the snow from the ground. Ten steps, and she blasted again, then stopped to send fire to warm her. It took a painfully slow time to get across the barren ground—fire was giving way to earth, so a mark had passed when after perhaps her twentieth blast she saw stone.

A heavy sigh channeled the relief that washed through her, and she stumbled the last few steps when she tried to trot. When she reached it, she pushed her palms against the frigid wall to convince herself it was real. Okay; now she needed to go right, toward the front doors.

The granite walls blocked the brunt of the wind, but ribbons of icy air slid down from the blind skies and whipped her hair around her face. Cold seeped from the wall as she walked it, and since her exhausted brain couldn't manage to both walk and sustain a fire flow, she had to keep stopping to warm up. Frustration, which apparently did not require brainspace to flourish, had won the war, and its prickly fingers urged her to hurry and get inside.

She increased her pace. It couldn't be much farther.

A stone, an ice-slickened remnant of the construction, caught her foot and she fell sideways, away from the wall, and hit the ground hard.

Before she could even cry out, something landed on top of her. Grabbed her hair and smashed her head into the ground. Stars flew across her vision. Almost instinctively, her free arm shot up to grab her attacker, and found naked skin.

Adrenalin shot through her as rough hands flipped her onto her back. With one quick shift his legs trapped her arms next to her body, but she bucked up, tried to dislodge him. A hand smashed into her mouth and she tasted the warmth of her own blood.

She opened her eyes wide, tried to lift her head to see through the snow clotting the air. Who was this? Why? The effects from the cold and the adrenalin kept scattering her thoughts, but enough sense remained to bleed the alarm she felt into panic, because too many things were just too wrong.

His second blow to her jaw sent a scream tumbling from her lips. And then he leaned close, she saw his face, and her heart exploded in her chest.

"When I let you up, you will get Alex and bring him here," Hunter, her dead sister's husband, her dead sister's murderer, told her quietly from a face as mild as milk. His green eyes stared into hers, an incongruent, warm color that invited a second look, a return smile.

His eyes lied. A monster lived inside this man, a man who had battered his wife, beat her for trying to leave him until he'd crushed in her skull.

Her mind balked, denied this impossibility. Not here. It couldn't be Hunter. Not in the city. Not near the front doors of the manse. Soldiers guarded every break in the wall. No one could get in. No one.

She heard herself wheezing as she hyperventilated. "You know that I won't," she managed, then closed her eyes and sent out her sight.

A thin strand drifted above her, weak and frail, and fell back. She screamed her frustration and sent it up again, pushed with all the strength but like her body, like her mind, the walk, the snow, the overuse had exhausted it.

When she opened her eyes Hunter smiled down, his face patient and almost tender, and it frightened her more than any look she had ever seen him wear.

"Yes," he told her conversationally, "I do know. As I know your magic is spent." He leaned back and considered for a moment. "But I'll have him back anyway."

His next blow broke her nose, and thick liquid choked her as it filled her throat. Another came, and she bucked and tried to turn her face, but her strength had fled. She spat blood and tried to bury her face in the snow, but the target was her head, any part of it, and his blows continued to fall, and she felt her head bounce each time his fist found her skull.

A blackness erupted around the edges of her vision, an inky flow that somehow blocked the pain as completely as it threatened her sight. The sound of her breathing, so fast, seemed to drift away, as if she were traveling away from it.

Someone screamed, a silken sound from miles away, and then something ripped away the pressure holding her to the ground. She turned her head. Her blood choked her, so she opened her mouth and let what breath remained in her lungs push it out. Each spasm triggered an excruciating jolt of pain in her jaw, but she forced it further open. A red mist erupted twice more and she could breathe again.

The snow had stopped, and someone was yelling, both of which seemed curious, so she narrowed her eyes and tried to focus.

Her heart thudded. Alex. Alex stood not twenty feet away. Her eyes closed on their own as she sought the strength to rise, but nothing remained in her but a yawning abyss of impotent terror. Unable to bear her own feelings, she forced her eyes open and found Alex. His arm moved violently up and down as he screamed, a nonstop flow of sounds from his ever-open mouth. Wait, wait! Was that Kuruk behind him? Relief flooded her and she let her head fall back. But even from the ground, she could see. A group of what must be other soldiers crowded behind them. A standoff? Against one man?

Her gaze drifted to where they stared. A group there, a handful of naked men stood, a barrier between Alex's group and the wall, and where she lay. Even further, closer to her, Hunter crouched. Blood leaked down his face as if he'd been hit, and she wondered who could have done so.

Hunter stood in one fluid movement. Alex's words began making sense as her mind cleared, a blessing and a curse.

"Get out!" Alex screamed. "Get out of here! I will kill you dead if you ever touch Kiera again! Get out! I hate you!"

"Son," Hunter broke in, and raised a placating hand. "She is a witch. She cast a spell on you. She hasn't told you the truth about what happened to Mama. Come with me, Alex, and I will tell you what really happened."

"Liar! You're a liar, Dad! Get out! I hate you!"

"Alex, you belong with your father."

"I hate you!" Alex screamed, and squirmed out from under Kuruk's hand on his shoulder. Both hands up, he charged toward the line of naked men and screamed wordlessly. A gasp left Kiera's lips, and she managed to get one arm under her, but Kuruk got there first.

Something, an incandescent ball of—was that air?—flew from Alex's outstretched hands at the same moment Kuruk's arms wrapped his waist and lifted him from the ground, and back.

It hit the group of standing men like a giant bowling ball and knocked them flat, and slammed into Hunter a heartbeat later. He flew back and smashed into the wall.

"Take them!" Kuruk shouted, and soldiers flowed past him, a squirming Alex still tight against his chest.

But before the first soldier could reach them, Hunter's men changed,

Shunakah the lot of them, and the soldiers slid to a stop. "Swords!" Kuruk shouted, unnecessarily since most had already drawn them. A shriek from the sky tore everyone's gaze upward, and a collective gasp erupted as a clot of giant black birds descended into the field. Some dove at the soldiers, who either ran or dropped to the ground. Others plucked Shunakah from the snow with monstrous claws and flapped heavily as they lifted their prizes into the skies and away.

With a final look at Kiera, Hunter changed and leapt into the waiting claws of the biggest one. *A raven*, Kiera despaired. *They're raven shifters.* A sound from Alex drew her eyes, and her heart broke into a hundred pieces when she saw the look on his face.

It was her fault. She should have told him.

KIERA WOKE TO FIND SAMAN standing over her. "Quite a fight, my lady," he told her cheerfully and patted her hand. Was he kidding? Since her jaw seemed to be stuck shut, she didn't even try to answer, but instead let her eyes drift across the room. Sterile, white walls meant that someone had brought her to the healer's unit. A good sign, one that meant she probably wouldn't die. A small, bare window broke the smooth seam of the wall to her right, and streamers of sunlight speared the glass and pierced the dimmer light diffusing the room.

"I would have pushed you into sleep, my lady, but to heal a broken jaw I need you to be awake," he told her as he collected tools, or did whatever made that noise. "At least for a time, although I have blocked most of the pain, I believe," he continued. "If I have not, please do say so."

How, she wondered, more than a little crossly since she couldn't seem to open her jaw, would she do that? With hand signals?

The genuine concern on his face when he turned back softened her anger, which she knew was in truth anger at herself, and she tried to push the ragged edges back into the darkness. Before she could finish the thought his firm hands moved her jaw, and despite his assurances, she arched as agony shot through her mouth and into her skull. "I am sorry," he told her, almost absently, and rested a finger on the sorest point. Relief flowed, as did her breath as she relaxed back on the bed.

Her jaw made a nauseating crunch when he next moved it, but no pain followed. After another adjustment he seemed satisfied, or so his face said as he drew his hands away. "Open, please," he commanded, and she did.

"Any permanent damage?" she asked as she moved her jaw from side to side.

His brows drew down. "I do not believe so." His voice was a question, a query as to why she might think so.

"Sorry, Lord Saman. I know your healing knows no equal. I have just never had my jaw broken before, and where I come from, it takes a very great deal of time to heal, even with medical help."

His face said he thought her home a barbaric place, but he instead said, "Please lay back, Lady Kiera. You needn't be awake for the rest."

"Am I hurt anywhere else?" she wondered. "I don't think he hit me anywhere besides the head."

"Your nose is still broken, my lady," he told her, all business, "and there may be other damage that your head injuries caused you to overlook." He laid a hand on her chest and urged her to lie flat.

When she woke the second time, Saman's face again hovered above her. Her eyes caught his, and what she saw there, saw on his whole face really, made her heart stutter. He wore the look she imagined doctors across time wore when they had to balance a compassionate mien with the need to create enough distance between themselves and their patients so as to not get caught in the tumble of emotions that followed the words that she knew waited in his mouth.

"Tell me," she said.

CHAPTER 7

Alex stood staring at her when Kiera opened her eyes the next morning. Her eyes swept the still-dark room and found no one else. She opened her arms and, after a moment's hesitation, he climbed in, boots and all. When he had snuggled up against her she wrapped the blankets around him, cocooning them together and away from the rest of the crazy world.

His shoulder shook and his tears wet her nightshirt. Unable to bear his pain, and her fault in it, her eyes closed and she squeezed him even closer. A time passed, air gave way to water, and the sun broke the horizon and started its trek across the sky. They dozed. No one interrupted.

Her bladder's urgent need woke her some time later, and she slipped out of Alex's arms and padded across the carpet to the bathroom.

"Am I a shifter, too?" Alex's small voice asked from the bed. Her stomach clenched, the flow of water stopped, and she had to close her eyes and make herself relax to get rid of the morning's excess. When she finished she washed her hands, found a packet of the pain powder to try and catch this-turn's headache before it overwhelmed her, and poured it into her mouth. She grimaced at the bitter taste, and reminded herself that she would have to go get some more from Saman. A lot more, since she'd likely be needing it every turn.

Her thoughts skittered, but she didn't try to call them back since this was not the time to think about that, so she cleared her mind and walked back into the main apartment. That Alex was afraid and confused was her fault, and she would do all she could to make things right. Now.

"Are you hungry?" she asked as she climbed up on the bed.

He waited until she lay back, then scooted so she could cradle his body next to hers. A warmth, the gentle scent of love, drifted up from her middle, filled her chest. This boy would be one hell of a good man someday. His bravery, his strength, his heart. The pain he had been forced to endure, the loss, had shaped but not broken him. He wasn't bitter, or mean, or even angry at the world. What anger rose was short, spent quickly. When he hurt, he sought love, comfort. Almost always. Most importantly, he had a good sense of what was what, an ability to see through the smoke much more clearly than many adults she knew, and she hoped his courage and good sense would get him through this, too. Anything he needed she would give, even if it meant moving heaven and earth to do it.

"This is my fault, Alex," she told him, and tried to keep her voice neutral. She wanted him to understand but not feel like she needed his comfort. This was the time for him to hurt, to seek answers, and to find relief from both, she hoped. "I should have told you before, and I am so very sorry that you had to learn about your father this way."

"So will I turn into a—a Shunakah? Like Dad?" His voice still sounded small, as if he was afraid of the answer, which he probably was.

"Yes, I think you will become a Shunakah," she said flatly, using the name she never wanted him to associate with shame. "But being a shifter is a very good thing. Look at Laszlo. Amba. Kuruk. You will be strong, Alex, and fast. Shifters, the Alaks, can hear much more than others, and can smell things others—" she had to speak slowly, remind herself not to say we—"can't. Someday I will rely on you to protect me," she said, and prayed it was true.

When he turned so he could face her, she read confusion, and no little pain. "But Kiera, I did it! I called air! When—when Dad was sitting on you, I called air and blasted him off!"

She felt her face soften. "Can I tell you a secret?"

Curiosity twisted his lips. "Yeah."

"You have to promise to keep it a secret. Swear it."

"I swear!"

"Laszlo can call fire." His jaw dropped, and honesty demanded that she add, "Not as well as you can call air, but he can call some fire, and some air, too."

Eyes narrowed. "Why doesn't he ever use it?"

"I don't know, Alex, but the important thing is that you understand that you have the best of both worlds. You can call air, and you will be able to shift, while I, on the other hand, can just do one thing."

Despite his mixed feelings her words drew his smile, one that looked like he could feel proud, and prickles of relief slid across her skin. Everything was going to be all right. It really was.

"Should I tell Kuruk to change my soldier training?" he asked, thankfully oblivious to the way her traitorous feelings waxed and waned.

Her neck hurt, so she pushed up on an elbow and looked down at him. "How would he change it?"

A shrug was his only answer.

"Laszlo uses a sword, and so does Kuruk, I think. A staff is the first step to learning the sword, Alex, and don't forget that the man training you is an Alak, so I would listen to what he tells you."

"I want to learn more tai kwon do."

"I don't think anyone here does TKD but you and me, but the soldiers do train in hand-to-hand. The man I trained with yesturn fought as well as I do, maybe better, though it was a different style than I'm used to."

They both sat up when the door banged against the wall. Laszlo strode across the carpet, eyes blazing, and swept Kiera up in his arms.

Without a word he rocked her, back and forth, arms so tight she had to squirm to breathe.

"I'm all right," she whispered against his chest, but he ignored it. His body radiated tension, or anger, or perhaps both.

"I saved her," Alex announced proudly, and Laszlo stopped. "I called air, Laszlo, and knocked Dad off her. I saw him punching her in the head and he made her bleed really bad. I made air come and knocked him off her."

"Where was Kuruk?" he asked Alex in a voice that frightened Kiera. Not for Alex, but for Kuruk. It was a voice that promised death.

"I told—" she started, but he squeezed her until she squeaked.

"Where was Kuruk?" he asked again.

"He was with me," Alex answered obediently.

Only then did Laszlo let her draw away, and when he did a woman came into view, a woman standing on the carpet just a few feet away. A dark-skinned and -haired, young, and rather petite woman who wore a look that promised trouble.

"Who are you?" Kiera asked.

"I am Muukwa," the woman answered. "The savior of your villagers."

Laszlo snapped a phrase at her in their native tongue and she had the grace to color. "I beg forgiveness," she said a touch sullenly. "I am Muukwa of the Denaa, Laszlo's tribeswoman, a cousin, and I came to his aid at Ta-lium."

"Why was Kuruk not with you?" Laszlo asked Kiera.

"We'd practiced hand-to-hand all morning. Alex staff. I told Kuruk to let Alex bathe at the stables and bring him up when he'd finished, and the storm hit just as I left. Laszlo, it's my fault he stayed, not his, so don't take it out on him."

He stared into her face, his thoughts locked tightly behind a bland façade. All at once, he looked at Muukwa. "Go into the hall and tell Kuruk to bring my wife her breakfast."

Her brows raised, but she nodded and stepped back toward the door.

"How did he get in?" Laszlo wanted to know.

"I expect the same way he got out," she told him, then slid a glance to Alex, who she expected to be upset by this. Instead, he looked interested. If only everyone possessed such resilience. "Some raven shifters, very big ravens, picked them up, lifted them right out of the courtyard, and flew away."

Tension rippled across his chest.

"Yeil," Muukwa spat. "From southwest. The gods-forsaken Yeil have paired with the whoreson Shunakah."

"Was it Vrishka?" Kiera asked, wanting to change the subject. "Attacking at Talium?"

The wry smile that lifted Laszlo's lip told her he knew what she was doing, but he answered anyway. "I do not know, *a'kala*. The men Muukwa caught did not wear colors."

"He would not permit me put the fire to them or we'd know who sent them, dear cousin," Muukwa added. "But since none were Alak, it seems fair certain who they call lord."

"We do not torture prisoners, Muukwa," came Laszlo's tired reply, and Kiera looked between them and wondered how long they'd had to argue.

"Did you know each other before—" Too late, Kiera realized this was probably not the cheeriest topic to bring up. "Uh, before?"

Muukwa grinned, a slow smile filled with something wicked. "No, no, Kiera. I am far too young to have lived in the long ago time when Laszlo roamed free."

Marco walked in, his face creased with concern, and saved her from the onerous task of excavating her foot from her mouth. With only a sidelong glance at Muukwa, he walked around the bed to Kiera's side and stood looking at her for a long moment. "Are you all right?" he asked, voice tight.

Laszlo's arm tightened around her, and she looked up at him first. "I am okay," she told both of them, hating the lie but unwilling to reveal what Saman had told her. The truth would cause tremendous upset, and she knew that they would both coddle her and try to force her to stay out of everything even potentially dangerous, and as Vrishka's armistice would end in eight turns that was simply not an option.

SAMAN STOPPED BY EARLY THAT AFTERNOON with a bag filled with packets of his pain-relieving powder. Knowing he was coming she'd pled a headache, and all had left her to rest. After giving her explicit instructions, twice, and a series of warnings, and after she made him swear to hold her secret, he left, and Kiera lay back on the bed and wondered whether she should laugh or cry. Why did things happen the way they did? Did God, or the gods, roll the dice and let things lay where they fell? Did something she had done render her deserving of this fate? Or was this—was everything—part of some bigger plan? Or was the truth that it—everything—was all just happenstance?

And really, which would be worse?

By the time Emmy brought her dinner, Kiera had done nothing more than tie her own stomach in knots. Maybe there was no answer, she thought, or at least none a mere mortal could fathom. Concern radiated from Emmy as she fussed over Kiera, laying out dinner, pouring wine, and Kiera realized she was going to have to lock this —her feelings, her secret—down tight or everyone would know a very large something had gone amiss. That would lead to questions, and then guesses, or even answers, and that would not do.

The fire, blissfully unaware of her torment, crackled cheerfully, and she made herself focus on its warmth, its strength, and as she did she forced her feelings down into the box in which she kept all the things she couldn't, wouldn't, let herself think about. Her childhood, and her mother's death. Julia's murder. Hunter. The turn the Shunakah had almost killed Laszlo, and Alex, and her. The turn she tried to send Vayu and Valen away.

Many cycles' practice served her well, and by the time company began to arrive, she was back to being just a woman recovering from an attack.

Marco came first, with a sweet-faced Allie in tow, and Amba brought Alex a short time later. Laszlo came in with Muukwa and Kuruk, sweat soaked and smiling, which lifted Kiera's spirits. He brushed her head with a kiss before retreating to bathe, and Muukwa joined them at the table and didn't wait to be invited to dish herself something to eat. Kuruk stood a good ten feet back, perhaps hoping she wouldn't notice him.

"I can still see you," Kiera told him over her shoulder between bites. "Come and sit."

"Yes. Come, *pinqaya*, and sit," Muukwa sneered.

From the bathroom Laszlo roared a word, but Kiera couldn't tell what he said because at the same moment Amba stood, leaned across the table and yelled into Muukwa's face, "Muukwa! You are a guest in this house! You will not use such language while you are within these walls or it's your hide I will stretch from the ceiling! Do you hear me?"

Muukwa made a sour face. "Of course, Amba. My apologies, Kuruk."

Muukwa's taunt was apparently the spur Kuruk needed. Face taut, he strode forward and sat deliberately into the chair next to Kiera. After shooting Muukwa a venomous glare, he reached across the table and snatched the steaming dish from in front of her. Using the spoon set next to his empty plate, he pushed the serving fork stuck in the dish that Muukwa had used aside with small movements, as if loathe to touch it, and dished himself some salmon pie using his own fork.

A smile threatened, but Kiera smothered it, pleased that Kuruk had sat on his own. Amba met her eyes across the table and grinned for both of them.

"What did she say?" Alex asked no one in particular.

A silence fell as Kuruk shoveled a bite into his mouth. Muukwa pretended she hadn't heard him and continued to eat dainty bites. Amba held her grin as well as her tongue, and kept her eyes on Kuruk.

"She called me a shit lover," Kuruk said after he'd swallowed. "And the shit are the Skani." He lifted his eyes to Muukwa. "That is what the outlier Alak call those of us made slaves."

A snake of anger slid into Kiera's gut. Her mouth opened, but she shut it. Amba had already said everything that needed said.

Marco, however, was apparently not satisfied. He sat his fork gently down and stared at Muukwa, and Kiera flinched on the inside from the blow she saw coming. "Muukwa," he said in his Vayu voice. "My name is Marco, and I am Skani. I am also a co-ruler of this deconn, which is peopled by both Skani and free Alaks. Your slander insulted both my person and my peoples." He leaned forward, just a little, and his voice dropped to a dangerous tone. "Use that word in this house again and I will have you whipped and thrown outside the walls."

Silence thundered.

With a hand that shook only a little, Marco picked up his fork and continued to eat.

Muukwa dropped her head and made a face at her plate, which nearly startled a laugh out of Kiera. Amba had caught it, too, and when her gaze met Kiera's she looked decidedly displeased, though whether at Muukwa, or Marco, or everything, she just didn't know.

Laszlo emerged from the bathroom, wet hair hanging across his shoulders. "And I will be the one doing the whipping, should I hear that word even once more," he told Muukwa sternly as he claimed the chair on Kiera's other side.

Marco shot him a look of thanks, to which Laszlo nodded before scooping fish pie onto his own plate.

"So tell me how it went," Kiera asked, praying the change of subject would lighten the mood threatening the whole table. "You returned at least a turn sooner than I expected you to."

After leaning over to kiss her cheek, Laszlo took a bite, chewed and swallowed it. "I believe Vrishka sent a small force to harry the villages in order to draw us out. He wants to watch us work before launching a full attack." One shoulder lifted as he shrugged. "It is what I would do as well."

Warmth radiated from Laszlo's body, and Kiera leaned against his arm, both to ward off the slight chill she couldn't quite shake thisturn as well as to draw solace, and perhaps courage, from the touch of his skin. His eyes found hers and his face asked if she was all right. It took no effort whatsoever to summon all her love and send it out on a smile, and she watched his eyes soften.

"He does not care that you know his men broke the armistice?" an oblivious Kuruk wanted to know.

He answered Kuruk but held her eyes, promising sweet pleasure when the others had gone, and a chill slid across her skin. "They wore black and claimed to be of a clan called the Shatru. We cannot prove they are Vrishka's men."

The clatter of a dropped fork drew all eyes to Marco. "What did they call themselves?"

"Shatru," Kiera answered, and wondered where she'd heard that name before.

"It cannot be the Shatru," Marco insisted, and when he registered the confusion on their faces, added, "The Shatru are the people who drove the Skani from our ancestral homeland over a hundred cycles ago." He picked up his fork. "I agree, Laszlo, if only because *Shatru* is the name we gave them. They called themselves—well, something else."

Laszlo nodded. "And Vrishka would know this. Perhaps he would tell them to use this word to frighten our Skani."

"Again, I agree," Marco told him with his mouth full, then reached over and squeezed Allie's hand. Only then did Kiera notice that Allie's eyes were huge and filled with fear. "This is a trick of your father's, Aliyah," he told her in a gentle voice. "Do not be afraid."

"So what will you do?" Amba asked.

"For now we do nothing," Laszlo told her, but his eyes swept the table. "I expect the next blow to come close to the end of the armistice."

"And?" Kiera prodded.

His smile sent a shiver down her back, but not from pleasure. Here sat a man who would take the devil's own satisfaction from thrashing Vrishka.

"We crush him inside the jaw."

Kuruk nodded, and then, after a moment's consideration, Amba followed suit.

"A good plan," Kuruk commented in an admiring tone and took a long drink of wine.

Guilt goaded Kiera to try and not to look confused, since she knew she'd probably know what he was talking about if she'd paid attention to any of his lectures. Uh, lessons. She meant *lessons*.

And Marco would know if he'd ever shown up for any, but either his conscience was clear or he saw no reason to feel guilty about it. "What jaw?"

A small frown creased Laszlo's brow and she knew he battled whether to point that out. After a surprisingly short fight, civility won. "For the jaw, we divide the army into two or three segments and send them in different directions. The main force travels straight to the battleground, but goes slowest. The others ride," he nodded at Muukwa, who'd been silent since Laszlo's chastisement, "or run to the sides and wait for the enemy to pass them. Once they do, they close off the enemy's retreat and move in." Marco still looked a little confused, so Laszlo added in a very patient voice, "The army makes a circle around the enemy and holds him inside it, then attacks from all directions."

"What a good idea!" Marco exclaimed, which sparked a snort from Amba. Laszlo met her eyes and they traded a look. Muukwa muttered something that was undoubtedly uncomplimentary, but no one looked her way besides Kiera.

Kuruk spoke, a veritable fountain of words tonight. "It is good when it works, my Lord Marco. We hold hope that our enemy is not as clever as we are, but we must expect him to be. This plan is one we have spoken of many times but have not used in my cycles in Fairbanks, which gives me hope it will work." His eyes met Laszlo's. "Because he cannot have heard that we used it."

"What about—" Kiera paused, because although she needed to point this out, she dreaded Alex's reaction. All eyes turned to her, but hers stayed focused on Alex's face. "What about the Shunakah?"

Alex lifted his head and met her eyes for a moment before dropping his gaze back to his plate. "My dad is a Shunakah," he said to no one, *sotto voce* and yet heard by all in the tense silence. With a gasp Emmy snatched his hand, then raised an alarmed face to Kiera. Muukwa even looked up and stared into Alex's small face.

"Alex," Kiera started, voice gentle, but Amba interrupted her.

"Grandson, there are good people and there are bad people," Amba told him, and her tone brooked no dissent. "They are not divided by name, or by sex, or by what shape their bodies take. It is even so with our enemies. I am very certain that there are Shunakah who are very good people, who kiss their children and wish each turn for peace. We do not meet them because they are our enemies, but it will not always be so. One turn I will take you to meet your father's people, and on that turn all doubt will be erased that you can be proud of who you are."

Hot tears slid down Kiera's face, but she didn't dare wipe them away or else everyone would notice, so she picked up her tea and drank the rest, and sniffled inside the cup. Laszlo slid a hand under the table and squeezed her leg, but kept his face forward to help her preserve her dignity.

When she'd gotten her emotions under control, she told Alex, "Amba is right, Alex. But you can be proud thisturn. No matter who your parents are, you are, thisturn, a very good boy who will grow into a very fine man." In a quiet voice, one that wobbled only a little, she said to Amba, "And we will succeed in Fairbanks because of those ideals."

But Alex stared at Amba, warring emotions on his face. Amba held his eyes, let him take his time to sort through his fears and his feelings. A grin split her face when he finally nodded, and he smiled back, but then, and to Kiera's surprise, Amba turned her eyes to Muukwa. "You have something you wish to say?"

"I do not," Muukwa answered in a tone that added *but if I did I would say it*, and sipped her wine.

Time to twist the subject back to where she wanted it. "So, Laszlo," she said, and watched her husband's handsome face turn. "Do you think the Shunakah are working with Vrishka?"

"I do not," he answered. "But that does not mean they will not be nexturn, or that we can discount them thisturn." His eyes held a spark of anger, though Kiera knew it wasn't for her. "Be cautious, *a'kala*, and for a time I ask that you and Alex stay together, and indoors." His eyes flicked to Kuruk's, who nodded his understanding.

He'd get no fight from her on that, though that he thought he had to firm it up with Kuruk chased a zing of annoyance through her midsection. A thought struck, and melted her pique. "But what about the ravens— what did you call them, the Yeil? They will be able to see the army as it moves, won't they?"

When he turned to answer, Laszlo's eyes held a spark of what might have been admiration. "The uniformed men will march where all can see. The soldiers who will serve as the jaws travel separately through the trees and shifted. I do not believe a skybound eye will find them until too late to warn the enemy."

His words soothed her worries, or as much as they could be anyway. The table had gone quiet again, so she turned to Marco. "Is there a party tonight?"

"There is," he told her. "I expect one every night until, well." He paused to look at Allie for a moment. Smiled at her. "Will you come, Kiera?"

The fire snapped and sizzled as the last log broke, and Laszlo got up to put more wood on the fire. Kiera watched his broad back, and marveled at how smoothly his muscles adjusted the position of his body as he squatted down to arrange the wood. "No," she said. "I think I'll stay in tonight." Alex watched her, so she smiled at him. "And play games with Alex." His return smile, both sweet and vulnerable, was both a blessing and a hurt, and she prayed for the turn when she could spend time every night with him. But especially now, he needed support. And love. "Amba, will you stay?"

"I will stay for a time," Amba agreed.

"I will show Muukwa to her room," Laszlo added, and moved to stand behind Muukwa's chair. "I am certain that she is tired."

"Oh yes, Cousin Laszlo," came Muukwa's reply. "I can think of nothing I would prefer at this moment than to lie abed."

With an effort, Kiera kept her mouth still and brows both down. Despite Muukwa's prickly exterior, there was something about her that Kiera liked, not least of which that she'd come to help Laszlo in a dangerous setting without being asked, and Kiera wondered how long Muukwa would stay, and if they would become friends.

Kiera turned. "Oh, Marco," she began, then paused. How to say this? "Will you please make sure that we have guards tonight? Especially because I won't be there, I worry." And now for the delicate part. "And, uh, maybe you could make sure no one drinks too much? We do still have early mornings."

His eyes crinkled. "Oh, absolutely, Kiera. You need not worry a trifle."

Oh, if only that were true.

CHAPTER 8

A SOLDIER INTERRUPTED THEIR BREAKFAST in the great hall, something Kiera had never seen before. Incongruous in his black and red-striped uniform, voices fell as all eyes followed his steps across the carpet. He spoke quiet words next to Laszlo's head, then waited as Laszlo stood.

"Meet me in our apartment in a mark," he told her brusquely, then turned and followed the man in black out a side door, the one that led to the barracks.

There was no way she was going to be able to finish, so she pushed her plate away. The weight of a hundred gazes pressed her almost unbearably down. They, too, were as frightened by this anomaly as she was, and she fervently wished she had reassuring words for them, and for herself.

Since she didn't, she stood and told them, "I will give you the news when I have it," and left, Marco and Allie in her wake.

"VRISHKA HAS MOVED TO TAKE TALIUM," Laszlo told them after he'd shut the door.

"What?" Kiera sputtered as she rose from her seat on the couch.

"It is not unexpected, though the timing is sooner than I would have liked," Laszlo answered grimly, then poured himself a glass of wine.

Marco, who'd gone pale, shook his head. "But he offered an armistice! We have six more turns!"

With a snort, Laszlo upended the glass and drained it. "He has not moved on Fairbanks and thus has not violated the terms."

"He wants us to do something," Kiera realized. "He wants *us* to break the agreement, to come and fight him, and if we don't, we look afraid. To his soldiers and to ours, and to the whole deconn. Hell, to Alaska. So we lose either way."

"It is a good move," Laszlo reluctantly acknowledged. Only then did

Kiera notice that he wore his armor underneath his coat, the one that covered him like a cape, and her stomach clenched. It was what he wore when they rode to Fairbanks together. "It will keep his men feeling confident, the stronger, and strike fear in our own."

A hand lifted and Marco ran it through his hair. "But I would think he would seem a bully," he disagreed.

Laszlo's eyes scanned the room as he looked for something. "A bully is still the stronger, Marco, and most admire strength. Kiera, where is your warm coat?"

"Emmy took it to be cleaned." Realization dawned before the last word left her mouth, and even to her own ears her next ones sounded strained, afraid, and she hated it, hated her fear. "This is it. We're all going out, aren't we?"

For a long moment his eyes held hers, then he turned to Marco. "You will stay here at the manse," he told Marco. "Summon Amba, and take her advice in all things. I do not expect Vrishka to get to the city, but if he does, listen to what she tells you. He has five tou, so I am taking six, four to march, which leaves three to keep him outside the walls." Perhaps sensing Marco's fear, his voice gentled just a little. "One could keep him out, Marco, for many moons."

Even though they had talked about this, planned for this, Kiera's fears rose high, twisted and roiled and whispered horrors in her ear. So many things could go wrong. She voiced the scariest because she had to. "What about Alex, Laszlo? I can't leave him here. Not with Hunter able to get in."

In two steps he stood in front of her. He put both hands on her shoulders and stared down into her face. From this close Kiera could smell his spicy bath soap, could see the coldness in his eyes. "*A'kala*, I have already hidden him." His hands slid down her arms, and his gaze softened as he watched her face. "Hunter can track you, but Alex is no longer near. He is safe, my heart, with many guards, who will take him farther should the need arise." It wasn't enough—what would ever be enough?—but the confidence in his words softened her fear, and when she sighed, he kissed her softly.

"You will ride with me, and with Kuruk." His gaze sharpened. "You will do what he tells you, Kiera. Tell me you will."

How could he ask her to do that when she didn't know what was going to happen? "I don't know, Laszlo." She lifted a hand and hated that her voice sounded tight. "I will promise to listen, but sometimes things happen. You know that."

"Kiera, he understands war far better than you, and sometimes the better choice is to wait, though it is the more difficult." An urgency colored his tone. "I do not want you to strike, Kiera, unless I tell you to. I want you to take my orders, and Kuruk's should we be separated. There will be a great deal of fighting, and Vrishka will want you used up before he enters the field." The look he cast urged her to understand. "Kiera, you are the only one who can stand against Vrishka should he use his magic."

The pictures his words made horrified her, sickened her. So she was to let people die so she wouldn't use up her strength and her magic. That it made sense, that he was right, made it worse.

When he saw she understood, he continued. "You will stay behind the lines unless I need your assistance." His face looked so frighteningly serious. "I will tell you if I do. If I have to leave, Kuruk will remain with you, and you must promise to take his advice."

A nod was all she could manage, and then she stepped in and threw her arms around him. She loved the way he felt, and smelled, and when he kissed her head she smiled into his coat. "I love you, Laszlo," she whispered, knowing he would hear her. For a moment, in the silence of his embrace, her heart slowed, a knot untied. They would get through this together, and everything else that happened. Everything.

From over Kiera's head, Laszlo told them both, "Chanda will accompany us."

Kiera pushed back, and the sour amusement tugging her lips surprised her. "Does he know yet?"

He bared his teeth in what some might call a smile.

"Then we shall miss him at tonight's party," came Marco's lame sally as he helped Allie rise from the couch. After she stood, he turned, lines marking muscles in his pale face. "Have you already dispatched the jaws?"

"Yes."

FROM THE NORTH, HEAVY FOG ROLLED IN as another mark turned and water gave way to fire. A hundred yards ahead of Kiera, seated on her sorrel gelding, smoky billows swallowed the thick column of soldiers that marched and rode almost silently southwest and atop the thick ice of Fairbanks' River. A snake, she thought, slinking along the smooth river with its body of ten-wide foot soldiers and its skin of mounted uniforms, anxious to find Barrow's mice to gobble up.

*Otuk*s in billowing black capes galloped up and down the lines, checking men, and some stopped to share news from the scouts with Laszlo. *All clear*, they always said as they rode up.

It seemed odd that they rode here, somewhere in the middle of the line, instead of at the front. She could see the advantage of remaining hidden from the casual glance, but then her racing thoughts could list several potential advantages of riding up front, too. Did the soldiers up front feel scared? The men around her didn't seem to be, or if they were, they hid it well. Their postures seemed firm, and all the faces she could see looked determined. Eyes watched her, though, and Kuruk, who rode behind her, but Laszlo even more than them both. Maybe they, like her, took their cue from him, and he never seemed afraid. Even now, as they marched off to battle, he seemed nothing less than utterly confident. His gaze took in everything, even her perusal, and though he seemed tense, he radiated strength. He seemed so powerful, even omnipotent.

Could she be as strong? As far as she knew, she was the most powerful mage in Alaska. Marco had said it, but even more importantly, Agni had told her so. Would it be enough?

The truth was that she had never fought against another mage. Never *fought*. Oh, she'd practiced some with Marco, who hated every second of it, and that was something she was going to have to deal with, too, when this was over.

Had any living mage actually fought another? Would it be like in fantasy books she'd read where they flashed defiant stares across a ravine to one another, arms akimbo, and threw spells across the abyss?

Five marks. That was how long it would take to get to Talium at the pace they set. Half past noontide, a fire mark, and their projected time of arrival was no coincidence. Vrishka would have no strong source of water for nearly three marks, and since Kiera could use fire and air very well, she would likely have the advantage no matter how strong Vrishka was. According to Agni, no *sunwyr* could use earth energy well, so neither's magic would dominate during that mark, the one between fire and air. And surely they would have won before water pushed aside air to reign for its time.

Still she worried, worried and wondered how strong a mage he was, and whether he had other *sunwyr*, but mostly she worried that he'd be able to draw from the voluminous snow—frozen water—that blanketed the ground from horizon to horizon, giving him a sure source of energy during any mark.

Her gaze slid to Chanda, who bobbed along next to her on his mount and held his mouth tight. After his initial protest he had not uttered a single word since they'd left, and even if he had felt inclined to chat, she doubted he would be willing to reveal his honest opinion of Vrishka's strengths and weaknesses to her. It infuriated her that she couldn't count on him for help, that he wouldn't pull a single strand on behalf of the Fairbanks army. To be fair, he hadn't said that, but as Vrishka's messenger, as the person most strongly advocating their surrender, it seemed pretty unlikely that he'd fight against Barrow.

Why had Laszlo insisted he come? In the hurry that followed his announcement, she'd forgotten to ask him about it. Surely Chanda wouldn't do anything to sabotage them—would he? Did Laszlo think he might, and if so, did he expect her to watch him?

Could she take Chanda and Vrishka if they worked together? She prayed she'd never have to know.

THE MARKS WAXED AND BLED INTO OTHERS as they marched, fire to earth, earth to air, and air to water. Fat snowflakes whispered sullen complaints as they slid down her coat, an odd contrast to the rhythmic crunching of feet and hooves in the snow. They'd left the river a mark ago, and traveled now through the valley that gradually opened toward Talium. Less than a mark to go, and yet the gentle rocking atop her horse during the long trip had coaxed away both thought and fear, and even the knowledge that they were close couldn't spur adrenalin, though she didn't doubt that would soon change.

Both Kiera and her horse startled when Laszlo cut in front of her on his way out of the line to her left. Her hands flew to the saddle horn when the horse skittered, and the thin reins slipped from her fingers and fell forward. A black blur swooped in from her right—Kuruk, who'd leaned low off his horse and grabbed them. She tried to catch his eye, wanted to ask what was happening, but he avoided her gaze.

Without turning back, Laszlo barked a word she didn't understand and continued out of the line. All eyes watched the huge man on the black mammoth of his horse. As he neared, the foot soldiers stopped, and the ones who rode pulled up their horses, and some broke ranks, which left a wide space through which he crossed. Her reins in his hand, Kuruk led Kiera through the gap the line of soldiers made. She swiveled in her saddle, looked everywhere, trying to fathom what had happened, or what was happening, and her stomach tensed as she wondered if she should start feeling scared. Behind her, a third mounted soldier led the horse carrying the white-lipped Chanda through the gap. A dozen or so soldiers on foot broke rank to bring up their rear, and when they'd passed, the gap closed as the soldiers again began slogging ahead.

Their collective feet broke new snow as they crossed into the treeline. Laszlo led them through a flat barrier of hoar-frosted skeleton birches huddled together, and branches scratched her coat and caught in her hair as she entered the forest. Her mouth opened to whisper to Kuruk, but she shut it. One thing she did know was that Laszlo forbade talking while they marched, and silence would be even more important this close to Talium. Maybe they were going to set up a command area, or going to meet up with one of the jaws. In any case, she'd find out soon enough.

Inside the forest, thousands of the giant spruce she knew as black dominated the space, though some hemlock had managed enough sunlight to thrive in the lees between copses, and the green boughs of both narrowed the available walking spaces and caught most of the snow that fell. They'd only walked for a handful of minutes, but she'd already lost the sound of the army. Ahead, lightning had split one of the giant trees. It had taken several others down when it fell, leaving a forty-foot semi-circular break that bared the smoky sky. After Laszlo led them into the middle of it, he pulled his horse off to one side and turned it so he could watch. The thin light slinking through above branches made it hard to read his face.

Kuruk led her in, and the others followed and fanned out. When the last horse was in, Laszlo dismounted and walked to Chanda. Without pause he grabbed Chanda's coat with one hand and tore him off the horse, then backhanded him before his feet even touched the ground, sending Chanda flying backward.

Kiera's jaw dropped, but before she could react Kuruk urged his horse forward a step and raised a warning hand to her. He didn't have the skill Laszlo did in hiding his emotions, and she read satisfaction in the set of his mouth.

Before she could decide how to feel about any of this Laszlo took two steps, reached down and yanked Chanda back to his feet, then smashed his fist into Chanda's face. Crimson droplets sprayed from his nose as Chanda again fell back. A *whoomp* sounded as his body hit the snow, and he didn't try to rise. Horror roiled through her chest. "Laszlo," she whispered urgently, and Kuruk made another shushing gesture with his hand.

But he needn't have bothered, because Laszlo ignored them both. "That," he told Chanda in the coldest, most frightening voice she had ever heard, "is for laying hands on my wife. Touch her again, and I will tear out your throat and feast on your blood." Chanda flinched when he took a step forward, and he cringed and raised both hands when Laszlo reached down and dragged him by the coat back to his feet. "I name you traitor, Chanda," Laszlo continued implacably, "for consorting with Barrow, and the penalty for treason is death."

Why hadn't he told her that he was going to do this? Everything was happening too fast, and she had to stop it, or at least slow it down. Though she didn't know that she would choose differently, he should have talked to her, her and Marco, before making this decision—and further, she wasn't sure that what Chanda had done merited death.

"Laszlo," she called, and used heels to tap her horse's flanks, but before she could make it go forward Kuruk pulled its head back. With a hard grimace, she remembered that he held her reins. "Wait, Kiera," he told her quietly, and she shot him a look that she hoped reflected more of the anger and less of the upset she felt at him, and at Laszlo, and even at Chanda.

But no one besides Kuruk paid her any attention. She threw up her hands and made a frustrated noise. If this didn't stop, she would call air and knock all of these idiots flat on their asses, though she did not relish the thought of Laszlo's anger if she did.

His next words shocked her beyond thinking. "But during the past half cycle, I have learned the value of mercy." His eyes flicked to Kiera and he let go of Chanda, who stumbled back, lost his balance and sat down hard, but lifted a face that, despite the blood, looked as stunned as Kiera felt.

"To earn it, you will give me your oath that you will not raise a hand against Fairbanks from now until your death, nor will you provide aid to any who would."

After a moment, Chanda nodded.

Again anger threaded Laszlo's tone. "Say the words, Chanda."

"I give my oath that I will never raise a hand against Fairbanks," Chanda rasped, then wiped blood from his face with the back of his hand. "And I will not aid any who would harm it."

Laszlo nodded. "Then I will be merciful. Instead of death, I banish you, Chanda. You will wait with Atmak—" apparently meaning the soldier who held Chanda's horse—"until we have driven Barrow back. When we have finished, you may leave to join them."

Without waiting for acknowledgement, Laszlo turned and retrieved his horse. After he'd mounted, his eyes found Kiera. Apparently uncaring that the entire group could hear, he told her, "His life was mine when he laid hands on you, *a'kala*. This decision was mine, and I will not discuss it further."

Even gently delivered, his words both stung and sparked anger. Instead of answering, she reached down and yanked the reins out of Kuruk's hand.

CHAPTER 9

INSTEAD OF REJOINING THE ARMY'S MAIN BODY, they trotted alongside it and made their way toward the front. Kiera hated trotting, and being strung out on adrenalin, which had hit at some earlier point as they bounced onward toward the battle, made her want to scream her annoyance.

And fear, she admitted. This was nothing like when they fought the Shunakah, where adrenalin carried her, smothered her terror, emboldened her. Instead, sandwiched here between Laszlo and Kuruk and tailed by a handful of mounted soldiers she vaguely remembered from her trip to Fairbanks, all she wanted was to go home. For this to be over.

Dark clouds bore down from the sky, and spilled yet more snow onto the shoulders and under the feet of the winding column. Shouldn't battles be fought in the sun? Laszlo kicked his horse into a gallop, and hers followed his lead. The marching soldiers seemed to slow as her pace increased, and a pang wound through her chest. How many of these men would die here thisturn?

Damn Vrishka! Damn him to hell!

As if conjured by her thoughts a line appeared ahead of them, and Kiera's breath caught. Across the open valley, and there lay Nick's manse off to the right, the west, and near the foot of the hills. But south and eastward from the manse stretched a line of soldiers, a line that blocked exit from the south end of the valley. It was still too far to see how many, or even what color they wore, but there they stood.

Her horse slowed when Laszlo pulled his up, and he turned to her, and to the men. The color in his eyes had gone from the near black he wore as a human to the golden brown of his bear's, a color she'd only seen once before in a fight, the time the Shunakah had attacked, but his eyes had melted to golden every time they made love, and this change, now, disconcerted her more than any other thing she'd seen thisturn.

The bellow he made startled a flinch from her, and her horse snorted and took a step, then two. As she patted its neck and tried to calm both their nerves, two *otuk*s galloped up. "Spread them out," he commanded.

Like syrup, the men began spreading in liquid slow lines outward to cover the north end of the valley, seeping from the bottle of the valley behind them to both sides of where they stood. Within minutes a second line slid in behind them, then another.

"So he knew we were coming," Kuruk commented in a mild voice, one incongruent to the wild beating of her heart. How could he be so calm? Her mouth felt dry, and she reached for the canteen she'd hooked to a peg on the saddle, but it had either fallen or been knocked off during their jaunt. A sigh escaped her, but before she could ask, Kuruk handed her his. The lid took a hard twist from her shaking hands to dislodge, but the water tasted good as it slid into her throat.

"It will be all right, *a'kala*," Laszlo said without looking at her, and she made a face and handed Kuruk back his water.

"Thank you," she told Kuruk, and was surprised her voice sounded so tight. Chagrined, she wished she knew how to lock down her feelings—well, her fear—so Laszlo didn't feel like he had to worry about it. She wanted his whole focus on this, on the important things, so that nothing went wrong.

"Feeling fear is expected, Kiera," Kuruk told her, and she lifted her eyes to his. "There is no need to wish it away. It will not go."

She drew down her brows. "Is it so easy to see everything I'm feeling, Kuruk?"

It was a rhetorical question, a self-effacing attempt at humor, but it drew a snort from Laszlo, who turned and traded a look with Kuruk before meeting her gaze. "My heart, you wear your every thought on your face, and only rarely fear to speak them." Offended, and not a little embarrassed, she opened her mouth to argue, but when he saw it, he offered her a smile that was surprisingly sweet. "I cherish your honesty, Kiera," he told her gently, then turned his attention to an *otuk* who had just ridden up.

That smile, a tangible reminder of the love from which she knew it sprung, smoothed away the jagged edges of her fear. As it waned a thought struck, albeit an odd remembrance at this place and time, and she turned in her saddle. "Kuruk, I need to say thank you for keeping Alex safe when Hunter, the Shunakah, attacked, and for saving my life. I owe you a debt."

Her words surprised him, she could tell, but he inclined his head.

"And not to question what you did, but why were you there? I mean, it was a blizzard, and I thought you'd keep Alex in the stable until it passed."

One side of his mouth quirked, and Kiera wondered if he was suppressing a smile. "My lady," he began, and she could hear the amusement he struggled to hide, "*you* were out in that blizzard."

"So you followed me?"

Again, he nodded, just once.

"How could you expect to find me in a whiteout?" She knew she sounded disbelieving, but maybe he'd thought one of them would run across her between the stable and the manse, a trek that didn't seem like a very good idea. As it turned out, she'd made it to the house, but she wondered what he'd have done if she'd gotten lost.

He hesitated. "We followed your scent."

"Turn out!" Laszlo roared, and she turned to him, heart thudding. What did he mean?

Any words she might have had died as she took in the field ahead. The soldiers were coming at a full run.

On either side of where they stood, *otuk*s bellowed, and men stepped forward, moving farthest at the ends, making a U with her at the dip in the middle. If they did more, she couldn't see. The sound of thousands of swords being drawn came next, then small sounds followed the pops of color as groups of men dropped coats and shifted into bears, and wolves, and coyotes. And then the only sound was the one her breath made as it passed her lips.

"Steady," Laszlo said quietly, though for her or only a voiced wish she didn't know.

Vrishka's army split and avoided the valley the ranks had created. Shields raised as thin shapes filled the air and hurtled toward the ranks—Were those arrows? Javelins?—and the crash of metal to metal came a second after the first wave crashed into her men.

From here she watched the men meet in a mix of fervent movement and blood. Her breath came faster. Axes. Some of Vrishka's men had axes. Or were those hers? All of the Fairbanks army carried axes and swords, but as the men mixed together it became impossible for her eyes to tell one from the other.

*Otuk*s came, spoke, Laszlo nodded, and they left. Kuruk watched her as much as he watched the battle, and she wondered if part of his job was to make sure she didn't intervene, and maybe it was a good thing, because the longer this went on, the harder it was to just sit here.

Clang, clang. Screams, rage and pain. Adrenalin had narrowed her vision and she had to keep turning her head to take in the field. She closed her eyes and sent up her sight. Fire, it was a fire mark, and fire flowed everywhere. As attracted to her as she was to it, outside strands split from their streams to wrap her sight. With barely a thought, she pulled those strands and returned with them to her body.

"No, Kiera," Laszlo was saying when she opened her eyes. "Let it go."

"It doesn't tire me to hold fire," she argued, and let the flames spin in her chest.

"You're frightening your horse," he told her, and she shifted her attention to the animal beneath her, who had splayed his legs and pinned his ears back. Did animals feel fire?

"You've gone hot," he explained, voice tinged with the slightest hint of impatience. She'd forgotten—how could she forget?—that holding fire made her become hot, made her skin glow. Maybe because no other mages used it much, not even Marco, so she never saw it, and air did nothing like that when inside the mage.

"Where are the jaws?" Kuruk interrupted urgently as fire escaped her, flew to the sky above, and after a brief look at her, then Kuruk, Laszlo turned back to survey the field. After a moment he made a motion with one hand and an *otuk* galloped up. She couldn't hear what Laszlo said, but the *otuk* nodded and brought his horse in behind them.

When Laszlo turned to her, his face looked hard. "Kiera, I must go see what's held the jaws before we lose the advantage." She shook her head. They had an advantage? How could he tell? And what was she supposed to do? Wait here?

"Take her behind the treeline," Laszlo told Kuruk in answer to her unspoken question, "and wait for my signal." His eyes met hers, and despite the battle, and the fear and the death surrounding them, he managed to summon tenderness, and she loved him for it. "Hold fast, *a'kala*, and listen to Kuruk's advice. All will be well."

Afraid her voice might break if she spoke, she nodded, and watched him gallop off until he disappeared into the morass.

EVEN JUST A FEW HUNDRED YARDS into the forest, the trees muffled the sound the battle made. As Kuruk led her into a small clearing near a cluster of skeletonized birch, a deer leapt across their path and surprised Kiera's horse. Her balance slipped as both she and the horse flinched, and she grabbed the horn, but the horse skittered back a few steps and Kiera felt herself falling. Kuruk whirled. Almost too fast to see, his hand shot out and caught her coat as she slid down the horse's flank. He held her suspended above the ground until the world stopped spinning, then lowered her carefully until her feet touched the ground.

The horse trotted a few steps, whinnied, and stopped to bury his nose in the snow. "Thanks," she said to Kuruk as she walked to the horse. "It seems I'm racking up quite a debt with you." She tried to sound light, but her heart still pounded and her thoughts just kept rolling. She hated this. Hated that Laszlo was out there somewhere. Hated that men were dying. On both sides. How in the world could she make this stop?

Marco had told her once that war was a Skani tradition. Laszlo had said that the Skani fought all the time. Whether this was her fault remained a question. Laszlo had assured her that Vrishka would come no matter what. And by the terms he offered, the only way he'd be happy is if she gave up the entire deconn to him. Was there no way that he would agree to just let them be?

A scream, long and sharp, sounded at the same moment Kiera put her foot in the horse's stirrup. After she mounted she held herself still and tried to hear over the pounding of her heart. Was that a person? It sounded close, but not too close.

The second time it rang out, both she and Kuruk turned toward the west, toward the hills bracketing the other side of the valley. It came from there. And it was a woman. Kiera grabbed the saddle horn with one hand and wrapped the reins in the other, then kicked her horse. "No, Kiera," Kuruk urged from behind her.

It took some effort to unwrap the reins, but Kiera managed to get them untangled enough to signal the horse she wanted it to slow down. "Kuruk," she said as she turned, "that's not a soldier. If you try and stop me I'll pull air and knock you off that horse." After a quick readjustment, she nudged the horse into a trot, then a gallop.

The horse stumbled, then slid on the smooth path when they entered the valley, but gained his balance before Kiera lost hers, and off they went across the bare ground toward the opposite treeline. Even if she'd wanted to, Kiera couldn't see if Kuruk followed, but she hoped he had. Strong mage or not, two looked better than one.

The horse slowed as he climbed, and soon Kiera heard noises. Laughter rang out, and it was close. A zing of fear stabbed her as she tried to untangle the reins—she needed to stop—but she fumbled and they slipped out of her hand. The pace was slow enough to jump off, and maybe she could get the damn horse stopped when she did, so she stood and lifted a foot out of the stirrup, then jumped down just as Kuruk's horse swept ahead and cut across her horse's path. A swift, black-gloved hand reached down to grab her reins and pulled both horses to a stop.

Kiera flashed him a smile of thanks and tried to pull her foot out of the snowdrift one leg had landed in. Pointedly ignoring the anger on his face, she started up the hill. After a moment, the sound of his feet breaking the snow followed.

Not fifty yards up the hill she found them, milling around an area where naked birch clustered loosely, framed by hemlock on the far side. A group of ten or twelve men sat or squatted in a sort of circle. Some talked. Others laughed. Vrishka's soldiers, for sure, in light blue uniforms. Kuruk's hand fell on her shoulder as she slid behind a tree. Shock made her foot hit the tree when she jumped, and she turned to flash him a look. His eyes had gone golden, and she flinched back from the unexpected sight. His brows drew down, and she realized he didn't know, or didn't understand her surprise.

With a small shake of her head, she turned back toward the clearing. There was no doubt that she'd heard a woman scream, so where was she? Should she just go marching up there? Why didn't they have a lookout?

One moved, a soldier, and she saw that something—maybe someone—lay in the snow in the middle of the group. No—it was two people. One of the soldiers leaned over them. Another made a comment she couldn't make out, and the first one laughed. The leaning soldier spoke sharply to the ground-bound figures, then reached down. Another scream sounded, and a knot in Kiera's chest clenched.

Her breath made a hiss as she exhaled, and she took another as she stepped out from behind the tree. She half expected Kuruk to grab her, to try and stop her, but he did not. The snow crunched as she marched uphill, though no one noticed her until she had covered over half the distance.

Her sight had gone up and back, and she carried a chestful of air and fire, and it warmed her as it churned and mixed deliciously together.

"Stop there!" one shouted. The others scrambled to see what had drawn his attention and lined up in a ragged bunch behind him. A lazy group, she noted absently, and knew that Laszlo would clout any of their soldiers who acted so incautiously and with such pause as these. He was merciless in his discipline, his insistence that the soldiers perfect everything, including their attention spans, which was something she'd chided him for in the past, and in that flash of thought it dawned on Kiera that she'd been extremely shortsighted.

Not that she'd ever admit that.

The first drew a short sword, one unlike any Kiera had ever seen, and took a defensive posture. Ten feet out she stopped.

"Put down the sword," she told him in a stern voice.

His foot slipped when he stepped back. "Yer a woman!"

Oh—the pants. She'd never seen another woman besides her wear them, but it would be silly to wear a gown to war. "That's right," she told him slowly, and held her voice calm. "So please put down the sword."

Didn't he see Kuruk?

His arm dropped as he lowered the sword. Maybe Kuruk had waited? "Just go on now," he told her in a different voice, one she didn't like.

She took a step forward. "What's your name?"

A rather lecherous smile rose and split his face as he pushed his sword back into its sheath. "Do ye wanna know me then?"

God. In her attempt to settle his nerves, she'd forgotten the singular importance of that custom. "Well, soldier, I'd like to know what you're doing here," she evaded as she took another step.

"Ye need to stop," he told her, shading to harsh, and took a step of his own. "And ye need ta turn around and go back."

Mosha! He sounded like Mosha! Is Barrow where Mosha came from, then, or someplace near it? And even if so, did that mean anything?

Not that it mattered. Not really. But something inside her wanted to understand how her friend, a man she had trusted with her life, could find it in himself to betray her. To offer her life to another.

Anger rose as her hands lifted. "Relax!" she commanded, then grimaced at her own tone. So much for nonthreatening. Surprise washed his face before anger, and he came in a rush, and after the briefest of pauses, the others followed.

Like notes of music through parted lips, air-encased fire burst from her hands, and like a song played, they fell with clothes on fire. Screams erupted as she stepped between the writhing bodies, but she passed them and walked to where they had first stood.

Two naked bodies lay splayed in the snow, a woman and a man, their hands and feet tied with a thin cord that stretched to hitch to four trees. They held their eyes tightly closed, as if afraid of what she would now do. "Kuruk," she called as she patted her waist. Apparently her canteen wasn't the only thing she'd lost on the trip down here.

The black-clad Kuruk slid out from the trees ahead of her and trotted down, as easy on his feet in the snow as a rabbit. "My lady calls," he offered and bowed deeply from the waist. Prepared to be offended, she waited until he rose to gauge his face. For a moment he held her eyes and she read something mysterious, but wasn't sure what, but then he smiled, bared his teeth, and she felt shock roll through her as she realized he was teasing her.

"Can I borrow your knife?" she asked, and traded smile for smile. Maybe he was just as happy as she was to be able to help. Without a word he unsheathed a straight ten-inch knife from his waist.

The eyes of the man on the ground locked on Kuruk and he made a frightened sound. Kiera lifted her hands, palms out, to try and soothe his fear, but he cringed and scrunched his face into a mask of terror. "We're not going to hurt you," she soothed, and dropped her hands. She shook her head and looked at Kuruk, hoping for an answer. He must have seen her magic, and then came Kuruk, a large man in black clothes wielding a big knife. To a man tied naked in the snow, that had to be a fright.

But apparently not to the still-silent woman, who stared not just defiantly, but with murder in her eyes. Kiera knelt down next to her, though too far to touch. "We are not going to hurt you," she said slowly, but the woman didn't seem to understand her words.

A noise turned her attention. One of the soldiers behind them had gotten the fire out, and he crawled to his feet, then stood staring with mouth agape.

With a hand on her leg, she pushed back to her feet. "Go," she told him, and lifted an arm to point southward and hardened her voice. "But not back that way. Stay out of the battle, or I will come find you. Go to Fairbanks, soldier. We don't enslave people there."

His head bobbed as he nodded a half dozen times. "Canna fetch the others, my lady?"

"Take them all," she said, and as he turned away, the world tilted. Her arms came up, but there was nothing to grab, and she fell to one side and watched the earth turn. Within moments pain shot into her temple, crossed her forehead, and filled everything in-between. With a groan, she lifted both hands to her eyes.

Kuruk's hand grabbed her shoulder. "What is wrong?"

"A headache," she ground out. "Give me a second." Damn! Her horse, and the saddlebag it carried, was how far downhill? "Kuruk, I need you to go down to my horse."

"For this?"

She pried her eyes open to find one of her packets of pain reliever dangling in front of them.

Even through the pain, outrage rose large. "You searched my saddlebag?"

"Yes." Unrepentantly. Well, he sure had come a long way from the man who'd been too afraid to talk to her. The bastard.

With a hand she snatched the packet and, eyes closed tight against the light, tore it open. The taste nearly gagged her, but she made herself swallow it, then scooped up a handful of snow and shoved it into her mouth, which helped wash down the rest of the bitter mess.

Ten heartbeats was all it took before the pain stuttered, then two more to fade to nothing. Her breath escaped in a harsh sound, and she opened her eyes. Kuruk had knelt down in front of her, and he looked troubled.

"I am fine," she said slowly, and started to stand. "So don't worry about it."

"Then explain why Saman came to you in secret."

She froze, then shook her head and pushed to her feet. "You spying bastard," she said without malice. "Have you told Laszlo?"

The answer was impossible to read, but his face held a stubborn set.

"No," she answered herself as she brushed snow from her pants. "You haven't, because if you had, he'd've questioned me about it." She lifted her eyes to his. "I'll tell him, Kuruk, when all this is over. Just please." A sigh escaped and she turned back to the still-bound couple in the snow. "Just please don't."

Without answering he followed her back, then stepped ahead of her. In one fluid movement he drew his knife, knelt, and severed the cord holding the man's hands, then the woman's. He lifted back to his feet and took two steps, then sliced their feet free.

After a moment the woman rose, then helped the man find his feet.

Kuruk spoke sharply to them in his native language, and Kiera realized that these two were shifters. Alaks. Although why that hadn't been apparent was a mystery. What was wrong with her?

The woman answered, then turned to Kiera and spoke in a stiff tone.

"She says that she offers thanks to you and—" Kuruk grinned—"your mate."

"Kuruk, tell her that I and my *friend* accept her thanks and offer our apologies for the treatment these soldiers gave her. Oh, but do say that they aren't our soldiers. I don't want them to think we did this."

"Am I your friend, Kiera?"

His words surprised her, and then they gave her a funny feeling. "Yes, Kuruk," she said. "I consider you my friend."

One corner of his mouth lifted, but it slipped away as he turned to relay her words.

"And please also say that they should go either east or north, because there is a battle south of here, and probably more soldiers west of here."

Kuruk's smooth voice continued to clip the harsh, deep-in-the-throat sounds that made up their language. The man broke in, motioned to Kiera, and Kuruk answered, used her name.

Without moving her body the woman's head swiveled smoothly, an eerie motion, and she stared at Kiera with hard, yellow eyes. She said something, a word.

Kuruk answered, then told Kiera, "She asked if you are the fire mage."

"And did you say I am?"

He sounded surprised. "Yes. You are."

True enough, though she wasn't sure how she felt about nadeconn Alaks knowing who she was by name. For one, was that good or bad?

With a stiff, and final, nod of thanks, the woman took the man's hand and led him uphill, north, and into the forest. After they disappeared into the trees, Kiera asked, "What kind of Alaks are they? Did they say?"

He sounded surprised, as if she should know. "They are Cha'ak," he paused, then continued in a different tone, as if he'd reconsidered her meaning, "but they did not invite me to ask their names."

Kiera made a face. Which were Cha'aks? Not a tribe from Fairbanks, she didn't think, since she wasn't sure she'd heard that name before. "How did they manage to get caught by Vrishka's soldiers, do you think?"

A shoulder lifted when Kuruk shrugged. "The man is very sick, but I do not know if that is why, Kiera. Their backs both bore fresh arrow wounds." Another shrug. "They did not tell me."

"Well, it doesn't really matter. Let's head back down the hill and go see if anyone's come looking for us."

CHAPTER 10

THE MARK HAD TURNED TO AIR BY THE TIME they made it back into the forest on the other side of the valley. An occasional sound slipped past the sentinel trees as the battle raged on to their right and down the hill. Perhaps as unsettled by the noises as she was, Kiera's horse slid and stumbled as they climbed higher. A little desperately she clasped her hands tightly around her saddlehorn, but the reins fell through her gloved fingers and slid to dangle from the bridle.

"Kuruk," she breathed as quietly as she could, trusting his superior hearing, and he nudged his horse ahead, leaned over and snatched the twin strips of leather from under her horse's jaw. Instead of handing them to her, he wrapped them around one hand and continued up the hill, leaving her with mixed feelings.

Before she could decide whether to ask for them back, a voice rang out from far away, and Kiera strained to hear what it said.

"A man calls your name," Kuruk whispered over his shoulder as he pulled their horses to a stop. "I cannot tell whose voice it is."

Her lips pursed as she let a breath escape from a chest that had gone too tight. She nodded, then drew another to replace it. Was this it? Was someone coming to bring her to the battle? With an eye on Kuruk, she pulled off a glove and reached into the saddlebag that hung on the left side of her saddle. *Of course it was on the side closest to Kuruk*, she grumbled, but then let the frustration slip away. Of course he'd see her regardless, though she might have been able to explain it away had he not searched her saddlebag. Well, and seen Saman come.

This made two thisturn, though this was prophylactic. She'd never needed to use it twice in a turn, that was true, but she'd never been in the middle of a battle either, not done anything this serious since this had started, what, a few moons ago, and the last thing she needed to happen was for the blinding pain to start out on the field.

Fingers closed around one of the packets, and she pulled it free and re-tied the thin string with two fingers. Grimacing, she used her teeth to tear it open and poured the contents into her mouth, gagged, and made herself swallow. Without thinking she used her tongue to get the residual powder off her lips, then made a face.

Kuruk watched impassively. "Will you die?"

Those words made her heart skip a beat, and she wondered inanely if shifters could hear heartbeats. Well, if he'd heard hers, his face didn't reveal it. "Eventually," she evaded, then tried to smile. "Though I hope mine is a long way off."

His eyes held hers for a long, long moment before he nodded, though whether he believed her or not she could not tell.

Someone shouted her name, much closer this time. "It is Chanda," he told her with a thread of distaste.

"Why do you dislike him, Kuruk?" she wanted to know.

He ignored her question. "Should we tell him where we are? If you pre-fer not, we must move or he will find us."

"Here!" she shouted, and felt surprised that her tension had eased. But if it was Chanda, she still had some time left. "Chanda!"

His horse emerged from a copse of trees to her right, mouth open and breathing hard. "You must come," he told her, as breathless as his horse, as he tried to pull it to a stop, but it backed up, took a step to one side, and shook its head.

Alarm rose and she sat up in the saddle. "What's wrong? What is it, Chanda?"

His hand lifted and he wiped sweat from his forehead, and as he did, she noted that his face looked clean. He'd been healed, and she wondered who'd done it. "Lord Vrishka has stopped the group Laszlo sent to the back side, and things are going badly, Kiera," he told her heavily. "We need your help."

Her breath caught. "Oh my God." Kuruk tossed her the reins, and she wrapped them around her hand like Kuruk had done. "Take me, Chanda. Go!"

The horse seemed to sense what she wanted, and it followed Chanda's out and down the hill toward the battle. Bare branches snapped her face, but she dared not let go of the saddlehorn. Even at a something between a trot and a gallop, the terrain made her seat uneasy, and she had to use her feet in the stirrups more often than not to stay in the saddle.

Sound exploded as they cleared the trees, and she flinched hard from it. Chanda kicked his horse into a run, so she gritted her teeth and did the same. The world lurched, then bobbed, and she clung with shaking thighs to the horse's sides and prayed she wouldn't fall.

Everywhere she looked, men fought. She was going too fast to make out uniforms, and except for the occasional stark white of a polar bear, she couldn't tell which shifters were which. With a loud whoop Chanda led her through a tangle of men, and some fell and others parted as his horse hit them. She followed as closely as she could inside his wake to take advantage of the space he made, and wished she'd taken a drink before leaving. Her mouth felt like a desert. And gone to the bathroom, but it was too late now for either.

Pain followed a swift movement she couldn't quite see off her right side. Had someone struck her? She darted a glance to her stinging thigh and saw a line of blood staining her pants. A sound followed, a man's roar, and an azure-clad soldier flew through the air across the edge of her vision. Beyond shocked, she gripped the saddlehorn in both hands and turned her head to see behind her. The wind made it hard to see with her head held this way, but her eyes found Kuruk, white teeth bared, his naked sword stained red, riding closely behind her. A wicked smile spread across his face when he caught her glance.

Apparently it wasn't just the Skani who liked to fight.

In marks, or minutes, Chanda led them away from the fighting and around a large rock, and everything happened. Her horse slipped on an icy patch in its lee, stumbled hard, and she lost her grip and fell. Someone screamed bloody rage. Kuruk, she thought as she fell. When she landed her head smacked the ice, but someone leapt atop her before she could lift it.

Vrishka. She knew he was near.

Eyes closed, her sight shot up and, with every drop of energy in her soul, she called for fire. And fire came. Not even waiting for her sight to return, and from all directions, hundreds of strands leapt to her, wrapped her, shot down the thin cord tethering her sight to her body, and filled her chest.

A cord? Her sight had a cord?

"Stop!" a voice commanded, and she could tell it was a voice used to giving commands. *Well, fuck you*, she thought as the fire spun and warmed her.

The weight suddenly lifted off as the man pinning her jumped off. "Tha bitch is right hot," he snarled, and kicked her in the stomach before stomping off.

"Ugh," she breathed, and pushed herself to her knees.

Oh yeah. It was Vrishka, all right. Vrishka, with his icy blue eyes and his hands on his hips, standing belligerently in front of a clot of uniformed men. Vrishka, a too-thin, sixtyish man whose sunshine-yellow hair draped round his face.

"Fuck you, Vrishka," she spat, and stood. Her eyes found the solider who'd jumped her, and he paled under the weight of her glare.

To her surprise Vrishka smiled, but it was a Vayu smile, a condescending, lordly smile. An evil smile.

Fire flared as it spun, and she let it fill her, knew she'd be a frightening sight.

"Let it go, Kiera," he told her. "You have lost."

Anger took as much room in her middle as the fire. She motioned to the field with her head. "Step out with me, Vrishka, and we'll see who's lost. Surely you're not frightened."

The sounds of steps caught everyone's attention, and as she turned Chanda emerged from behind another pile of granite slabs, slapping snow off his sleeve. He nodded at her, as cordial as if they'd met in church, and walked to stand behind Vrishka.

Her jaw dropped. "You oathbreaking bastard!" she yelled. "You gave your *word!*"

"Let go of the fire, Kiera," Vrishka interrupted coldly. "Or I will have your dog butchered."

Kuruk!

A river of thoughts raced through her head as she turned slowly. Yes, indeed. Kuruk lay pinned to the ground on his stomach by a very large man, and just beyond the two, a group of soldiers hovered with swords drawn and points down. Could she kill Vrishka, and apparently Chanda as well, before these men killed Kuruk? She fervently didn't want him to die, but what choice would she have but to gamble? An entire army was at stake—her army, the men who'd made snow angels with Alex and her on one frigid winter afternoon—but her heart was threatening to crumble under the weight of two golden eyes whose fate she held in trembling hands.

As if in answer, his face said he saw her ambivalence and the pain it roused, and he smiled a little. Though she sympathized with the chagrin his capture had meted and that shined through his smile, it was the acceptance in his eyes of whatever choice she would make that left her ragged.

"Allow me to ease your choosing," Vrishka said from behind her, and she spun away as much to sever Kuruk's gaze as to listen to Vrishka's words. "Discuss a matter with me thisturn, Kiera, and I will withdraw my troops from the field and leave this—" he waved a hand—"for another. Hmm?"

"How many have you killed thisturn, Vrishka, so that we might talk?" she asked with more than a trace of bitterness. But she sent the fire up, up and away into the clouds pressing the sky into the snow at each horizon.

Lightning flashed. Before it struck she closed her eyes and used her sight to shift the energy up and into the pregnant puffs lingering above the snow-clouds blanketing the seen sky.

"Your skills have improved," Vrishka noted dryly when she opened her eyes, but his face held something she felt tempted to call contempt. Oddly, or perhaps not, his voice held a trace of the accent she associated with Mosha, but it had been smoothed out. Again she wondered if Mosha had once come from Barrow.

"Speak, Vrishka, so we can all go home," Kiera said tiredly.

Something sparked in Vrishka's eyes, and he strode the five steps between them, then slapped her face so hard she stumbled back. Kuruk bellowed from behind her, and her hand lifted to her face and covered her partly open-jawed mouth as the sounds of a struggle ensued. Without looking back she lifted a hand and held it, palm out, behind her to tell him to stay calm.

In a deliberate voice, he told her, "You will address me as Lord Vrishka." Chanda's brows raised, but he wiped all expression from his face when Vrishka turned and stalked back to stand in front of his cluster of men. "Kiera," he continued blandly, as if the slap had never happened—and she noted he didn't bother to call her Lady Kiera, much less Governor Kiera. The jerk. "The situation in Fairbanks is nothing short of unseemly, and we simply cannot allow it to continue."

We? Was that the royal "We," or was he saying he spoke on behalf of some group? And if so, who? The Skani?

"What sit—" she began, but he lifted a finger, and his brows, a fatherly expression meant to tell her to shut up and wait to speak. Annoyance snaked through her, and she pressed her lips together and let it rise to her face. Regardless of the men standing guard over him, if he didn't have Kuruk pinned behind her, she would have knocked him on his skinny, arrogant ass.

A very slight smile lifted his lips, and she knew he'd read every thought on her face. Good. She hated him and hoped he knew that, too. How had she imagined that this arrogant bastard would ever agree to treaty fairly with them, and with her? He was Vayu all over again. Did he pick mistresses from groups of frightened children, too?

His hair blew across his face when he shook his head. "Emotional," he commented to no one in particular, and though she tried not to let it land, his stab prodded a zing of anger.

"Fuck you," she snarled. "You piece of shit," she continued slowly, and as calmly as she could manage, but her temper had snapped. "You slaving, raving lunatic. You ride on the backs of women and slaves."

Eyes opened wide on many of the soldiers standing behind Vrishka. Shock rolled across Chanda's face, and from behind Vrishka he shook his head quickly, urging her to stop.

Vrishka did not walk. He leapt to Kiera, grabbed her around the throat with one hand, and the crack from when he backhanded her stung her ears almost as much as his hand on her face, and then again, and again, and again. And although he wasn't the strongest of men, the third or fourth slap tore open skin inside her mouth.

Blood-filled cords stood out on his face when he'd stopped, and she watched as he struggled to regain his composure as they stared into each other's faces and breathed each other's heavy breaths, a strangely intimate ritual that set Kiera's stomach churning.

"This," he told her between heavy breaths, "is why a woman must not rule." She opened her mouth to argue, but he interrupted, spoke very deliberately. "Say one more word, bitch, and your dog dies."

Kiera shut her mouth, but let the satisfaction his continued loss of control evoked paint her face. With a hand he shoved her backward, and she fell onto her hands and her bottom as he walked back to the place from which he apparently preferred to address her.

From the ground Kuruk barked a laugh, and she turned and met his eyes. Admiration, pure and clean, shone in his eyes, and she grinned back. One or both apparently offended the giant man atop him, and in one violent movement he pressed the flat of his hand into Kuruk's face and forced it into the snow.

"Stop it," Kiera ground out as she climbed to her knees, adrenalin still singing in her veins. "Or I will burn you alive, you motherfucker, and fuck the consequences!"

"Leave off," Vrishka called impatiently, but when the man released his face, Kuruk surged up and threw him off, then rolled smoothly to his feet and crouched, knees bent, hands raised.

"Let him be!" Kiera shouted, then spun to Vrishka and screamed, "Tell your man to leave him alone or I will bring fire and burn this entire valley to ashes!" She flung out an arm and pointed to the field. "People are dying out there!" she sobbed, still more in anger than with the grief that threatened, "while we play these stupid goddamned games! Speak your fucking piece and leave, or call your fucking water and let's finish this!"

Chanda stepped out, hands raised placatingly, and looked from Vrishka to Kiera. "Well," he said quietly, "I would venture that this is officially not going well. Please," he turned to Vrishka, "my lord, allow me." After the slightest of pauses, Vrishka nodded regally, though anger still pinched his features.

The underling's smile Chanda wore dropped away as he turned and walked to Kiera. His hand took her arm a little roughly, and he led her aside, closer to the rocky hill, and further from the battle. "Sit there," he barked to someone behind her, and Kiera's backward glance revealed that Kuruk had followed, and now stood staring at Chanda with brows raised.

"You'll hear everything anyway," she told him, and he nodded without releasing Chanda's eyes, then shifted his weight to stand *contrappostos,* a false relaxed stance, with one hand on his sword.

Ignoring Kuruk, Chanda led her farther back, sight if not sound apart from the others, and wiped the snow from a fairly flat rock before motioning for her to sit. The smooth gesture reminded her of how he'd acted at brooding, and she grimaced at the memories. Unaware of her thoughts, he squatted down in front of her, far enough to allow her heart to slow, and offered a bland smile.

"I know you feel I have betrayed my oath, Kiera, and so first let me tell you that I have not. I have done this for Fairbanks, for the good of our deconn."

Her mouth opened, and he paused to wait for her words, but she closed it and shook her head. She would hear him out before wasting time chasing down the philosophical aspects of his goddamned promise. Vrishka promised to withdraw after she'd heard him out, and she wanted this over now. Now.

When he saw she meant to stay silent, he continued, and he sounded very earnest. "Kiera, I know you realize that the Fairbanks Skani are unhappy. But it goes deeper than just adjusting to a change, which I believe you think is their concern. The truth is that a woman ruler, a woman, a boy and a—an Alak ruling the Skani is not, well, it will not work. And some would say that it is, well, unnatural."

Bait or not, Kiera couldn't resist that. "What about it, precisely, is *unnatural*, Chanda? It goes against *nature*? Oh, for Christ's sake!"

He laid a hand on her arm and squeezed, but she jerked out of his grip and flashed an angry look. "I am not saying that I think it unnatural, Kiera, understand me. I am saying that is what some say."

Her breath made a hiss through pursed lips. "You coward," she called him. "If you think having a former slave as a ruler is unnatural, at least be man enough to admit it."

Instead of taking offense, he paused and seemed to appraise her. "You have become very outspoken, Kiera," he told her, and it didn't sound like a compliment.

She shook her head, both weary and exasperated. "Chanda, I am tired of this. *So* tired of it. Tired and afraid and—" She felt her eyes go wide as she rocked back. *Sick!* She'd almost said sick!

"And what?" came his quiet question.

It took every ounce of her self control to not leap to her feet, though what she'd do after that was a mystery. "I'm just—worried, Chanda." Breath in, breath out. "So many people are dying out there." That was the truth, and as the fear rushed back in to fill her, she turned to plead. "Please stop trying to charm me and just tell me what Vrishka wants me to know."

His mouth puckered as he thought over her words. When he'd come to a decision, he nodded. "Here are the terms, the real terms, and I ask that you listen to all of them before you speak. Agreed?"

That sounded dire, but she nodded.

He looked so sincere, so intent on making her believe what he had to tell her. "First, you must understand that Vrishka will be lord of Fairbanks, Kiera. His army is the stronger in both numbers and experience. He fights often, in Barrow, against the Alaks on the north coast, and our army has never fought more than a ragtag pack of Shunakah."

Kiera felt her jaw harden. How dare he? And even if what he said was true, they had plans, and discipline, and a lot of men who would fight to stay free until their breath stopped. When Chanda saw her face, he raised a hand. "Kiera, I am telling the truth when I tell you that his is the stronger." He offered the hand. "Pull water. Am I lying?"

She refused his hand and looked past him to the unbroken snow behind where he stood, then lifted her gaze to the ashen sky. When had the snow stopped falling?

After allowing himself one small sigh, he continued. "Vrishka will rule over Fairbanks, Kiera, but from Barrow." His voice tightened when he spoke his next words. "He has chosen to leave me as regent." Her gaze flew to his face, and he grimaced. "I did not ask it, Kiera. It was his choice, but it is a good one, I think."

"I just bet you do," she muttered darkly, but he continued as if she hadn't spoken.

His next words shocked her beyond all belief, especially delivered in the same, even tone. "And you, Kiera, will marry me." He ignored her open mouth and plodded on. "The freed slaves will remain free, Kiera, a fact that should please you very greatly, though they will be asked to continue in the jobs assigned to them. And Marco will be given a mayorship. You may visit him as often as you wish, of course."

"Chanda," she told him, and meant every word. "I will not marry a man who breaks his oaths." She held his eyes and slowed the tempo of her words to make sure he heard and understood every single one. "And who beats slave women to death after taking his pleasure with them in a barn."

Genuine shock washed his face. "I have not ever beaten a woman, Kiera, nor taken one against her will, not even a—" Recognition changed his mouth. "Ah. Now the pieces come together." His knee made a pop when he stood, and he stopped to rub it before turning to take four, then five steps. His chest expanded as he took a breath, and he spoke to the hills he faced. "It was Valen, Kiera, who did what you speak of, and not me." When he turned, he looked hurt, and a little sad, and despite everything else, including her better judgment, she felt embarrassed, and a little ashamed for attributing that horror to him despite that he hadn't seemed, well, like someone who would do something like that. *But he's a Skani man*, the other half of her mind argued. One who sees women as possessions, baby machines, and who even this moment didn't seem particularly outraged at what Valen had done. And what had he said? That women look for men to protect them or something? That men needed to seek their pleasures with various women? And besides, he'd tried to force himself on her.

Well, the other half argued, *he did let you push him away*.

A hand flew to her face. Oh, good God. This entire exercise was ridiculous. Beyond ludicrous. And so she told the truth from behind her hand and hoped her words would dam this river. "Chanda, even if everything you say is true, even if I was forced, I could never marry you. I'd be supremely unhappy and I'd make you just as miserable."

"Why?" Quietly.

"Because then what? For one, you'd have me set up house while you went off fucking, oh, pardon me, *taking your pleasure* with whichever woman catches your eye. According to Marco, you're quite the ladies' man, and Chanda, I could never live like that."

He closed the distance between them and took her hand. "Kiera, I am willing to reach an accord with you."

She stood and pulled her hand free. "I am not trying to negotiate with you, Chanda. And why me, anyway? There are abundant—" Her head shook as realization dawned. She really was slow on the uptake lately. "Ah. I get it. I'm a fire mage. You see fire mage children, or powerful mage children anyway." Annoyance drew her lips together. "No thank you, Chanda. I am so much more than a brood mare, and besides all that, you seem to have forgotten this most important fact. I am already married. Happily. To Laszlo. The former slave. And did I mention *happily*? I am not willing to divorce—er, put him aside, even for the sake of the deconn." Her head fell back and she stared into the darkening sky. Snow would soon fall. More snow. Where the hell was the sun? "I will leave, Chanda, if Vrishka defeats us, and take Laszlo with me."

"That will not be permitted," came a voice, and Vrishka emerged from behind a cluster of rocks to claim it. "You will marry Lord Chanda, Kiera, and bear him many sons. Further, to keep temptation at bay, you will send half of your army to serve in mine." As he spoke, his voice dropped to shade into sarcasm, and she felt a slip of admiration for a man who could hold anger that tightly. Despite being an utter prick, he was probably one hell of an adversary, and she bet he never forgave a wrong. However, and all that aside, she would enjoy watching him die, because she, too, never forgave a wrong, especially one where her men had to die so he could spend a mark driving home his oh-so-important points.

Surprise popped as she realized that she had become every bit the barbarian as any man in this country. The thought made her laugh, a completely inappropriate reaction, and both men's brows raised as she slapped a hand to her mouth to try and stop it. Her emotions had just seemed to heaved and sway with the wind, and had since—well, since.

With a mental shove, she pushed that aside. On the bright side, it had stopped her laughter. "*Lord* Vrishka, I thank you for your kind offer," she said, and struggled to hold the sarcasm from her words. "But I will never voluntarily send Alaks to you to be slaves again. Never. They fought to be free, and as long as I draw breath, *I* will fight to see that they will remain so. Surrender would be their decision, and not mine, but I am certain their answer to whether to return to slavery will be *no*."

"Kiera," Chanda broke in, "they are dying now, and so many more will die before this is finished if you say no. Which is worse? Really? Wouldn't you want to live? And the ones we send will go into the army, do the same thing they do now, and so nothing will change for them. Not really."

"Ours have chosen to fight, Chanda," she shot back. "No one makes them! And ours can marry, and own things, and make a life for themselves!" Tears welled up. "They can complain if someone hurts them, Chanda, and we will do something!" Her hand lifted to brush a stray hair from her mouth as she tried to regain her composure.

A handful of men came from behind the rocks. One spoke quietly to Vrishka. When he'd finished, Vrishka turned his attention back to Kiera. "I have told you the terms, and now I will withdraw my troops and await your answer." He paused to exhale through his nose. "You will marry Chanda, Kiera, and you will send half of what remains of your army to me, a fair mix of and shifters. There will be no further compromise."

"I have heard what you plan for me, and for Marco, but what about Laszlo in all of this, Vrishka? What of—" she hesitated, searching for the right word, and when she found it, she used it with emphasis. "What of my *husband?*"

It was Chanda who stepped forward. Who answered. "Kiera," he told her, not unkindly, "Laszlo is no longer a factor in this matter." He held out a hand to her, offering something. Her heart began to pound, but she lifted a shaking hand, palm up, and watched him drop what looked like a small, wood-cast star, roughly made—the comb that Laszlo had made for her in the first turns she met him. The comb moons later she'd used magic to infuse with her love and left for him when she thought she might be swept back to the old Alaska, or die. The comb he always carried. Every turn. "He is gone, Kiera," he said quietly, and stepped back.

Her ears roared. She held the comb up to her face, and from a distant place felt tears sting her cheeks. Tears that she knew would never stop.

Vrishka's final blow pierced the bubble wrapping her, the one forcing despair down her throat, for the smallest of moments. "He carried that, yes? Well, he carries it no longer." He stepped in front of her. Made sure she saw him. Heard his words. "You have what remains of the tenturn to make your choice," he told her, then strode away, Chanda behind him. The men surrounding them began bleeding away, and Kiera fell to her knees.

"No," Kiera whispered as she rocked back and forth, the comb now clutched in the fingers of both hands, not caring who saw her. If the world ended. The snarling black mass of grief had wrapped her tight, strangled her eyes, her lungs, her heart, her soul. "No. No. No." Over and over, and over. A chant, a prayer. A plea.

"No!" she screamed. Gasped. "Oh God, no! No, no, no!"

Laszlo's face filled her mind, but he was gone. She would never get to touch him again. Never hear his voice. Feel his hands. Tell him she loved him. Sleep next to him, his breath on her shoulder.

The world went dark, and she lost her balance and fell to her side. Icy water filled her mouth, and she pushed her face into the cold as deeply as she could and begged Death to claim her, and the hand It held at that moment was crueler than the scythe that had cut Laszlo from her life.

CHAPTER 11

LIKE TEARS FROM BLACKENED EYES, DROPS of icy rain slid down silver lines to the ground, where the somber hooves and feet that marched back to Fairbanks crushed them into the dead earth under the snow. Fog lay wearily across the hilltops and slid like sleep into the gullies between them. As dispirited as the turn, the brown horse she rode bobbed his tired head while he walked, and Kiera hunched over the saddlehorn and watched her tears stain his neck.

Emptiness echoed across the night-dark valley, and Kiera felt lost inside it. A chill that not even sunfire could warm wrapped her, and though tears fell, they came from nowhere. Her fingers twitched inside her gloves. Some small sliver of sanity kept her from screaming, but barely, and only because she knew that if she started, it would never stop.

Kuruk rode just ahead of her, head down and her reins wrapped in his hand.

When they passed the gates, the soldiers who guarded it took off their helmets and bowed their heads. Did they grieve, she wondered, and felt her face tremble, felt cold rain mix with the tears on her cheeks.

At the manse, Kuruk dismounted and walked to her. His eyes met hers, deep and black and filled with compassion. She held out her arms and let him lift her from the horse. Sobs racked her body even before her feet touched the ground, and he pulled her close.

Strong arms wrapped her from behind, and Marco's voice, a soft stream of nonsense sounds, filled her ear. A river rose, wave after wave of pain and sorrow, and she cried out, sobbing, and only their arms kept her from the waiting ground.

INSIDE THE MAIN DOORS MARCO led her up the left stair, and not the right, and relief left her nearly too weak to climb. Maybe one turn she could face their bed, and his clothes, and his smell, but at that moment she couldn't bear even the thought—and even that much, the considering, pulled her shoulders down. Wearing patient faces, Marco and Kuruk waited for her to wipe her face and take the steps upward.

Wood had already been laid in the fireplace of the room Marco chose for her, one that was thankfully done in yellows, and not blues, and one that was laid out nearly opposite her own. Kuruk led her left to the bathroom and opened the door. Before she closed it she heard the fire burst to life, and after she'd closed the door she used the toilet, washed her hands, and burst into tears.

He was gone. Gone. God, how could he be gone? Heavy sobs racked her chest, and she leaned back against the wall and let them come.

The door opened and Marco came in. Without pause he pulled her up and crushed her to him. "He's gone," she sobbed. "He's gone."

"Come, Kiera," he soothed, and helped her limp out of the bathroom and to the bed. The covers were already pulled back, but she shook her head because she didn't want to get in there.

"I have to tell Alex," she whispered. Pain rose as she realized something else, and her eyes found his. "And Amba."

He pressed his lips together and sighed through his nose, but he nodded. "Sit, Kiera, then, and let me find them."

"Stay with her," came Kuruk's quiet voice, and he stood and let himself out.

Kiera walked to the couches and sat facing the fire in the smallest, palest, and waited.

In less than a half a mark the door opened and she found Amba staring in, her face a mirror of Kiera's heart. Without a word Kiera rose, Amba walked in, and they fell together. Something broke, and something healed, and some bar of strength lifted Kiera from the depths of the darkness.

When their sobs eased, they made their way to the couches and sat, touching, hands clasped.

"I have not told Alex," Amba said, voice tight, and stared at the fire. "But I will when I return, and then I will have Emmy bring him to you."

"Stay," Kiera whispered, and squeezed her hand.

Wearing a half smile, Amba turned to Kiera. "No, Kiera. I have no warmth to give this night, and neither do you." Her eyes shifted back to the fire. "Sleep, Kiera," Amba murmured. "And take warmth from those whose blood is still hot." She paused to sigh. "Kuruk," she said, eyes still captured by the flames, and spoke as softly as when she had to Kiera, "stay with her." With a final grimace she stood, and pulled Kiera to her feet. After squeezing Kiera's hand one last time, Amba let herself out without looking back.

WHEN THE DOOR NEXT OPENED KIERA stood and braced herself, but it was Allie. Like Amba had, she entered without a word, but instead of coming to Kiera she whispered, "I'm sorry," offered a sad little smile, and walked straight to Marco and wrapped her arms around him.

Kuruk's brows raised, and he looked from Allie to Kiera, then back at Allie again. With a shrug Kiera sat down on the couch. "Kuruk," she said, and he walked to where she could see him. "Will you please do me a favor?" she asked in her quietest voice. When he nodded, slowly, she continued. "Will you get my—um—supplies from my saddlebag? I'll need it in the morning."

The smile that lifted his mouth was as small and sad as Allie's, but the eyes above his were warm.

"Allie, I am staying here tonight," came Marco's voice from behind her, and though he was trying to be quiet, Kuruk shook his head as he let himself out. Kiera turned and watched as Marco led the pouting Allie around to the far side of the bed so they could argue out of Kiera's hearing.

Tears filled Kiera's eyes, but not because of Allie. Or not really. Life was going on, rolling like water over rocks, but it shouldn't be. Night had fallen, thick and black, and bled in through the open curtains. Out there, someplace out there, Laszlo had died. His ears would never hear again, and his eyes would never watch the sun rise, or set.

Pressure filled Kiera's chest, and her eyes closed as the tears washed seeing away. Self recrimination rose, and fell. She would accept blame for this. No one else besides her, and Vrishka, and the man who had taken his life held blame, though many others would owe—what was it they called it here? Recompense. Yes.

But she knew that the largest fault was hers. If she hadn't left him there, let him ride away, he would be alive. Here.

The dark drew her, and she stood and walked to the window. A memory bubbled up, one of a dark winter night at another window, and the warm hands that drew her from the press of the cold glass. Unable to bear her thoughts, she pushed them aside and stared out the window, where skeletal fingers of the city's lights shot up and pierced holes in the velvet dark that wrapped the sky.

A creak sounded when the door opened, and she drew a breath and turned. Kuruk—it was Kuruk, but then Alex followed him in, eyes huge in his swollen face, and then Emmy, her hand locked around his. Her eyes found Kiera in the dark shadow first, and a world passed between them in that moment, a sharing of sorrow and sadness and regret. Emmy felt pain first for Alex, and Kiera loved her for that in part because Amba was right. For now, she had precious little warmth to spare.

After one more breath, Kiera left the window. Alex ran to her, and when her arms captured him he collapsed, sobbing, and she lifted him and carried him to the bed. Still in her bloody pants, she struggled to climb up, but this bed stood higher than hers, and she slid back. A hand caught her arm, another rested against her back, and the men helped her into bed.

As she held him Alex cried loudly, angrily, and didn't try to stifle the sobs that racked his small body. Kiera closed her eyes as she rocked him and let her own tears wet his back.

The door slammed when Allie left, and both Kiera and Alex jumped. "Shhhh," Marco soothed as he sat on the bed. With gentle fingers, he brushed Kiera's hair.

"Emmy," Kuruk called softly, but it was a command, and he pointed at the bed. Kiera watched as she came and stood beside the bed in front of Kiera. "Climb up, and lay next to Alex," he told her, and she obeyed, albeit slowly—knee, then hand, then knee—with a puzzled look. When she had lain down, he turned. "Marco, go there," he motioned with his head, "and lay behind Kiera."

With a small smile, Marco shifted on his feet and stared at Kuruk.

"Please," Kuruk urged.

After one final look, Marco nodded, then walked around the bed. When he'd climbed up, he pressed his chest against Kiera's and wrapped his arms around her.

Her lungs felt tight, and breathing was hard, but something small unwound as the collective warmth, the comfort from their touch, bled into her, and she closed her eyes. The bed moved when Kuruk climbed up, but she didn't bother to see what he planned for himself.

In a moment his hand found her hair, and lay still in the mess it made above her head.

After a time Alex's sobs melted into hiccups, and she felt him relax as he fell into sleep.

"Don't be angry with Allie," Kiera murmured, and felt a little surprised that her own voice sounded so even. "She's no more selfish than I am."

Marco spoke quietly. "Kiera. No."

"Shhhh, Kiera, and let sleep come," came Kuruk's soft words. "Let nexturn be nexturn."

"I don't want nexturn to come," she said into the stillness.

Marco squirmed closer to her and squeezed her hard. "Oh, Kiera. I am so sorry."

"I wish it had been me who died. I wish I knew where death takes us, because I—" her voice broke—"I would follow him."

Kuruk's voice sounded both thick and far above her. "Your grief honors him, Kiera."

"He loved you so very much, Kiera," Emmy whispered. "Love like I have never seen."

Her sobs came, pulled her body into the rhythm of her breathing, and she held Alex tightly and tried to keep from waking him. Marco rocked with her and made sounds meant to be soothing while Kuruk kept a hand pressed to her cheek.

After a time Kuruk spoke, and sounded chagrined. "Pull up the blanket. Your ear is cold."

His words surprised her, the incongruity made her laugh a little, and the sally interrupted her grief enough to let her drive the sobs back. With a sleeve she wiped her nose, then turned her face and found him sitting above her on the bed.

"No. I'm fine. It'd be hard to be cold in the middle of all of you," she told him.

Even in the half light, the relief on his face told her his words' purpose.

Emmy fell asleep first, arms still wrapped around Alex, and then Marco.

"Sleep, Kiera," Kuruk whispered above her some time later, his hand still cupping her face.

Instead of answering, she closed her eyes. "I want to get up," she finally whispered. "Will you help me untangle Marco?"

"So you can do what? Pace the floor? Walk the grounds? No, Kiera."

With a huff she unhooked Marco's arm and twisted her back a little as she eased away from Marco's chest and up from Alex's. Kuruk laid a hand on her shoulder as Marco woke.

"No, Kiera," Kuruk said again, and his voice held a warning.

"Don't tell me what I need to do," she ground out. "I need to get up."

Marco slid his arm around her and pulled her back to his chest. Each exhale of his breath lifted her hair. "Listen to me. It would grieve Laszlo very greatly, even more than it grieves me, Kiera, to know the pain this has caused you."

Her eyes closed and filled.

He continued mercilessly. "If not for yourself, do this for Laszlo. Do not let this grief destroy you, Kiera. Let us share it, lift what we can."

"I don't want to."

"You are too cold," Kuruk told her as he stroked her hair. "Let us warm you."

"Kuruk," she said tiredly, answering his meaning rather than his words, "I feel grief, tremendous grief, because I lost my husband. I can't help it."

He did not sound convinced, or maybe it didn't matter. "Perhaps. But do not turn from comfort when the pain is nearest, Kiera, or it will swallow you."

"I don't care," she said, but she did care, and she hated that she did.

"Please Kiera," Marco said as he tucked the blanket around them both. "Just lay here with me."

With each exhale her arms felt heavier, so she let Marco wrap her. "I love you, Marco," she murmured as her body relaxed. "Please don't die."

"Shhh. I am not going to die," he whispered into her hair, but if he said anything else, she didn't hear it.

Kuruk's harsh whisper came from above Kiera's head. "Go! Go now! And close the door! " Behind the lump of Alex and Emmy, from the glass in the west wall, dismal light wafted in and slunk around the room. Instead of warmth, it cast a sickroom pallor.

With consciousness came the pause, that moment the morning after devastation when the whole world waits, breath held, for the flood to begin. "I have come to share sorrow," Muukwa muttered, annoyance snaking through her voice, and still it waited.

"She is *sleeping*, *kishtangi!*"

Equal parts of jagged emotion and physical pain exploded at the same moment that Muukwa abandoned all pretense at politeness and shot back a full-voiced reply. Kiera cried out, thrashed violently, knocked Marco off the bed, and stumbled to the bathroom. Guts heaving, she collapsed in front of the toilet. Agony sliced across her forehead each time her stomach pushed waves of thick liquid out her mouth and nose. When nothing remained, she collapsed on the floor and covered her eyes with both hands. Great rolling sobs shook her chest.

Warm hands lifted her and helped her lean against the toilet as she garnered what control she could find. Fingers wiped spittle and vomit from her trembling lips. "Open your mouth," murmured Kuruk, who poured bitter powder between her lips and tapped her fingers with a filled cup. Her stomach threatened to reject it, but she washed it down with the water, willed her stomach to ease, and prayed.

Even in the darkened bathroom the ambient light stung her eyes when she dropped her hands. Kuruk stood when she did, and as the pain melted away she saw Marco framed the doorway behind him. Her head dropped. All of this—all of it—was a nightmare. Thisturn she would have to pull herself into the great hall. She would have to tell the Skani and Alaks what happened. Vrishka's terms.

The Skani would say to give in, and the truth was that she was terrified that she would want to. That she might do it, even if the Alaks said *no*. She lifted her eyes to Marco's silhouette. Kuruk's. These men, so many, could as easily die as Laszlo had.

Laszlo.

Her chest heaved and she leaned forward, head in hands, and let the sobs come. Marco pushed past Kuruk and dropped to his knees in front of her. She clung to him and cried her anguish as he rocked her.

When the worst of the storm had passed, Kiera pushed back. "I have to go to the bathroom," she hiccupped, and Marco rose and led Kuruk out. When she had finished, she washed her face and hands and padded short steps out to the bed. Emmy and Alex lay awake, but still, and when he saw her, Alex's lips trembled.

"Are we going to the funeral today?"

It took long seconds for Kiera to wrestle her raging emotions, harder because everyone watched, before she could answer. "I—I don't think we will go thisturn, Alex." She looked at Marco, then at Kuruk.

Marco furrowed his brows. "What is a *funeral*, Alex?"

Alex cast troubled eyes to Kiera.

She swallowed. "It's the—a ceremony for saying goodbye to someone who has—has passed—who has died."

After a pause, Kuruk spoke carefully. "Here we have a *ta*, if a family wishes it." He waited until Kiera nodded to continue. "A time to share memories, and to wish the dead well in his next life."

Raw sorrow welled, but she had to ask. For God's sake she couldn't leave all the details to Amba. "And what—what do you do with—" Chest tight, her hands lifted as she begged for a moment. When she could speak, she asked Kuruk, "What do you do afterward? Do you bury them?"

But Kiera had forgotten about Muukwa, who still stood by the door, face contorted. "Bury them in the *ground?*"

Sharp words exploded from Kuruk's mouth, words Kiera did not understand, and Muukwa shrugged, but dropped her eyes.

"No, Kiera," Marco told her, but he looked a hard question at Kuruk. "No one buries the dead in the ground. Their bodies are burned."

"To speed them to their next life," Muukwa added as she walked over.

Pointedly ignoring Muukwa, Kiera spoke softly to Marco. "What? What is it, Marco?"

Kuruk put a hand on Kiera's arm. "Kiera, this is too much for now. Take a bath and then we will walk the grounds. Let us decide these things after."

Heart sinking in a chest bound with steel bands, Kiera looked between Kuruk and Marco. "Where. Is. He?"

Kuruk would not meet her eyes. "I do not know, Kiera."

Agony and fury flashed, tangled as they caught, and sent words she couldn't stop. "You left him out there! You left Laszlo laying out there!" Stumbling back, she caught the edge of the bed with a hand and let it keep her upright as she stared disbelief at the men.

Kuruk took two steps and then her arms. "Kiera, it is very common for an enemy to refuse to return the bodies of the *otuk*s they have taken in battle. I am sorry. *I am sorry.*"

She lifted her eyes and felt tears stream down her cheeks. "Will they—" Images rose, horrifying images she'd seen in history books, and her breath caught in a sob. "Will they do something—terrible to his body?"

Too hard, he crushed her to his chest. "No. No," he soothed. "They will burn him."

A small sound, like an injured bird, erupted from behind her, and she turned to find Alex, weeping quietly, and shame washed through her. This boy had lost his mother less than a cycle ago, and now the man he considered close to a father. What had she been thinking? Of nothing but herself. "Alex, I am so sorry. We aren't going to talk about this anymore." With both hands she pulled him over, then wrapped him inside her arms. Murmuring soft words, Emmy scooted until she bracketed his back, and put a hand on his shoulder.

"Marco," she said, and forced her voice calm, "I have to talk to the Skani and the Alaks thisturn. Can you bring everyone together this afternoon?"

His eyes appraised. "For what purpose?"

"Vrishka gave me new terms." She looked to Kuruk. "But this morning, I think we should do something else." She nodded her chin to Alex. "Something that—that isn't horrible."

A sour smile lifted one corner of Kuruk's lip. "Fight."

BLOOD SANG THROUGH KIERA'S VEINS as she stepped around the edges of the square they'd marked with heelmarks and stones behind the stable. Kuruk had made her spar against him, and after he knocked her down twice, she stopped pulling punches.

A dozen yards away, Alex sparred against a shifter she didn't know. Even without her coat sweat soaked her shirt and dribbled down the back of her pants. Alex's hair lay stuck to his forehead.

Stars sliced across her vision when Kuruk's palm slapped above her ear.

"Jerk," she growled as she rubbed her head.

A shoulder lifted. "I took the opportunity presented." After a pause, the skin between his brows wrinkled. "Do not worry that the Yeil may return with the Shunakah, Kiera. Las—uh, after your attack soldiers were sent to every roof, and I have closed the gate for this time."

Abruptly, Kiera gasped and leaned over, fist squeezed into where her stomach curled.

In two steps Kuruk stood in front of her, hands out and face filled with concern. Using her grief and the anger that wrapped it, Kiera *kiai*ed as she surged up and drove that fist into his midsection, then, as he began to stumble back, followed up with a front kick to the inside of his hip.

Before he could return a strike she slid back, cocked her left leg and side-kicked his thigh.

Nearly too fast to see, his hands caught her leg, wrapped her shin, and lifted her boot to his shoulder. Kiera hopped and swiveled on the leg on the ground and, from the right, drove two hammer fists into his forearms. Either she knocked her leg free or he let go, but she charged in, punching his chest as fast as she could. She blocked his open-handed strikes and drove him back two steps before he caught one, then the other wrist.

A small smile. "Better."

"Better than what?" she snarled, angry, no, *furious* that he so easily bested her every single time. That nothing was fair. That Laszlo was gone. With a tug, she yanked her arms free. "I can't pull earth like you and—" Both the words and her anger died and the bitter wind carried them away as she stared into his broad-jawed face. "Hold on," she said, and stepped back. Eyes closed, she sent her sight out and down, down into the earth.

Thick, green strands moved sluggishly through the frozen earth, perhaps slowed by the ice gripping the dirt. Filmy hands reached for it, called it to her, and she pulled it up and into her. Unlike fire, and air, it wouldn't actually spin. It more soaked in and had to be used quickly. She pulled more, fed it into her legs and arms, and one thigh jerked as the earth disappeared inside it. And unlike air, she couldn't actually feel it when she carried an excess. Not really. How much was too much, and what would happen if she overloaded? Air came popping back out, though she had yet to pull too much fire. Water she had not tried. Even a little was too much and made her feel like she couldn't breathe.

Despair roiled underneath as she pulled, but she waded through it and forced herself to focus. She would give her due to Laszlo later. Every turn.

In moments, after perhaps ten pulls, her body began to tingle and the big muscles in her legs began to tremble. She opened her eyes to find Kuruk watching her with equal measures of curiosity and concern.

"Do you need some time to cry now, Kiera? We can stop if you wish."

Instead of answering, she screamed wordlessly as she charged. Green light sparkled in the corners of her vision as the world faded, slowed, and became surreal, almost dreamy. Like a bubble from a pond's depths rose the thought *But I am crying*, but then green haze washed it away.

Crisp snow crunched beneath the flat of her foot as she pushed off for the next step, syrupy slow, the pop as her boot crushed it into the frozen earth almost surreal. She remembered earth having this effect on her before, but that, too, slipped away like a fish in her hand as her heel left the ground.

Kuruk's face, slowed by the time warp of earth, slid from concerned to surprised to shocked. Before he had time to lift his hands she hit him like a football player, shoulder to chest. She dug in her toes with the next step and surged forward, still screaming, and he flew back. One foot flew up, caught her knee, but she pushed, and he fell. Unfortunately she had come too fast to stop, so when she tangled in his legs as his back hit the ground she fell forward and landed hard on his chest, knocking the breath from her.

Face to face, his eyes opened wide and stared into hers.

"Earth magic," she rasped breathlessly, and rolled off.

"Earth? Did you use earth?" came Marco's incredulous voice from somewhere behind her.

Still strong legs pushed her up and Kiera whirled to find him watching from the corner of the stable. Next to him stood Muukwa, and a handful of soldiers had gathered as well.

Tears rose, a stab of grief unattached to any particular thought—or if there was a thought, a memory, she didn't want to chase it down. With a hand she wiped mud from her arm and tried to blink them back. "Yep."

"You moved as fast as an Alak," Muukwa accused. "Is that your magic?"

It took a second to think through what that might mean. "No, Muukwa. I'm a fire mage. I am most closely connected to fire."

"You truly loved Laszlo," came Muukwa's non sequitur in a tone that said she found the idea incredulous.

Kiera's breath caught. "Yes," she breathed, and turned toward the gristly white Pi'tahs, the mountains below which Fairbanks crouched, and brushed the rest of the mud from her coat. When tears fell, she wiped them away with the back of her hand.

"Do you have this magic, Marco?" Muukwa asked from behind her.

"I have other magic," he answered tersely.

"Well, you must spar with me anyway," Kiera heard the smile in her voice, the challenge, "and I give my oath that I will treat you gently. Once only, until one falls to the ground."

"I do not have time to play with you, Muukwa."

"You have time to stand and watch, but not to fight?" Her voice was one shade short of a sneer. "Are you frightened?"

"No, Muukwa, but if you do not shut your mouth—"

Kiera spun around. "Muukwa. Don't." She shook her head. "Leave Marco alone. And Marco—" But Marco's face gave her pause. It held anger, sure. But fear lay there, too, a great deal of it just below the surface, and Kiera wondered why. "Please."

All heads turned as Alex came running over, sliced the space between Muukwa and Marco, and tension bled away as attention turned to him.

"Don't be mean to Marco," he told Muukwa matter-of-factly, but before she could answer, he spun to Kiera. "I saw you, Keer!" he exclaimed. "How did you do that?"

Staring at Alex was like looking at Julia, and his seeming nonchalance reminded her of the turns following his mother's death. Like herself, he buried his grief. They had both lost so much in the last cycle. Lost and gained and lost. "I used earth energy, Alex."

Marco's voice drew her back. "We will gather at fourth air—" *two p.m.*—"and you can speak Vrishka's terms to all at that mark."

Chapter 12

Back in her room, Kiera forced Alex to eat his lunch. After she'd sent him to bathe, she picked up her coat and sat holding it on one of the couches next to the fire. With one final breath, and trembling fingers, she pulled the wooden star from her chest pocket and held it in front of her face.

With jagged claws, memories climbed from the depths, ripped holes in her chest and her throat. Eyes closed, she drew his face to her mind. Broad and bronze-skinned, she'd held that face in her hands and watched the walls behind which he hid his heart fall, watched his eyes fill with tenderness as he brought his lips to hers.

Abruptly she stood, clutching the comb between her fingers, and marched to the dressing table. A handful of red ribbons lay forlornly atop it, and she grabbed one and strode to the window. Her fingers trembled as she slipped an end through the comb's empty center and tied the ribbon around her neck.

The deathly cold bled through the glass. Chest tight, she pressed fingers to its transparent face. Wished she could hold the cold like it did, wished she could summon cold like fire, pull it inside and let it still the shearing grief winding her heart like razor wire. A maelstrom, a lifetime of tears waited, but she stared dry-eyed out the window at the grimy town below and the fingers of fog gripping the mountains beyond them.

Her lips trembled and she leaned forward and rested her forehead against the glass.

A hand on her shoulder startled her, and she turned to find Kuruk standing behind her. "Is your head hurting?"

For a moment she stared at his face before she shook her head. "I have to take a bath and go to court," she told him as she walked to the bathroom. "Alex, are you finished?'

"Almost," he yelled.

116

Someone had made the bed, and a cheerful yellow coverlet lay smoothly across its width. Kiera sat atop it at the edge of the bed and brushed the fabric with the pads of her fingers.

"We will have a *ta* nexturn if you wish it," Kuruk told her carefully.

Back and forth her hand stroked the bumpy fabric. "I wish it." She lifted her eyes. "Will Amba?"

His lips thinned as he considered. "She has not said so," he finally admitted. "But it is very common to hold a *ta* for a fallen son. I do not believe that she will object."

The bathroom door slammed open and startled Kiera. A towel-clad Alex emerged, but before she could inquire into his door-slamming the front door opened and Emmy bustled in carrying an armful of clean laundry.

Too heartsick to make further conversation with anyone, Kiera took a bath, and as she soaked she wondered what she was going to do about everything.

AN EASY FOUR HUNDRED FAIRBANKS CITIZENS crowded the great hall, a fair mix of Alak and Skani, every one anxious to hear Vrishka's proposal. Even Amba came, though she stood close to the doorway and spoke to no one. Tension buzzed through the air, and people speculated in voices made too loud by the room's acoustics.

From atop one of the tables, Kiera delivered Vrishka's terms. Her even tone surprised her, as did the way her mind drifted as she said the words. Mouths dropped, both mage and shifter, and silence thundered when she'd finished. Without waiting for questions, she took Kuruk's outstretched hand and stepped down, then sat and lifted a glass of wine to her lips. Before the ruby liquid touched her lips the heady scent told her it was Lorgda's good wine. She lifted her eyes and found him sitting at the next table, eyes sad, likely for her, and she offered a smile she didn't feel and drank the entire glass. When she finished it, she plinked the glass on the table and dredged up another smile because he deserved it. He didn't often come out of the greenhouse, and his kindness both touched her and sparked the tears she had hoped to hold at bay.

Naga's voice rang out, outrage large. "Make Marco a mayor? Why, my lady, that is outrageous!"

Kiera stood and let her eyes find the source of the voice. Leith stood facing away, but Naga's face was pinched with what looked like real shock, and it made Kiera laugh. Just a little, but a laugh nonetheless. Of course the damned Skani—well, Leith and Naga, she amended—would completely disregard all but what affected them. To her surprise Allie stood with them, looking every bit as affronted as Naga, but it was just a little too emphatic, and Kiera found herself doubting the girl's sincerity.

But then, who else's side would she be expected to take? Everyone knew that Marco backed Kiera in most everything, which left him less than popular with the majority of the Skani. And Allie was what, seventeen?

With a sigh, Kiera let her gaze drift to the main group of Alaks. And of course they looked frightened, and angry, and many of their eyes sought hers, perhaps hoping for reassurance. She wished she had it to give.

A sudden wave of longing rose. At this moment the loss of Laszlo felt so keen, so complete. Here she stood in a sea of people, alone really, left to face this increasingly agitated group and to try and find a way to calm them. To solve their—these— problems. She loved Marco with every fiber of her being, but here he sat, useless, across from her wearing a sullen look as he drank his wine.

Chanda—Vrishka—was right. Neither of them knew a single important thing about running a deconn. Sure, she had the courage to do what needed done, and Marco had more than enough heart, but they were idealists—inexperienced, ignorant, and failing miserably. Without Laszlo, without someone who understood the intricacies of how to run something as unwieldy as an army, or a city, they were doomed to fail.

And so. Her eyes lifted again to the Alaks crowded into the far side of the room, and tears blurred their faces. Sorrow filled her, and shame. And loss. So much loss.

There was no way she could shear away these people's freedom. But what? What could she do against a man who not only knew how to run a city, but an army, and who had more soldiers and experience than she— than anyone here—did?

Wait, a voice warned. Maybe she could talk to Amba. Ask her for tactical advice. Laszlo relied on her, told Marco to take advice from her when they left the city. That turn.

The thought pushed aside her grief, some of it anyway, that and the next glass of wine, and she ignored everyone as she drank it.

But what did the Alaks want? Yes, they very likely did not want to die fighting a battle they were all destined to lose, but how could she make that choice for them? Maybe there was another way. Maybe she could smuggle them out somehow. Send them out to the nadeconn. Would the tribes take them?

The feeling of being watched interrupted her rambling thoughts and drew her gaze from her hands atop the table. Marco watched her, gauging her face.

"Is there more?" he asked quietly.

"Only that Vrishka has more men, more experience, probably more mages, and is going to crush us if we resist," Kiera answered bleakly. "Do you want to talk about this?"

His head turned as he stared out at the people gathered in the hall. His despair was palpable, and Kiera squeezed his hand. "I'll be in my room," she told him as she stood.

ON THE WAY BACK, KIERA TOOK the stair that led to her old apartment. Kuruk followed and offered no comment. When she arrived, she strode in without allowing herself the pause she wanted. Everything was still the same. Same as the morning they'd left. Yesturn morning. In a pile near the bed she found what she wanted: Laszlo's shirt from yesturn. She wound it into a roll and carried it out, and let Kuruk shut the door.

When she returned to her new room, she lit the fire and dropped into the pale gold chair near the window. Eyes closed, she let the afternoon sun warm her, Laszlo's shirt in her hands. Alex returned with Emmy a mark or two later as Kiera drowsed in the chair. Energy, will, thought, all had fled. Marco, too, seemed to have deserted her. When dinner came she refused it and instead watched the dark creep in from the corners and steal the blue from the sky.

Pale pricks pierced the encroaching dark as stars raised defiant faces and refused to succumb. The sky offered itself to her, a living work of art, and she wished it would lend her its wisdom, sing its hymns, and reveal the peace that must surely come from an eternity of waiting.

A Van Gogh sky, she thought, for the first time in moons. Her mother's song, the one she'd sung to Laszlo that first night together. She tried to fling it away, but it lingered, pressing its words in until they filled her thoughts. Yes, it hurt. A ragged, tearing pain. But still she found herself saying the words in her mind, repeating them over and over, like a mantra, a spell against the ravening dark.

Softly at first, she sang it to the waiting stars.

Beneath a Van Gogh sky,
We stand watching, you and me.
We wait for stars to sing the song,
To seal our destiny.

They light the sky on fire,
The sound of bloody light.

BLOWING EMBERS

Our shadows stretch, immortal;
Devouring the night.

The stars, they burn the skies,
Burn my eyes, white December.
My heart, it floats like ashes,
Fallen embers, blowing embers.

We stand so strong and purposeful,
Our hands stretched toward the moon.
And who would blame me if, perchance,
I gave my heart so soon?

Fiery stars streak toward us,
Shooting, spinning through the skies.
Flame chars the past to soot,
We see through newborn eyes.

The stars, they burn the skies,
Burn my eyes, but I remember.
The stars, they float like ashes,
Fallen embers, blowing embers.

Against the blazing heavens,
We lay watching, you and me.
The sky too small to capture us;
Love is infinity.

The stars, they burn the skies,
Burn my eyes, white December.
The stars, they float like ashes,
Fallen embers, blowing embers.

Fallen embers, blowing embers
Love burns all life to ashes.
Resurrection. Rising embers.

Alex padded over and stood next to her chair. "That's Gram's song," he told her solemnly. "I heard her sing it."

His eyes looked sad, so she offered a hand, but he ignored it. "Yes," she answered tiredly, and let her hand fall to the arm of the chair. "Gram taught it to me when I was littler than you."

"What does it mean?"

"Come sit with me and I'll tell you what I think it means."

After a glance over her head, probably at Emmy, Alex jumped into her lap, landed on her stomach, and forced out what breath she had. This was the same anger, the same pain as when he'd lost his mother, and while Kiera understood, she found herself weary at the thought of trundling through another handful of moons of its stuttered risings. She loved him, though, more than anything in the world, and she knew the goodness in him, and her love, would slowly smother it, or burn it away. But regardless, she'd do it, so she pushed aside her turmoil and wrapped her arms around him. What else could he do, really? How else to rid himself of the pain of yet another loss of someone he loved?

"I think that song tells us that when you love someone, really love them with all your heart, it changes you, and it changes them, too. For the better." Satisfied, he snuggled down and rested his head against her shoulder. "I also think," she continued, voicing her meandering thoughts, "that it means that when you love like that, it makes you stronger. Like someone new, almost. But in time. The time it takes for that love to burn all the bad things away."

Her words were wasted on Alex, who had fallen asleep in her lap. Carefully she stood, lifted his sleep-softened body, and carried him to bed. Emmy pulled back the covers and she slipped him in, then kissed his sleeping face.

"He is just so upset," Emmy defended without meeting her eyes, and Kiera smiled wryly.

"I know," was all she said before she returned to her chair. Kuruk brought her a blanket, which she wrapped around herself. Without asking, he dropped down on the floor next to her and stared out the window.

Filmy light from the city below highlighted his nose but hid his eyes. Did he hope that she would love him, someday when this pain had faded? She should tell him not to, that she would never love another man, but the right words, any words, escaped on the back of the sigh she breathed. It was just too big, too much, just one more thing in the mountain pressing her shoulders into the cold, dead earth, and she didn't think she had the strength to rise and bear all of this up, much less carry it while she struggled just to walk.

A part of her wished that she could leave. Take Alex and go back to the old Alaska. Find a job as a lawyer, worry about depositions and discovery, fret over trials and Christmas plays, and forget every single thing here.

But she knew she couldn't, and that in truth, despite all the pain, she didn't really want to. Not only had she had nothing in her old life, nothing besides Alex that mattered after the earth swallowed Julia, but these people, even some of the Skani, trusted her to see them through this horror and any that followed. *Perhaps undeservedly*, she made herself add. But what could she do? her thoughts wailed. One woman who knew nearly nothing against a man like Vrishka. She hadn't lied when she told Marco she knew he'd crush them if they resisted.

Another sigh escaped, and the bathroom beckoned, so she rose, got a drink and used the toilet. When she'd finished she came back to her chair and pulled the blanket up to her chin, then laid her head back, stuffed Laszlo's shirt where she could rest her cheek against it, breathe his smell, and let her thoughts drift with her consciousness out the window and to the stars spinning in the Van Gogh sky.

VIVID, FEVERISH DREAMS FOLLOWED KIERA as she half-slept through the turns. Laszlo's hands, so strong—hands that held her too tightly even during the night, as if she were a treasure he was afraid might slip away while he slept. Marco's ironic face when he explained why Fairbanks had no water mages. A giant bear rocketing down the snowy field, and her fear as crisp as the air. Agni's admonition as she lay with Laszlo atop her after he'd breached her shield. Chanda's face in the dark of the barn. The horror she felt at the touch of his hands, and he wearing the same face when he told her that Laszlo was gone. Kuruk's face while she wept.

Words, past-spoken sounds laced with amber firelight, exploded from a golden treasure chest, swirled, muddied, as voices spoke over each other, warring to be heard and understood.

> *You must not give up just because your first line of defense has been breached.*
> *There is always a way in, a'kala.*
> *It is very common for an enemy to refuse to return the bodies.*
> *There is a lot of lying in this court.*
> *There is always a way in, a'kala.*
> *You lay vulnerable to his next attack.*
> *There is always a way in, a'kala.*
> *You simply gave in.*

"SON OF A BITCH," KIERA GASPED and opened her eyes. "Son. Of. A. Bitch." Chills washed her, skidded across her skin, up her neck, and she exhaled, then stood. The blanket, and Laszlo's shirt, slid down to puddle on the floor at her feet.

From next to the chair, Kuruk thrust to his feet and took her forearms in his hands. "What is it, Kiera?"

"I—" she struggled to find the words, to fit this maelstrom into something that would make sense to him. "Wait," she said, but stumbled over the blanket. Kuruk caught her arm and she smiled her thanks, a real smile, and surprise washed his face. Kiera untangled her feet, then padded to the table. Marco lay asleep on the far side of the bed, and tenderness for this man rose high as she poured herself a glass of water, then lifted the carafe to offer Kuruk a drink.

His nod came slowly, and she smiled again at his confusion. No, they weren't out of the woods, not by even the kindest assessment, but fiery hope flared and dug excruciatingly joyous hooks into the walls of her chest. Laszlo lived, she knew he did, and if she had to burn the entire country to the ground, she'd bring him home.

As if feeling her need, the wood in the iron fireplace burst to life, and she smiled again, a smile that rose from the fires of the rage that lay churning in the pit of her stomach.

She took a moment to sip the water before walking across the room and handing Kuruk's to him, then dropped into her chair.

As for the rest of it—well. She'd need help for that.

"Kuruk," she asked, "will you please wake Marco? I want to speak to both of you."

She had to have proof before telling Alex and Agni. It was still possible, she made herself admit, that Chanda had told the truth about that. But it, like everything else he—they—had said was most likely a lie. She knew it was. Knew it like she knew the cleansing sun would soon rise and incinerate the darkness.

How much had she just accepted? Everything. Every goddamned thing.

And she could attribute the whole thing to laziness. Laziness in learning what Laszlo had to teach, in not bothering to question what Chanda told her so earnestly, in what Kuruk told her, thinking his words true—in every single goddamned thing.

At Kuruk's urging, a bleary-eyed Marco rose and stumbled to the bathroom. The first twinges of her morning headache threatened, so when he emerged, rubbing his eyes, she pushed past him, but no place in the sparkling clean bathroom revealed the packets of powder. "Kuruk," she called, but he was already behind her, a packet of her powder clenched in his hand. "You can leave those in here," she whispered, but he shook his head and stalked out.

As bitter as usual, she choked down what she could in the bathroom before walking back to her chair and washing it down with the remaining water.

Laszlo's shirt still lay tangled in the blanket, so she leaned over and plucked it from the floor. "Let's move to the couches," she told them as she wrapped it over and again around one forearm. When they'd settled, she on one couch and they on the one across from her, she paused to listen to the fire crackle in its bed on her left as she stared into the shadows that painted their faces. Both looked very concerned, and she tried hard not to laugh, though she wasn't sure why it should be funny.

A shaky breath escaped from pursed lips. "I love you both," she told them very seriously, and watched shock ripple across their faces, albeit likely for very different reasons. Kuruk looked a question at Marco, whose face said he had no answer but fervently wished he did.

High on her joy, her lips curved in a wide smile as she waited until they looked back to her to continue. "You are both my loyal and good friends. And because you are, I am going to ask that you listen carefully to what I am going to tell you, and think about this." Her chest expanded as she drew a deep breath. "Really think.

"How many soldiers does Vrishka have, Kuruk? Or Marco, if you know."

Marco looked to Kuruk, who looked at Marco, and then to her. "Chanda said—" Kuruk began, hesitantly.

The fingers of her left hand lifted from the arm of the couch. "No. I know what Chanda said. He said that Vrishka has more soldiers than we do. But have we asked someone who would know? Counted? Found someone who would have done that?"

Kuruk's eyes hardened as he realized Kiera's meaning, and he leaned forward, anxious to hear more. As he did Marco's hand raised and covered his eyes.

"Could we have been that stupid?" Marco asked from behind his hand.

"I think we were," Kiera answered, and sipped her water. "I think we made two mistakes. First, we took others' honesty for granted, which was pretty stupid of all of us, and second, I think that we have been exceedingly lazy." So many things, ideas, needed to be said—she struggled to sort and put them in the right order. If she was going to make this work, she first needed these two to believe her.

"Laszlo—" his name still made her chest tight, "If Laszlo were here, all those *otuks*, our soldiers would have someone to talk to about what happened out there. To tell them what they saw and how many they counted. I'm positive that's something he did with them. But there's no one. I came back broken, Kuruk with me, and Marco, you stayed here. Amba, too, is in no shape to ask questions. Alex is shattered, and Marco, Allie's been fighting with you since before all this started." Her mouth had dried again, so she drank down the rest of her water and rose to pour more. "In short, my friends, I think we've been played."

"'Played'?" Marco asked from behind her.

"Intrigue, Marco," she explained as she returned to the couch, but the fire needed wood, so she walked between the couches and tossed two, then three quarter-cut slabs to the hungry tongues. "Psychological warfare. I'm the only fire mage in this country, and as such I pose the greatest risk to Vrishka's victory." A smile rose as she conjured Laszlo's words. "'There's always a way in,'" she echoed, "a way to breach any shield to get to the tender meat inside." Dismissing her reverie, she walked back and stood in front of the luxuriously soft canary couch.

"Everyone in this deconn knows what Laszlo means to me," she continued when she'd plopped back down again. "And you, Marco, and Alex. But Laszlo is strong, strong enough to keep fingers from either of you. So take him and solve all problems. Take him and what happens to me? I fall completely apart. Easy to step on, and over, especially when I lay there on the ground and let them. That's what Chanda and Vrishka believe women do when their men are taken, and it seems in that at least they were right. For both Amba and me, taking Laszlo crippled us.

"Second, and, no offense, but he is the strongest leader of the three of us. Kuruk, you heard Chanda—Vrishka, too—disparage Marco and me. 'A woman and a boy' or something. And we have been little better than either believe, Marco. You never come to train, or to magic lessons anymore. You spend nearly every moment with Allie."

Marco opened his mouth and started to object, but Kiera raised a hand. "It's true, Marco, but I'm not judging you any more harshly than I've judged myself. I have done little but focus on myself, and my projects. Oh sure, I've taught some of the Alak soldiers to make shields, and that is a good thing, but I have purposefully tuned out any advice Laszlo offered about armies and about ruling, and although I did go to the *otuks*' meetings, I never listened. I have no idea how to run a deconn, or lead an army, or fight a battle with more than just me." She held Marco's eyes. "And neither do you."

"I hold blame as well," Kuruk interjected before Marco could answer. "I have lost focus." He shook his head in disgust. "I did not consider what is now made so obvious it shames me. If Vrishka was that powerful, why did he not take us on the field?"

That hadn't even occurred to Kiera, but she nodded when Marco did. It sure made a lot of sense.

"Yes. That's quite a mystery if he does have more men. And—" this was the risky part, and she prayed they'd listen as avidly to her, trust her on this as they had on everything else. "I do not believe Laszlo is dead," she told them, and braced herself.

Marco's jaw dropped. "No, Kiera," he told her as he rose, only to sink down next to her on the couch and wrap her shoulders with his arm. "Don't. Don't do that," he told her very seriously. "I cannot bear to see your heart broken again."

Her hand lifted and touched his cheek. She loved him so much, loved that he hurt for her, loved her back. But he was wrong.

"No," Kuruk said into the stillness. "I think Kiera has the right of it."

Chills skittered up her back. "If he's dead," she whispered, "where is his body?"

Marco sent Kuruk a look, perhaps pleading for sense, but Kuruk had abandoned him.

"This is no skirmish. Vrishka means to take Fairbanks. It would be a great thing, a powerful tool," Kuruk said, eyes staring inward. "It would crush all our hearts to see—" his eyes lifted and focused on Kiera, as if gauging whether to use words to paint the horror, and she nodded, knew she could hear it because *Laszlo wasn't dead*. "—to see the broken body of the man none could best dragged across the field," he finished, and though he's said the words, Kiera knew he had softened his picture for her sake.

After casting Kuruk a thankful smile, she closed her eyes. First water, three-something in the morning. "And Chanda. He knows I can pull water. Thinks I'd know if he lied. He never said 'dead.' He said 'gone.' Hmmm. Where do the *otuk*s sleep?" she asked Kuruk when she opened them. "I need you to take me there. Oh—and I need someone to wake Muukwa."

CHAPTER 13

THE *OTUKS* APPARENTLY SLEPT ALL OVER THE CITY, some in each of the handful of barracks that lay in the lee of the city walls, each with the hundred or so men he commanded. Kuruk suggested bringing all the men, and Muukwa, to a place in town that served as an Alak eating house during the turn, but that had good lights for the winter moons. They'd need a fair space to hold them all, and likely no building would hold all eight hundred—*eight hundred*—called to manage the eight thousand or so soldiers Fairbanks held. As Kiera marveled at the number, Marco suggested the open house— the coliseum—and on that they agreed. All could fit on the field.

How did Laszlo keep up with all these men? How did he make sure they trained, and did all the other things that needed done? How did he get word to them when he had to go out, or dispatch some here, or to the gates? Who set their shifts, and decided who was best for which jobs? She intended to answer all these questions as quickly as she could, and hopefully some she hadn't thought of yet.

In less than a mark nearly all the *otuk*s had dressed and gathered in the snowy field of the coliseum.

And here, later thisturn, would be Laszlo's *ta*. What to do about that. Should she cancel it?

No. Maybe she could use it. Based on what she learned here, she had decisions to make. If she chose to fight Vrishka, she would be using the men, her soldiers, and they deserved to decide what they wanted since it was their lives as much as stake as her own. No matter what they said, she was going after Laszlo, but she refused to act like a goddamned Skani and use their lives like tools for her own ends.

A suspicion lurked that they, at least most of them, would want to fight. Those who didn't she would find a way to smuggle out so they could make their way into the nadeconn.

One of the *otuk*s, one she hadn't seen before, approached her. Broad shouldered and dark haired, he stood a head above her. "We are all here, my Lady Governor, and await your questions."

"It's just Kiera," she answered absently, and looked around for a place where she could climb above their heads, all taller than hers. The stand where Vayu had watched tournaments was closest, and she made her way there, Kuruk on her heels. "Please help me up," she asked, and before she could raise a knee to start her climb he wrapped hands round her waist and lifted her so she could put her feet on the four-foot high balcony. "Thanks," she grinned, and turned to face the crowd.

Hundreds—eight hundred—upturned faces stared at her in the watery moonlight. Ice crystals danced in a playful breeze above their heads as Kiera drew both a breath and air to carry her words.

"I am going to ask some questions, and if you have the answer, please raise your hand—" she lifted an arm—"like this. If many have answers, let's start on this side—" she pointed left—"and at the back." This was going to be very time consuming if she let every single man answer. "No," she amended. "Let's do it this way. If your answer is 'yes,' move to this side—" she pointed right—"and if it's 'no,' move to this side."

The faces waited.

"Of those who fought Vrishka's army, how many of you faced more men than you commanded? How many of you felt outnumbered?"

Bodies moved, shifted, and snow crunched as hundreds of feet broke it as the group moved left. Some remained, stayed in place, perhaps a third. None moved to the right.

"Of those of you who did not move, raise your hand—no, move this way—" she pointed right—"if you did not fight."

After a hundred heartbeats, the center of the field lay bare. None—not one *otuk* who had fought had faced more than they had brought.

"Shima's tit," Marco exclaimed. Kuruk looked up at her, and she grinned down.

"Where is Muukwa?" she asked him.

"I am here," Muukwa said as she walked up from the side of the field. With her head, she motioned to the men on the field. "A good idea, but recall that I, too, fought, and I saw many more men than I led, and I believe the *otuk* who commanded the other jaw still sleeps in your healer's hall."

"How many did you lead?" Kuruk asked her. "And how many in the other jaw?" Hadn't Laszlo told her this? It seemed like he had. God, she so wished she'd paid attention to what he'd said.

Amusement rose high on Muukwa's face, perhaps for the same reason.

"I had near a tou, as rode your other jaw. I cannot say how many your man met, but we faced half again as many." Math told her that there had been about five or six thousand total soldiers facing Vrishka. So. Pretty close to the same number.

And she had another three thousand—wasn't that what he'd said?—that had stayed here.

A question needed to be asked before she let hope soar, but dread's fingers threatened to close her throat. For so many reasons this answer was utterly crucial, so she swallowed them down, then again, before opening her mouth. "Another question. How many of you lost men? Lost more than a quarter of your command in the fight?" None moved, so she pointed to the middle and slightly right. "Please move and stand here if you did, and will those of you on this side—" she pointed to the far right—"please move farther that way so I can get a good count."

Most of the *otuk*s stood on the left, and none of those moved. Not one moved.

Relief, so sharp it stung, slid across her shoulders, and she let out the breath she'd been holding. "Praise God. Oh, praise God."

The whites of smiles flashed like lights across the field, and she realized she was still pulling air, sending every word onto the field.

Well, good that they knew she didn't want any of them, not one, to die. "I am so proud of you," she murmured, meaning it, and let air carry her words to these men who fought so bravely, men she loved so fiercely, and heads bowed, perhaps in embarrassment, but white again flashed here and there before they did.

So. Not even his "more experienced" soldiers could take a bite out of this army. Pride rose as she stared out at the men waiting her next words.

Before her next question formed, a thought struck. "Muukwa, Laszlo told me—" *right before he rode away that last time,* she thought with some pain, "that the jaws had not come. No—" her eyes found Kuruk. "You said it."

Muukwa's voice held scorn. "They waited for us."

Disbelief lifted Kiera's brows. "What do you mean 'waited' for you?"

Muukwa moved to stand directly in front of her. "I *mean,*" she said deliberately, and with some heat, "that your Skani lord's men knew we came and waited in our path to stop us."

Those words struck Kiera dumb. It could not be. "How?" she managed.

Even in the scant moonlight, Muukwa's disgust was plain on her face. "Well, I am no governor," exaggerated patience slowed her voice to that of a parent's to a particularly slow child, "but I believe that someone told them."

Both Marco and Kuruk barked different words, but at the same time so she could understand neither. Kiera lifted a hand. "Hold on." That was to the men. "Muukwa, how do know that they didn't hear you, or see you from above, or scouts saw you and told the army? There are many other ways they could have found out."

With a shake of her head, Muukwa turned her attention to Marco. "You, young Skani governor of the two peoples. What would you believe if I told you that we, changed all, slunk through the trees on quiet feet, that our own scouts checked our forward, side paths? That the forest hid our passing, but that not halfway to the field a tou plus half waited above and below with arrows and spears, shooting at every cursed thing that moved in the forest?" When he didn't reply, she added, "And this *marks* before the battle was to begin. Before even you marched. Both jaws—" she emphasized— "*Both jaws* met ambush." Her eyes turned to Kiera. "It shames me to say, but perhaps one might have been seen and met. But both?" Muukwa shook her head. "Both spotted, and time to send a tou plus half to meet each? Just enough to ensure victory against both? No, Kiera. You were betrayed."

Abruptly Marco turned and stalked away, entered a doorway under the stands and disappeared.

"He should be angry," Muukwa commented to no one in particular, then turned and flashed Kuruk a disgusted look, for what reason Kiera could neither fathom nor cared enough to explore. She had one more matter before she began gathering the logistical information she needed.

But it frightened her. No—it terrified her. Even though she knew—mostly knew—she was afraid that one would say the word, and if someone did, she prayed with every fiber of her being that she could still find the strength to do what needed done. This was bigger than her grief, and she had taken an oath to protect these people until she no longer pulled breath. Even worse—*God, please*, she prayed, *don't make me have to choose between Laszlo and this deconn.* Even though she knew what she would do, it would kill her, steal all will to live.

Enough. This was not the time. "I have one final question before you go back to your beds, though will four or five please stay after to explain some things to me?" A breath. Another. "Any— any of you. Did you—did you see Laszlo fall?" Her tongue wet her lips and she hoped they'd forgive the shake her voice made. "If you—saw him fall, please come forward, here, in front."

Her heart threatened to pound out of her chest while she waited. A second, ten. And then one, one from the back, began moving, making his way to the front, and Kiera's breath caught.

All eyes watched him, waited breathlessly for the hundred thousand marks it took for him to make his careful way to the front. Bands wrapped her chest, but she fought down tears and the despair that lay below them. *Not yet*, she told them. *Wait and see what he has to say.*

When he breached the front row of men, the *otuk* bowed his head once, then strode the ten steps to stand in front of Kiera. A tall man, this one stood half a head over any she'd seen. A Skani, *nuwyr*, with a wiry build and hair the moon bleached white. The pulse of silence made the only sound for a long moment, and then he spoke.

"I saw him riding, my lady." He lifted his face to meet her eyes, but the dark hid his. "Behind our lines. I saw him go into the east forest, skimming the trees on that black demon. He rode like the hells' dogs chased him. He—" he stopped, breathed. "He must have heard something. Or saw it, maybe. He turned south and rode in between the trees, and I did not see him come out." He looked back over his shoulder. "No one did, my lady. None saw him since."

Kiera's eyes closed, but tears still fell. "Thank you," she breathed, but more to God, and to Fate, than to the *otuk* below her. "Thank you."

A hand gripped her shin, and she opened eyes to find Kuruk grinning up at her. Did he feel disappointed, she wondered, but shame at the thought swiftly followed. His face held joy, and reflected her own relief, and nothing more. Maybe—well, maybe Laszlo was wrong. Maybe his love meant something else.

And maybe it just didn't matter. Not right now.

"Ahhhh," Muukwa said as she strolled over, then stopped and made a point of staring at Kuruk's hand on her leg with a face she probably meant to look puzzled.

"Help me down," Kiera asked Kuruk, ignoring Muukwa, and when he did she strode to the brave *otuk*, the last man to see Laszlo, and wrapped her arms around him. Startled, he stiffened, then raised a hand to pat one of her shoulders in an awkward tempo. "Thank you," she said into his coat before letting go.

From there, where no one but those in front could see her, she told him, told them all in a voice barely more than a whisper, "I don't believe that Laszlo is dead." Lips parted in surprise on the *otuk* in front of her, but discipline, that damned discipline Laszlo had drilled into every man, closed its iron fist, and none said a word, none made a sound. "But that is a secret for now, a secret between us. I think they took him to try and break us—break me—and at least for me, they very nearly succeeded." She took a breath. "Go to your beds. Thank you for coming. But will a few stay, please, because I have questions that only you can answer." She severed the feed of air, then took Muukwa's arm and led her away from the others. "But first I have to beg a favor of you."

THE FIRST SLIVER OF THE SUN washed creamy light across the snow at the same moment Kiera took the first of four steps leading to Amba's door. This house, the same house Kiera had brought Alex to all those moons ago to beg Laszlo's protection when she'd thought Amba was Laszlo's wife. Despite repeated invitations to take a room at the manse, Amba loved her house, and refused to leave it. Kiera suspected that, at least in part, Amba didn't want to be associated with the rest who lived there, present company excluded.

"Please wait out here, Kuruk, or go back home," she told the tired-looking man who'd followed her here. "I'm fine." After he nodded, and she knew that meant he'd wait, she lifted a hand to the door. Ice crystals burned Kiera's knuckles when she rapped them against the weather-worn bare wood. Sooner than she expected the door opened, and Kiera lost her breath. Gray lines etched Amba's face and rendered her ten cycles older. Eyes sunk deep in that face stared at Kiera for a handful of heartbeats before recognition registered, and when it did she stepped back and opened the door so that Kiera could come in.

Hatred for Vrishka's scheming, and for Chanda's, burned in Kiera's gut as she stepped inside and rested a hand against the wall so she could take off her boots, something Amba insisted on. As she did, she looked around, and shame swept her. The blue interior, usually almost frighteningly tidy, lay in complete disarray. The curtain hiding the bed had been pushed back, as had the covers atop it. Clothes lay here and there on both floor and couch. No dishes cluttered the sink, but an untouched plate of food some kind soul had probably brought sat long cold on one of the round tables.

She should have insisted Amba stay with her. Good God, grief's stone had weighed Amba into the ground.

Without waiting to be asked, Kiera sat on the couch and waited for Amba to join her. Instead Amba ambled to the sink and poured a measure of water into a cup, then drank it all down. "I have no warmth to give you, Kiera," Amba told the wall behind the sink, then rested the cup, and her hand around it, on the shelf. "But do not sorrow for me, daughter. A grievous wound steals all strength, and we must lie still until the worst passes. I will rise again."

Sorrow tempered Kiera's anger and smoothed her voice. "I have warmth, Amba. Come sit with me."

Maybe something in Kiera's tone got through, because Amba turned and limped across the floor. When she'd sat on the azure couch, she turned bleak eyes to Kiera, whose hands lifted and wrapped Amba's. "Listen to this and tell me what you think," she started, then paused to calm her trembling heart. Sort her thoughts.

It didn't help. The words, and her tears, tumbled out, all ajumble and out of any semblance of order. She told it all, including her own secrets, which tumbled out on their own, and Amba waited, did not interrupt, or show surprise, but as Kiera spoke a light lit in her eyes, and some of the gray lifted from her features.

"And then Muukwa left," she finished, and sat back to wipe her eyes and await Amba's response.

For the first time in Kiera's knowing, Amba seemed at a loss for words. A minute passed, and another, and Amba dropped her gaze and stared at her hands.

Heart sinking, Kiera leaned up and wrapped one of Amba's hands between hers. "Am I wrong, Amba?" she whispered.

"No," Amba told her hands, then lifted furious, tear-filled eyes to Kiera's. "I am just so angry," she continued quietly. "Like you, I feel I hold blame in this game as well. So easily we accept the tellings of the lords, and they play with us like children with dolls." Her hand slipped from Kiera's as she stood. "You have done the right things, Kiera. We will find him."

"I will do anything—everything—Amba," Kiera whispered, "*everything* to bring him home, and if there is no home left, I will find him and take him far from here."

Amba crossed the floor and poured more water. "And what of the Alak, Kiera?"

"I will do whatever they wish," she replied, a touch defiantly. "If they want to fight, we'll fight. If they want to leave, I will find a way to get them out of here and into the nadeconn."

"All this and save Laszlo, too?"

"I will need help with both," Kiera admitted, "but I refuse to give one for the other. I *refuse*."

Amba faced away, but Kiera saw her smile.

"What am I going to do with Marco?" Kiera asked because she knew she needed advice on this first.

"Marco is a good boy, Kiera, as you know," Amba turned and rested her back against the platform holding the sink. "But divided loyalties are hard to balance." She took another long drink. "And now that he knows who betrayed you, and him, his heart is breaking as yours did when you thought

Laszlo had betrayed you. Walk softly with him, Kiera, and give him your love and your understanding. His first loyalty is always to you, and though he may twist, that will not change. But you must ask him," Amba added, "why he will not fight."

"Wait, wait, wait. What do you mean by 'divided loyalties'? Do you mean because he is Skani? If that's what you're saying, I know that—of course I know that—but I don't think he would choose them over me, over Fairbanks, and I don't think that's what you mean at all."

"What I mean, Kiera, is that that boy is smarter than you think, and I believe he suspected what Leith did from the first turn. I know that I did. But imagine, Kiera, how heavy a stone to carry that must be—the knowing that your mother's blood is as cold as your father's after all, and how it would cast doubt on the state of your own. You are his salvation, Kiera, you and the love that grows, hesitant as a spring flower, between he and his brother."

Kiera's jaw dropped. "Love? *Valen?* What love? Valen is gone!"

Sound lay quiet as Amba's brows lifted. After a moment she crossed the floor and sat next to Kiera. "Tell me again what you heard Leith say to Vayu before he pulled you from the water."

"Um," Kiera closed her eyes and tried to remember the words. "The first thing I heard was her telling him that Marco offered to trade his life for mine, and then—"

Amba interrupted. "Were those her words, 'Marco will trade his life for hers'?"

Her lips pursed as she struggled to remember. "Noooo. I think she just said 'he.'"

"And then what did she say?"

Oh, God. The pieces fell together, and Kiera lifted a shaking hand to her cheek as her eyes opened and overfilled. "She said that if he agreed, if Vayu agreed, he would stand them—the army—down," she whispered. "She said, 'My lord, he is your son,' and told him that if he took the city, if *Laszlo* took the city, even the Skani would accept him as the eldest." She turned to Amba. "He offered his life for mine," she told her needlessly, but it had to be said because it was beyond belief, and only saying it would make it real. "Offered to give up everything, the rule of Fairbanks he knew he'd win, his *life*, to save me from Vayu."

Wrinkles from Amba's smile spread across her face and crinkled the corners of her eyes. "And you, daughter, unworthy as you believe you are of such sacrifice, what would *Kiera* have done if her legs wore Laszlo's pants on that turn?"

Her own smile rose and surprised her, and startled more tears.

"On that turn Laszlo spoke the same words you said thisturn, Kiera," Amba answered for her. "'I will give everything,' he told me." With that, she patted Kiera's knee.

She had to stop this or she would never stop crying. "Dare I ask, Amba—and does everyone know but me?"

"You speak obliquely, but I take your meaning," Amba gently admonished, which sparked a wry smile from Kiera. "I do not speak of it, at least not for many, many cycles, but I will tell you that once Vayu the boy, near then to Marco's age, took a fancy to one of the slaves, and when she found herself breeding, she escaped into the nadeconn to try and save her child. When her son was taken a tencycle and two later by slavers, she followed them to Fairbanks and lived close until they found her as well, though, she is proud to say it took another tencycle for them to catch her. As to the latter, I am certain Laszlo believed you knew. That Marco told you, or I did. And, like they, I believed another had. Do others know? Not widely, at least among the Skani. Leith knows, as you know, and perhaps some others in the manse, but children beget by slaves are a shame to a Skani man, and especially to a woman, though it does happen with some regularity."

"That's stupid," came Kiera's heated reply. "And why in the world do they, the Skani, do that when they can, uh, have as much sex as they can stand with each other during brooding moons?"

"Who can say?" Amba answered tiredly. "Though there are near a third as many halfblood children as full Alak, and far more than full Skani, and if for no other reason than that, we will be free of them one turn." With a small shift in her seat, she turned a sharp glance at Kiera. "But more importantly, you must tell me this, Kiera. What odds did Saman give that you will survive this?"

Without flinching, Kiera met her eyes. "I don't want to talk about that. Not now. Please. I'll be able to do everything he wants me to when this is over."

Mouth pursed, Amba nodded once as she gave in, and the ease with which she did surprised Kiera. "And so on to the crux of the matter. What is my role in this plan of yours, Kiera?"

Kiera opened her mouth to answer, but then stopped. "Hold on a second. I got sidetracked, but you said that Marco knows who betrayed us, which means that you know not only that we were betrayed, but by whom. Please. Tell me it isn't Allie."

One brow arched, a sure sign of disappointment in Kiera's refusal to accept what, to Amba, must seem the obvious. "You know as well as I all who heard Laszlo's plan. Could it instead be Kuruk, who at this moment waits outside in the snow for you like a lost pup? Or perhaps Marco himself, or me?"

"Maybe a servant overheard?" But even to Kiera, that sounded weak.

"Do not malign the people who stayed to serve you, Kiera," Amba admonished as she rose. "*You*. Not even in jest. Now may I ask him in? He is doubtless cold."

Of its own accord, a hand lifted and covered Kiera's eyes. "And I am doubtless an ass. Of course."

Whatever lined the doorframe scratched as Amba pulled open the door. Without a word Kuruk kicked snow from his boots and came in. After he'd pulled them off he padded across the floor and sat next to Kiera on the couch. Cold radiated off him, but he smiled at her without the least sign of resentment.

"I'm sorry I left you out there so long," she told him, meaning it. "Did you know that Allie is the traitor?"

Her question didn't seem to shock him, but he gave it due consideration. "She is the most likely," he finally evaded without meeting her eyes.

"You knew," she accused softly.

His eyes sought Amba, but she offered only a wide smile to both of them.

And then she knew why. "You heard everything. You heard every word we spoke here."

Again he shot a desperate plea to Amba, and still she smiled but offered no hand up.

"Deny it," Kiera hissed. "I dare you."

Defeated, he turned sorrow-filled eyes to Kiera. "You know I cannot."

She broke his gaze and lifted her eyes to the ceiling, a blue so soft it looked whitewashed. "You can't tell what you heard," she whispered, knowing he would know exactly what things she meant. "Promise me. Give me your oath."

His hesitation drew her eyes back to his. "Promise me," she hissed.

Reluctantly, he nodded once. "But won't the powder—"

"Stop," Kiera interrupted. "And the other thing is that we will not discuss it. Not here, not anywhere. I am quite sure you heard me tell Amba that after this is done I will do whatever Saman says I need to. But for now no one can know." She lifted her hands in exasperation. "Think how Marco would react, Kuruk! Think how *everyone* would. And I would do nothing but fight with everyone just to walk down for breakfast. The powder—" she directed this at Amba, who would ask anyway—"is to take the pain and the—the rest away. I won't have to take it forever." She hoped.

As always, Amba's eyes saw too much, but the look she gave Kiera said that she wouldn't push it for now. "So what is the plan, Kiera?"

"I don't have a plan. Only a goal. And I don't know what the Alaks want yet, Amba. Laszlo's *ta*—" even saying that word caused her chest to clench—"is in, um, about three marks. I will ask them then. Fight or flee, and I will help them do either, and then I'll need both your help in working out how to do it." She turned to Kuruk. "Did you tell me that the gates are closed, that no one is permitted in or out?"

He nodded.

"Good. No one must leave until we've decided what to do. And," she sighed, "no one must mention Allie to anyone either. Not yet. If she's in this, others are too, and if Leith can arrange to get me out of the manse, others can get someone out of the city." She let her eyes drift to the mess of the house, the clothes tossed so carelessly on the floor. "If anyone can find Laszlo, Muukwa can. I believe that. And when she does, I will make plans to get him out as well. But no one can get out now and take word to Vrishka that we know." And now she regretted whispering her confession to the *otuks*, not that she didn't trust them, but anyone could have followed them to the coliseum and overheard. "Amba, I know you'll hate this, but I trust you above all others to keep all who remain in Fairbanks, including Alex, safe, and I will have to leave the city when Muukwa finds Laszlo. Hunter, his father, is still out there, and he will kill to get Alex."

Amba's return smile lifted the hairs on Kiera's neck. "If he comes looking here, *see'a*, I will rip the throat from that filthy Shunakah boar." Her gaze hardened further. "He lusts for your blood, Kiera. Take care outside this city."

"I know," Kiera admitted, but avoided Kuruk's pointed look. "I won't go alone."

She hoped that she could keep that promise.

CHAPTER 14

JUST BEFORE EARTH TURNED TO FOURTH AIR, Kiera and Kuruk left her room, both with coats tucked over two layers of the soft brown pants the servants wore. Kiera swore she wouldn't wear another damned dress until Laszlo was home, and maybe not even after that. It had been marks since she'd seen Marco, since early this morning, and her heart felt an empathetic heaviness for him. But going to find him would mean running into Leith, and that she could not do right now. After this, she swore, she'd go find him, and stay with him all night as he'd done for her more times than she could count.

Maybe Amba was right. Maybe he did wonder if his blood destined him to be a bad man. God knew that nearly every Skani man, and many of the women she'd met, were callous, selfish and even cruel. But some—in some she had met, promise seemed to lay quietly. Marco, of course, stood as the stark exception, with his kind heart and his laissez-faire attitude about most everything. Instead of craving pleasure he sought peace, put needs of others above his own, and though his temper ran hot at times, his laughs came as easily as his love. That didn't mean he wasn't a brave man. She'd seen him take arrows to save children from what would have doubtless been a terrible fate.

As they walked she realized that something had changed, though. He ditched magic lessons, and for moons he'd pointedly avoided anything related to fighting. And his face—she kept seeing his face when Muukwa had challenged him to spar.

Fear. Stark fear. But why?

But the time for parsing possible reasons passed as they reached the coliseum—the *open house*, as the Skani called it. The susurration of thousands of voices whispered from the gaps made by doors and slid over the open top. Corpulent haze skulked around the western horizon, but clear blue reigned the sky above. Instead of taking the main door and the stairs leading up into one of the stands or open rooms where one might enjoy the beauty of the turn, she marched around to the south and slipped inside one of the ground level arches. Their boots on the stone made the only sound as they paced to one of the inside doors.

Men covered the field inside, bunched so closely in some places that she couldn't see snow between bodies. Above them more men, and some women, filled the bottom levels of the stands. So. It looked like nearly all of the Alaks had come, and bless each one of them. She tried not to feel disappointed that she didn't see even one Skani, not anywhere, who wasn't a soldier, but maybe some *awyr* waited in the stands.

Right.

Well, the bright side was that this would work to her benefit. Without stopping to talk to anyone, she skirted the stone concave footing the dome above until she reached Vayu's box. "Help me up," she asked Kuruk, and he lifted her so she could stand on the ledge, just as she had earlier that morning.

"You are losing mass," Kuruk chided when she'd found her footing.

Despite everything, a smile rose from someplace. "Do you mean that I weigh less than I used to?"

His nod looked somber.

"Do you know that where I come from, even now I weigh far more than most women, and it is not generally considered attractive—er, beautiful—to weigh as much as I do?"

His face held disbelief. "Your men favor scrawny women?"

Many thoughts came to mind, but she held them all and shrugged instead. Eyes closed, she sought air. Now was near the middle of an earth moon, and for these turns air faltered even during its strongest marks. Still she found a strong flow and diverted a handful of strands into herself, set it spinning softly in her chest, and opened her eyes.

Marco stood below her, face more somber than she'd ever seen it. With a flicker of thought she released the air, jumped down to the ground, and took the steps separating them. His eyes warned her from making a scene, but she wrapped her arms around him anyway. After all, she was supposed to be sad, and everyone knew that he was her dearest friend.

She expected a pause, maybe a stiffening, but he melted like a child into her embrace. With a small sound he returned her embrace too tightly and gave in for the briefest of moments to his desperate need for her warmth, and her love. "You will stay with me from now on," she whispered into his shoulder, knowing he would understand her ambiguity, and the reference to all the times he'd said some semblance of those words to her. "I love you,

Marco. So very, very much."

With that, he pushed her back and gave her a dry-eyed smile. Although still pained, his eyes held something stronger than they had before, and that warmed her.

Without waiting for her to ask, Kuruk lifted her back to the wall. Air came quickly, strands from a small but strong stream whooshing overhead, and she set it and turned her attention to the Alaks and *nuwyr* below. Well, the Alaks, the *nuwyr*, and the most profoundly decent Skani mage man in this country.

"I know that you came here thisturn to wish Laszlo well in his next life," she began, hoping she had rightly remembered what Kuruk had said, "and to offer comfort to those he left behind, which is all of us. But instead, I want to talk to you all very briefly about something else." She stopped to breathe, and was pleased to note that no one spoke, or shifted, or seemed anything but intently interested. "Thisturn I am once more going to tell you the terms that Vrishka has offered for you, and for me, for the rest, and then I am going to ask you to think very hard about what you want—because the time has come to make decisions, Fairbanks, and I will not make them without you telling me what you want us to do.

"The turn I stood in this field and accepted the governership you gave me, I told you that you must never kneel again. I won't lie and tell you that Vrishka offers anything else. He says that if we surrender you will remain free, but he also said that you must agree to stay on and work the jobs assigned you. Now, I have asked you to do essentially the same thing, but please consider the difference. No one in Fairbanks as it stands thisturn will make you stay if you choose to leave. No one in Fairbanks as it stands thisturn will turn their face if you have a grievance. You can marry, and keep your children, and build and own your homes.

"But Vrishka would have me send half of our army to Barrow, where Alaks and *nuwyr* remain enslaved. Vrishka has tried to soften this by saying that armies are armies, and our soldiers' lives would not change. But I ask you, Fairbanks soldiers, have your lives changed since that turn you took your freedom from the ruling Skani? If your answer is yes, then perhaps your answer to Vrishka should be *no*.

"Vrishka would take Fairbanks from me, and from Marco. For me, he would force me to put Laszlo aside and marry Chanda, the Skani mage you know, who would stand as regent for Vrishka. Marco he would banish to the edges of our deconn, too far from all of us. As for the Skani mages, their lives would continue as before I came, and you will better know what that means than I do.

"Now, I know that you have probably heard that Vrishka has more soldiers than we do, and his man told me that his army has more fighting experience. I do not believe the first to be true, that he has more soldiers, and I cannot answer the second because I do not, cannot know what battles he has fought. I can say that in the few battles that I have seen, our soldiers have fought bravely and well, and I feel nothing but the keenest pride in every one of them.

"But as to what would be the outcome of a battle is something I absolutely do not know. I cannot assure you of success because the truth, Fairbanks, is that I do not know if we can win. Laszlo is—is gone, and I don't yet know if anyone else can do the things he did. God knows I can't.

"Fairbanks, I will not take this decision from you because it isn't my life at stake here. It's yours, and your way of life, and so I need you to decide. Your choices are these: Fight, agree to Vrishka's terms, or flee. If you choose to fight, I will stay with you, give you my heart and fight alongside you until we either win or I die. If you wish to surrender to Vrishka, I will tell him. And if you wish to flee, I will help you escape into the nadeconn before I make those decisions for myself.

"I am going to leave here for a mark. Please think about this. Talk to each other. When I return, I want all who wish to fight to stand on this side—" she pointed to the right—"of the coliseum. Those who want something else stand on the other side. First I must know if you wish to fight—and please, even if everyone else wants to fight except you, do not feel shame because there is none. Not everyone can or wants to fight. If you wish to flee, send me a message and I will arrange a time to meet with you later tonight."

But when Kiera returned to the coliseum a scant mark later, not one soul stood to the left of center.

WITH DELIBERATE EFFORT, KIERA could keep her worry for Laszlo from dominating every thought, but only just, and even when she beat it back it lay cringing on the floor of her mind and waited for her attention to turn so it could rise and bay its venom across her every imagining.

And when it did, ugly, horrifying pictures, scenarios of torture and torment and pain, reached claws into her heart and ripped pieces from it. Instead of waiting for Muukwa to return, she wanted to go out herself and find him.

But how would she do that? First, where would she look? How would she know what lay beyond Fairbanks' gates, where someone would imprison someone, and for God's sake *who would she ask?*

Muukwa was the best choice for this—she'd known that before she'd even asked for the favor. Muukwa was nadeconn, which meant that not only could she find her way around outside the city, no one knew her, and few in Fairbanks had actually seen her, which gave her a distinct advantage over any other person Kiera might send, including herself.

And since Laszlo, who was the harshest judge she knew, trusted her enough to let her lead a jaw, she must surely be strong, resourceful, and competent.

And all that—and it was a lot—lay dwarfed by the hulking responsibilities she had here in Fairbanks. Her people wanted to fight, to keep their homes, and so she needed to focus on how exactly she might help them do just that.

But *God*—it roiled and twisted her guts into the thinnest of strings.

Only by focusing on the tasks at hand could she keep herself from collapsing under all this weight, and so she spent as much energy as she could muster, as well as her worry, on the now.

First, she needed to learn how to fight Vrishka and any other mages he had with him. Water magic claimed Vrishka, and likely his sycophants as well. Would water-based spells make her feel the same suffocation that water energy inside her did? But surely her fire frightened water mages as much. It must.

Agni. *I need Agni for this*, she thought as she passed the back gate again and nodded to the soldiers guarding it, again, her third time around the inside wall's perimeter, Kuruk on her heels. Maybe Agni would agree to go out with them. Help them fight. God, she hoped so.

No one had mentioned any use of magic so far at all, and that both reassured and scared her. That withholding meant she had no idea what power Vrishka held—though he must surely be a *sunwyr*—and whether he had other mages with him, and if so, how many.

Chanda was with him, and although she knew that he was a *sunwyr*, she didn't think Chanda would fight her.

She hoped.

But she had Marco, and his skills awed her. He wasn't as strong as she was, but then apparently no one was, or at least no one Marco or Agni had seen. But he could make firestorms, a mix of air and fire, nearly as well as she could, and he could summon and direct energy from farther away than she. Perhaps because of his age, his strength seemed to continue to grow, though she had no idea whether a mage peaked at a level of ability.

Books. She needed more books, too. The authors of the ones Agni recommended often spent a great deal of space pontificating about drivel, but gems lay inside each one, too. Some odd-named man had explained how to mix air with fire safely outside a body in excruciating detail, and when she'd tried it, it worked, and following his instructions allowed her to spin a separate spell inside her at the same time. Two workings at once, though minding them both took every atom of her attention.

She had also learned how to mark enemies with tattoos like had been done to her, allowing the one doing the marking to track the victim as Hunter seemed able to do to her. And as much as she wanted this lion off her shoulder, to her great chagrin the author hadn't thought explaining how to remove one important, and never mentioned it.

When she got Laszlo back she planned on tattooing him whether he agreed or not. And maybe she should do that to Alex, too. No one besides her should be able to use it. Well, someone who shared her blood might, since the spell linked the victim's blood to the marker's.

Kiera's jaw dropped, and her hand raised and stuttered in the space in front of her chest as she stopped. Kuruk came around in front of her, looked his concern into her face, but she waved him off.

Hunter could track her. But there was no way that he had hijacked her tattoo because he had been in prison when she received it, and he wasn't rich or resourceful enough to find someone on the outside to arrange for Kiera to receive a spelled tattoo. And even if he'd escaped by then, there was no way he could have known her plans. She'd made them—what, two turns before she flew out? In her office. Only a handful of people, none of whom ran in Hunter's circles, knew the details.

But someone related to him had done this. Probably closely related.

She'd thought all this time that Jim Asana had some role in this. After all, Jim had arranged for every aspect of her tattooing, and the clan leader—governor, or whatever his title—of Bethel shared the same name, and it simply couldn't be that common. She had never heard it aside from when someone spoke of Bethel.

But Asana and Hunter were worlds apart. Further, they looked and acted nothing alike.

With a shake of her head, Kiera resumed her walking. This was not the time for that. After she'd settled everything else, then and only then would she spend precious time parsing the strings of this mystery. No one besides Hunter had ever come hunting her, and so for the time being he remained the only related threat, and avoiding him was all that mattered.

Fifth air. Dinnertime. And Kuruk was presumably very hungry since they hadn't eaten all turn. It was too late to go to Agni, and she had—what—four turns left. Jesus. Well, she had books at—well, back in her real apartment that she should stop and pick up to read tonight.

She knew she should probably just move back there, but the courage to do so evaded her. What if. What if Laszlo was dead? What if she found him and they killed him to keep him from her? What if—

"Let's go in," she told Kuruk over her shoulder, and found herself smiling at the relief he tried to hide. "You don't have to follow me everywhere, you know," she told him sternly.

Back in her new room, Marco sat on the floor playing a game with Alex in front of the fire. The image they made reminded her of the turns before the ill-fated tournament, but those turns before it had been good ones, and when they lifted their faces to her as the door closed, she smiled her love to them both before dropping her books onto the table nearest the door.

Emmy had brought dinner, and although the others had obviously eaten, plenty remained in the dishes pushed together in the center of the table. Tummy rumbling, Kiera took a plate as she sat down and dished herself some of the lukewarm fish pie. By late winter, she'd been told, rations ran short, and so everyone ate fish since the deconn's anglers harvested so many during salmon runs.

"There aren't any salmon shifters, are there?" Kiera asked Kuruk with her fork halfway to her mouth.

A grin split his face as he slid into the chair next to her. "No, Kiera. No salmon shift." He dished himself all of what remained in the bowl and shoved a heaping spoonful into his mouth. "There are," he said with food in his mouth, "twelve tribes, and none shift to salmon."

"Really?" Kiera asked, both fascinated and slightly ashamed that she didn't already know that. And she should, since her soldiers would be facing shifters. God—she wished she had more time to learn, and to prepare. "Well, I know the Denaa, and uh—the black bears, and the wolves. Coyote. And the Shunakah. Oh, polar bears."

"Yes. The Denaa are the great brown bears. Tungak, my tribe, are the black bears. Wolves are called Tikaani, and Nanuk is the snow bear."

"And the others? Oh, those scouts we—um—found were something else, right?"

"Cha'ak. White-haired eagles."

"Eagles? Are their animals bigger than—uh—other eagles like you and Laszlo are bigger than the bears that don't shift?"

Amused, he nodded again. "Just as the Yeil you saw, the ravens. The same size."

Kiera gulped. Eagles bigger than people. "Are any enslaved?" Would Vrishka have any? She hadn't even thought of how to deal with a threat from the sky.

When he shook his head, her stomach unclenched. "No. I do not know of any Cha'ak, or even Yeil, whose children slavers catch. They do not often speak to others, and I am not even sure where the Cha'ak live, though I have heard that they now claim Anchorage, the old Skani city, as theirs."

"And the others? The ones I haven't seen?"

"Kaviak, the coyote—we have some, all soldiers, though not many as their homeland is far east of here. Kidjuk, the great goshawk, and Gakut, the lynx, live far south. I have never met one from either tribe. Your mark—" he pointed his spoon toward Kiera's shoulder—"favors the Gakut, from what I have been told." He took another bite. "North," he said when he swallowed, "live the Nanuk, the Aivak, who live in the water—" he shuddered—"when shifted to sea lions, as do the very great Aabluk, the black and white whales."

A hand rested on her shoulder and Kiera turned to find Marco standing behind her. Sadness lay behind the bland look he cast her. "Well, that's more than I knew," he told Kuruk.

"It seems unlikely that Vrishka has brought sea lions and whales to fight on the Fairbanks plains," Kiera told both of them. "And so our soldiers will face polar bears and *nuwyr.*"

"I saw Tungak." Kuruk grimaced. "And wolves. Though I do not believe either will fight one of their own tribe on the field, even to avoid the lash." He lifted his eyes to Kiera's. "I would not, though I would let none harm you, either."

Since she couldn't think of a suitable response to that, Kiera patted his hand. She couldn't imagine how it must feel to see your own people enslaved and forced to fight. But how did tribes form anyway? What mechanism marked one as a shifter?

"Do you mark your date of birth? I mean," she explained when Kuruk wrinkled his brow, "do you know on what turn of which moon, and during which mark your mother birthed you?"

"I came into the world three tencycles and two apast on the twelfth turn of the first fire moon, during second water."

Kiera looked at Marco, who shrugged. "That is a target moon for birthing babies," he told her, "though if he were Skani I think he would have been *nuwyr.* I do not understand it either, if the stars rule their lives as they do ours."

After they finished eating Kiera snuggled on the couch with a book, and Marco laid his head in her lap and watched the fire burn while she read. Her mind's recalcitrant meanderings made it difficult to digest the words, which infuriated her because she desperately needed to. The key to victory could well lie on one of these pages.

But should she talk to Alex? Tell him that Laszlo wasn't dead? But then what would she say when he asked where Laszlo was? *Oh, he's being held by our enemies, and they're likely torturing him, and now goodnight and sweet dreams?* Which was worse? Thinking he was dead or knowing he was being hurt? And they could easily kill him, and then, like Marco had pointed out, they'd all get to watch him fall to pieces all over again. What would that do to a boy who'd lost his mother, faced death himself and his murdering father? Who'd been swept away to this brutal land and had everything he had known turned upside down? Who now had to deal with the double stigma of being a shifter and a Shunakah?

And just how was she going to defeat Vrishka if he had a cadre of mages?

Was Laszlo hurting now? Did he bear his suffering by clinging to the frail hope that she'd figure it all out, rouse the troops, and come save him? She both hoped so and desperately hoped not. What if she failed? Could she bear to go on if she did?

The fingers of Marco's hand closed around her wrist, and she looked down into too-knowing eyes. "Stop," he told her softly. "This is my time to be comforted, Kiera, and I will not have you filling it with other worries."

Tears rose and led a heady wave of tenderness to crest. How dare he be so kind? Every worry she had he shared, and while she had a chance to save Laszlo, Marco had lost Allie forever.

"I'm sorry." Despite his teasing, she meant it, and she let her fingers brush his hair when he'd settled back. She watched him watch the fire, dry-eyed, but drawing strength from her touch.

They'd get through this, she swore. Together, all ten thousand of them.

CHAPTER 15

PERHAPS BECAUSE YESTURN HAD COME SO EARLY for Kiera, her daily sickness raised its ugly head just as second earth turned, and before she even woke. When she did, it was to an agonizing drumbeat that matched her heart's, and though she tried, she couldn't make it out of the tangle of bodies on the bed before her stomach's revolt manifested itself all over her shirt, and Marco's.

The noise—and likely the feel of hot vomit across his back—startled Marco, who jerked back, and Kiera lost her balance and toppled as the world spun off the bed to the floor, where she lay with both hands across her eyes and begged the roiling, the room's spinning, to stop.

"What is wrong with her?" came Marco's shrill voice from somewhere above.

"She is sick," Kuruk told him as his hands found Kiera and lifted her from the floor.

"Goddamn it, Kuruk," she ground out as he carried her cradled body into the bathroom.

"I said nothing he could not see with his own eyes," Kuruk told her softly as he sat her on the toilet. "Open your mouth."

"And what, exactly, is that?" said Marco from the doorway. Or so she presumed, since she still could not open her eyes. She also presumed he meant the powder that Kuruk poured into her mouth.

"Fetch her a cup of water," Kuruk ordered, and when he had gone, Kuruk whispered, "You must tell him, Kiera. He will think of worse if you do not."

Her tongue rubbed the roof of her mouth, seeking saliva to wash the bitterness away, as she considered what to tell him.

When the smooth coolness of the cup touched her hand she took it and drank the water inside. The powder had already started working, and in moments the pain, the spinning, the nausea had fled. She exhaled as she opened her eyes and found Marco's inches from her face.

"Do not lie to me," he commanded in his Vayu voice, and Kiera knew that meant he was very, very upset. As she knew he would be. Christ.

His eyes were so blue, almost icy, and set in such a handsome face. He had grown again—his chest had filled out and he now stood a hair over six feet, and she didn't doubt he'd clear that by another inch or two before he finished. Such kindness, such profound goodness lay underneath that face, and such vulnerability, and she loved him so very much for all of it.

Which meant she had to lie. Lie to the boy who'd once lessoned her in lying. But the truth would frighten him. She couldn't do that. Not right now. He would insist that she do what Saman said she should, and she could not. Would not.

Maybe just minimize it, then?

"I see the lies rolling around, Kiera," he told her, still in Vayu mode. "Do not, do *not*, lie to me."

"Kiera," Kuruk pled, and she flashed him a furious glance. He had *promised*.

"I have contracted a sickness," she told Marco, and had to force herself to keep her eyes from Kuruk, whom she prayed could keep his goddamned mouth shut. "It is serious, and made worse because my genetics, my body, is different from everyone else's. I didn't tell you because I knew it would upset you, Marco, and because I'm not doing what Saman says I should right now, and I knew you'd try and make me."

From this close Kiera could see Marco's pupils blow open and the color drain from his face. A very big Not Good. "And? Will you die, Kiera?"

"I—I don't think so, but I will need to rest more when this is all over."

"And what else?"

"I don't know what you're asking me, Marco."

The muscles in his jaw flexed as he clenched his teeth. "Now is the time to tell me the details you have so carefully left out of that recitation."

"No," she whispered.

His chest blurred and then he was on his feet, towering above her. "No!" he shouted. "What do you mean, *no?* You will tell me!"

Kuruk put a hand on Marco's arm and steel into his voice. "Do not yell at her."

But there was no offense to be taken. She knew that he was just profoundly upset, and afraid of losing her, because that was exactly how she would feel, which made lying to him even worse. But she had to. If he knew, he'd never let her leave this room. "I mean, Marco," she said quietly before Kuruk and Marco fell to blows, "that there is nothing else to tell."

She lifted her eyes to his and told as much truth as she could. "It's serious. And I am afraid. And as soon as all this is over, I swear to you that I will spend as long as it takes in bed, or on the couch, and I'll do whatever else I need to do to beat this. But right now Marco, I can't. And I won't, no matter what you or anyone else says. I can't just lie in bed all turn while Vrishka knocks down the door and Laszlo languishes in some—some prison or something. I love you, Marco, more than my own life, but I won't even do it for you."

His eyes measured and weighed, and as they did Kiera prayed it wouldn't occur to him to just go ask Saman. *I bet they never addressed that in ethics*, she thought inanely. *What to do when one governor forbids you from telling and the other orders you to spill the secret.*

"How long will it take to recover?" Marco finally asked.

"Moons," she said wearily. "Now get out, both of you, because I need to take a bath before I go see Agni."

"Hurry up," Marco told her, equally drained. "I have your spit all over my back."

KIERA FOUND THE FLAME-HAIRED AGNI sitting alone in the main room of the magic chamber on the bench closest to what Kiera would forever think of as the altar. It had been turns since she'd been here, to the room laid out like a church where she had learned and practiced magic, but even when she came every turn she never quite got used to the flash of the rococo décor. *Who designed this?* Kiera wondered, then dismissed the thought and walked the aisle to Agni.

Agni turned when she heard Kiera's footsteps, then rose when she saw who it was. "My Lady Governor," she said, and stepped into the aisle. Her brow furrowed as she took in Kiera's pants, and Kuruk trailing behind her, but Kiera ignored the look and strode forward.

"I need your help," she told her teacher briskly, "and not in the usual way. May we sit?"

With a nod, Agni led them between the closest pair of benches.

"Okay, let me explain all of what I need because I'm afraid I'll miss something if I don't, and then we can talk about each one, okay?"

Another nod and more furrowed brows.

"I know you have heard that Vrishka, the Barrow governor, wants Fairbanks. He's offered terms, surrender terms, but we have decided to fight." Kiera expected shock, or at least surprise, but Agni's face showed neither. Maybe her teacher had good sources. Or knew her better than she thought. "And so, since he is a water mage, I need you to tell me, in great detail, how to defeat a water mage. I also need to know if you know if he has other mages, and if so, how many, and what element they claim. And how powerful they are, if you know that." Kiera took a breath before asking the biggest question. "And finally, I need to know if you will join us. Help us fight Vrishka to keep Fairbanks free. Oh, wait." Kiera interrupted herself. "I also need to know how to use sigils, Lady Agni. I can't fight a war relying on just my own magic. I have to be able to call more."

Agni's gaze slid to Kuruk.

"This is Kuruk, Lady Agni, my—um—bodyguard, I guess. Well, more my friend. Anyway, I trust him—" *mostly, and except with Marco,* she added silently—"and you may speak openly in front of him."

The chagrin, the profound *something* that slid across Agni's face surprised Kiera for many reasons, not the least of which was that Agni almost never showed any feeling on her face. A good courtier.

"I can help you with five of six," Agni told her with the stone back in her face. "Greatly. But the one with which I cannot will not please you."

"What do you mean?"

Agni's face was unapologetic. "I will not speak of it with him here."

"Why?"

"It is—it is personal."

Oh, for heaven's sake. Kiera turned to Kuruk. "Please wait outside," she told him, and knew he'd stay close enough to listen anyway. "I'll be fine." Didn't Agni know how well the Alaks could hear? Well, *she* hadn't, she supposed, until Laszlo had let her in on it.

When Kuruk had gone, Kiera turned to Agni and waited.

"I cannot," Agni told her, and Kiera saw the struggle, "I cannot go into the field with you. Or, more precisely, I should say that I could go, but I would be of no use to you there."

"How is that true, Agni? You're the strongest mage, the most skilled, I know. Do you have an aversion, or a fear of fighting?"

The fuzzy curls crowning her head bounced when Agni shook her head, and when she spoke, her voice held shame. "I cannot, my lady. My magic has been bound. I cannot call more than a handful of strands at any time."

Twin spears of shock and outrage pierced Kiera's middle. "*Bound?* Someone *bound* your magic?"

"They did," Agni told her as she regained her composure. "And so now that you understand, I will move on to the areas in which I can help you."

"Who did this?" Kiera hissed.

"My lady," Agni said helplessly, "it is so long past that it scarce matters anymore. May we please move on?"

It would be unfair of Kiera to make Agni spill the secrets, and the shame, in her heart, so she nodded reluctantly, but promised herself she would find out. And maybe help Agni find a way to fix this. God—how cruel would it be to bind a mage's magic? And how much worse for someone who had obviously been as powerful and skilled as Agni, the one mage who could parse the smallest strands of air from fire, who knew the answer to almost every magic question, and who saw every mistake the mages she taught made?

"Vrishka is a *sunwyr* water mage," Agni continued, either ignoring or oblivious to Kiera's thoughts. "He is powerful, but not as powerful as you are. His skill is brute force workings as he has never acquired the skill and finesse required to do more precise spellwork. He is not a patient man. To defeat him, use these weaknesses. He will call sheets of water and snow to bury the men, send waterstorms to freeze them, move snow to frighten them, and so on.

"He does have other mages, a handful, and all water mages, though he will not have more than one or two with him. None are as strong as even Marco, who could defeat two of them. Some will be very young, no more than two tencycles, though I do not expect him to bring more than one of those. He seeks glory, and craves admiration, and will not allow his other mages to address your magic directly.

"Use fire, my lady, as much as you can carry, and cunning. He cannot shield, and fire smothers him as much as water will you. I have no doubt that you have the strength and the intelligence to defeat him. And now, let us go into your room and I will show you the sigils, but you must practice them as often as you are able before using them because if you do not you will confuse them or make other mistakes. And I will suggest that you use both your own power at summoning as well as sigils, as the energy you call with sigils will mix with what is already spinning and thus be easier to control."

Agni stood, and Kiera followed.

"You know Vrishka very well," Kiera commented quietly as they walked to the door marking her room. Agni paused, then opened the door without answering.

"Attend. For fire, use the fingers of your right hand to trace this shape," Agni told her once she had closed the door and walked to one side of the room. "Call fire first," Agni admonished when Kiera lifted a hand to follow along.

It took less than a heartbeat to find and coax a handful of strands into her chest, where they spun softly and warmed her insides.

"You improve so rapidly it sometimes frightens me," Agni admitted with a small shake of her head. "Now follow my fingers with yours. You must draw it exactly as I show you. In the same direction. Bottom up. And the same size. Smaller will summon less, and larger is not needed." With that, Agni lifted a finger and traced an angled line leaning to Kiera's left, about twelve inches, then paused before drawing down at the opposite angle, then connected the bottom two edges.

Kiera followed along, but nothing happened. "Um, I'm sorry, Lady Agni, but I got nothing."

The purse of Agni's lips told her that she had missed something. "That was a demonstration of the shape, my lady. Do it as one continuous flow. Do not pause."

Using her finger, Kiera traced a foot-high triangle, and a fist of fire hit her chest at the same moment she connected the bottom legs. "Ah," she said, and smiled her pleasure because this, for once, would be easy to learn.

After sending the fire to burn out in the middle of the room, she turned to Agni and awaited the next. Air came when she drew the same triangle over a horizontal line, and earth came, precious earth that she had so much trouble with, when she drew a simple square, always starting at the bottom left, and done with either hand. Water frightened her, but she tried it anyway—not surprisingly, it came when she drew an upside down triangle, one that pointed down.

When she'd sent the last to the floor, Agni nodded, pleased.

"But let me ask you this, lady Agni," Kiera said as she wiped sweat from her hands. "You did more—I don't know what to call it, ceremony or something, the raising of hands and so on—when you tested me. This is, well, pretty simple."

"I only used stronger invocations, Lady Kiera," Agni said quietly, "Which I will teach you another turn. I require a more complicated summoning because my power to do so is bound."

"What did you do to Vrishka to earn that, Agni?" Kiera asked equally quietly, and Agni's face froze. "I am asking as your friend, as someone whose heart hurts for you, and who would share your pain, and not as your governor. Do not answer me unless you want to."

Agni turned away. "You will enhance the power of the sigils if you call colors to your mind as you trace their patterns. For fire, think red, fill your mind with it, and the fire that comes will be stronger and more pure, more cardinal, which helps most during mutable marks if you need strength. Air is yellow, earth is green, and water is blue."

A breath escaped in a sigh. "Thank you, Lady Agni. Your help is priceless, and I do not have words to thank you for all that you have done for me, and for Fairbanks. Without your help, without what you have taught me, I have no doubt whatsoever that we would fall to Vrishka—and if not him, to someone."

As Kiera's hand touched the doorknob, Agni spoke so softly that Kiera had to strain to hear her words.

"I loved him."

Struggling to keep her jaw closed, Kiera turned and strode across the floor and stood facing Agni's turned back.

"He was my husband, Kiera. For more than a tencycle. He was never a kind man, but he had this way of finding his feet in even the most difficult of things, of cleaving the blackness. Early on we lost a son, a child, to a sickness, and without his tender care I dare say I would have not found my way back from the dark.

"But his lusts ruled him, and he took many mistresses. I admit this because I know that only you will understand, Kiera. I loved him, and each one pierced my heart. After a time I gathered my courage and asked him to refrain, but he would not." Agni paused to draw a breath, but she did not turn. "My magic was very strong, and I taught magic then as well. One night I and my best student, a young woman, designed a spell. One that altered my face, and my hair, and even my body. It made me appear to be the woman with whom he spent his evenings at that time." Agni's breath rattled when she exhaled. "And I used it, and he discovered it, and I think that he would have forgiven me, in time, but because my student knew, soon all knew, and so his anger burned fiercely against me because all knew that I had tricked him. As I said, he craves admiration and cringes from all that might detract from it."

Anger made it hard to keep her voice quiet, and calm, but Kiera somehow managed it. "How did he discover it?"

Fiery curls tossed and one caught a stream of light that had snuck in from the high, slotted window, changing the color of both to a warm, soft orange. "I did not leave his bed for two turns, and at the end of the second his hand wiped the ink from my skin, and the spell lifted, leaving me instead of her."

"And how did he bind your magic?"

Agni turned, tears on her face, and raised a hand to her chest. "With gold, Kiera."

"Gold? Inside you?"

"An oversimplification, but essentially correct. There is a spell attached, or many spells. It renders me as trackable as you, Kiera, and also sealed my sight inside my body."

Horror made Kiera shake her head. "And how did you end up here?"

Agni's courage failed and her eyes fell to the floor, but she found it, and raised them again. "He traded me to Vayu for a thousand slaves. I can still teach, after all."

And now Kiera's jaw did drop, and so did her fear of offending propriety. With a clenched jaw she wrapped her arms around Agni, tiny Agni, no taller than five feet, and squeezed her tight. And after a moment, Agni hugged her back.

"That son of a bitch," she whispered. "I'll kill him. I promise you that. For what he did to you, for what he did to all of us, I will kill him." *And I will find every slave he took.*

Agni's chest shook, and Kiera pushed her back, alarmed, but Agni was laughing. "Oh, Kiera. Bless you."

"No, Agni. Don't thank me for caring about what happened to you. It was wrong, and anyone, any decent person, would be horrified at what he did to you."

Agni's eyes held amusement, and perhaps sadness as well, but she smiled and moved on as she always did. "Practice the sigils, Kiera. Do not call water when you mean fire, or fire when you mean air. It is easy to mistake one for another in the heat of battle, or worse, to forget which way to draw them and get nothing. Every turn, as often as you can, practice until it takes no thought."

"Your advice is, as always, exactly what I need to hear. But I also want more books, Agni, though I don't know which would be best. Do you have suggestions?"

"I do, but first, please—" Agni laid a hand on her arm—"allow me to tell you how very sorry I am at your loss, Kiera. You are bearing it surprisingly well, if you will forgive me for saying so, but I know it must be very difficult, and made more so by the current crises."

And now it was Kiera's turn to smile. "Thank you, Agni. But I think all will be well."

AFTER LUNCH KIERA, KURUK AND MARCO walked the grounds and met with *otuk*s all over the city. After each meeting Kiera silently blessed Laszlo. This was a well-oiled machine. Soldiers trained in shifts, and on certain turns, based on a central schedule. Everyone got time for everything. The newest recruits had twice the work, twice the training, and less guard duty, though all walked the walls or guarded the entrances. They had been spread across the city, a few for each *otuk*, though they met together for weapons and hand-to-hand four times each turn. Veterans trained twice, then spent time learning new skills—arrows or the little javelins Kiera had seen on the field, or practiced moves on horses. Except for meals and the few marks granted free each night, no one had time to sit. And now that Laszlo had added archers to the rooftops to keep out the Yeil, spare time had become even more scant.

But everyone seemed happy. Not joyous-burst-into-song type of happy, but no one she met complained, or seemed dour or resentful. Fear lurked below the surface of most everyone she met—the few in whom she detected none scared her just a little—but none seemed consumed by it.

On her treks she learned the secret of communicating with eight thousand-odd soldiers in a nontechnological society. Once or twice a turn if needed, Laszlo met at a prearranged time with a group of about fifty *otuk*s, who carried concerns, complaints, and requests of the entire army. He answered them, and they carried the answers to ten more, who carried them to ten more, and so on, and in less than a mark the entire deconn's soldiers knew his words. And too, he made rounds, rounds and rounds and rounds. All turn.

Which explained why he wasn't there that turn she and Marco had climbed into the hayloft, but somehow showed up in time to catch her. The luck of a very thorough man.

And everywhere she went, men brave enough to speak to her, or Marco, or even Kuruk now that he was branded as hers, praised Laszlo, sometimes outright, and sometimes offered polite suggestions for her consideration, and perhaps her implementation. What a good leader he was. Always listened. A hard man, hard to please, but always fair. No one worked harder. Dug to the bottom of every problem. Always had your back. Addressed complaints. Stopped trouble before it started. Made them work hard, but made them better, maybe the best army in Alaska.

The hardest part, even harder than keeping the unceasing stream of words extolling Laszlo from crushing her, was the hope. In every eye its light burned back the fear of what lay ahead. With every step, with every handshake, Kiera prayed that they could find a way to do this. That it wouldn't be in vain. That these men wouldn't die, or feel the yoke of slavery ever again.

Despite that they had no wisdom to offer, Marco suggested setting a time each turn to meet with *otuk*s like Laszlo had, if for no other reason than the soldiers needed to know someone still listened. "And besides," Kuruk had argued, "you need a way to call them to arms when the time comes. When you meet, design a call that you can remember."

By the time they finished nighttide beckoned, just scant minutes away when the trio made it back to the room. None had eaten since lunch, and they hoped someone, namely Emmy, had been kind enough to set something aside for three hungry people.

But more than dinner waited when they opened the door. Muukwa, who wore a wide, bare-toothed grin, and naught else.

"I found him."

PART II

Chapter 16

"**I** found him," Muukwa repeated, this time more slowly, and looked from face to face. "I have found where Vrishka is keeping Laszlo."

Kuruk recovered first. He strode across the floor to the bed and pulled the yellow quilt from atop it, from off of Alex and Emmy, then tossed it to Muukwa. "Put this on," he growled.

For Kiera, breath wouldn't come, and if she didn't remember how pretty damned soon she was going to collapse. Marco's arm wrapped her shoulders, and she stared into his face as he led her to the couches and found a shock that must match her own. *He never believed it*, Kiera realized. He hadn't thought that Laszlo was really still alive.

Kiera's voice cracked when she spoke. "I—I—where?"

Marco picked up a cup, and then the carafe of wine in his other hand, but after a pause he sat it down and poured water instead, which he carried to Kiera.

Muukwa sashayed around the arm of the couch wearing the yellow quilt, obviously pleased with herself. With a hand she parted the fabric to free a leg, then climbed onto the couch and sat on the arm with feet on the cushion.

"Wine, please," she told Marco, who waited for Kiera to finish the water.

Anger crept up his face and he opened his mouth to respond, but Kiera laid a hand on his arm and pled with her eyes. He made a face, but took her empty cup and returned to the table and poured more water and a cup of wine for Muukwa.

"Where is he, Muukwa?" Kiera asked in a voice that shook only a little.

Enjoying the drama, Muukwa smiled sweetly and took her wine from Marco's hands before turning to Kiera. "You will be shocked," Muukwa predicted, and took a drink through grinning lips.

"Shima's tit, Muukwa!" Kuruk shouted from behind the couch. "Just tell her!"

Anger pushed the smile from Muukwa's face. "You listen to me, *pini*—Kuruk! I have done much for this information, including taking the cock of your mage—" she waved a hand as if trying to recall his name—"Chanda."

Water sprayed across Kiera's shirt and the carpet in front of her, and she choked and sputtered and tried to breathe. A hand, Marco's hand, patted her back, but when she caught her breath laughter came, and blossomed, and slid toward the hysterical. Between breaths, she managed, "You—you—had sex with Chanda—for this information?"

Uncertainty colored Muukwa's face as she tried to decide whether to be offended or to join in Kiera's laughter. Kiera couldn't see Kuruk, but Marco was studiously avoiding her gaze, as if embarrassed, though for what reason Kiera could not imagine.

By focusing on the logs in the fire and then starting a burn, Kiera was able to pull her emotions back, but a small trickle of completely inappropriate hilarity remained and colored the world. Well, who knew? If she'd known it was that easy, she would have been knocking on his door turns ago.

Laszlo was absolutely not dead or Muukwa wouldn't toy with her—with them—like this. So focus. Focus and Muukwa will tell all. "So how was it?" That slipped out before she could catch it, and hearing her own inanity caused her to collapse into laughter again.

This time Muukwa smiled with her, caught the lunatic fringe of Kiera's hysteria, and let herself laugh with her.

"Have you considered him, then?" Muukwa asked after they had subsided, through the largest smile Kiera had ever seen.

"Actually, yes," Kiera admitted, and wiped tears from her eyes.

"Kiera!" Kuruk sputtered from behind her.

"Oh, Kuruk, this was while Laszlo and I were—separated, I guess. Not seeing each other."

"Save yourself for my cousin," Muukwa advised, and took a long drink of her wine. "His cock is too small, and he drives it like a fox-chased hare." She snorted as she kicked out a leg from under the blanket, then cast her gaze on Marco. "And not one time did he touch my *kuula* with anything but his tiny cock."

With a groan Marco shielded his eyes with a hand, and Kuruk pretended Muukwa had not spoken. "I remember this time. But I cannot believe that Laszlo permitted you to consider another man even then."

Kiera turned to glare at Kuruk. "Laszlo does not 'permit' me to do anything. Then and now, I do exactly what I want."

"Well spoken, cousin," Muukwa said, and raised her cup in toast to

Kiera.

Kiera was beginning to catch on to the madness in Muukwa's means. "I'm not going to like this, am I?"

A somber tint crept into the edges of Muukwa's smile. Before answering she drank the last of her wine and held the cup out to Marco, then waited until he noticed her before smiling and dipping the cup up and down.

With a sour look at Kiera, he pushed off the couch and snatched the ceramic from Muukwa's hand. Kiera watched her watch Marco, and wondered if Marco had caught Muukwa's drift.

With feigned patience Kiera waited until Marco returned with more wine for Muukwa, which she drank before once more turning her attention back to Kiera.

When Muukwa finally spoke, she shed the smile and the pretence. "He is being held in the pit of Talium, Kiera, but he is whole, at least for the time." When she took another drink, her face hardened for a moment with the anger that the knowledge she carried had lit. Yes, of course she was angry. They all were.

And Nick. Of course it was that slimeball Nick. That son of a bitch.

But whoa. Wait.

"What pits?" Kiera asked. "Do you mean in a—a cell or something underground?"

After assessing Kiera's face for the smallest measure of time, Muukwa spoke rapidly to Kuruk in their native tongue, her voice taut.

"No," Kuruk answered pointedly in English. Or Skani. Or whatever. "She is new here, from far away, and does not know."

After heaving a heartfelt sigh and casting her eyes to the ceiling, Muukwa adjusted her position on the arm.

Before she could speak, Kiera realized she'd forgotten something very important. "Kuruk," Kiera said, then leaned back until she found his face, "please fetch Amba, or send someone to. Please."

It took effort to lift her head, and Kiera realized another headache was coming. And was this one early. "Wait," she told Kuruk, who had nearly reached the door, and stood. To be polite she raised a finger to let them know that she'd be right back and walked over to Kuruk. With her back to the couches, she mouthed, "powder."

His eyebrows raised, but he slid a packet from his pocket and handed it to her carefully, so no one would see what he did. "Thank you," she mouthed, then hugged him. "Give Amba my love," she whispered, a very poor cover for her odd behavior, "and don't tell her anything. Just tell her I have news, and bring her."

With a nod, and one quick disapproving look, he disappeared through the door and Kiera walked to the bathroom. She used the toilet, thankful for once she had to, and used some of the clean water from the handwashing pitcher to wash down the bitter crystals. How many more did she have? Not many, she guessed, and like it or not, she was going to have to find time to go see Saman.

Marco's eyes watched her when she walked back to the couch, and his face told her that he knew, but he held his tongue, and she hoped the excitement to come would soon replace this in his list of important things to think about.

What a twisted path I walk, she thought dismally. *Hoping for more to cover the lesser*. With a sigh she retook her seat, dismissed her thoughts, and smiled at Muukwa.

Without making Kiera wait, Muukwa launched into her explanation. "The pits are where fights are held, Kiera. Shifter fights. To the death. Skani—Skani and I am ashamed to say that some nadeconn Alak come to watch." She leaned forward and let the blanket split and slip off either side of her legs. "To place bets. They have tournaments that last many turns. Near all of the pits are filled by taken Alak—slaves, I would call them, though some—" she made a face—"come because they wish to fight. The pits are shitholes. The men who own them fill rooms with whores, taken Alak all, or so I hear, and let the men who bet dip their cocks in whichever they want during the dark marks after the fights have stopped for sleeping."

Alex woke at the same time Muukwa stopped to drink her wine, and called to her from the bed in sleepy voice. "Emmy," Kiera pressed though numb lips, "keep Alex in bed. Alex, go back to sleep. I love you, but you need to sleep right now."

"Do not unhand your hope, Kiera," Muukwa said, the most sincere Kiera had ever seen her. "Laszlo is lifelong unbested, and I do not believe any there will be able to kill him. But that is their plan. To force him to fight until someone does so."

That had to be something Nick thought up. Laszlo had humiliated him in his own court and publicly stole the woman promised him from under his nose. "I have to get him out," Kiera whispered, and reached a trembling hand toward the cup in Muukwa's hand.

Once she understood, Muukwa handed her the cup but caught Kiera's wrist with her other hand. "He is strong." Muukwa held her eyes. "He is very strong, Kiera. And your love has made him stronger yet. I have seen it. None will kill him, and he will not be broken."

Against her will, Kiera's eyes closed but did not block the tears that threatened. "How do you know that, Muukwa? You came, what, a handful of turns ago? How long had it been, or had you ever seen Laszlo before?"

The mischievous smile that was Muukwa rose. "I bring my pack to fight with him when he leaves the city. We have known each other, cousin, for near my whole life."

The door slammed open and they turned to find Amba, breathing hard, and Kuruk behind her. Alex slid out of bed and ran to her. With open arms she leaned over and scooped him up. "Gramma," he told her, "Muukwa says Laszlo is in the pit and isn't dead and I want you to go get him."

The sound Amba made hurt Kiera's ears, but she had to wait until Amba put Alex down to tell whether it was anguish or joy. Even then it was hard to tell, but Amba marched over, grabbed Muukwa from the couch, yanked her down and pulled her into an embrace that would have crushed Kiera's bones. "From this turn, Muukwa, all that is mine is yours," she told her in a voice that brooked no dissent, but her eyes were closed, her face wet.

Muukwa waited to smile until Amba released her, but the look on her face she tried to mask, the childlike joy at Amba's high praise, lifted Kiera's heart. Muukwa, however, cast a sly glance at Marco, whose eyes stared at the floor.

Of its own volition, her head shook and a smile rose. Marco had a surprise or two in store, ones she hoped would help heal his heart. But she forced herself to put that aside for now. The time had come. "We need to make our plans," Kiera told them as she sat down next to Marco and took his hand in hers. Her eyes found Amba's. "But first we need someone to fetch that young woman who came with the messenger. The one from Nick's."

She had much to learn before the sun rose and set on this, the eighth turn of the armistice.

THE YOUNG WOMAN SEEMED QUITE FRIGHTENED at being made the center of attention. After gentle prodding, she had again admitted that her name was Dula, that she had been Nick's slave, and only after a spate of tears agreed that she had escaped and followed Nick's messenger to Fairbanks.

"No one is angry with you, Dula," Kiera told her for the tenth time. "We all admire your courage very much. But please, I need you to tell me about what's going on at Nick's."

Shoulders hunched further as Dula tried to melt into her corner of the couch.

A cup made a solid clunk when it met the table. "Enough," Amba said. Amba radiated anger, and impatience, and an angry Amba was a scary

Amba. Even Muukwa leaned unconsciously back when Amba walked past her.

"You will raise your head and look at me," Amba commanded, and to Kiera's amazement Dula's head popped up like Amba had pulled it. "You will now answer my questions, Dula. Do you know of Nick's pit?"

"Yes, my lady," Dula whispered.

"Did you work in it?"

A hesitant nod. "Yes, my lady."

"Does Nick keep enslaved Alaks, shifters, in the pit?"

"Yes, my lady."

"Does he make the shifters fight?"

"Yes, my lady."

"To the death?"

A grimace. "Yes, my lady."

"And men come to bet on those fights?"

"Yes, my lady."

Impressed, Kiera couldn't help but think that Amba would make a great lawyer. But Amba was far from finished.

"How often does he force the shifters to fight?"

"Every night of tournament, my lady."

"How long does the tournament last?"

"Five turns, my lady."

"How many tournaments during each moon?"

"Two, my lady."

"When is the next one?"

Dula's mouth opened and stayed open. "I—I do not know, my lady."

"How many turns pass between tournaments?"

"A tenturn, my lady. Sometimes just nine."

"How many turns had passed between the last turn of the last tournament and the turn on which you escaped Talium?"

"I—am not certain, my lady. Four? Five?"

A ripple of some emotion washed Amba's face, but she didn't even pause.

"How many fights happen each night of the tournament?"

"Many, my lady. Eight. Ten."

Lips pursed, Amba nodded her head over and over as she sorted and analyzed this information. "It is turn one, two or three of the tournament." The girl stared up at her and Amba looked to her again. "What was your job in Talium?"

Dula's lips trembled. "I worked in the kitchen, my lady."

"What did you do in the *pit*, Dula?"

Dula's face fell.

"Dula. You will answer me."

And after a moment she did, but even straining Kiera could barely hear her. "I—I was to walk up and down it. Let the men take their pleasure with me if they wished it."

Silence thundered, and the black of a storm tightened Amba's eyes, but when she spoke, it was gently. "And here, what do you do?"

The young woman's eyes rose, and dropped, and rose again. "I work in the kitchen here, too, my lady. But that's all." Her eyes flicked to Kiera and she found a shred of courage, but not enough to raise her voice above a whisper. "I know I should not have run from my lord Nickinum," she told Kiera before dropping her gaze back to the carpet in front of her feet, "but one night my lady governor took a man from atop me in the stables and beat him with a shovel for trying to force me. I—I knew that she would show mercy if I came."

Muukwa raised both brows and whistled though her teeth. "Cousin, my esteem for you grows by the moment."

A wide smile rose on Amba's face. "Yes, Muukwa, our Laszlo chose well," she agreed.

A little embarrassed and not quite sure how to respond, Kiera grimaced and changed the subject. "Do we need Dula any more tonight?"

"No," Amba said, assuming Kiera had asked her. "Send her back to bed."

"Oh. Wait," Kiera said as a thought struck. "Dula, how does Nick get the slaves, the Alaks, shifters, and women for the hall?"

"Many ways, my lady governor. Most times, he buys them." She shrugged still too-thin shoulders. "At times, oft around tournament, people bring one or two for him as recompense for debts, or to pay entrance."

"Thank you, Dula. You may return to your bed." Kiera laid a hand on the girl's arm and gave it a soft squeeze. "And Dula, you always have a home here."

When the door closed, Amba turned to Muukwa. "You will go to assist Laszlo in his escape from the pits at Talium."

"Not alone she won't!" Kiera broke in with some heat.

As if rehearsed, both Marco and Kuruk spoke her name.

Annoyed, she raised a hand to still them and addressed Amba. "If Muukwa agrees, then I, too, think she's the best one for the job. For many reasons. But Amba, how will she get in without getting caught? She is, I am sure, a very great warrior, but these are the people who took Laszlo, and who still manage to keep him prisoner. No offense, Muukwa, but she isn't

Laszlo."

Kiera got up and paced the space between the couch and the fire. "We need two plans, and I'll need all of your help with both. I think I may know how to get someone into Nick's, but I need to talk with someone first before we work out that part." Her hand shot up again to ward off any arguments. "Hear me out. I am sure I'll need all your insight, but please just listen for now. I think I may have the genesis of a plan to defeat Vrishka, and I want to know what you think."

All the excitement, and the lack of sleep, had dried her mouth to ashes, and so she walked to the table and poured herself a measure of water. As she did she cast a mournful look at the new bottle of Lorgda's good wine someone had delivered while they'd been out walking Fairbanks. But her headache had come very early, and it seemed likely that the sip of Muukwa's wine had set it off. Saman had warned her off wine, though he hadn't explained exactly why she should avoid it. Well, she would from here out for sure.

After drinking half, she walked to stand in front of the fire where she could see everybody. "Vrishka, and Chanda who so helpfully advises him, believe that we stand beaten thisturn, and have since the turn he took Laszlo. He thinks that without Laszlo we can't do it. Anything. To him, I'm just a woman, and near worthless in his eyes for much more than magic and birthing babies, so if he cripples me with grief, he believes I will not have the strength, or the will, to fight." She did not add that he had nearly been right. "Marco he believes too young to be effectual, and for insurance he inserted some significant conflict into Marco's life as well. And when he removed Laszlo, he knew he took our strongest leader, the one who could actually tell how many men he had, who could accurately gauge what risk his army posed to ours. And then he lied, they lied to us. About everything. Inflamed our grief and our fear."

"But Kuruk, smart Kuruk, God bless him, had the gates shut and in and out passage barred when we returned, and to our knowledge none have gone out to spill our secrets to Vrishka, and so for all he knows we languish here, swimming in our grief and trembling in our fear of the mighty Vrishka, whose army he told us has more men, which it does not, and that he has more experience, which may be true, but Laszlo has trained and left us an army worth its weight in—well, whatever you hold dear, and I really believe we have a good shot of kicking his ass.

"But my point is that in Vrishka's mind none of us, not one, has the knowledge, much less the courage, or anything else needed to fight him off. I'm sure he believes that we'll surrender in two turns."

Kuruk stirred, and she smiled at him before continuing. "And so I propose a return charade to thank him for the one he forced down our throats. Agni told me that Vrishka is arrogant, and wants everyone's admiration, and we can use that." She paused, took a drink. "He believes that he has us beaten. He absolutely won't expect a trick, not from a—what did he say to me, 'a mere woman and a boy.' No. He expects us to give in with trembling faces and both hands raised. I don't think he believes we'll try to fight, but here's the thing—I am sure Vrishka believes that even if for some reason we do, without Laszlo to lead the army it would be less than even a pitiful effort."

Even to Kiera, her smile felt wicked. "And so I propose that we send out half our soldiers to him just as he has so kindly asked, but armed. We'll say that we send their weapons, too, in tribute or some bullshit. Play to his ego. Laszlo told me that one thousand, a tou, soldiers can keep an enemy from this city, and so a tou is what we'll leave for Amba. The other three tou will sneak out and come around like the jaws Laszlo explained—"

"No," Muukwa interrupted, and showed her teeth. "Not behind. Vrishka will take the Natuvik Pass to go north because it is the easiest passage for ten tou to the north slope. We will ambush him from the heights when they pass."

"Where is it? How far, I mean."

Muukwa leaned forward and used her hands to help tell her story. "It lies a hard quarter turn north and west at the Skani pace, but the marks favor us. Vrishka must march as slow men march. Even so, Vrishka will reach Natuvik Pass before the men who will find Fairbanks closed can warn him."

Hope caught fire in Kiera's chest. "Oh, Muukwa. Yes," she breathed. "And one of those who find Fairbanks closed will be Chanda, which means they'll be separated. Every mage out ups our odds. And in the meantime we let our soldiers march obediently with him for a while. After a mark or two their obedience will settle any fear that remains."

As they traded nods, Amba added a point. "We will need a signal for our marching men, and many arrows for the men in the trees."

"And now we need to send a messenger to Vrishka with news of our surrender." Kiera looked at Marco, whose face she could not read. "Do you have a suggestion?"

He ignored her question and asked his own. "Who will lead the men who sneak through the forest, Kiera?"

A smile lifted her lips. "You will. With Kuruk. I'll be coming from another way, and I want a mage waiting in the trees, my friend."

Kuruk stirred again, started to stand, probably to object to something, but Kiera watched Marco shake his head, and that same fear she'd seen when Muukwa challenged him rose. When he couldn't keep if from his face he stood and stalked to the table.

"Why do you fear battle?" Muukwa asked him in what sounded like astonishment, and Kiera closed her eyes. She hadn't considered this, that Marco's fear was of *battle*, and although she suspected she knew why, she did not want Marco demolished in front of these people. Especially not now. With quick steps she crossed the floor, but before she reached him, he turned a furious face to Muukwa.

"I was torn and broken, Muukwa," he shouted, "in a fight with a pack of Shunakah! Not only did they almost kill me, even with healings it took over a moon to find the strength to stand on my legs. I beg your almighty forgiveness if I am not anxious to repeat that!"

Muukwa's brow wrinkled, and the room stood silent and still. With a shake of her head Kiera took the steps between them, but although Marco let her take his hand, his arm barred her from coming any closer. Instead he stared defiance at Muukwa and dared her to shame him.

"Once," Muukwa answered a long pause, and although everyone could hear, she spoke to Marco alone, "I nearly lost my life in a battle with a Cha'ak, a white haired eagle. I had led my band into her lands, and the Cha'ak do not forgive a trespass. I, too, required a span of moons to heal, and for a cycle," she shrugged, "or perhaps two, I felt great fear in considering even the smallest of battles. But I did not give in to that fear, Marco, and now it has fled because I defeated it."

Marco dropped his eyes first, and then his arm, and Kiera wrapped hers around him. "Kuruk can do it," she whispered, and prayed that she could do this without him.

A low voice came from close behind Kiera's back. "Walk with me, Marco." And then Muukwa smiled. Kiera could hear it in her voice. "And you will tell me how you drive your cock, hmmm?"

A snorted laugh she couldn't quite catch erupted from Kiera's middle, and from above her Marco sputtered and made a strange squeak as he presumably sought for a suitable response.

But the pressure from his arms eased as he released Kiera, and Muukwa took his hand and led him toward the door, tossing words and casting sultry smiles.

"Does 'genesis' mean birth?" Kuruk asked from the corner into which he had fled.

"Yes, it does," Amba told him as she poured herself a glass of wine.

Kuruk seemed confused. "I think I do not understand. What more needs planned?"

From the bed rung Alex's impatient voice. "Are you going to get Laszlo, Gramma?"

"We will get Laszlo back, grandson. Now sleep."

As the last of the adrenalin burned away, the exhaustion it had vanquished rose and sucked the marrow from Kiera's bones. With a little wobble she stumbled to the bed, where Alex and Emmy lay wide-eyed and wide awake. At more than half past first water, or 3 a.m. back in the other world. "I need to sleep, too, and so do you all." This more to Alex than Amba. "Did Muukwa take that yellow quilt? Damn it. Well, let's try to get some sleep anyway. Someone can sleep up here with me if you don't mind being cramped." A hand shook when she tried to peel back the blanket from her side of the bed, but she knew she'd be fine after she slept a little. Mid-pull, she paused. Maybe she should doze in the chair so the sun would wake her. That would come early, but nexturn—no, this one—she needed every mark she could squeeze out. "I have to have a few marks at least—"

"Kuruk, go fetch us some blankets," Amba barked as she plunked down her cup. "Now!" she added when he didn't move as fast as she liked. With pursed lips and a determined mien, she stepped around the bed and took hold of Kiera's upper arm. "You will lie on the couch," she announced as she half-dragged Kiera back around the bed.

"I want to sleep in the yellow chair," Kiera whined, and hated that she sounded like Alex. "I can't sleep long, Amba. I have so much to do this-turn!"

"Hush." With a meaningful look, Amba gave Kiera a gentle shove when they reached the closest. "Lie down and sleep. I will wake you at third water."

"Third—no, no," Kiera said, shaking her head. "That's way too long. I need to be awake by, oh, second water at the latest."

Arms crossed. "Third air. And if you do not lie down and quiet your tongue before I draw my next breath I will see that no one wakes you until noontide."

Both because she knew that Amba meant every word, and that no one, Alak or Skani, would dare defy her when she waxed imperious, Kiera lay back. "We'll get him back, Amba," she promised as she closed her eyes.

A hand, Amba's hand, brushed the top of her head. "Sleep, daughter. Leave nexturn to nexturn."

But it is nexturn, Kiera thought, but it fell with her, unspoken, as she tumbled into the velvet dark.

CHAPTER 17

B Y NOONTIDE, AND THANKS TO THE THREE weather *awyr* Kiera inter-
rogated and then set to it, mounds of gummy fog had rolled down
the mountains to gulp down Fairbanks and at least ten miles around
it like Jonah's whale. Since several complicated spells regulated water and
airflow overhead, it took precious little tweaking to collapse one along the
edge. A vacuum instantly developed and drew clouds into the lee of one of
the mountains. Almost frighteningly fast, the collected water vapor grew as
heavy as a gravid storm and avalanched down the slope. And until she fixed
it, the thick mass would feed itself and live on indefinitely.

With luck, everyone would think a spell had failed. Which it had, with
help. Kiera forbade the weather workers from leaving their thankfully spa-
cious workroom for three turns, promised them food and water, and then
set a guard on them to keep them in and others out. They were working,
after all, on "fixing" an emergency situation.

Luck. She was going to need a lot of luck, but she took a lesson from
Laszlo and tried to make her own. By fourth air the first fifty soldiers had
slipped out the back gate and into the forest beyond. They had to get over
a hundred out a mark to get all three thousand in place by the time Vrishka
made it to the pass, and she did not want any going out during the last
night just in case Vrishka decided to watch her. As one of the *otuk*s had gently pointed out, most armies set up the night before, or early the morning
before the battle, and their plan would have a much better chance of being
a surprise if Fairbanks lay still the ninth night.

God bless Laszlo, and the *otuk*s he had trained, fifty of whom came to
speak with her, Kuruk and Muukwa within a half mark of when she called
for them, and who almost instantly understood the plan better than she
did. She trusted them to choose who went with Vrishka and who would go
to await the party at the pass, to know who would be best where, and to
divide the right number of Alak and Skani for both. She had to.

Kuruk would go out at the set of night nexturn with the last of them, and Fairbanks would then silently wait though the night. At second earth, 5:00 a.m., of the next morning, the tenth and final turn of the armistice, almost half of the *otuk*s who stayed would march the "surrendered" men out Fairbanks' gates and send them to Vrishka's camp, which lay in the valley just this side of Nick's. A good five mark march. The shakiest part of the plan lay after he received them. If Vrishka left immediately—and she prayed he would leave the cleaning of Fairbanks' messes to Chanda—they would enter Natuvik Pass sometime during the cardinal marks.

Allie she planned to send out nexturn with a small escort to deliver her message, which she still had to craft in a way that wouldn't invite them in to collect the men themselves. But leaving matters to the last turn seemed even riskier.

The final afternoon marks she spent practicing sigils behind the stable while Kuruk folded his arms and watched. Even when they all met in her room for dinner, no one asked her where she would be, whom she would lead, or when she would meet up with the army, perhaps because they knew the answer to the first. But she wasn't ready to tell them the details of her plans, because she needed to talk to Agni first. And Saman. Find out if she could learn what she needed from both in a few marks—because if not, she was in very serious trouble.

AFTER DINNER KIERA SOUGHT SAMAN FIRST, faithful Kuruk on her heels. To her very great relief, learning what she needed from him took less than a mark. Mastering it would take cycles, but before she left she knew she could do what she needed.

Locating Agni required Emmy's help, since Kiera had never been to her apartment. And then it required having Kuruk fetch a female servant, and then another, and another and another. After she found the right one, Kiera traveled with Agni, Kuruk, and the female Skani to the magic rooms, but Agni made Kuruk wait in the chamber while Kiera learned and then practiced two spells under Agni's careful eye.

Nighttide came and birthed the ninth turn. Mid first air, Kiera sent the woman to her bed and Agni brought Kuruk in. He left one mark richer and a bit of blood lighter, and for that matter, so did Kiera.

On the way back to her room Kiera wished she had another place to sleep, but on this tight schedule she'd waste more time getting her things than taking the extra sleep she knew Amba would force on her.

As their feet mushed spots into the runner bisecting the great hall, Kiera told Kuruk, "I finally remembered where I've seen you before." Since he walked behind her it took a full minute to realize that he'd stopped, just stopped walking, and when she did, she turned and made an exasperated face at him. "What?"

Her breath caught at the look on his face. With hands up, *I surrender*, she took slow steps back to where he stood. Too-bright eyes set like pebbles in a stone face watched as she came, and he flinched when she put a hand on his arm.

She made her voice soft. "Does it embarrass you, Kuruk, because if it does, please don't. Valen hurt lots of people, including me."

His jaw clenched, and he whirled and marched toward the main doors.

"Kuruk," she called as she trotted behind him, "I now know where you are at every minute, remember? And if you run, I'll just come find you. We can't fight tonight. Please! Please stop!" And even though she wasn't sure why this upset him so much, she added, "I'm sorry!"

The sound he made echoed the hall, something between exasperation and resignation. After exhaling again, he turned and stalked back to where she stood. "Do you know why Laszlo chose me, Kiera, to guard your life?"

Oh shit. What, *exactly*, was she supposed to say to that? After a nearly useless half minute in which her brain seemed to pump out nothing but detritus, the safest thing she could think of was, "Tell me."

And why the hell did this have to happen now?

He watched her as she thought, and he listened when she spoke. But it was the wrong answer, she could tell the moment his ears registered it. His lips closed and pressed together, and when he spun and stalked out, she let him.

BACK IN HER ROOM, ALEX AND EMMY slept in the bed while Amba sat drinking wine in the yellow chair, which she'd pulled close to the fire. Neither Marco nor Muukwa had come, and Kiera wished them both joy together on this last night. Without waiting to be told, or dragged, Kiera obediently undressed and lay on the couch.

"Where is Kuruk?" Amba asked as Kiera pulled a blanket over her.

A sigh escaped before she could catch it. In a whisper she hoped only Amba could hear, she told her what had happened.

"He feels shame, Kiera, but his fear for your safety will draw him back when the sting wears off."

"Why should he feel shame?"

"Did you not find him naked and the object of torment at the hands of the governor's son? Helpless ?"

"Well, yeah, but—"

"He is an *otuk*, Kiera. A leader of soldiers. A man who commands respect. A great fighter."

"And a man," Kiera added with a snort.

Amba pursed her lips. "He should come and sleep."

"He's right outside," Kiera told her through a yawn.

Amba leaned sharply forward. "How do you know that?"

Whoops! "Well," she said slowly, "I asked Agni to give him a mark so I could tell where he is. I just—know, though I'm not sure exactly how the spell works, but he knows where I am, too. Since I don't know where anything is outside Fairbanks, it will help me find the army after I rescue Laszlo."

Amba's eyes closed as she shook her head. "A map was not an option, then?"

"I'm afraid of losing it. And I'm not very good at maps."

"Muukwa knows the way."

Another yawn. "We might get separated."

A sigh—a good sign—but then, "Tell me your plan," which was not.

"I'd rather not. You'll just worry."

A mild voice answered, but the tiniest thread of steel wound through it. "That was not a request."

"Do you know what I tell Las—" Pain sliced and stole her words, and then it was hard to breathe, because for that moment she had forgotten. Forgotten that Laszlo was gone. Forgotten that he lay in some pit, some dungeon—forgotten that his life could be extinguished at any moment. Forgotten that it was the ninth turn, that soldiers slipped out every mark, that some of those men she loved would soon die—*everything*, and when it came crashing back, it was an ocean under which lay nothing but darkness.

Amba rose and lifted Kiera's shoulders off the couch so she could sit down, then wrapped Kiera in her arms. Tears didn't come. Instead they rocked together, back and forth, and tried to find their breath.

After a time, Amba murmured, "Tell me your plan," and despite everything else, the smallest of smiles rose on Kiera's face.

"Laszlo will survive this," Kiera told her quietly, "because of the strength you gave him."

"And the love you gave him. Now tell me."

As good as her word, Amba again woke Kiera at third earth. To her relief, she made it to the bathroom and had time to mix the powder she'd found stashed in the bin next to the toilet—thank you, Kuruk—in a cup of water in time to head off the headache. Thoughtful Kuruk had snuck in while she slept, and relief poured through her as he returned her smile when she emerged from the bathroom, though his looked as shaky as hers felt. Emmy had already brought breakfast, and Marco and Muukwa strolled in together, arm in arm, as Kiera sat down at the small dining table and dished yet more fish pie with a spoon.

But her stomach knotted as she began considering all that she had to do thisturn, and she pushed her plate away. "Muukwa," she said, and waited until Muukwa pulled her gaze from Marco, "I need you to go with me this morning." Her gaze slid to Marco. "And I have tasks for you, too." The tea had cooled, but she sipped it anyway. "Marco, I need you to go find me some money—vayans they're called here, but I don't want vayans. Surely someplace someone has stashed some coins from someplace else, or something like that. Something valuable. Enough to make someone look like they just made a sale, or a score, but not so much it looks obviously fake. And I need ink, good ink, that won't wash off. Stain, maybe, in blue or black, and something to write with."

"What you need is to eat," Amba commented as she strode behind the table on her way to the bathroom.

"My stomach is upset," Kiera explained, then hated that she'd felt the need to plead. How was it that Amba could reduce her to a child with a handful of words?

With a deliberate frown, Kiera continued. "Emmy, I need you to take me and Muukwa to where clothes are stored. We both need a couple sets, and a pack to carry them in that I can carry on my back, and if I can't find what I need, I need you to find me someone who can sew both well and very quickly." The heat in the cup in front of her had leached out, so she pushed it away, too.

"Do you want more tea, Kiera?" Emmy asked.

"No—"

"Yes." Amba spoke as she came out of the bathroom. "And bring some cheese and the freshest berries you can find. Go now." She shooed Emmy with a hand until Emmy scampered out.

"Amba, I need to get going," Kiera told her tiredly. "I have so much to do thisturn, and I don't have time to sit here all morning waiting for food and then eating it."

"And what, brave Kiera, will happen when more than a turn passes and you have not eaten? Come now," she frowned, "every soldier knows better. Your strength will fail. You will eat now, and you will eat before you leave."

When both Marco and Muukwa hid smiles, Kiera glared at both of them.

Kiera compromised by having Kuruk send someone to bring Aliyah.
If she had to sit here, it was going to be doing something she could tick off
her list. First, she had Emmy take Alex to play outside. There was no way
she would take a chance that he'd say something he shouldn't in front of
the girl.

"Marco, you don't have to stay," Kiera told him when Kuruk closed the
door. "And Muukwa, I don't want you here unless you can stay quiet. I
don't want any—drama."

"I have no words to say to her," Muukwa announced as she threw herself
into a chair, but she watched Marco.

His face was hard to read. "I will stay," he finally said, but moved to sit
on one of the couches, where his back would be to Kiera when he turned
to face the fireplace. This had to be hard for him, and Kiera's heart went
out to him. He'd done so much for Allie, faced his father's rage and a traitor's sentence to save her, and she had betrayed him over something that, to
Kiera, seemed so small.

"Remember," Kiera told them, "we are broken. Broken and giving up.
We don't know that Laszlo is alive. Try and look—crushed."

Muukwa snorted, but Amba shushed her. "Listen to her," Amba warned,
"or I will take you outside."

It didn't take long for Kuruk, who had fetched her himself, to return.
"They are here," Kiera breathed, and then the door opened.

Kiera let her head drop as it did, and only lifted it when Allie stood in
front of her.

Aliya curtseyed. "You sent for me, my Lady Governor." To Kiera, Allie's
voice sounded so sweet, so tender. So unlike her father's. And yet.

It took very little effort to summon her grief to the surface. "Aliyah,"
Kiera said quietly, "I asked you here because I need your help." She took a
moment to look around the room, to take in every face. Kuruk's watchful
eyes met hers, then Amba, who stood near the window with hands curled.
Then Marco, who sat with his back straight and turned away, and who
stared dejectedly at the floor. Whether that was an act or not, Kiera didn't
know. Muukwa, whose stony face gave nothing away. Then back to Allie.

Kiera's chest expanded when she drew a slow breath. "I want you to go
tell your father that we accept his terms."

Allie's lips parted and her eyes grew large. "So my lord Chanda is to
govern Fairbanks?"

Kiera let her eyes drop to the floor, and waited ten heartbeats to raise
them, just long enough to stop the aching to slap the smile that trembled at

Aliyah's lips. And wondered if anyone had told this besotted child the rest of the details, including who had to marry him.

Somehow she doubted it. Again, and with more fervor, pity for Marco rose. Well, better to be rid of her, Kiera supposed, that for him to marry her and be stuck with her.

"Yes," Kiera murmured, then said, "yes" again and rose and paced behind the table and laid her hands on the back of a dining chair. "I have no choice, Allie, do I?"

Allie's head shook. "No, my lady."

Kiera rubbed her brow with a hand. "Will you take a message to your father, please, tonight, Allie? Tell him that I agree to his terms. That we surrender." She raised both hands this time and washed her face. "And please, for me, beg his mercy. I lost—I lost my husband just a few turns ago." Kiera let her shoulders drop. "Please beg him for this last night. I will send out half the army nexturn at first light and send them to him. I'll give them all the weapons they can carry, so he'll know we're keeping very little. But he will have to protect us, please remind him of that, Allie. We—well, we need a strong man to lead us, and—" Kiera turned away and let her voice drift off. "And we will do all he asks if he will just keep Fairbanks safe. With Laszlo gone, I am so afraid, Allie."

Allie walked around the table and laid a hand on Kiera's shoulder. "I will tell him, my lady, and do not fear. My father is a strong man, and will keep our deconns safe."

Kiera did not turn. "I'll—I'll ask Kuruk to find someone to escort you to your father's camp later this afternoon. Thank you, Allie. Now, please, if you don't mind, will you—let me—"

"I understand, my lady," Allie told her gently. "And I am sorry. But this is the right choice."

"I know," Kiera whispered, and used her shaking hand to wipe imaginary tears.

"May I tell the others?" Allie asked as she walked toward the door.

Kiera sat down in the chair. "Of course."

Instead of the Amba she expected, when the door closed Kuruk came from the recess near the bathroom and dished cold food onto a plate for Kiera. She made a face when Kuruk pushed it in front of her, but lifted a spoon of something dumpling-thick and whitish to her mouth. Sawdust in a milk and flour base, as it turned out, but she forced herself to swallow it. Apparently they were out of fresh fruit.

"You did very well with that child, Kiera," Amba told her, but something in her voice made Kiera lift her head.

"But?"

"No. I mean those words." Amba heaved a sigh. "The time grows short and I find myself fearful."

"'We need a strong man to lead us'?" Muukwa snickered from the couch.

"It was all I could think of," Kiera said, and forced another lump into her mouth. "Do you think it was too much?"

"Please swallow before speaking. I think that it may not have worked for another—" Amba told her, but she admonished from autopilot. Kiera could hear Amba's thoughts drifting. "But the words were right for Aliyah."

Marco turned to face her across the back of the couch. "Agni told you about Vrishka."

"Yes, she did."

"You know she came from Barrow?"

"She told me that, too."

Marco's eyes narrowed as he considered. "Do you think she told you the truth?"

"Yes." This stuff was awful. One more bite and then she was finished. Didn't people in poor countries eat less than this every turn and still do all right? With an eye on Amba, who still looked lost in her own thoughts, she pushed the mess around to make it look like she'd eaten more. Kuruk turned his head and watched her, and she ignored him.

"Did she say who is more powerful?"

Kiera lifted her eyes so he'd know she told the truth. Well, most of the truth. "She said I am. And that even if he has other mages, I can take them." *So please don't agonize*, she begged with her face. *Don't worry. It will be all right.*

Marco struggled, she saw he did, and she loved him for it—but if he was that scared, she didn't want him out there anyway. Silently she prayed that after the dust had settled she and Marco, and maybe Muukwa, could work on making this better. But not now. In the field he would be a liability, and she couldn't take care of him, or ask anyone else to. Better he stayed here with Amba.

Using her feet, she pushed the chair back so she could stand. "Since Emmy isn't back yet, Muukwa, why don't you and I go check in with the *otuk*s, and then go see about some music?"

AT FIFTH FIRE KURUK SLIPPED OUT the back gate with the last group. After a quick hug, Kiera stood at the guard post and watched the fog swallow them. When the gates closed, something more than the mark on his back made her ache, and she prayed with every fiber of her being that this gentle man would last the battle. But surely he had to be tough, right, and a strong fighter to become an *otuk*?

With a heavy heart she turned back, alone for the first time in turns, and slid as her feet broke the wind-shaved snow quilting the back fields. What if Vrishka had told the truth? What if he hadn't used all his men in that little skirmish? No one had even mentioned that possibility. And what if he really could outfight them? What if his ability to summon water had grown stronger in the last decade, and he had learned spells Agni knew nothing about? And his mages—some of them had to be his children. Agni's children. Could she—could she do what needed done, inflict that—what had Agni called it, *darkness*—on Agni if the need arose, especially with her own grief so raw?

Dark thoughts led her up the right-hand stair and down the hall, and it wasn't until she stood outside the door to her old room that she realized what she'd done. It was a silly mistake. She'd been lost in wondering. On autopilot. Kuruk, her bodyguard, her friend, would have stopped her, tapped her shoulder, before she lay one foot on the stairs. Would have offered raised brows in question—*do you really mean to go this way?* But now there was no one.

After a moment of indecision, she opened the door. Hoar frost climbed one window, and the air smelled a little stale, but she walked to her closet—their closet—and pulled down one of Laszlo's big, black shirts. Her coat slid off when she shrugged, and she pulled the shirt over her head, then put her coat on over it. Even so, it hung a black stripe below the coat's hem.

Almost reluctantly, she turned to go. A seamstress awaited her in her other room for one final fitting before she and Muukwa left. Maybe she'd ask the woman to cut a few inches off this so she could wear it. And maybe, if she did, some of the luck of a man who made his own would rub off on her.

As her fingers left the latch, she prayed that the next hand that opened this door would be Laszlo's.

CHAPTER 18

FOG SQUATTED ON THE GROUND, SO THICK that Kiera had to push an elemental breeze in front of her and Muukwa as they walked to avoid even near obstacles. Even with the walls of Fairbanks less than a mile behind her the still air felt eerie, and Kiera shivered and adjusted her pack as she led the way toward the foot of the mountains.

"I can carry that," Muukwa told her.

"No, but thank you. I need you to be as light as possible."

"Tell me again what I must do."

"Well, for now you need to walk. When we get to the spot I found, I'll need a few minutes. When I tell you, you need to come stand in front of me, as fast as you can, then wrap both arms around me and hug me close." After a second a spark of mischief made her add, "You can pretend I'm Marco."

Instead of any one of the snappy retorts she expected, Muukwa har-rumphed. And then, five, maybe ten minutes later, as if she'd been thinking about it, she muttered, "He will be safe here."

But the underlying question in her voice surprised Kiera, and she stopped and turned to the woman wearing a snug-fitting, sleeveless dress in which Kiera would have developed hypothermia ten steps from the manse. "Yes, Muukwa, he will be safe. Laszlo told me a tou could hold the city from an army for a long time, and we left him a tou."

Snow started to fall after another half mark or so. That was good; it meant they were almost clear of the city's main spells. But it made walking difficult, at least for her. Fluffy puffs dusted the ice the ceaseless wind sculpted atop the ground, and although the snow lay less than a foot deep, a third of her steps started with a slip as the new snow melted and further slickened the surface.

Like a soft breeze, Muukwa sighed, "I am afraid for him."

Kiera was glad Muukwa couldn't see her face. "I am, too."

The climb grew steeper. A tree popped out so suddenly Kiera almost ran into it. Good—they'd hit the treeline. Now to find a path up. With a flicker of thought, she increased her airflow to clear more fog from their path.

A hundred hard steps later. "He isn't a man like Laszlo. He will do my bidding."

The gravid wind slapped wet fingers across Kiera's face when she turned. "I agree that Marco isn't like Laszlo, Muukwa." She paused to brush the clump of snow off her cheek, but didn't try to keep the sting from her voice. "But don't mistake kindness for weakness. Marco is just as strong as Laszlo, just in different ways, and you had better understand that I won't have you twisting him around just for fun."

Before Muukwa could answer Kiera started back up the hill—well, the mountain now. After another half mile the beating snow forced her to pull and send more air to clear her path and keep her going in the right direction, but they were almost there.

When the ground leveled off, Kiera stopped to catch her breath. Eyes closed, she sent her sight out and ahead and found the spot she'd scouted that afternoon. Another quarter mile up, but there lay her deep pond, frozen all the way to the granite chalice in which it slept. Her thoughts tumbled as she started up again, and mixed with the worry she'd been crushing. Could she do this? Sure, the idea seemed sound. But so many things could go wrong. So many things, and she offered thanks to all good things that Marco hadn't asked her for details, because he would have—well, after he'd stopped shouting, he would have told her that she was crazy. And maybe she was.

With a shake of her head, she pushed that away. This would work. She knew it would. She'd done something very similar once, though not to this scale, but over the past moons she had grown a great deal stronger. There was no reason to think it wouldn't work.

When they reached the pond, with careful feet Kiera stepped onto the relatively flat surface. Her sight followed her sigh out and dove into the ice below her.

"Muukwa, stand at the edge and wait for me to call you. When I do, come as quickly as you can and wrap your arms around me."

Muukwa strode out and stood in front of her. "Would our children be Alak or Skani?"

The ludicrousness of discussing Muukwa's feelings for Marco while she attempted perhaps the strongest spell of her life, done in the hope of saving her imprisoned, probably tortured husband in time to meet her army, left Kiera feeling more than a trifle annoyed. "Muukwa, I need you to wait over there. And really, is this the time to discuss this?"

At her tone, arms crossed and Muukwa's mouth closed in what Kiera might be tempted to term a pout. "I hate this, Kiera. I cannot stop thinking about him."

Kiera let her brows raise, but sympathy stirred and melted the edges from her ire. "From what I know, they would be both, and would probably be able to shift and might have some magical ability, too. Now please shut up. Since you're out here, wrap your arms around me. No, higher. Around my neck, but use my shoulders to hold your weight. I'm going to have to rely on your strength, Muukwa, so do not let go. If you feel yourself tiring after we go, tell me. Remember that I'm not as strong as you are and I don't know if I can catch you if you fall."

Face to face, scant inches apart, Muukwa sounded mournful. "Why can I not stop thinking about him, Kiera?"

Chagrin rose, then fell on the breath she exhaled as they stared into each other's eyes. Something in Muukwa's tone, something in the set of her mouth, reminded her of how she'd spoken about Laszlo, how he had dominated her every thought, not so long ago really, and how she still felt. "That's how love starts, Muukwa," she said softly, and closed her eyes.

A lick of fire came without being asked, and simmered as it spun contentedly in her belly. A flicker of thought, and orange light slid from her hands and into the ice below. In seconds ice popped and spit as the pond around her began to melt, and she sent her sight to direct the sluggish water into the concave she wanted it. Higher here, behind her, but smooth, then lower and lower beneath her feet. Open in the front. It took minutes of careful heat to bring the pond to the ground in front, then lower. With one last blast she smoothed the surface. Steam rose as she finished and water washed her boots, but she used fire to burn it away before any soaked in.

After lifting her right arm, she filled her mind with thoughts of fields of green grass, of spring trees bursting with heavy leaves, and used her index finger to draw a yar, the square that called earth. A gossamer softness, a green bar of earth, pierced her, met the waiting fire, and melted in the white flame. Using the fire for elemental ballast, she used a finger to draw another yar, and stumbled back a step when the second stream sunk in.

Unlike air, or even fire, it felt almost massless inside her. Not slick, but it wouldn't stay together here in her chest, where she needed it to wait, and without wrapping it in fire she couldn't have held it. Worse, it slowed her thinking even as it strengthened her body. But as she bound and wrapped it inside the circling fire her thoughts began to clear, and she let out a breath. Unlike an Alak, her body wasn't made to process this much earth, and without fire to bind it, earth would have flowed into every cell, infecting her until she burned it off.

When the earthfire spun slowly, tamely, Kiera's sight shot out of her body and rose like a shooting star called back to the skies. Higher, and higher yet. Air waxed heavier than she'd thought—it was an air mark, after all—but during this earth moon she dared not rely on any of the streams for something this major. And besides, for what she planned she needed a steady, strong flow that wouldn't weaken as the mark turned.

Almost too soon she found them. Twin streams, the mother air streams that traversed the planet. So much larger than any other flow. Miles and miles straight across, zooming hundreds of miles per mark toward some destination off to the west. Not that direction mattered for her purposes, except for the effect on the angle, but her water bowl would help her get that right.

After a handful of tries, stripping strands from the mother began to seem impossible. Was it that they were wound together, she wondered as her sight skimmed the surface? No, she decided, they were just being pulled so quickly.

Like a swan, she dove in. The flow hit her freight train hard and shoved her sight hundreds of feet west in two heartbeats. From her chest, miles below, she called to the air, *come with me*, and clawed her way to the edge. Strands followed her out of the flow, poles larger than summer trees, spun and twisted and wound like cyclones as they stripped themselves from the main stream and wrapped giant fingers around her sight—and once they did, after that pause they whipped toward earth, and her body, faster than anything she'd ever even imagined.

"Hold on," she whispered as her sight sank into her body, one heartbeat ahead of the air.

And that fast it overfilled her. She struggled, strained, to catch it, to spin it, but it crushed her sight, drove a knee to the ice.

Her lungs stopped even as her heart thundered. Panic threatened, made her want to thrash and push back, but she needed this air, and she knew she probably couldn't push this flow out even if she wanted to. Muukwa cried out, but hung on as Kiera opened her mouth and held her eyes closed.

No, she needed it, but not in her.

On both knees now, Muukwa kneeling in front of her, she pulled forth her fire, and the earth that threaded it, wrapped it round her sight, then sent the fire away.

Even with eyes closed, the green of earth filled her sight. Muscles ticked, spasmed as strength filled her. Earth met the air in her chest, softened it, and her lungs burst open. With a shaking right hand she drew a xan, and fire came before she finished the shape. Molding a sheet, she used white flame to catch the drifting earth, hold it as shield to the air pummeling her from above even as she drew another yar.

After four, then five gasped breaths, her lungs relaxed. After drawing one more yar, she managed to croak a warning to Muukwa, then surged to her feet and *kiai*ed as she thrust the air out, out of her chest, and sent the tornado wind down and into the cup below her feet.

And shot into the air. The upward thrust tore Kiera's head back, and Muukwa's hands slid up Kiera's back as the force pulled her down. Kiera wrapped her arms, still earth strong, around Muukwa's middle and squeezed as hard as she could, but even so, inch by inch Muukwa slid down Kiera's middle.

Out went her sight, and teased a strand of the air beneath her feet up, leveled the fist-sized bumps around them into something smoother, then raised the edges to waist height in a series of fingers around them. Only then did she relax her grip on Muukwa. They stabilized as they passed the fogline, and Kiera slid her sight back down the flow and reangled the air so that they traveled more *south* and less *up*.

Hot breath wheezed on Kiera's neck, but when the thrust eased, became less of a launch and more of a long fall, Muukwa whooped, evidently pleased, and Kiera's hand flew to her injured ear. When she turned her head Fairbanks, and the cloud that covered it, already lay so far behind them that she could barely see the mashed potato mounds in the dark. At this rate she would need to bring them down in just a handful of minutes, and she hoped she could find someplace close to Nick's that was safe.

Safe being free of soldiers, villages, and out of sight. She had no doubt that Vrishka's soldiers kept careful tabs on the entire area between his camp and Fairbanks, which was why she had refused to stalk through the dark, even with Muukwa leading her. It would take untold marks at the snail's pace they'd have to travel, and besides it would be ridiculous to chance being spotted, and caught, when she knew she could get them there in minutes without anyone seeing them. No one, here or anywhere, expected to see people flying through the air, and providing they stayed quiet, no one would likely even look up. And no mage, not even a *sunwyr*, would see a change in the flow of the elements, because no one, to her knowledge, used the mother air streams. Agni had told her so. Pointedly.

And understandably. Pulling too much air would crush a mage, and as she now knew intimately, these streams traveled so quickly that without a buffer even a strong mage wouldn't be able to use streams from a mother flow. But she'd only used the tiniest of bits from one, and after she ceased her pull the mother would call it back, or let it drift away. It wasn't like she'd diverted the entire stream.

But even if Vrishka did manage to detect her use of air, he couldn't use it to find anything except her spot on the mountain—the place where she sent it to manifest. She was riding the wave, so to speak, and even when she watched their trail with her sight, it just looked like an air flow. A normal, albeit fast, flow.

The lights of Nick's manse came into view, and from up here she could even see the yellow specks from the thousand lamps in Vrishka's camp, which still lay south of Nick's and blocked egress through the valley that squeezed that end of the plain. Eyes closed, she sent her sight sliding back to the angle point and shifted them lower, and they dropped to perhaps a hundred feet and to the west, toward the hills behind Nick's. A knowledge of the terrain would have come in handy, but since she didn't have one, she made her best guess.

And praise all good things, no fog blanketed these hills, which was something she hadn't thought about, but should have. Just over the first hill the trees opened up, and she sent her sight back, angled the flow, and prayed. This was the dangerous part, for many reasons. Soldiers might see them fall, scouts might be nearby, they might hit a tree. But things took too long and she missed the opening. She grimaced as they skimmed the trees, falling lower at every second, and at this angle she couldn't correct their trajectory without calling for more air—air from a local stream, which she refused to do. Vrishka would find her if she did, and Laszlo would die. Fairbanks would fall.

Because earth flowed so weakly, no mage would detect her calling it from local streams, as long as she avoided using yars anyway, and she'd use it to mask any wounds her fall caused. Muukwa wouldn't even need her help if she healed like Laszlo and Alex.

There! There ahead lay another clearing. Two hills back from Nick's. Her sight shot back, tore and severed the strands as she released her call to the air, and they fell. Was it too fast, she wondered, then realized it was, and still forty feet from the ground, but it was too late. "Hang on," she whispered urgently, and felt pleased that Muukwa didn't even whimper.

Rocks. Oh God. Let there be no rocks.

But then one of Muukwa's arms struck her in the face as she stripped off the dress, and to Kiera's eyes it seemed to stop where she'd thrown it off, then twisted in a parodic dance thirty feet above the ground before the earth called it down. Ten feet and forty miles a mark, and Kiera's mind, slowed by cold and fear, pondered why Muukwa would chose to land naked in the snow.

But then, just before the ground rose to meet them, Kiera's arms expanded as Muukwa's body, her chest, exploded outward. Muukwa wrapped Kiera inside enormous paws, pulled her head tight, and jerked and twisted until her back faced the ground. The snow made a soggy snarl as Muukwa skimmed the top, and then she caught and they tumbled once, twice, and hit a tree.

The furry arms wrapping Kiera relaxed, and she slid free. Muukwa pushed up, shook the snow off her coat, and cast her eyes at Kiera. A big bear—not quite as big as Laszlo, but she'd weigh in at close to a ton, Kiera thought. And beautiful, with the large, humped shoulders marking her as Denaa, and a rough, ruddy coat that in the pale moonlight looked a few shades lighter than Laszlo's dark copper.

The adrenalin she'd spent left her legs a little wobbly. "Thank you, Muukwa. And I'm fine," she said, and felt surprised that it was true. "Are you okay?"

Without answering Muukwa turned and galloped off through the snow back the way they'd come. Belatedly, Kiera wondered if anyone had seen them fall, or heard them land. With a small sigh, she shrugged off the pack and knelt down in the snow. The cold stung through her thin pants, but she ignored it and sent her sight out and down. Earth was always hard to grab, summon, but she wrapped strands from the stream flowing just below the snowline and after two tries managed to pull a bit into her.

Air flowed out as she exhaled, and her thighs stilled as the earth chased the sharp fear from the large muscles. Like an ache, she could feel Kuruk when her thoughts stilled—so many miles away, and not moving. She started to wonder how he was, if he had felt her leave, but pushed it away. Chin to chest, she drew a breath, held it, and concentrated.

From a quarter mile away Muukwa's feet made an even crunch-crunch as she ran. A small animal, perhaps a fox, trotted amid the trees behind her. An echo sounded as an owl cried its frustration from somewhere in the trees.

But no voices. No sounds of leather, or metal, as a soldier shifted position. No human steps. Yet Kiera made herself sit still, listening, for long minutes, until her knees numbed and her feet burned.

Farther sounds drifted, then died as earth wore off, and as Kiera stood, Muukwa came trotting back, her dress blowing to cover either side of her furry face from where she clasped it in her jaws.

The sight made Kiera smile, but she ducked her head and dusted snow from her pants. When she looked up Muukwa had changed, both from a bear and into her dress, the hem of which she held up, then turned to face the moon. "I may have torn it," she mourned. With a sigh she lifted the seam higher, tried to find the open seam, which bared her—well, bare behind.

Kiera turned to the trees and stared into the waiting dark. Down that hill, and up another, then one more, and they would be at Nick's. Less than a mark. Could they do this? The plan was complicated, which meant lots of things could go wrong, but no matter how hard she'd tried, she couldn't think of a better one, not one she knew would guarantee Nick allowing two women into his home and to attend the gruesome tournament below it. For many reasons Muukwa was a good choice for the role Kiera cast her, the best choice. But could she quiet her own heart, play her own role, well enough?

The pack lay on the ground, and she squatted down and pulled it open. She should do this now, rather than wait. That way even if someone discovered them, they could keep their cover, hopefully avoid capture, and continue on their way. But if someone saw her before she disguised, chances were someone would recognize her, even in pants. Before she started, she dug out one of Saman's packets, tore it open, and poured it into her mouth. When the snow had washed it down, she found the hand-sized paper inside the pack on which Agni had drawn what looked like a celtic puzzle, then lifted out the carefully wrapped bottle of ink. Her clothes, her costume, lay below, and she pulled them out, too.

In this cold it took determination to let her coat slide off, but it took steel to lift off her shirt. "Muukwa, I need your help now," she whispered as she laid the paper inked with blood and soot against the snow. When she saw the lines soften as the snow melted into them, she lifted the paper and pressed it carefully against the skin between and just below her breasts, where her costume would cover the mark, though God knew her clothes would leave little else to the imagination.

As the ink set she cast a glance at the red silk clump lying innocently next to her feet. It would cover about a third of her breasts, and a band of stronger cloth had been sewn inside that would, she hoped, keep them from falling out. But although the—ahem—*dress* would fall to cover her bottom, it ended a ways before her knees, and the seamstress had cut large gaps out of both sides, leaving the outsides of her breasts, her waist, and the tops of her hips bare, though the thinnest of gold strands wove and crisscrossed through the entirety of the fabric, and was the only reason the dress would stay on.

And on, it looked like a costume she'd expect to see at a strip club back home, which was exactly the look she'd hoped for. To her knowledge, and everyone else's she'd queried, and to her very great surprise, no one had yet thought up naughty dancing girls. She planned to present, or rather have Muukwa present her, or sort of her, to Nick. And offer to trade. Nick would be so pleased. She knew he would. The lecherous, slimy bastard would love this. Love what she could do.

A hand, Muukwa's hand, turned Kiera to face the moon and pulled the paper from her chest. As Kiera held her bitterly cold breasts inside her crossed arms, Muukwa's inked finger began tracing the pattern.

"Begin at the bottom," Kiera reminded her quietly. "The bottom right."

Muukwa snorted. "You have now given me that same instruction seven times."

"Sorry, sorry," Kiera whispered, afraid her voice would carry. "I just don't want anything to go wrong, Muukwa."

The ink felt cold against her skin, and tight when it dried.

Muukwa spoke softly, and without looking up. "Would it please you if I came to love Marco?"

"I—I would be pleased if Marco was pleased."

Another snort. "Shall I tell you how he drives his cock?"

Kiera's shoulders jerked when she flinched. "Um. No. But thank you."

The snow crunched when Muukwa leaned down and wet her finger in the inkpot. "But surely you have considered him."

Even whispered, Kiera's voice sounded tight, even to her. "I have not."

Muukwa looked up, eyes assessing. "Why have you not?"

"Muukwa," Kiera hissed, "I do not want anyone to hear us, so please keep your voice down if you insist on talking. I have not considered him because, well, he is like a brother to me. I love him, but not like that."

"No one is near." Muukwa waved a hand dismissively, but her eyes held Kiera's. "If you do not love him, why have you shared his bed?"

With pursed lips, Kiera leaned down until she was face to face with Muukwa. "I don't even know where you heard that, but let me tell you that yes, we sometimes slept in the same bed, but it was to protect me from harm. From being forced to have sex with men during brooding moons. But never, not one time, have we ever had sex, or even touched each other in anything other than—than the way a sister would touch a brother." Kiera leaned closer. "And let me tell you one more thing. I have loved Laszlo since, well, since the first time I saw him ride up on his horse. My second turn here. And Muukwa, I will never, ever, love another man. Whether Laszlo lives or dies," she whispered furiously, "I will never love another man!" Kiera stood and stared into the needle-thin trees, jaw set hard against the chasm of sadness that lay waiting, underneath everything, for her to stumble. "Now please finish this so I can go get my husband out of that fucking dungeon."

CHAPTER 19

WITHOUT THE ABILITY TO SUMMON a constant flow of earth, Kiera would have died in the mark it took to cross the three hills. The long black shirt she wore atop her dress kept out nothing but the headwind, and a twisting breeze slid under the shirt to press icy fingers to the bare skin beneath. And even with it her legs numbed, feet and face and fingers burned, and even her thoughts slowed, shrunk to nothing more than regulating her breath and the steps she took, ten behind Muukwa, who strode barefoot in her tiny dress through the unbroken snow.

Lights shone through the trees as they descended the last hill, and Kiera's heart had enough remaining sense to pound a staccato. Past the treeline the ground leveled, and at last the manse of Mayor Nickinum of Talium, protectorate of Fairbanks, came into view, a scant half mile from the hills from which they'd slid and scampered. Even from behind it stood palatial, a flat-topped pyramid rising to defy the flat of the plains, and doubtless designed to strike awe in the hearts of all who looked upon it. None of the supporting buildings, stables and storage stood more than a story high, and all were dark. But from the manse lights shone from dozens of arched windows on each of its four aboveground levels, giving the entire structure an almost ethereal glow.

The moisture in Kiera's mouth dried, and she stopped to scoop a handful of frigid snow in bare fingers and washed out her mouth. Muukwa turned to watch, but said nothing. After Kiera spat, Muukwa turned and they walked the last hundred yards to the manse.

The main doors lay on the far side, and as they approached them Kiera panicked. Did one knock on doors here, or did visitors just walk in and wait to be greeted? What was the right protocol? She had never before had to think about that, and making the wrong move, even hesitating, would raise suspicion, and maybe give her away. To her knowledge she, and Alex, were the only people in this land who weren't born here, and although many things were the same, some very fundamental differences set this Alaska apart from the one she knew. And Nick knew that.

But Muukwa stole her indecision by striding up to the door, flinging it open, and without the slightest hesitation walking inside. Kiera followed, head down, and tried to slide into her persona even as she soaked up the precious, glorious warmth of the hallway.

From beneath her lashes she looked around as her fingers thawed. It was exactly as she remembered it. A wide, two story entry, painted a soft gold, floored with marble and bisected by a white and gold runner that led guests into the bowels of the house. Lights shone cheerfully from lamps set atop small, rounded tables cast of what looked like stained spruce.

While she stood silently Muukwa used a hand to brush snow from her dress, her hair. When she'd finished she strode into the next room, a sitting room apparently—one in which Kiera hadn't lingered during her last visit. This time, people—well, men, maybe twenty—sat on or stood between the five-odd plush gold couches, perhaps awaiting entry to the great room beyond to which the two grand doors stood closed. Some sipped wine, others talked with those nearest, but eyes lifted and all talk ceased when Muukwa cleared the threshold.

Undaunted, Muukwa showed her teeth and added a definite sway to her hips as she sauntered across the room. The men's eyes followed her, but some turned glances on Kiera as well, whose oversized shirt covered her completely, neck to knees. The attention stiffened Kiera's muscles, jilted her steps, but she shushed her thoughts, made herself watch Muukwa's feet and follow behind. When Muukwa threw herself into one end of a couch, Kiera shuffled to stand behind her and kept her eyes on the floor. It took effort to keep her breath quiet and hands unclasped, but she concentrated on drawing deep breaths.

It took only a handful of seconds for conversation to resume, a forced laugh to sound, and for most of the attention to turn back. Eyes lingered, though—Kiera could feel them assessing.

With steps that ticked on the marble floor, one of the standing men, a tall blond in very fine tan pants, walked over and leaned in to lift Muukwa's hand, which he kissed. "I would be pleased to know you, my lady." His voice was smooth, silky, the voice of a rake. Lips curled as Muukwa smiled, a predatory smile that should have sent the man running. But then, Skani men never considered the risks a woman might pose.

Beginning at his feet, Muukwa took her time looking him up. Her gaze lingered at the juncture where his pantslegs met, but lifted, up and to his face. "You may call me Iyya," Muukwa told him as she removed her hand

and leaned back to cross one leg over the other. "You appear a wealthy man," she commented baldly as she laid an arm across the back of the couch, "and I am always pleased to know a wealthy man. You may sit with me until my turn is called."

A smile ghosted across his face as he took the space next to Muukwa, and Kiera breathed a silent thanks that it was Muukwa on that couch and not her. Her own heart thudded, her lips stuck together, and her legs would not stop trembling. Earth, she needed earth to strengthen her overtired muscles, and for once, she'd welcome the way it slurred her thinking, soothed her worry. Eyes closed, she sent out her sight. Gently, softly, she stripped off a finger's width from a flow wending across the floor. She didn't even try to spin it; instead, she drew it in, into her legs near her ankles, and only then drew it up to chest, arms, face and then called more. Carefully, little by little she summoned, so that no one would notice the slight pull of earth.

"And what is this?" the man was asking Muukwa as Kiera opened her eyes, but earth had slowed her heart and she tried to look as if she hadn't noticed the shift of attention in the room from Muukwa to her. "A gift for my lord Nick?"

Muukwa tilted her head and stared at the man. "Perhaps," she said. "And perhaps not. She's a fair one, no?"

"Her clothes hide her," he told her seriously. "But her face is fair. Are you selling, then?"

A wide smile broke across Muukwa's face. "Perhaps." She leaned forward and let her breasts fill the space her dress bared. "But she will fetch a high price, Len, perhaps even more than a wealthy man can afford."

The smile he returned said he didn't believe her. "She is fair, but not that fair, Iyya."

"Ah," Muukwa laughed gaily, and adjusted her shoulders, let a gold strap slip down her arm as she addressed the room. "But she has talents other slaves do not. Talents my own lord wishes known, for he plans to open his own pits by turn of next moon, and she is far from the only girl he has grown to please the men who come."

The way his breath filled his chest said she had him. "Tell me."

Another predatory smile. "Nah, nah, my friend. You will wait until the mayor presents her."

As if summoned by the call of his name, the twin doors opened and Nick strode in, gold and purple robe waving behind him. Unsmiling, his eyes took in everyone, but he stopped mid-stride when he found Muukwa half-lying on the edge of the couch closest the door. Kiera's heart thundered as keen blue eyes assessed first Muukwa and then her, the eyes of a man to whom she had been betrothed. His handsome face looked flushed, perhaps from too much wine, and someone had recently cut his thick, dark hair. She hadn't realized how big Nick was, perhaps because she measured every man against Laszlo, whose enormous chest made even strong-shouldered men like Nick look small.

Perhaps nothing could flummox Nick, the king of the smooth. A smile lifted his lips as he took the steps separating him from Muukwa. He reached for her hand, lifted her to her feet, then raised her hand to his mouth and watched her eyes from above it. "My goodness," he told her through a half smile. "The gods have smiled on me tonight. Tell me that I am not dreaming, dear girl, that such a beauty has found her way into my humble home."

Muukwa's lips parted and breath slid out, and Kiera wondered whether he was spelling her. "I am Iyya, my lord Nick," she breathed, "and I would discuss my business in private."

Teeth ground as Kiera searched in vain for some sign of magic and found none. How did you tell if someone was spelling someone through touch? It would likely require knowledge she didn't have, an understanding of how bodies used elements. But Muukwa held her own, slid a silky smile across her lips, and waited Nick's judgment.

"Of course," he told her after the briefest of pauses. "Of course, my dear." Still holding her hand, he led her out the way they had come, but before they reached the door he turned left and led her down a hallway. Kiera trotted behind and kept her eyes down.

"She is yours?" Nick asked as he slid Muukwa's arm into his.

"She is," Muukwa confirmed in a stronger voice. "And what I have come to discuss with you, in part."

Nick opened a door on the left and stood so that they could pass. Kiera could feel his eyes on her. "Mmmm. Really? Well, if you are selling, I may buy her." He closed the door and stood blocking it. "Tell her to remove the covering."

Muukwa lifted her chin to Kiera, *do it*, and Kiera turned away, then lifted Laszlo's shirt and let it drop to the floor. Now she would see how well Agni's spell worked. If Nick would see someone else, a twenty-something girl with short golden hair and dark eyes—for some reason the spell could not alter her eyes, but her face now held a slightly smaller nose, larger lips, and a sharper chin. A pretty face, all told, and one set above a body that mostly matched Kiera's, which made the spell easier, stronger, and, according to Agni, more likely to last. When the shirt splashed at her feet she drew a breath and turned, then lifted her arms, palms up, for inspection.

Eyes narrowed, but a smile lifted Nick's lips as his eyes touched her legs, her belly, the bare skin on her sides, and lingered at her breasts. His bald perusal made her hands want to lift to cover herself, and when she met his eyes for the briefest of moments, his said he saw it. Liked it. "I will buy her," he told Muukwa in a silky voice when Kiera dropped her eyes to the carpet at her feet.

And now Muukwa smiled. Kiera heard it in her voice. "I am pleased that you find her fair," Muukwa told him, all business now, "but how she appears is the least of her gifts, my lord. I came to show her, to perhaps offer her for sale if the price is right, in an exchange. My lord wishes an accord with Talium."

Nick stepped from the door and to what must be a bar built in front of the far wall. Glass clinked as he lifted the top from a carafe, and from it he filled two glasses with opaque liquid. A white wine, presumably.

"Leave that off," Nick told her gruffly when Kiera leaned down to pick the shirt from the floor. Her hand unclenched from the fabric and she stood, then cast her gaze to the legs of the couch upon which Muukwa sat herself. Nick brought wine, then sat next to her, but angled himself so he could keep an eye on Kiera as well.

"I await your words, my dear," he told her as he sipped his wine.

Muukwa leaned back and rested her shoulders against the corner of the couch, then lifted a bare arm and laid it behind Nick. If she wasn't relaxed, she was the best actor Kiera had ever seen. "My lord, who asked not to be named as yet, works to open a pit before the next moon turns. But not just fighting, my lord, though we know the real money lies there. He has grown girls—" a smile—"talented girls, who will fill the eyes and soothe the fears of even the most cautious of betting men." Muukwa paused to sip her wine, then made a face. "This is piss, Nick," she commented without inflection and lifted the glass to Kiera. After the heartbeat it took to decipher what Muukwa wanted, Kiera took the glass from Muukwa's fingers and walked back to the bar and set it gently down.

Nick's brows raised, but his eyes tracked Kiera.

A shiver slid down her back, and not just because the room was so cold.

"Shall I tell you how, Nick? Because you will find that you must have her after you see what she can do."

Nick shifted his attention to Muukwa and let a spear of anger color his words. "And what, Iyya, is the exchange you offer? So far you have told me that a competitor rises and that he will fill his stalls with girls that will draw more men than mine. You offer a girl for sale, but then speak in riddles about an ability she has to drive up the price." He leaned forward. "Speak your purpose, girl!"

Muukwa ignored the dangerous tone. Her legs crossed and she drew the predatory smile across her mouth. "Nah, nah, my lord. I have but tried to tell you all of what I was told to say. My lord offers an accord. He will sell you some of his girls in exchange for spreading word here about his pit, which he will run when yours does not. So," Muukwa's smile widened, "not a competitor, my lord, but an ally." Kiera watched Nick's shoulders relax as Muukwa's words soothed him, and she wished fervently that Muukwa would stop playing games. "But you will not believe my words when I tell you what she can do. I ask that you let me show you. But first, I require music. A space as big as this room. And men." Using her finger, Muukwa traced an O on Nick's hand, then lifted her face to his. "And then you will tell me how much you will pay for her, my lord, and four like her."

THE GREAT HALL AT TALIUM, when compared to the one in Fairbanks, was not quite as great, but it would earn a close second. It must have taken builders ten cycles just to decorate the two-hundred-foot three-story room. Thin gold beams traced lines skyward and broke the stain-darkened walls into sections. Murals covered some higher spots, and relief had been cut into other places. Head-sized balls of light hung at the end of thin poles and burned just brightly enough to create a sense of dusk for those two or three hundred bodies, nearly all male, milling around or sitting at the many dark tables spread across the room. Servers in purple and gold livery ferried wine and empty glasses across a somber gold and plum rug that clung to the floor, all but that room-sized space below the podium on which the band played in one corner of the room.

So slowly as to be a torment, Nick wound them through the room. He stopped a dozen times to shake hands, to greet or share a laugh, and Kiera's heart would not stop pounding. Her sight told her that unlike Fairbanks, inside Nick's no gold had been laid inside the walls. Elements flowed as freely through the building as outside it, and for that, Kiera was grateful. She wouldn't need much, but it would take a great deal more concentration if she had to keep seeking what she wanted. This way she could pull the smallest of flows, build it up, and set the flow to keep filling her as she spun her spell and concentrated on other things.

Her mouth dried when her bare feet took their first step on the dance floor. *Relax*, she told herself as she followed Muukwa and Nick. It was just the start of fifth water, and no one had begun dancing yet, but when Nick reached the center of the floor the band abruptly ceased their rendition of a slow, vaguely Celtic song. Heads bowed as he reached the stairs leading up. "As you requested, my dear," Nick told Muukwa through a smile and rested a hand on her shoulder.

"I require that you play two songs without a pause between them," Muukwa told them. "Do you know Kusaxan? And Kusook? They are Alak songs, but widely known, I believe."

The man in front, the one who must have been the leader, a thin but well-dressed Skani man, looked to Nick, who nodded once. "I do, my lady," the man told her somberly.

Nick turned to look into Muukwa's face as his hand slid a slow path down her back and finally stopped just above the rise of her buttocks. "So, my dear, your lord is a shifter? Hmmm. An interesting development."

Mukkwa shifted a shoulder and leaned into the embrace Nick offered. "Perhaps," she answered with a coy tilt of her head. "And perhaps money is the more important of the two, my lord."

From behind them Kiera saw the fingers of Nick's hand squeeze Muukwa's hip. "There are many important things, my dear," he told her softly, intently. "So many things that bring pleasure."

The teeth that Muukwa showed shone white in the near dark of the band's corner. "Do you offer your cock, then, my lord, for my pleasure?"

A hand flew up, Kiera's hand, to cover her mouth, to stop the hysterical laugh that threatened, but she recovered, pressed lips together, used shaking fingers to adjust the shirt she'd pulled back on and tried not to believe that Muukwa had just used the word *cock* in a sentence with the mayor of Nickinum.

But if Muukwa had shocked Nick, he hid it well. Instead of any of the dozen reactions she half-expected, Nick's hand squeezed again, harder this time, and a smile lifted his lips as he leaned in and kissed Muukwa. It lasted a long time, and Kiera felt her stomach clench and turn as his hands wrapped Muukwa's hips, pulled her into his, and as he did she wrapped arms around his neck and opened her mouth.

Ignoring the open stares, the leering grins from the men who watched, and with her eyes glued to the ground, Kiera took the opportunity to call yet more earth, adding it to the store that spun inside a dozen strands of fire in her chest.

It was Muukwa who broke the kiss, whose mouth lingered near Nick's in a seemingly reluctant parting. "Let us save our pleasure, my lord, for later. Let me show you what my girl can do."

The pink of his tongue touched her lips, licked a line to her nose. "Mmmm, Iyya," he said to her lips. "How delicious you are. Allow me to be so bold as to tell you that your lord chose his messenger oh so well." But his arms released her, and he stepped back.

Facing Nick, Muukwa ran her tongue between her teeth, then turned to face the band. "When we leave the floor, commence Kusaxan," she told them brusquely, and led Nick off the floor.

The time had come, and Kiera's stomach knotted hard. As the first notes started she popped some of the earth, let it fill her, and took a step, then another, in time with the low beat. *Relax*, she commanded herself, and closed her eyes against the sight of hundreds of eagerly waiting eyes.

By the third step, earth filled her, slowed her heart and the worry that wound it. Many cycles ago Julia had taught her a dance—well, several dances—meant to be done for Kiera's then husband. In private. But she'd practiced this one thisturn, added moves from all, the steps she remembered, and as she relaxed her hips swayed, her arms lifted to caress the lover she dreamed, her body turned in time with the tempo. But this was a dance anyone could do, her moves so far, which was why she needed two songs. One to get going, one to whet the appetite. The real treat, the hook upon which she meant to catch Nick, was yet to come.

Eyes still closed, she turned, parted her lips, and lifted the shirt—slowly—let it catch and free on the strings winding her dress, catch and free over her hips' slow gyration, then her waist, her breasts, higher and higher. She turned slowly, let her hands caress her body as she pulled the shirt in time with the heavy beat, step by step, up her body and over her head.

Against her will earth made her hear the sharp intake of many breaths as the shirt slid to the floor, and more when she turned away, faced the band, bent at the waist and ran hands down the back of her thighs as she swayed her bottom in time with the beat.

But Nick said nothing, perhaps waiting for the something more he knew must come.

As this first song wound down Kiera continued her dance across the floor, but pushed all thoughts away and began the hardest part. Water. Keeping them separate, the water from the fire, was something she'd been practicing all turn. Earth—thank God for the earth she'd held, which she released from fire and bound with the string-thin strands of water she peeled off a local stream. Agni said it wouldn't take much, which was good since no matter how desperate her need, Kiera couldn't hold more than a few strands without choking.

Too soon, far too soon, the first song ended, and then it was time.

Chapter 20

As the first song ended the second began, a heavy, slow, seductive song, and Kiera sent water through the mark Muukwa had painted on her chest, keying the final part of the spell. One to which Agni had added something special. A mark designed, like Nick's Danse, to create—or perhaps call—lust. From another mage she'd learned how to draw water from people, to feel what they felt, and this worked essentially the same way, except instead of pulling she would send the lust she created to wash across the crowd, where it, bound with earth, would sink into all it touched. It took no trigger, like Nick's, except the touch of the magic she sent, and she could send it across the room.

A brief introduction started the song, just long enough to fling the first wave into the audience, but the drums began a heavy beat, and she stepped to match each. Step, bounce a hip, step, bounce. *Sex*, she thought, *sex*, and sent another.

The lust she sent infected her, too, which she hadn't known was a risk, but the earth she continued to pull kept her calm, and she did not fight it. As the singer began his part, words she didn't understand, Kiera gyrated, twisted hips, ran fingers and hands down her own body, rubbed her stomach, clenched her fists, pushed out her hips, and imagined release. The pace increased—this was the Alak song of sex after all—and as she sent another wave into the audience, she let herself fall further inside her own spell.

From somewhere off to her left Nick laughed, a low, sexy laugh, and though she knew he was well pleased, she couldn't make it matter. Frenzy-fast the drums beat, the singer cried, and Kiera sent the last of the lust into the crowd as she turned, lost in her own, and used hips and arms and face and fingers to imagine taking her pleasure, to show the audience how it felt, and how hard she craved it.

The song began its crescendo, neared climax, and Kiera's body followed it up, locked when it peaked. Her back arched, fists clenched, and she cried the pleasure she imagined, then fell to her knees on the floor as the notes stopped, head bowed, mouth open, and tried to catch her breath.

"A tou vayans," Nick said into the silence that followed, and maybe it was just the earth and water still stirring inside her, but his voice seemed both overloud and unbearably heavy with unspent emotion. Or something. "For each."

Muukwa laughed delightedly and ran a hand up Nick's arm. "Five. Each. And two of your fighting slaves. My choosing."

"Oh, my darling," Nick said thickly, and captured her hand, led her from the floor and toward a doorway set in the back of the room. Kiera grabbed her shirt from the floor and pulled it over her as she trotted to keep up. "You will bankrupt me. Two, and one fighter."

Muukwa flashed a wicked smile as Nick motioned for the band to begin playing. "Three, and three."

The door stood slightly agape, and Nick pushed it open and let Muukwa, then Kiera pass into the well lit hall behind it. Muukwa waited for Nick, then took his arm. Kiera kept her eyes down and followed behind. She knew that she should feel elated, or at least relieved. So far, everything had worked. Nothing had gone wrong. But she felt sick. Sick at this house, sick that beneath it Alaks waited, enslaved men whom Nick forced to fight to the death so the men she'd just danced for could bet. So Nick could make money, he made Alaks fight and sent his slave women to walk the halls for those men to bed. Halls he surely intended for her to walk as well.

And Laszlo. That Laszlo lay someplace, in some cell, somewhere beneath her feet was nearly more than she could bear. If she thought she could get to him, find him and free him before Vrishka could cross the few miles to get inside this place, and to her, Nick would already be lying on the floor.

Near the end of the hall Nick motioned to a door, and Muukwa opened it and stepped inside. It looked similar to the one he'd taken them to before, except this one was far larger and set up more comfortably. A set of overstuffed, luxurious couches V'd in front of a fireplace maw. Muukwa plopped down into one as Nick poured red wine from what looked like a metal decanter, which he carried to her, but stayed standing. Eyes assessed from over the top of his glass. "Is she a whore?"

"Will you light the fire?" Muukwa countered, and Kiera wondered if she was trying to evade his question. Did she wonder what Nick wanted to hear? She hoped Muukwa wouldn't look to her for an answer, because she didn't know what Nick wanted, either. The safest answer seemed to be *no*, since a woman could always be made to service men, and she readied to shake her head if Muukwa looked her way.

But she did not. Instead she watched Nick's nod and how he started the fire using long matches and paper. "Are you a mage?" Muukwa asked him, voice bland.

"I am," Nick answered with his back still turned. "But water calls me, my darling, and so fire is not something I can summon. Are you an Alak?"

"I am," Muukwa parroted, but kept her voice smooth.

"From where?"

"Tungak. From an island to the south."

Nick rose, a smile on his face that Kiera did not like. "My goodness. A bear."

Apparently Muukwa did not think that required an answer, so she sipped her wine and watched him over it. "She is no whore, nor are any I offer. You saw her flinch from your eyes and knew it then. I wonder why you ask me then, Nick."

Nick's eyes glittered in the firelight. "From where did you find her, Iyya? A water *nuwyr*, she must be. That is what I cannot help but wonder."

Instead of spooking Muukwa, for which Kiera knew his words had been meant, Muukwa smiled, then let it blossom into a grin. "You wish you knew. I will not tell you, Nick, but if we can reach an accord, my lord will sell you four more who can do the same." After a pause in which she stretched her shoulders and leaned back until the ample cushions cradled her back, Muukwa added, "and the part that will best please you is that she is simple, Nick. She rarely speaks, understands even less, and does what she is told. But she has been well trained. When the music starts, she will dance."

Nick's eyes flicked to Kiera, who dropped hers to avoid them. "What is her name?"

Even though this was a detail they had forgotten, not even a pause passed before Muukwa told him, "We call her Kala," and Kiera lost her breath, but neither paid her any mind. "It means *lover*, in the sense of *beloved*," Muukwa explained. "For she will fast become your favorite. I am sure of it."

Kiera's eyes closed. *My beloved.* Not just *my woman*, or even *my lover*, at least not in the sense she had understood it. *My beloved.* A knot tightened, another loosened, and she opened eyes to find Muukwa staring at her. A gift, in the middle of all this madness. A gift for strength. Her eyes closed again as she blinked, but she dared not acknowledge the gravity of the word in any other way.

The glass spun in Nick's fingers as he considered. "Tell me who else your lord is considering an accord with, my dear. I would know how many others will have—" he nodded toward Kiera—"such a girl."

But Muukwa just smiled, which made Kiera want to jump up and down. *Tell him it's just him*, Kiera's thoughts begged. *Don't do this, Muukwa.*

"My darling," Nick drawled, "if everyone has one, or more—"

"Then everyone must have one or else the men will go elsewhere," Muukwa finished for him, a dangerous look in her eyes. "But I will tell you that you are the first, Mayor Nickinum. And if you can pay enough—" One shoulder lifted as she shrugged, sipped her wine, and let the words hang between them. "But I must thank you," she told him after she'd swallowed, "for this wine. It is very good."

It surprised Kiera when Nick laughed. "Yes, it is, my dear. Very good wine indeed. Mmmmm. Like you, simply delicious. And a beauty to match. Well, sweet Iyya, perhaps we can reach an accord after all. How many fighters does your lord have, hmmm?"

Muukwa's head shook as she smiled back, but it looked less than friendly. "Some. But he wants more good ones, as all lords do, I would imagine."

"And that, my darling, is why he sent you to me," Nick said, and nodded as though he understood, at long last, what Muukwa had come for. He came around and sat on the couch arm opposite Muukwa, wine glass still in hand. "I will trade you three fighters for every girl, good ones, and two tou vayans. I will add my guarantee that the fighters will last a half cycle at least. I will replace any lost before that time."

An icy band wrapped Kiera's chest, leaving the coldness of death where it touched her skin. *Lost.* Like a sock in the laundry, or a set of keys during a hectic turn.

"My choice must be the final one," Muukwa insisted, and held up her glass for Nick to refill.

The cap sealing wine inside the decanter clinked when Nick removed it. He bought it to her and poured out a half glass before returning it to the bar. "Are you an expert then, my dear?"

"I am an Alak," Muukwa said as if that explained everything, then drank down her wine, all of it in one long swallow, and stood. "Take me to where I can see them."

With a nod Nick turned to the door. "Leave her here," he said as his hand pulled the blackened door toward him.

No! Kiera's mind screamed, and she took a step toward Muukwa, begged her to look back. *No! You can't leave me here when you're going to see Laszlo!*

"I will not," Muukwa told him in a voice that said she knew a game was afoot, and Kiera's stomach unclenched. "She is worth a cycle's business, Nick, and so she will stay where I can see her until ours is finished. When we have reached an accord, you can leave her anyplace that pleases you."

Eyes narrowed a fraction, and Kiera wondered whether her words aroused his suspicion or whether she just annoyed him, but then Nick smiled, washed it away, and motioned her out. His eyes lingered on Kiera, she felt them, until he walked past to join Muukwa.

Head down, she followed Muukwa's feet through a doorway at the end of the hall, and down as they descended the stairs to the pit.

THE AIR HEATED AS THEY STEPPED DOWN two, then three flights of stairs. The smell of unwashed bodies, grease, and sex wafted up in a breeze that traveled the steps, perhaps seeking a way out. After one final turn the stairs exited onto a twenty-foot-wide walkway, two tiers separated by four steps, with the widest being the top, that surrounded a hundred-foot circular arena that lay overlit and empty below. There was room up here for hundreds, perhaps more, people to stand. Someone had scrubbed the rails and the floors, and the walls bore no handprints, but the air stank of filth. Singular doors opened on the building side of the walkway, dozens and dozens of pine doors set into the stone walls, painted black to match the railing, and Kiera knew that most, perhaps all, would lead to bedrooms of some sort, places for the men to take the women they chose. Did they wait for intermissions, she wondered, or would some take a woman when the bloodlust overwhelmed them during a match?

If there was a hell, it was something like this.

Since this pit had been dug from the earth's belly, streams of that element wafted through, many more than Kiera had ever seen above the ground. Using her sight, she pulled some into her and used it to strengthen her trembling legs, and let it soothe her jumbled nerves. Hadn't Muukwa told Nick she was simple? Well, she felt like a waiting firestorm, and she needed to calm herself or she was going to give everything away the moment she saw Laszlo.

Where the tiers curved to angle the room, Nick opened the one door painted white. Narrow stairs lay behind it, actual torches lit it, and soot-blackened walls bracketed the stone steps. Without waiting to see if they followed, Nick stepped inside.

Heart thundering, Kiera followed third. No one had cleaned the floor at the bottom, and down here the stink was almost unbearable, especially with earth still thrumming through her veins. But unlike the Alaks, she could no more tell one person's smell from another's, and in this stink she doubted that down here even they could.

Before they reached the first cell, Nick looked behind, perhaps to gauge Muukwa's reaction, and asked, "What is that thing Kala wears round her neck? It looks like wood."

"She made it," Muukwa answered easily as she picked her bare steps to avoid a mess of something Kiera refused to think about on the floor. "I do not know its meaning to her, but I gave her a ribbon to bind it and she has not since taken it off."

"Hmmm. Is it spelled?" Nick wondered aloud, his eyes on Muukwa, and Kiera knew he hoped she'd react.

But Muukwa raised a hand, palm up in an *I don't know.* "I do not understand magic, Nick, but perhaps you would like to see it?"

Eyes hooded, he nodded and motioned for Kiera to approach. Head down, heart pounding, Kiera walked carefully until she stood in front of him and stared at his boots, now dirty with the shit and blood he hadn't bothered to step over. The wood held no magic, she knew that, nothing more than sentimental value wound its circle, but she'd been stupid to wear it, and she silently cursed herself for forgetting. It must look suspicious, a slave wearing a piece of wood around her neck. She'd never seen a slave wear anything but the clothes their lord gave them, and this made her stand out as very peculiar indeed.

His hand slid inside the neckline of Laszlo's shirt and plucked out the wooden star Laszlo had made her. When she wouldn't raise her face he jerked the ribbon tight, hurting her neck, and pulled the star to the side of her face where he could see it.

Of course if he had been a *sunwyr* he wouldn't need to touch her to search out magic—or maybe he just wanted the chance to frighten her. Since that seemed more likely, she cringed from his hand and kept her eyes on the floor.

After one final jerk he released the star and used two fingers to lift her chin. The look on his face, the naked lust, sent a snake of real fear boring into her gut, and she flinched back and pulled her chin out of his hand. With a chuckle he turned and walked past Muukwa, whose ebony eyes watched Kiera's face.

Her eyes flicked to Nick's back, and she offered Muukwa a small smile— *I'm fine*— before letting her head drop back down.

They passed four or five cages—and cages they were, tiny rooms fronted with metal bars and sporting holes cut in the stone floor for waste. Nothing besides what looked like one filthy blanket, and one man, peopled each. As they passed, when Muukwa came into view, men stared, Alaks who must have come to stand at the bars when they heard her voice, but no one spoke. Except for the footfalls, hers and Nick's, the entire room lay inside a blanket of silence.

When Nick stopped and waited for Muukwa to come see what he wanted, Kiera stopped, heart breaking, and tried to breathe. When she cast a sidelong glance at the man closest her, he stared back, face washed blank, and she wondered what he thought. Was he—this large, coal-haired man—shy and gentle like Kuruk, she wondered, or fierce like Laszlo? Did he long with every breath for one last view of the stars, or had he given up? Did someone outside pray for his release, would mourn his death, like she did for Laszlo? Her face must have given something of what she thought away, because the stone in his eyes softened for the briefest of moments before he turned away and stalked the three steps to the back wall, but he did not turn to face her again.

"He will be a champion," Nick was telling Muukwa, and she stepped closer so she could see him, though she knew it wouldn't be Laszlo. She didn't even know if Nick would show them Laszlo, but she knew he was here, down here somewhere, and now she knew how to get here and back out. She hoped that he would, though, because if he did she was going to use the spell Saman had taught her then—the final part of her plan—and take the chance that Vrishka would feel her close, get Laszlo and Muukwa out and flee. She'd call a grand, skywide firestorm if necessary to keep Laszlo and Muukwa safe, but she dared not do more than follow them like Kuruk had followed her until she found Laszlo, because the miles separating Vrishka from Talium looked less than two, and on horseback he could be here in fewer minutes than it would take her to find Laszlo.

But if he did not, if Nick didn't show Laszlo to them, she would wait until later, until the right moment, and use Saman's spell at the appointed time, a mark when Vrishka would be far less likely to feel it, then search out her husband and free him.

The man Nick offered was a large Alak, not as big as Laszlo, but close. Probably a bear, she thought, and wondered if Laszlo had found any of his tribesmen here. Kuruk had said he wouldn't fight another of his clan, and she wondered if that rule held here, too. But perhaps not, she thought dejectedly, when the lord would undoubtedly never permit it. These fights were one on one, and death visited so often here, and so easily.

Thoughts twisted, came round and presented themselves for reinspection. Could she really just cast Saman's spell if Nick showed them Laszlo? Could she really just leave these men down here, fuck all, and flee, leave them staring silently between their bars?

And what, exactly, would acting that rashly do to her plan for Fairbanks? Vrishka would know she was here, that she knew what he'd done, and was not mourning her loss in her bed back in Fairbanks. And if she couldn't get back to Fairbanks in time, warn the remaining soldiers, they would march out in a handspan of marks and directly into Vrishka's waiting hands, and four thousand unsuspecting soldiers was at least a tou and one important fact less than Vrishka would have.

Teeth ground as she clenched her jaw. She had to stop this. She was going to have to hold her feelings and bide her time, and do exactly what she had planned with Muukwa.

Nick walked them to another stall and offered a stream of commentary on another caged Alak, but Kiera tuned him out. Instead she stared at the floor and called earth, peeled tiny strands from the stream winding past one of her feet and fed it into her leg, then up and into her chest. Her heart slowed, but sounds become louder—the shuffle of feet, someone using their toilet, a snort as someone stifled a sneeze.

And a smell. One wafted to her in the filthy air so very like the one even a washing hadn't banished from the shirt she wore.

Her head lifted as she sought its source. Her lips parted so she could suck in more air. It was over there, she was sure of it, somewhere around the turn and down further than they'd walked this direction. She strained to see into the cells, but earth didn't help her eyes. Did Alaks see better, she wondered absently, and if so, why didn't earth help her? Maybe not, she thought, since she'd never noticed any she knew seeing any better than she did.

But did the others, like the eagles she and Kuruk had found? Did they have senses like their animals when they weren't shifted? And if that's how it worked, maybe she was just more like a—a monkey or something.

Kuruk. Thinking of him made her feel him, but that feeling told her that he was far, miles and miles, and that he was moving, but not quickly.

Instead of considering that, she wondered why her thoughts would not stop tumbling like pebbles in a stream. Was it nerves? Worry about the now, and nexturn? Maybe just the leavings from the fear that caught her every breath, and would there ever come a time when it lifted, or broke, and she felt safe again?

And thoughts of safety led her back to Laszlo. She exhaled, drew another breath, and used her tongue to wet her lips. Another breath, a long one, and she drew another few strands of earth into her leg and summoned it up. Eyes closed, she waited until her heart again slowed from well above a hundred beats a minute to let out her breath.

Could a mage develop an addiction to earth, she wondered inanely, and had to stifle a laugh. Using elements wouldn't hurt her, but even if they did, whom would she call for help? Agni? Would they have a group? *Hi, my name is Kiera and I'm an earthaholic.*

Nick's voice, the use of her name, cut through her thoughts and stabbed a spear of terror into her chest. The good part was that all thoughts of laughter died on that spear. "Is Kala all right?" he asked Muukwa as he walked to her. "She looks sick."

Muukwa followed behind him, eyes blazing, but whether from the treatment of her kinsmen or in anticipation of a threat to Kiera, she did not know.

Head down, Kiera waited until Nick approached her. He lifted her face, but she avoided his eyes.

"She does not look ill," Muukwa said matter-of-factly, "though the smell down here is nearly beyond bearing. Perhaps she choked." She laid a hand on Nick's arm, pulled him away from Kiera. "Let us not dawdle in assessing the slave's health. You can poke her with your cock until it shrinks after we conclude our business, if it pleases you." Muukwa paused to wave her free hand in front of her nose, as if that would wave away some small portion of the smell. "Ugh. You have shown me three fighters I could take in your pit," she told him as they walked. "I want you to show me your champions, Nick, and no more of the leavings."

Nick sputtered, then laughed. "Oh, Iyya, you are such a delight," he told her as he patted the hand lying on his arm. "And so fierce! But surely, surely, you see the strength in the one I just showed you. He is—mmmm—so strong."

"He is weakened, Nick, and will not recover."

Nick stopped. "Why do you say so?"

A shoulder lifted. "I have seen it before in those who fight. My grandmother would say the spirit has left them, but I say they are weak." She lifted her eyes to his. "Cull him, or spend him in the next match. You have one tonight, yes?"

Brows raised, Nick nodded and followed as Muukwa led him around the arched end and stared into a cell toward the front. "This one, he is one I want. See how quickly his eyes lift to mine when he hears my voice? And strong shoulders. Good legs. He will be fast, and tear the throat from any who face him." She pulled Nick from the cell and resumed their walk. At each, Muukwa stared in. "Why do some have women?"

His shoulders lifted when he shrugged. "A winner's reward, my dear. I have found it keeps them content."

"This one," Muukwa said as she gazed between bars. "I want this one, but not the woman."

"Ah. In this, I must decline, my sweet," Nick told her, and something in his voice lifted Kiera's eyes.

Muukwa snorted through her nose. "Even after seeing my Kala," she gestured to Kiera, "you would hold a champion from me? Surely, surely, a man as wealthy as you can find many more."

With small steps Kiera shuffled forward, but Nick blocked her view into the narrow cell. She edged toward the arena so she could see around him, but it didn't help. If she took one more step she'd be inside it, and if nothing else raised Nick's suspicion, her—the supposedly simple slave's—interest in one of the Alaks would, so she made herself slide back toward the wall and prayed no one could hear her heart.

Nick's hand captured Muukwa's. "You must know that I am loath to refuse you anything, my darling, but this one I must keep. Let us move on."

Wearing a disappointed look, Muukwa sighed and let Nick lead her past the cell. Nick's hand slid around her waist and pulled her close. Face near hers, he said something Kiera couldn't hear, and they both laughed.

It took every ounce of self control she had ever possessed to keep her steps slow as she walked to the cell. From beneath her lashes she cast a look in. But the sight that filled her eyes stopped her feet, and nothing, not Nick, not Vrishka, not God, could have made her lift even one of them.

Oh, yes. It was Laszlo. Pinched into a corner, hard-eyed, wearing a look of death, which he turned on her. Stripes, half-healed whip wounds, covered his bare chest and one cheek. And clinging to him was the singularly most breathtaking woman Kiera had ever seen, a young woman with dirty blonde hair and upturned eyes, and their arms wrapped each other as if warding against all the threats the world posed. Her head lay against his chest, and she stared hatred at Kiera, threatened death if she even looked at her man.

Thunder roared in Kiera's ears. Strength slipped out, bled away as if pumped through a torn artery, and her hands lifted, though she didn't know why. Someone screamed—maybe it was her—and the floor rose up as she fell.

CHAPTER 21

NICK WAS LIFTING HER, SHUSHING HER, and only then did Kiera realize she was still screaming.

"Pull her away," Muukwa urged, and Nick half-lifted Kiera and dragged her away from the sight. "The beast has frightened her."

"Barbarian," Kiera whispered as she struggled to gather her thoughts, calm her emotions. Reckless in her grief, she called as much earth as she could hold and fed it into her legs as Nick dragged her through a puddle of black liquid—blood perhaps—and further down the shit-stained floor.

Nick laughed in genuine amusement. "Mmmm. He is at that, Kala," he told her once they were out of eyesight of the cell, and held her arm while she stood. "Now calm yourself. I will not let him hurt you. Do you understand that?"

Her hand trembled when she pushed the hair from her eyes, but she managed to nod. Another breath, and earth slowed her heart. After one final look at her face, Nick turned from her and walked back to Muukwa, who stood with lips pursed and a hand on one hip. "I now believe I should have left her in that room," Muukwa told him. "The fighting does not upset her, but perhaps being this close to the beasts has done it."

The look on Nick's face said he didn't care, but he tried to sound concerned. "He is simply the worst one—mmmm—so vicious, which is why I cannot let you take him, my dear," he lied. "But here, look at this one, and tell me what you think. There are two, yes, that you like? Let me find another and we will conclude our accord for the girl."

"I have chosen one, Nick, but before I consent to take others, I want to see them fight," Muukwa told Nick as she threaded an arm through his. "I will choose the final ones during the matches."

A smile lifted Nick's lips and he leaned to press them against Muukwa's. A hand slid across her back and down to cut across a buttock. "Perhaps you will join me in my room, darling, before the games start, hmmmm?"

Muukwa raised a slow finger and pressed it against Nick's open mouth. "Not yet," she breathed. "Please me with the fighters you trade me, and I will take your cock until you cannot raise it." With that, she turned and led him back toward the stairs, but she caught the look he flashed over his shoulder at Kiera. "Nor her, Nick," she admonished through an open smile. "Buy her, and you may poke her until the thought of her *kuula* no longer lifts your cock."

BACK UPSTAIRS THE BAND PLAYED, and dancers turned and smiled into each other's faces as they spun each other on the floor, but it seemed less real than a film, a colorless caricature of life, and Kiera could summon no feeling for any of it. She should have been surprised at all the women, so many more than when she'd left for downstairs, but it didn't seem to matter. A brief wondering slipped through her thoughts, a curiosity at whether Nick had had a tournament going on when she'd last been here.

She hadn't known to ask.

But that, too, wafted away when her mind refused to hold it.

Instead of thinking, she stood behind Muukwa's chair and let her sight search the strands. Some part of her knew that the numbness was a blessing. Underneath, the black ocean roiled, crested, tried to break through, but a silver barrier held its waves from reaching high enough to fill her belly.

She found herself wishing for Amba, and Marco, and even Kuruk, all of whom could have been on another planet, or dead, for all the good her wishing did.

Well, at least Laszlo wasn't dead, and she knew that now that she was here, he wouldn't die. But despite that very great relief, things—well—things had changed. She would free him, free the others, but she would find her way to the army with Muukwa, or alone. And either was fine. They had enough men, and a good plan, and Laszlo—well, he could go someplace else. And if he wanted Fairbanks after all this was over, she would. Of all the betrayals, of all the things he could have done, this stabbed the most deeply, and he had known it would.

As her sight danced in the large band of fire a hundred feet above the manse, she supposed a better person would forgive him. Find a way to understand that in the worst situations, sometimes these things happened. He had loved her, after all, and she did know that, just as she knew he still did.

But love wasn't enough. And even if he thought he was going to die anyway, even if he thought she'd never know, neither those nor any other set of facts would raise her mercy high enough where she could forgive him. And it never would. Time would, she knew, dull the pain, tease her into forgetting the blood that gushed from the open wound his betrayal had cut. And maybe in different circumstances she would have found a way to see past it, given time.

But not this time. Not after what had happened between them in the past. He knew, knew as intimately as one could know another's pain, what the betrayal he had let her believe he had committed had cost her.

When the band ended its set for the night, ten or twenty songs later, dancers slipped off the floor, and in a susurration of cloth and movement people drifted out of the great room. In mere minutes, when the room stood half empty, Nick rose, lifted Muukwa to her feet, and led the way into the entry and down the right-hand hall to the end, and down the stairs to the pit.

With tired feet, Kiera followed. Men jostled her, and some used their proximity to sneak a hand to brush a breast, or her buttock. Sometimes she flinched away, but she refused to lift her eyes until Muukwa's hand found hers and dragged her forward through the throng.

After exiting onto the tiers Muukwa pulled Kiera to the top level and down toward the white door, following in Nick's wake. But he stopped short of the door, turned and gestured for Muukwa to take the steps down to the railing where she would have the better view. Kiera did not want to follow, but standing up top with Nick would be even worse.

A hand on her shoulder stopped her first step. She turned to Nick, who motioned for her to remove the shirt that covered her. After just one deep breath she used both hands to pull it over her head, and watched his eyes take in her body as it slipped to the floor. Hot lust burned in his eyes, and she turned away and tried not to feel shame, and fear, but the loathing would not be banished.

On both sides men stepped close to the railing, but Kiera squeezed as far inward as she could, close enough to touch Muukwa, and put Nick out of her mind for the time. A snake of nausea twisted inside her when a group in livery emerged from the stairway, spread out, and approached the clots of men. Similar to Vayu's tournament, the ones she could hear provided the names of the next set of fighters, laid odds, and collected money. On a paper in one hand they made quick notes following each transaction, probably who bet on whom and for how much. And women, slave women of varying ages and looks, followed the bet-takers, all wearing clothes that hugged hips and revealed breasts. Some seemed truly interested in attracting the men's attention, while others avoided eyes and shrank from touches. And different men, she noted, liked different reactions. Some smiled when a bold woman approached, used a hand to rub her back, touch an offered breast. Others' eyes lit when a woman avoided his gaze, and broke away to follow.

Horror, then rage flamed and consumed disgust, leaving white flame and dusty ash inside Kiera's heart. But not yet, she told herself. Hold fast.

A voice turned her head. Someone on her left spoke in a familiar voice. Her eyes lifted and her heart stopped.

Chanda.

Eyes wide, she stared down into the empty arena below, wrapped shaking hands around the thin pole that topped the stone rail, then forced herself to slow her breathing. She was wearing a disguise, she reminded herself. And Saman's spell would work as well on him as any. It worked on her. Sure, this complicated things, but she would just have to be careful, she told herself as she exhaled a slow breath, and not pull earth, or anything else. Was Vrishka here, too, she wondered, and hope rose. Wouldn't that be wondrous—

But then her heart exploded in her chest. *Oh my God*. Muukwa had said—

"Iyya!" Chanda exclaimed, surprise in his voice, and from under her lashes Kiera watched Muukwa's head raise, and turn. A smile that didn't look forced raised her lips, and Muukwa stepped behind Kiera, slid between Chanda and her, and pushed Kiera back with one hip.

From behind Muukwa, and with her head down, she couldn't see how Chanda took Muukwa, or if he thought it odd to find her here. His words were cautious, his tone teasing, but she knew Chanda lied well, knew he hid his thoughts even better, and it made her worry.

And then, just to further complicate things, Nick clicked down the stairs—Kiera knew the sound his boots made from their earlier walk—and stepped to where he completed a triangle with Muukwa and Chanda. "Good eve, Lord Chanda. Well, well. I see you two know each other." Kiera heard the smile in his voice, but she also heard the something else underneath—the annoyance, perhaps even jealousy, that he couldn't quite banish.

Muukwa's arm raised—had Chanda lifted it?—and after a slight pause Chanda said, "Yes. I am acquainted with the lovely Iyya, Lord Nick. She came seeking my advice. Enjoying the pit, my dear?" He laughed then, and Kiera wondered why. "But I have come thisturn to make money." His clothes rustled against the rail as he shifted, and Kiera imagined he'd turned to look out into the arena. "I have a propitious inkling, Mayor. On the third match, is it not?" He laughed again, and this time it sounded ugly. "I have vayans that will bring more before my eyes close. I feel it."

Nick had relaxed as Chanda spoke, but Kiera could not banish her worrying. What if Nick wanted her to dance here, say, between matches? She couldn't, not with Chanda standing there. He'd know instantly she pulled water and how she cast the spell, if not the mechanism through which she fed the energy. And what if Vrishka was here, and she just hadn't seen him? She couldn't just ask. What if she missed him, missed her chance to end this war without a single soldier's death?

This way lay madness, she knew it did, but she could not stop her thoughts. And the turning of water for which she waited was still marks away. Five long marks. In one mark it would be first water—3 a.m.—but she must wait until second water so the rest of the manse would be asleep. She didn't know if she, or the spell, was strong enough to work on the manse's entire population, or would even travel far enough to do so, and she hadn't thought to test it and see. And she could not do it except during water, during those first ten or so minutes when it pushed air aside and burst heavily forth before slowing to a steady flow. Only then could she hope to shadow the spell, which would profoundly affect the flow of local water streams, from Vrishka and all the other water mages camped a few miles away.

But when she cast it, Chanda might still be here. Not that she cared, but Vrishka, if he waited chastely back at his camp for morning, would. And likely very much.

The face of the man Kiera had seen through the bars rose, and her teeth ground. As she waited, one man each match would die. That man, who had something good in him—she'd seen it—and others.

Someone—Nick maybe—said Vrishka's name and Kiera's attention snapped back. "And did Lord Vrishka accompany you?" Muukwa asked, sounding like someone trying to be polite, but Kiera's exhale blessed her. Smart Muukwa, to whom she would never be able to repay this night's debt.

"He did not," Chanda answered smoothly. "Though I believe that he may consent to come nexturn. Will you be here? He would enjoy knowing you, I am certain."

A barb? Either way, Muukwa pressed on, a smile in her voice. "I would be pleased to know him, Lord Chanda." She shifted to face the arena, and Kiera could see her profile, and her face, which looked clear. "And now I shall anxiously await nexturn."

Behind her a black door opened, and a light-haired man emerged, then walked to one of the liveried men, one hand in a chest pocket. When Kiera's gaze turned back, she found Chanda watching her. She felt her eyes open wide, tried to stop it, and dropped her face.

She watched him take a step, tried to edge around Nick, but Nick's hand fell on Chanda's arm. "My lord, she is not yet one of mine," Nick told him in a tone that tried to sound mournful, but Kiera knew he wouldn't let Chanda touch her in any case, not until he had finished with her.

She tried to feel happy about that, but all she felt was sick.

But then the games began, and gave her stomach a better reason to twist.

KIERA BREATHED A FERVENT THANKS skyward that she had waited. It had not occurred to her, though it should have, that the cages holding the Alak fighters were magicked. What had she thought, she wondered—that the doors just closed and the men waited politely inside for an invitation out? The idea of keys, at least, should have occurred, but not even that possibility had teased her mind.

Before the fighting, a tall, heavily built man in livery had approached Nick, who dug a small amethyst bar from a hip pocket and handed it to the man, who'd nodded his thanks before opening the white door that led to the dungeon. And now she needed to mark that man, follow him so she knew where to find him when she manifested her spell.

After a handful of minutes the first two men entered the ring, but they did so without the fanfare of Vayu's. No mounted horsemen cried welcome, and even the men did not posture, but came out slowly, warily, and strode toward each other with no evidence of malice.

Kiera saw Muukwa's hand clench the rail as they met, one jumped the other and down they tumbled, but her face remained serene, even interested, though her eyes belied it. After a half minute of fisticuffs, one changed beneath the other's arms—a wolf—and then the other, also into a wolf.

Men around her began talking in excited voices, and until they did she hadn't realized that all had lain mostly silent. But Kiera closed her eyes and sent her sight skyward.

Below her the snarls of fighting dogs broke her thoughts again and again, brought her sight tumbling from the sky, but each time she sent it back up, urged her ears to close. She could do nothing, not now, but pray that would end quickly, and she dared to hope that neither would die. That none would before the next water turned, because she was finished with this. So much hung in the balance, but she had another plan, one that had hatched as her sight meandered the streams biting into the earth surrounding this pit of hell. One that she prayed would soothe any suspicion Vrishka might feel when Chanda did not return.

When it ended applause erupted, some hooted, and Kiera forced herself to look into the field below her. One lay clearly dead with his throat torn out, one stood over him, head hung low. Even to the fighters, then, there was no victory. Only a chance to live another turn and to die in the next match.

Liveried men, some with wine, some taking bets, rushed to fill the pause that followed. Chanda's attention turned to one of the bet-takers, and Kiera took the opportunity to pull just a few strands from an earthstream that flowed near her nose. Valen was a *sunwyr*, but of air, yet even so she knew he had been able to use earth, at least a little. She'd seen him trying to force Kuruk to change in his magic room that long ago turn. And Chanda was a *sunwyr*, Agni-trained, and might too be strong enough to know if a mage disrupted a flow, even of his opposite. To minimize the risk she stepped into it, as if unknowing, and peeled off a few strands.

A knot relaxed in her chest as it filled her, and she released the breath she'd held. Thoughts slowed, a blessed lift of the worry and the sickness she felt. Another half mark or so was all she had left. She could do this.

Eyes opened to find Chanda staring at her, and the breath she'd been exhaling caught. She dropped her eyes to the floor in front of him, heart pounding even through the earth, and cursed herself. *Stupid, stupid, stupid!* Just what would she do if all this was blown because she couldn't deal with the sight these people saw every turn?

Oh, God, she prayed, and felt her fists clench. *Please let me think of a way to salvage this.*

A foot lifted as he took the first step toward her, and then another. But then bared feet stepped between them, and Kiera raised her eyes.

"She is not for the taking," Muukwa told him, and her voice said she meant it.

Without changing expression, Chanda stepped around her and approached. "I have seen her before," he said, perhaps to Muukwa, and perhaps to Kiera. "Though I cannot remember where."

Holy God. She had not even considered that by using a servant from Fairbanks for this spell, someone from there might recognize her. Well, she rationalized a little desperately, she hadn't actually thought that she'd run into anyone from Fairbanks.

And at Chanda's words Nick turned and walked to stand at his elbow. "Lord Chanda, did you say that you have seen this girl before?"

Stark fear and anger warred in Kiera's chest, and she put her head down to hide them. It wouldn't help anything to stare defiance into Chanda's face, even less so with Nick watching, and the trembling bow string upon which her emotions balanced was leaning that way at the moment.

From behind Chanda Muukwa laughed in genuine amusement, then wiggled between Chanda and the rail to where she could see Kiera. "You have not seen her before, my lord, though perhaps you have seen one that brings her face to mind. Her stock is Barrow, I am told, and are you not camped with their army? Surely it is one of the many whores in whom you poke your cock whose memory rises."

A laugh, hysteria no doubt, snaked through Kiera's belly, shoved terror aside, and she pulled her chin closer to her chest and tried to still her mouth.

"'One of the many whores'?" Chanda echoed, shock ringing his voice, and Kiera nearly lost hold of her laugh.

A smile stood high in Muukwa's. "Oh, my lord," she told him, and ran the fingers of one hand down his arm, "yours is such a strong body, and a strong body has strong needs. Tell me you have held your pleasures, but I will not believe you."

Only Muukwa could turn whoremongering into a compliment, Kiera thought, and had to force herself to keep her head from shaking in disbelief.

And then the next fight started.

SOUNDS FROM THE THIRD FIGHT drew both Kiera's sight and her eyes down, and when she looked, really looked, her heart stopped.

Laszlo.

Was this the fight Chanda had come to see? she wondered as her gaze slid left and to his intently watching face. Hadn't he said the third? That son of a bitch. God help him, because when this was over his ass was hers, and there was no more mercy left inside her, not for him.

Movement drew back her eyes. Her mouth made an O, the start of a "no," but although she pressed her lips closed, her eyes refused.

Unlike the first two fights, this one seemed dramatic—and not just because it was her husband pacing the ring below. Instead of a cautious stride, both men—both very large, naked men—walked the edge of the field, circling, shoulders set aggressively, lips peeled back from teeth.

The cuts on Laszlo's body had healed, and despite her anger her heart wept, wondered how many times during these turns his body had been forced to heal.

Shouts sounded, one here, one across the field. Caustic tears rose and burned her eyes. How many minutes remained, she thought desperately, and at last her eyes closed and she reached out to test the air. Minutes. A handful of minutes.

A rush of feet, and her eyes opened when the two met, both changed into their bears, one black, one shading to brown. Frenzied claws ripped flesh, jaws snapped through skin, screams tore the air, and cheers rose on all sides of the tier.

Another scream sounded and the black flew back and smashed into the smooth stone wall beneath her feet. In less than a heartbeat the brown, Laszlo, leapt through the air and landed on him, sent them both crashing to one side. From this angle she couldn't see the fight unless she leaned over the rail like most everyone around her was doing, but she refused. Instead she prayed, begged God to keep her husband alive for the minutes that remained.

Water came. A gush, then an ebb, but it was too little, and still too soon.

Yet another scream sounded, this one of unmistakable pain, and shouts erupted, then cheers. Eyes closed, then opened just as the locked pair rolled away from the wall and into her clear sight.

Blood was everywhere. The floor, their bodies, and it sprayed off in a ruby mist as they struggled. Who was winning, she wondered desperately, and then hated the thought, and herself for thinking it.

This had to stop. *Stop*. She was finished.

Eyes slammed shut. Water was coming, a gush, another ebb, but it was going to have to be enough. A deep breath. Hands fisted as she drew down her sight, held to it as tightly as she knew, used it to shield her chest.

"Muh-lek," she whispered, and opened her hands before the last letter sounded. With both index fingers she drew the shape Saman had shown her into the air beneath her hands, a point-down triangle crossed by one then two vertical lines, top to bottom, and then she released her sight and pulled as hard as she could. Water from everywhere.

It hit her like a wave from all directions, felt as though it drenched her, but instead of holding it, trying to spin it, she held her breath and sent it out as fast as it came, out to join the water gushing as elemental water pushed and tore apart the last streams of air marking the former mark.

It took seconds—perhaps ten—and when the last of it had gone she opened her eyes to silence. A smile lifted her lips, the first real satisfaction she'd felt in too long, the first clean feeling she'd had all night. Around her, everywhere, bodies lay, eyes closed, breaths even, lost in deep sleep. Trays near servers still clanked as they settled. Shining puddles of wine trailed down the stone floor from broken glasses.

Perhaps a half mark remained to do all that needed done, but she doubted she'd need a fraction of it. Based on the way the spell had felt, and the amount of water she'd pulled, she knew that she had not touched one soul in the house above. But then, she didn't know exactly how Saman's spell worked, much less how to expand it. Instead, he had assured her she didn't need to understand, and he'd been right. It had worked well enough, and before it lifted she'd finish this, wake Muukwa, go out into the nighttime trees, and execute the second part.

She stopped to pick up the shirt Nick had made her strip off and slid it on before opening the white door, then looked back at Muukwa as she pulled the hem to cover her backside and wondered whether to wake her now for help. She decided against it. She wanted no one to hear what words she had for Laszlo.

The man with the amethyst key had not come back up. Kiera had stood so she could watch the white door, but she'd been afraid he had gone out another exit that she hadn't seen. Her fear was in vain, however, as he lay at an odd angle at the foot of the stairs. After she reassured himself that he hadn't hurt himself when he fell—though she really shouldn't care—she rifled through his pockets until she found the key in the one at his right hip. Instead of opening any doors, however, she walked onto the field.

Her breath caught at the sight of Laszlo lying there, crumpled, blood oozing from a dozen deep cuts in his side. Both he and the other Alak had shifted back—perhaps sleep triggered it, she thought. She made herself walk the floor separating her from him.

His back, which lay toward her, was filthy. Without the power of healing that lay in all Alaks, she had no doubt some horrible disease would be rampaging through his veins and stealing what life remained.

Knots filled her stomach, stones that weighed more than the manse in which she stood, but she forced herself to step around where she could see his face. That face, so sweet when relaxed in sleep, the face she loved more than her own life, and perhaps the life of anyone else.

But one she could no longer live with.

With a foot, she nudged his shoulder. Watched his eyes open, look up. Expressionless his face remained as he rolled to sit, then stand. His muscles stilled as he watched her from hooded eyes, waited for her words.

Kiera lifted off the shirt, his shirt, and handed it to him. With a hand he took it, but held it at one side. Trembling fingers lifted to her mouth, and she used her tongue to wet them, then reached inside the costume and rubbed the mark on her chest away. As she did, some strand of something popped, snapped inside her chest, and she knew she now looked like herself again.

Laszlo opened his mouth to speak, but she raised an ink-covered palm to stop him. With the other, she handed him the amethyst key. He took it, gingerly, his eyes on hers, but closed his mouth.

"Use this key," Kiera told him quietly, "to open the cells. Free the Alaks here, Laszlo, and then I want you to go with them. Someplace away. Do not return to Fairbanks." She expected surprise, something, but his eyes stayed on hers, his face expressionless. After a breath, an attempt to slow her pounding heart, to still her shaking hands, she continued. "Before I go, you will listen to me, to what I have to say, and you will not speak or I will send you back to sleep and wake someone else to do this."

She held his eyes, let him see that she meant every word, and lifted her hands. Used them to untwist the knot tying the wooden comb round her neck, and dropped it on the floor at his feet. "As of this moment, I abjure you." Despite her commitment to this, her voice broke, but she didn't let her eyes drop. "I divorce you. You are no longer welcome in my home, or my bed. Take your—your whore—and go. I wish you happiness, Laszlo, I really do."

His eyes closed and she turned to go, but pain rose, a jagged knife that sliced her heart in two, more words bubbled from the blood that flowed, and she wanted them said, so she spun back around. Struggled to keep her voice from the scream that threatened. "I want you to know that I know this was hell for you, a hell beyond my imagining. And that I'm sure you thought you'd die, and never see me again, and maybe that's why." At his impassive face, this face she loved, and wanted to hate, red rage and black despair rose and burned her heart to ashes. "But I died, Laszlo!" she shouted, and heard it echo inside the arena. "I *died* that day they told me you were dead! I pressed my face into the ice and prayed for death to take me!" A sob escaped, but she clenched a fist to her belly and wrestled herself back under control. A breath, another, as she stared, maybe for the last time, into the face that had named her *beloved* but had taken another.

"I risked everything," she whispered through trembling lips. "Ten thousand lives I risked to save yours. And God help me, but even knowing what you did, I'd do it again. I have loved you, love you so much, but I can never forgive this, Laszlo." Her head shook, and she heard her voice rising, but couldn't care that it did. "It is the one thing you know I cannot bear. The one thing we gave each other that we gave to no one else, and the thought—" Her breath caught, and she made herself stop. She lifted a hand, a signal that she had finished, then turned to mount to the stair and to wake Muukwa. "You have a quarter mark to get everyone out," she said without looking back. "And then I'm bringing this goddamned house down."

CHAPTER 22

FROM A SPOT INSIDE THE TREELINE, HIGH UP the first hill, Kiera waited for almost a half mark before calling the fire that ran beneath the ground. A shifted Muukwa had gone to fetch the pack—and Kiera's coat—but despite the bitter cold Kiera wanted to wait here to watch her handiwork, even though she could have done this as easily from two more hills back. Watching Nick's manse fall would help heal the sickening something she couldn't shake from a night inside it.

While she'd let her mind, or rather her sight, wander and trace the elements last night, including the earthstreams that constantly traversed the house, Kiera had discovered that Nick's manse lay atop a cavernous fault in the earth. Better, less than a mile below and around that fault, veins of liquid fire flowed. Apparently here, like the Alaska she'd come from, the earth still moved, changed, and volcanoes still erupted as they did back home.

Yet as angry, as sickened as she felt, she couldn't bring herself to murder innocent people—and even after Laszlo cleared out the enslaved Alak, some would surely still remain. Servants, slaves, women whom men brought, and even some of the men. So instead of bringing the fire all the way up to swallow the house in what would have been a beautiful, cleansing death, she used it, and earth magic, to carve away the support holding the ground in place above the fault, an upside-down V upon which Nick had unknowingly built his house.

The earth shook as the fire carved, a small quake, and she heard shouts as people ran from the house. A smile lifted her lips as she sank her sight back into the ground, let it call and direct a worm of fire to lick yet another slide of rock into its fiery red mouth.

Another quake struck as the rock fell, one so big that she would have lost her footing had she been standing. She held the fire, locked it in place, and sent her sight to examine the rock. Too much off—not enough space between the fire vein and the soft dirt filling the fault—and the fire would pop the thin skin and rush to fill the gaping space, slide both up and down, and it was the up that would pose the problem. And as strong as she was, Kiera didn't know if she could stop it. A lot of force, pressure from the earth's belly, pushed the fire up toward the surface as if it wanted it birthed into the air above. Perhaps she could seal it inside, dead end it somehow, but on the chance that she could not, she'd best not gamble.

But, oh—the waiting was hard. The nibbling and testing, and nibbling and redirecting and testing again.

The best part—well, the second best part—was that neither Vrishka nor any mage would see her working, even if they looked underground, which no mage she knew did. But even if they did—even if Vrishka suspected treachery and looked into the earth, all he'd see was lava. She used no elemental fire energy, pulled from no streams. She had just used her sight to urge earth wending the rock to weaken the stone, and to thus lead a flow of manifest fire to peel off stony layers in a slightly different direction. Showed it a weakness, urged it into it.

There. As another piece of support fell away, the thin skin of granite topping the V cracked—she'd kept the fire far from that part—and the underground waterstream that ran above it nosed its way inside, then tore back the skin and dumped untold gallons inside the open maw beneath it. When it did, the earth above it collapsed all at once, like a giant hand pressing into a series of brittle boards, and the ground shook again. A great thunder sounded as a sinkhole of sorts opened up and the earth supporting Nick's house fell to fill it.

A grin split Kiera's face as she opened her eyes and forced herself to stand on the shaking ground. The thin moonlight reflected on the snow, and on it people ran back and forth across the field. Screams filled the air as the house continued to sink into the ground. Even those inside it, she was sure, would be fine—the hole was a big one and wouldn't crush the house—but never, never would another house be built in this spot. Never would a pit be dug into the earth here, and never would men be celled and forced to fight for the pleasure of others in this spot. And that was something good.

The skin nearly jumped from Kiera's bones when, from behind her, Muukwa commented, "An impressive sight."

Hand over her heart, Kiera turned to face the fully clothed, grinning woman, whose eyes still looked bleak despite her smile. She had not asked, not once, why they had left without Laszlo. Inside, after Kiera had woken her, she had paused just long enough to stare over the rail at him. Offered no words, good or bad, but had turned then and followed Kiera out.

"Thank you," Kiera grinned back, and took the coat that Muukwa offered. "Even at night, a palace falling into the ground is a sight to behold."

"I will not argue," Muukwa told her, and turned to watch the people the moonlight showed running across the open snow from Nick's house. There had to be a hundred at least. And by the volume of sound, most were still screaming even though the ground had stopped shaking.

Without turning her head, Kiera said softly, "By the way, I would be very pleased if you came to love Marco," then turned, picked up her pack, and walked to crest the hill.

WITHOUT TALKING, THEY MADE THEIR WAY through the forest and north, Kiera following the pull that was Kuruk. They'd napped, a precious few marks, and ate the dried fish Amba had insisted they take, and then Kiera had made herself swallow another packet of the powder when she'd gone behind a tree to relieve her bladder. Using a near constant pull of earth, Kiera could keep a very fast pace—not quite Muukwa's best, she was sure, but then they didn't need to go any faster than an army marched, and she was sure they were still ahead by some miles, though she'd have to be careful and stay further even than Vrishka's forward scouts.

She had waited to make sure Vrishka did march before they left. After her men showed up he'd sent a hundred or so marching men toward Fairbanks, presumably including Chanda, then packed up and marched the remainder of his army, and those she'd sent, out and back toward Barrow, job in Fairbanks accomplished.

And she planned to join them, just her, at some point before they reached the Natuvik Pass. In her hat, and wearing her heavy coat and brown pants—the same ones the foot soldiers wore—she would look like just another. When she did, Muukwa would race off to join the others waiting in the pass.

The marks passed, one after another, as the sun rose higher in the sky, and the walking melted the fear that filled her belly, at least for the time. Another turn without fog, for which Kiera found herself grateful. Fighting in the fog would be a nightmare, especially for those waiting in the pass. Using earth, or more precisely, calling earth, didn't tire her the way using the other elements did, and she wondered why. Did it have to do with metabolism?

She watched Muukwa walking, almost carelessly, so light on her feet, and thought biology must have something to do with it. After all, the Alaks used it all the time, almost every minute of every turn. Catching it, however, was hard for her, and took effort, but the earth she caught, ironically enough, seemed to restrengthen whatever magic muscles she used to pull it. A conundrum, for certain, and one she meant to ask Saman and maybe Agni about when they got back home.

What would home feel like, she wondered, without Laszlo? She'd move out, have someone help her move her things to the new room. Would she be sad, she wondered, then knew she would be, but it wouldn't be the utter devastation that had claimed her when she thought Laszlo dead. She hadn't lied when she told Muukwa she would never love another man. It wasn't in her to do it, not after she'd given everything to him, and every turn she'd miss him, perhaps almost unbearably at times. But would she ever be able to stand the thought of touching him, of him touching her, even if she let him come back? Her gut said *no*, and she believed it.

And maybe he would know that—she suspected he did—and he would stay away. It would make things a lot easier for her, though she certainly wouldn't begrudge him visiting Amba, or Marco, or even Alex. Just not in her presence. And maybe someday she could bear to have him move back to Fairbanks, but not with her. And not right away.

Muukwa could carry her words to him. Or maybe once she got back, she'd write them down. That way she could be sure he knew exactly how she felt, and what she needed. She knew that he would respect that, and would try to understand, because he did love her. She had never doubted that.

Her breath colored the air in front of her as she stopped to gauge the mark. The high sun confirmed what her sight found—noontide had come, and during this, fourth fire, was the best time for her to join the army, if for no other reason than her magic ran strongest for the next mark.

Using nearly numb fingers she snapped, and Muukwa turned. Kiera gestured at herself, then down the hill. *I am going to await the army.* Muukwa nodded her understanding, sent Kiera a smile, then turned and loped ahead far faster than Kiera could have possibly have gone, even with all the earth she could hold, and Muukwa was still *barefoot.*

Still shaking her head, Kiera made her way down the hill. After a few steps, she found a fallen bough and used it to clean her tracks as she stepped down. This way the forward scouts, should one come this way, would hopefully think the person whose tracks he crossed still continued ahead. And if not—well, she'd send him to sleep and backtrack before anyone noticed, though she prayed that wouldn't happen. Vrishka was bound to miss a scout that didn't return, though she'd be gone before they found him unharmed and sleeping in the snow, and when he woke, he'd tell a story she hoped no one would believe. Further, she'd pushed her hair into her hat, and thought she could pass for a man in the bulky coat, so Vrishka would be looking for a man, and not her, and if she had to, she could strip off the coat and the hat, pull earth to stay alive, if not warm.

It wasn't a great plan, she knew, but she had no other. And the truth was that she really wanted to be with the marching men, her men, who risked their lives for her, for Fairbanks, and she couldn't keep them safe from up ahead.

As she waited and stared down into the flatlands below, it occurred to her that she could just head north, follow Muukwa, and avoid these risks—risks to both her and to her men should Vrishka somehow divine her presence. The more she thought about it, the sounder that seemed, and she stood.

A sound turned her head. From behind her. She sank back down, wedged herself into the lee of the two pines she'd found growing close enough to touch. But below her, sounds rose, too. The army was coming.

Her teeth ground. Was this a scout? Weren't forward scouts supposed to scout—well—forward of the army? Though technically he was ahead, just not very far. Maybe he was a side scout, then? She hadn't heard Laszlo talk about those, but it made sense to have some.

And speaking of that, who *exactly* would she get to manage the god-damned army? She didn't even know what to look for, or from whom she could—should—choose. Not really. As her recent treks around the city had shown her, a good leader needed such a wide range of skills, and smarts. Oh, and commitment. A hard worker. And very great strength. Did anyone in Fairbanks have all those?

She doubted it, and as she did, she realized that she was going to have to ask Laszlo to come back. Not with his whore, though. She would not let him bring that woman inside the city. If he did, she would leave. Things would be settled enough, she thought, that she could—though it would be a horrible thing, and she would miss those she'd come to love so very much.

Another sound, a foot breaking snow, she was sure, and this time closer. She cursed silently. *Just go on*, she urged him with her thoughts, *and scout over there.*

Her eyes closed. What if he was an Alak? Well, if he was, covering her tracks would hardly matter, would it? If Kuruk could follow her across a field during a blizzard, any Alak would surely smell her out here, a woman hiding in the trees during a clear turn. Why, she wondered desperately, did she never think of these things?

Below her, the army began to pass. Thousands of men, neatly arranged into squares, crossed the plain below as they headed north. How much farther was it to Natuvik, she wondered, then sought her link with Kuruk to find out. A handful of miles. Maybe five, she thought with some relief. Not far.

Eyes closed, she called earth. Teeth clenched as she pulled, more and then more, until when she opened her eyes she saw a green mist covering everything. She was close enough to the pass that even if she had to take out a scout, the army would likely reach the pass before Vrishka noticed.

Should she stand, she wondered, or just wait for him to find her? Both had advantages. If she popped up she'd startle him, and have a moment to suck all his water out so he'd fall. But if he found her, she could show herself as a woman, pretend to be frightened, beg him and so on—and in the interim, suck all his water out.

With a hand she pulled the hat off her head and let it fall to the snow. A Skani wouldn't hear it, and an Alak would already know right where she was.

A time passed, and she heard nothing. Afraid to relax, she pulled more earth and sent it to her legs. Just in case.

And that pull saved her life.

From above, a figure fell on her and knocked her face-first into the snow. An arm snaked around her neck and squeezed the bone against her throat, Alak hard, intent on breaking her neck.

Her hands flew up. She had no breath to scream. Fingers tore into flesh, then she wedged a hand between the arm and her throat and pushed it a micron off her windpipe. Enough air squeezed by to grant her a small breath, and she used the moment to pull more earth into her feet, closest to the stream. The wedged hand held the bone from her windpipe enough to wheeze small breaths, and she held him there until the earth filled her, and prayed he'd think she was weakening.

When it did, she used the unwedged hand to push down into the snow, brought her knees in, and surged back. They lifted, balanced together for a moment on both their knees, then fell back and tumbled down the hill, his arm still locked around her throat.

It hurt. The falling, over and over and over, snow-dusted rocks smashing her hip, her knee, and the arm squeezing her windpipe, but no matter how hard she tried, she could neither dislodge him or the arm.

And still, she dared not call fire. Not this close to Vrishka. So close—they were so close—the moment she did, he'd know. The five miles that seemed so close just minutes ago she now knew were too many. If it had been a mile, she would have. Would trust that she could signal them to come while she held off the bulk of the attack for the handful of minutes it took her three thousand to get there.

But five miles. Even if they could hear her scream—and who could scream that loud?—even on Alak feet five miles would take too long. She was a powerful mage, no doubt about that, but was she strong enough to hold four to five thousand enemy soldiers and who knew how many water mages? Not likely.

Near the bottom, the hill fell steeper than it looked. They hit the solid brown of a lone spruce and the jolt knocked the man's arm free. She slipped out of his grip. Gasping as she slid, one hand at her bruised throat, Kiera pushed out her feet, tried to stop, and finally did, then scrambled back up toward the spot near the tree where the man still lay, face down. Pulling earth as she stepped—and she was tempted to use a yar or two—she filled her aching body and prayed no one from the army, just a handspan of yards and a sharp drop behind her, would see her.

Scout or not, she was going to send this aggressive son of a bitch to sleep so he couldn't follow her. But for the smaller working, and not a group, she had to touch him—Saman had shown her both spells—and so up she climbed.

His back rose as he breathed. Silky chestnut hair covered the head of this average-sized man, but his clothes confused her. Thin, nearly white pants covered his legs, and a long-sleeved shirt of the same color and fabric clung to his back so tightly she could see the cut of his muscles. Did Vrishka's scouts wear clothes like this?

But all thought—all the world—fell away, leaving just two green eyes, when he lifted his head and turned a shark's smile to her. "Hello, Kiera."

Hunter.

She should curse herself, or rage at fate, or despair at the turn of events. But nothing came. Nothing except disbelief, even when he rose to his feet.

"You took Julia from me, Kiera," he told her nonchalantly as he dusted snow with both hands from the front of his shirt, and then his pants. "What happened was your fault. Your. Fault. You had no right to interfere. To take her from my house. *To tell her those things*." He raised his eyes, and for the first time Kiera saw the rage burning behind his eyes, a bottomless, black rage, and the hair rose on her arms, the back of her neck. "She was *my wife*." Seamlessly his face relaxed as his lips curled into a smile. "And then you lied to the judge so you could take Alex. You, the fat bitch with no life, wanted my son since no man'll stick his dick in you." His smile widened. "No man but that fucking James Asana, huh, and some fucking slave trash you scraped up?" He shook his head, still smiling. "Well, they can't have you. You're dead, bitch."

And then he was on her. She hadn't even seen him leap. Lightning fast they fell back, and breath gushed out when she landed on her back. His fists pummeled her face, blood flew, but earth kept her from passing out. Fire—she had to call fire. No, no, she couldn't. *And he can shield even if I do*, the sane part of her mind wailed. Belatedly she began fighting back. Fists, fingers, then with knees. She hurt him, surprised him, but even with earth to aid her he was the stronger, and the more aggressive.

A strained sound pushed past his lips as he shoved himself backward, out of the lock she had pulled him into to try and stifle his reach. She surged up, smashed a fist into his face, and he fell back, but not off her. With one hand he reached behind him, and when she saw that hand again he held a knife. A large knife, one that would slice the life from her body. Where had he hidden it? Her ears thundered and she called earth, called it as hard as she could, and felt the streams rise even from the earth beneath her and melt into her body.

When he lunged she was ready. She caught his arm with her hands, pushed it out, out and above their heads. His hand twisted and he pulled free, then stabbed down, down and into her gut, then again, and again. Blood splashed up with each blow, and her hands fought to catch his, but he jerked it away, smashed her face with the knuckles holding the knife, and plunged it in again, this time between her ribs and into her chest. She felt a lung stutter, and breath left her in a *whoosh* as it collapsed.

One moment he was on her, smiling obscene joy into her face, and the next a dark streak flashed in front of her eyes and he was gone. A hand—someone's hand, or their foot—caught the hem of her coat, and whatever had pulled him off jerked the three of them over the ledge.

The fall was short, perhaps a dozen feet, but Kiera's arms wouldn't lift to keep her head from the rocks below, and she hit them hard, then slid off the forward side and into the snow. Her head fell to one side, and as she struggled to breathe her eyes focused. When they did, her lips parted with a joy so sharp it stung. Fifteen feet away a bear—a giant brown bear—screamed its rage as it stripped the flesh from the Shunakah who had taken her life.

Laszlo had come.

She knew he would blame himself for staying just far enough behind her that he couldn't reach her in time to stop this. But all of it was her fault. If she had been thinking about more than herself, she would have asked him to come, made him wait until the battle was over. It would have been the better choice, not just for her, but for Fairbanks. And he'd known that, and followed her.

Thoughts drifted, made little sense as her life leaked away from the slices in her gut and chest, as the pierced organs shut down.

A shadow fell across her face, and she looked into Laszlo's. A shaking hand, his hand, found her face, wrapped her cheek in his fingers. A tear fell, and another, splashed on her nose, but his mouth stayed tight. Behind him soldiers bunched around, probably trying to see if she would die.

The army. She'd forgotten the army. Her army here, and the one that waited. And now she'd die before she could tell him what she'd done. Her eyes sought her soldiers, searched for an *otuk*. Someone had to tell Laszlo. And he had to leave. Where was Vrishka? Near—he had to be near.

Earth came when she called. She could still do that. "Natuvik," she wheezed after the long minute it took to strengthen her one working lung. His finger touched her lips. "No, *a'kala*, do not speak," he told her gently. "You must lie still and await a healer." His words were meant to reassure her, but she knew—they both knew—she was dying.

More earth, but even so her strength was fading, as was the light around the edges of her vision. "My—fault," she whispered, and watched Laszlo's eyes close, his lips tighten. "Love—" she started, and his eyes opened, over-bright, but she could not find enough air to finish. His eyes held hers, his chin quivered, and she knew he knew, and that would have to be enough.

A fast sound. Hooves. Running. Laszlo looked over his shoulder, but Kiera could not see that far. Eyes closed, she could no longer keep them open, and her sight burst forth, raised above her body, and when it did, she knew it was Vrishka riding up. Streams of water twisted, wound the figure that pulsed dark in her sight. She watched it thunder up, saw it pull a long something from its back. Saw it—

"Earth," she gasped, and opened her eyes. But if Laszlo heard her, he did not acknowledge it. His eyes unfocused as he concentrated, calculated the right moment to turn. *Look at me*, she begged with her eyes, *listen to me!* Desperate, she called earth, but fire fell away when she tried to grab it. Earth wound her, as obedient as ever, and she counted seconds and tried over and over to pull enough breath to make him hear her. Tears squeezed from her eyes as she struggled. *Listen to me!*

"Earth," she wheezed, but then, almost too fast to see, Laszlo spun and stood, and his arms lifted, perhaps to catch the sword he'd heard Vrishka unsheathe. But Vrishka had pulled earth, and Laszlo didn't know it, hadn't heard her. Had not understood. Laszlo stumbled back at the same moment the tip of Vrishka's sword cleared the skin of his back. A heart shot—she knew it was—as black blood, heart's blood, poured from the hole in Laszlo's back.

And he fell, next to her, eyes glazed open to the sky.

Her lung spasmed as she tried to scream, then her body did, a rictus of pain, of despair, tearing every fiber. The world went white, then black as her eyes closed against the pain they had brought her.

VRISHKA'S VOICE. Was he speaking to her? Kiera tried to open her eyes, but they would not.

"—know you can hear me, you slovenly whore." A shushing, then a clump of snow landed on her face. "You still draw breath, and before you go to the hells with your filthy animal lover, I want you to know that I will put your army to the sword, to the last man, and then I will take Fairbanks and raze it to the ground. I will send your boy to my men to use as they will, and when they finish with him I will cut his throat and hold his head to the ground until the last drop of your filthy blood leaks into the snow."

His words swam in front of her, melted into lights that dipped and sparked. Her heart had slowed, beat irregularly—a burst, then stutter, lapsing only to pound again. It sounded so loud in her ears.

"Do you hear me, Kiera? Hear my words, you putrid whore, filth of Alaska! You make a mockery of magic, and the Skani, and *I will cleanse our race of your depravity!*"

Someone else spoke, a smooth voice, one meant to calm, but the sounds ran together and made no sense.

"Marco? Are you certain it is Marco, son of Vayu?"

Her lips parted as she tried to breathe, and she used the last of her strength to pull earth, coax it to strengthen her muscles. As it filled her, the speaker's words, too, became clear.

"—a contingent comin' up behind. Mayhap a tou, ma lord."

Disbelief rose high in Vrishka's voice. "And you are certain that Lord Marco leads it? A *tou? One tou?*"

"The rear scout counted 'em, ma lord, and dinna haveta hurry ta do it."

The sigh Vrishka sent sounded too loud.

"Do ya want me ta—"

"No," Vrishka snapped. "He is a mage, and so I will go. Pull a tou plus half and I will meet them at the rear in a quarter mark. And keep this quiet until I return, Mosha. Put Fairbanks to putting up camp, and we will gullet the filthy lot when I have come back. In the interim, strip them of weapons and put a guard on the pile."

"Ma lord—"

"The deal is off, Mosha. Leith said she would hold him at home regardless. He dies."

A pause. "What da ya wanna do with—"

"Leave them here to rot."

CHAPTER 23

IT TOOK LONG MINUTES FOR VRISHKA'S WORDS to rise for recollection, but even when they did, they made little sense. *Filthy whore. Marco. Depraved. Raze Fairbanks. Your boy to my men. Put your army to the sword.*

Next to her Laszlo lay dead, and that knowing shadowed all else, blotted all other thought even as it sealed her inside the emptiness of utter despair. Each breath stung her nose, mocked the longing, the ache, for her own death.

Thoughts drifted. She drifted on an ocean and waited to die. Pain, physical and emotional, rose and fell back in waves. And still her heart slowed as it wound down.

Wrapped in blankets, Laszlo's breath in her mouth.

Alex's small body inside her arms as he slept, tears on his face.

Marco's head on her lap in front of the fire.

The green of Hunter's empty eyes.

The warmth in Marco's face when he smiled.

Marco had a tou.

The wind brushing a hundred white daisies that lay on Julia's grave.

Laszlo's hands brushing her hair.

A tou. A thousand soldiers.

The swish of Alex's arms as he carved his snow angel.

She should have tried to go back.

No. She'd left nothing.

She left Marco a tou.

Marco! Oh my God!

Terror shot adrenalin arrows into her belly and her heart pounded, erratic, and burned her throat. Fingers flicked when she tried to close her hands. Using the last slip of strength that remained, she called earth, whispered its name in her mind. Thought green. Jade grass that bowed to the summer wind. Soft leaves bursting from overripe trees. Flowers, red and yellow, enveloped inside a waving emerald field.

Her heart hammered when the earth filled her, stuttered, stopped, then hammered again. Focusing on her hands, she pushed them down, down into the snow beneath her. Gouged it with trembling fingertips.

Traced a square. From the bottom, with both index fingers, up, down, across—and her heart lurched, her chest convulsed, and she coughed, choked, gagged. Her back arched when pain seized her. Another square. Another. Another and another and another—and a puff of breath burst forth, a cough.

Larger squares. Over and over, and her sight left her body, drifted above it.

Found fire rolling and twisting just above her chest. Cardinal fire.

Pulled it, but all but a few strands slipped back.

The fire sank into her chest, wound itself with the earth, and still she traced squares.

Eyes closed, heart thundering steady and strong, she called fire, all the fire she could hold, and it came. Threatened to gag her—did gag her—and she retched.

Mixed it with the earth even as her fingers traced squares now into the frozen ground. Let it turn inside her.

God, she prayed, she begged, *please God, let this fire and earth heal me. Please God. Please.*

Beneath her, her fingers moved, faster and faster, and as her sight grew strong she sent it, reached out, strained, and pulled earth—and fire—strands from the ground and the sky and the fire beneath the earth and the bodies on top. All of it, waves and streams and pillars, she called into her body.

Her lung, the one that lay stilled, moved inside her chest, twisted sickeningly, *filled*.

A cloud of air burst forth and she opened her eyes and gasped, then gasped again. Still pulling, she watched the world through a wavering wall. A wall of fire.

On all sides of her, ground to a hundred feet or more, orange flames sizzled, spiraled and sparked as they shot skyward. But instead of surrounding her, it *was* her, and she was fire.

And earth.

Her fingers stilled, and she used hands to push herself to one elbow, then twisted to her side and pulled in her knees.

Weak. She was still so weak. But still her sight strained, pulled earth and fire.

A sound called her eyes. From the hillside where she'd tumbled a tree fell, crumbled into ash before it hit the ground. And then another. Her head turned and the world spun.

Behind her, beyond her fire, soldiers lay prostrate, thousands and thousands who had fallen when she stripped the earth from their bodies.

After exhaling, she stopped her pull of earth, and then of fire. The red wall surrounding her fell like a sheet of water, balled and *whoomp*ed as it died, leaving only a cloud of black smoke for the breeze to tear.

Her breathing made the only sound for long moments.

Using her hands for balance, she put one foot down and stood. She expected a wobble, but her strength was returning. She let her eyes fall on the nearly unrecognizable mass of torn flesh that had been Hunter, and then they dropped on Laszlo.

On his back, eyes closed and face serene, as if in sleep. Her nostrils flared as grief rose and filled her chest, and she dropped to one knee next to his torn chest. Laid a shaking hand on his arm. Words poured like water from her lips. "Oh, my love. Oh, God, how I love you." Breath stuttered as tears rose and spilled down her cheeks. Almost without thinking, she pulled earth and used it to send that love wending into his body, made him her charm like the one she had once left with Marco, the same one she had thrown at his feet just marks before. "Take my love with you, Laszlo," she whispered through numb lips, "wherever you go."

A wail rose from the darkness churning her guts, and she lifted her face to the sky and screamed her pain.

After spending her breath, and ten more, she rose on shaking legs and turned to face the fallen men, then used the back of one hand to wipe snot and tears from her face. Too much time had been wasted, and she used every scrap of strength she could summon to wrestle her raging emotions under control. She could no longer bear to look at him, because if she did a universe of grief would open and swallow her whole, and she could not give in to that. Not right now. When this was over—well. She would see where her feet took her—but for now, now she had two things that needed done, and their names were Marco and Vrishka.

Three, if she counted waking her army.

First, she sent her sight up and searched out air. She sent it past the first flickering stream she found, but another, steadier, flowed above it, and from it her sight captured a handful of strands and dropped with them back into her body.

It spun inside her, a gentle pressure inside her chest, and she threw back her head, sent a mass of air out and screamed as loud as she could, "Kuruk!" and heard sound echo through the canyons.

Something inside the spot that connected them moved—she felt him jump, and knew he had heard her. And the fire that had reached skyward—surely someone had seen that. But to be sure, she lowered her face, angled more north, and screamed her friend's name one more time, let air carry it down to where the plains narrowed into a valley.

And then he was coming. Fast. Faster than she could imagine.

She hoped he knew to bring everyone else.

While she waited she walked among the men, but none of these were hers. If she had been a different person, she would have killed them all as they lay unconscious, and a part of her wanted to, wanted to save even one death of her own men at their hands, but she could not bring herself to do it.

No. Instead she would leave them lay for the minutes it took them to wake, pray the other half of her army got here soon, and force them to surrender.

But Vrishka, she thought as she walked, would die.

Oh—here was one of her men. She used a foot to nudge him. If sucking out all a person's earth worked like pilfering their water—and she now suspected that depleting any one element would do this—a touch should wake them.

And it worked. His eyes opened, then widened when he saw who stood before him. She smiled and offered him a hand up. "Be careful," she warned as he rose, "and don't touch any of Vrishka's men. They will sleep for a bit longer, but come help me wake the rest of ours."

With one last look, one that bordered on awe, he tore away his eyes and walked to a pair of her men and nudged them. "Tell them to wake others, and hurry," she urged as she brushed another's leg with her boot. "Hurry! Get up!"

In a handful of minutes—ten, maybe—most of her men were awake. All still had weapons, to her relief. Hadn't Vrishka said to take them?

"Where are my *otuks*?" she called to the men. Two, then three cut out of the throng and strode to her. Each bowed a head before meeting her gaze. Her eyes filled, she wasn't sure why, and she used a hand to wipe the tears. Others then, ten, then twenty, then forty stood before her.

"The soldiers from the pass are coming," she told them, "and I hope they get here before Vrishka's men wake. He told one of them, Mosha, to take your weapons and kill you all. I am sure you know who he is. I want him found, found and held for me. Pull out their—their *otuks* and put them somewhere safe, away from the men. But listen to me. I don't want to kill these men, not unless we have to. Tell them that they can be free, ask them to give you their oath that they will, I don't know, swear allegiance to Fairbanks or something, and if they do, make them our soldiers. I leave the details to you, because I know you all know this stuff better than I do. Any that refuse, keep them separate. But keep our soldiers safe, and kill the enemy soldiers if you have to." She looked into their faces, each somber, as expressionless as Laszlo's.

Eyes closed as a ball of grief rose as high as her chest, and she breathed it out. "Laszlo has—Vrishka killed him," she told them, and she saw eyes widen. "And now Vrishka has gone after Marco, who rode out of Fairbanks with our last tou to guard our backs. As soon as the soldiers from the pass get here, I need two tou to go with me, the fastest you have because I will be flying, and bring none who can't shield." She stopped to breathe. "And please decide now, because we need to be ready to go when they get here. And please spread the rest of the men out, right away, and cover Vrishka's, and if they wake before the others get here, make them stay on the ground." She paused, realized she probably shouldn't be the one making these decisions. "Don't you think?"

One, a blond man in front, gave her both a nod and the smallest of smiles. Relieved, she returned his nod. "I am no soldier," she told them, "and so I leave this to you, the ones who know what to do. Keep us safe."

She turned, took a step, and froze.

Leaning over Laszlo's body was that woman. The one from the cell. She must have followed him. Rage colored the world red. Lightning fast, her sight shot up and into the sky, pulled a mass of air and dove back into her body as she took the steps toward her husband. A hand lifted as she sent a blast of air out, then another followed it. Both hit the woman—one sent her up, the other launched her back ten feet to smash into the ledge beyond where Laszlo lay. A crack followed the bounce of her head off the rock, and her dress caught as she slid down. But instead of trying to rise and fight, or run, the woman raised herself to hands and knees and bowed her forehead until it brushed the snow.

"Do not," Kiera snarled, "touch my husband, or I swear to God I'll kill you!" It took some effort to make herself stop, both the walking and the words, and it took even more to hold her gaze from Laszlo's face, but she had to. The grief was near, too near, and if she didn't turn away, it would take her. "I need a man!" she yelled over her shoulder, and one, then two came running. "Keep her—" she lifted a shaking finger—"away from my husband. And—and keep his body safe until I come back."

Lips pressed tightly closed, she brushed past a soldier and walked toward the south, and waited for her two tou to join her.

THE FEEL OF KURUK SO NEAR broke her nervous consideration of the state of the snow ahead, and whether what she planned would work. It would take a lot of work—would wear her out—but she would be pulling earth, drawing yars as she flew, and she prayed both that she could get there in time and that Marco would be fine when she did.

When she turned, more than a ton of solid black bear broke the treeline on the hill to her left, soared over the ledge, hit the ground, rolled headfirst, shifted before feet hit the ground, surged to his feet, and swept her into a hug that knocked her back two steps. Tears came, just a few, as she rocked in his arms. "Kiera," he said into her hair, and she hugged him closer, then pushed him away. "Marco came, Kuruk," she told him, and wiped her face. "That stupid fucking sapskull, and Vrishka has gone after him with a tou and a half. I—"

"Kiera!" Kuruk's hand touched her coat, the blood that still stained it, and he looked into her face. "Are you hurt?"

Her hand captured his as she shook her head. "I'm—all right."

His eyes blazed. "I smell the Shunakah."

"Hunter is dead," she whispered, and squeezed his hand. "I can't talk about this right now, Kuruk. Please." One breath, and she swallowed the pain back down. "I am taking two tou, and I need the rest of you to stay here, keep these men out of the fight. I've told the *otuks* to offer these soldiers amnesty—freedom in exchange for allegiance to Fairbanks—but if they refuse, and some will, cut those out and keep them separate. Kill them if you have to."

Kuruk nodded his understanding, then said, "I am going with you."

She wrapped fingers around his bare arm. "Stay here. Please, Kuruk, don't follow me. I have lost so much thisturn. If you come, I will not be able to stop worrying about losing you, too. Please, *please*," she pleaded, tears in her eyes, "stay here and stay safe."

The look in his eyes softened, and he nodded, though his face said he didn't like it.

From the valley behind him Muukwa came running, pulling a shirt over her bare chest. "Marco? He has gone after Marco?"

Jaw tight, Kiera nodded.

"Let us go!" Muukwa yelled, and flung her arms into the air. "Bring the wind. Fly us, Kiera! Now!"

"In minutes, Muukwa," she said, and laid a hand on Muukwa's arm.

"I need soldiers. Look, here they come." She turned eyes to Kuruk. "I am done waiting. Tell them to go south, as fast as they can—run. I need them there a mark ago."

BELOW HER THE FLAT GROUND RUSHED BY, though not nearly as fast as last time. Instead of using the mother stream to go flying, which wouldn't have worked without another mirror of sorts, and she hadn't had time to make one, Kiera used fingers to draw air, and fire, and earth, over and over and over. Air lifted her in one giant leap after another, and the farther she went the better she got at it. She'd send air to the ground just before she landed, which shot her up—and she'd gotten better at angles—then sent another to push her ahead. Leaps that at first must have looked like ink on a child's paper who'd been learning Ms now looked like rolling hills.

And earth strengthened her, soothed her frazzled nerves, both of which she desperately needed since Muukwa had arms and legs wrapped round her front. But Muukwa only tested Kiera's muscles. Even during the first several leaps, and the few near-crashes, Muukwa said nothing, just clung to Kiera in apparent trust that Kiera would keep them safe.

Fire warmed her, gave her a strength and a sense of peace that not even earth could. Though it made her body no stronger, knowing she held it helped her worry less. It would also make a handy weapon in case Vrishka popped into view.

Below her, and not as far behind as she'd feared, her two tou, all Alak, ran full out on legs of bear and wolf and coyote, weapons waving from the leather that strapped them to their backs. She hadn't known that shifted Alaks could carry weapons, though she knew she should have.

Ahead, a mile ahead, she found them. In the middle of a wide plain, two armies clashing in full-out battle. Since all hacked at others she didn't know how to tell who was winning, but she knew Vrishka had more men, and that was never a good thing. Soon, so soon, her men would come from behind, crash in and crush their enemies, and she left that to the men below her. As she started the arc down she closed her eyes and sent out her sight, this time to find Vrishka, and Marco. Find one and she'd find them both, she was sure of it.

Her heart pounded as she realized that she didn't know if Vrishka had brought other mages. If he had, they were probably back at the other place, but it was too late now. She prayed that her *otuks* would know them, recognize them somehow, and do whatever was necessary to keep them from using their magic against her men.

Her sight found a disruption in the flow of water and she opened her

eyes to see where, since her sight saw things, and distance, so differently. Behind the clashing army, around the side of a hill that poked a nose
into the plain, someone was drawing water from three streams. *Please*, she
prayed, *let Marco still be alive. Let me get there in time.*

Down they came, almost in the middle of the fighting men, but she
threw a fat spike of air to the white earth ahead of her, waited till she was
truly falling, and then used a burst of air to boost her to just where the up-
rising ricochet would catch her and Muukwa, wrapped inside her shield—a
new something she'd thought to do this time—and send them on what
looked to be their last hop.

As she rose cheers followed her up, and she turned her head as her two
tou spread to crash into the backside of Vrishka's army.

And as she fell, twenty feet above the snow, a headache hit, one that stole
her vision and her magic and tore a scream from her throat. Hands slapped
across her eyes to block the poisonous light's drill into her skull. Without
air to cushion their fall they crashed hard to the ground, and the impact
knocked the remaining breath from Kiera's lungs. When Muukwa left her
Kiera rolled into a ball, hands still wrapping her eyes, tried to breathe, and
willed her stomach to stop retching.

Muukwa's hands lifted her face out of the snow. "Kiera!"

"Pack," Kiera ground out between heaves. "Packet."

Hands tugged Kiera to one side as Muukwa dug in the pack strapped
to Kiera's back. The one thing she'd done right thisturn was to send a man
after her pack before she left.

Paper brushed her hand, and Kiera closed her fingers around it. Using
teeth, she tore it open, then poured the bitter powder between her lips.
Once she'd scooped some snow in it washed down, and she held her breath
and waited the moments until it worked. When the pain began to fall back,
she pushed to her feet and wiped spit from her chin, then used a shaking
finger to draw a yar before turning to Muukwa. "I am sick. Don't ask more.
We need to go." With one final shrug to settle the pack on her back, she
drew a yar, then another, and took off running as fast as she could toward
the hill.

And when she cleared it, there they were. Marco, on foot and backed
to the hill, had drawn a firestorm around his three open sides, and from
behind it he threw a hail of fireballs at Vrishka, who, from horseback, had
raised a thirty-foot wall of snow in front of him from which white fingers
shot spears of ice into the fiery wall. But Marco was alone, and Vrishka
wasn't. A good fifty, seventy soldiers formed a rough half circle around
Vrishka's, sparse behind the wall and heavy on each side, and the twenty

closest to Marco held bows.

Rage bled red across the world. Without waiting to see what Muukwa did, Kiera opened her hands and drew a xan, then a yar, then a xan, then a yar, then a vata. The excess felt intoxicating, soothed her fears, and she stepped toward Vrishka from behind, and before any could turn—he really should have set a watch—she sent a mass of fire into the sky and then called it down. Lightning. A sizzling, tree-sized flash of white blew Vrishka off his horse. She shrieked, screamed her rage because he had *shielded*, and strode toward him, hands raised. But he shouted when he fell, and as her second strike blew ten of his men to the hells, bowmen turned to her, and to Marco, and launched a swarm of arrows.

A smile lifted Kiera's lips as she drew another yar, then another, let earth slow time, and sent six-foot balls of fire ahead of her even as she drew another bolt of lightning to the ground. Airborne arrows went in them, but nothing came out of the forward-hurdling balls, not even ash. And when they hit the ranks, her fireballs, hair caught fire first, then the bodies beneath them just—melted.

Hatred and adrenalin sung through her veins, softened the horrors she knew would haunt her dreams, and fueled her steps. A man, then another, shifted into polar bears and leapt into the air toward her, whirlwind fast and earth-slowed, but she called skyfire and burned them to ash before their feet ever again crushed the snow.

And when she turned her head, men were running. Away from her. Disgusted, hating them all, she looked left, then right. Where was Vrishka? That cowardly bastard was not going to get away. He had killed her husband—twice—and her men, threatened to murder Alex and every other person she loved, and tried to take Marco away from her. Never, never, would she let him leave this field, no matter the cost. Never would she give him the chance to hide out, lick his wounds, and come back to try again.

Rage bled from red to black as she realized he'd fled this corner, and, trusting Muukwa to comfort Marco, she called fire to melt the snow in front of her as she ran back toward the field.

There, a hundred yards away—and he'd found another horse, the bastard. For a moment she wished she had one, too, and could ride it well enough to do any good. But she had neither horse nor skill, so she called air, which she could use, wrapped her shield like a blanket around her, and sent herself skyward. It might not keep arrows all the way out of her back, but it would keep them from going deep, and it would keep hands from touching her.

The arc brought her down near a clot of fighting men, and she took several steps, tried to tell who was who, but for uniforms it was nearly impossible. They were all mixed together so tightly she dared not use any magic to help anyone. Not that they needed help, right? Not now that they outnumbered Vrishka so heavily.

A man, one of Vrishka's, rushed toward her, sword out, and as he ran her eyes assessed and she knew she could take him, and would have stepped to him to embrace the joy adrenalin brought, but for time. As her eyes left him she lifted an arm, extended a finger as if in accusation. From her palm, from her fingers, grew a ball of air and fire, and a whispered thought shot it from her hand. She didn't see it knock him from his feet and ears tuned out his screams.

There! Across the field Vrishka had raised a fifty foot snow wall, hundreds of tons of frozen water, and when it tipped forward, she knew his purpose. Even as it came crashing down eyes closed, opened, and pure fire streamed from her hands, her face, her chest, over the heads of the soldiers, who to a man pulled shields or paws over their heads and fell to the snow. As the fire traveled she called earth, to slow time, and used her sight to spread the fire into an arc, a thin band, and the two met, fire and water, fewer than five feet above the heads of the cringing soldiers' heads, and thick, red ribbons wrapped the snow and rendered the falling avalanche to hissing steam.

Wild cheers erupted from all over the field, but Kiera ignored them, used air to bounce her up, and again chased Vrishka as he rode his horse north and away. *Ride far enough, you bastard, and meet the rest of my army!* her thoughts screamed, but she quashed it. She didn't want him anywhere near any of her men.

As if sensing her words, he stopped, turned his nearly blown horse in a small circle and waited for her to come.

And come she did. On her first bounce, while still a good fifty feet above the earth, hundreds of ice javelins rose from the snow beneath her and shot like bullets skyward. The fingers of her right hand drew a xan, and another, and she fed the streams into a convex of white-hot fire beneath her, then thickened it, and pops stung her ears as spears exploded when the elements met.

Another stream of air bounced her back up as she fell, and another fed behind her shot her forward. Air warbled in her ears as she fell too fast, and though she stumbled a few steps, she managed to keep her feet as she landed a scant twenty feet from the circle Vrishka's horse had trampled into the mushy ground.

For a handful of heartbeats they stared at each other, and hatred thickened the air between them. Wind had blown his hair askance and his eyes looked wild, but she knew he hadn't given up. Would never.

A rush of thoughts tumbled. Fire cancelled water. Water cancelled fire. So what was left? Strength. Who could call more. Push the other further. And even if Agni hadn't told her, their fights had shown her who held greater strength. So now. Now she would break his shield and send his body to the hells.

Kiera started to raise her hands, something she didn't need to do to work magic, but it was something she did when she didn't think to stop herself, probably because it seemed more natural that fire flowed from her hands. But as she did she saw with earth-slowed time an ugly smile rise on Vrishka's face, and before her heart could beat twice frigid water grabbed her feet, yanked her down as the ground beneath her feet melted to nothing she could stand on.

As water closed around her, her mouth opened, a scream started as time transported her back—back and into a small wooden barrel. Her back arched, panicked arms flailed as she tried to raise her face above the shimmering sapphire wall, but cold swept her, icy fingers wrapped her throat, stole her fire, and pulled her body down.

Instinctually seeking fire, up shot her sight, but water ravaged it, too, and it fell, a soft shadow that melted back inside her chest. Numbing cold slowed her arms and her legs and she slid downward. Arms rose above her, and eyes that refused to close watched the surface slide farther away as she sank.

No! her mind screamed. *No!* But cold wrapped her, and the weight of the water dragged her toward the waiting earth.

Earth! she screamed into the water. Maybe she couldn't call fire, but she could call earth, and with earth, she could bring fire. Fingers twitched, hands clenched and opened. Her mouth closed as her fingers drew a yar, and another and another. Lungs screamed, vision blurred as down flew her sight, down and into the ground beneath her. Faster than sound it raced, passed without pause through stone and water, and sought the fire she'd touched, the bottled up flow a scant mile beneath the surface.

And found it, and its sister, pressing impatient fingers into the slice of rock separating them. Using her sight, she used earth to coax hardness from the mass of stone walling the molten fire, atomized the manifested earth to weaken the rock, and the fire burst up those hundred feet she'd softened. Step by step she drew it up, eons and moments it took as her lungs burned and begged her to breathe. The ground shook when it came, then burst under her feet as ten thousand tons of lava spilled into the lake, rose faster than any tide, thrust her body toward the sky like a sacrifice. Throbbing earthfire burst the ice around the narrow hole she'd fallen through, and shoved her and a hundred red fingers above the waterline.

Mouth open, she gasped for breath and tried to find her feet, but the molten rock was too thin to stand in. After two tries she managed to roll free, naked because the fire had burned off her clothes, and onto the rapidly thinning ice.

With knees and hands she pushed to stand on the now blue icy rim covering the lake and drew a yar to stop her muscles' shaking, then a xan, a vata, another yar, and filled her chest as her trotting feet carried her off the melting lake.

North and two thousand yards away, the speck that Vrishka made rode at a breakneck speed.

Did he know what she had done? That she wasn't dead? Her head shook back and forth, icy drops of water spilled down her chest, her back, as she realized it didn't matter, because regardless, she was finished playing games.

Eyes closed, she sent her sight down, back into to the lava and the rock that cradled it. Using her sight she teased the sister strand, the one feeding the flow that spilled joyously into the lake, to follow a trail of rock she weakened. Up and up, and north, and up again. Eyes opened, gauged distance, closed again.

A patter, *pat-pat-pat*, drew a slice of her attention to the ground behind her. Feet, she was certain. Running feet. Without looking back she sent a chest high sheet of air behind her. Air in case it was friend.

Eyes closed again and up popped her sight, just ahead of where Vrishka was drawing a cyclone of earth and water to power his flight. A cavern blew open in front of him, bubbled molten rock to the surface. The horse's head lifted as Vrishka yanked the reins, and the horse skidded, dug feet into the snow, stumbled, fell, and over its head flew a screaming Vrishka into the waiting arms of her fire.

Ten seconds passed, then twenty to be sure the man drew water no longer, before eyes closed for the briefest moment as she breathed her thanks. When she turned she found a cadre of about a dozen soldiers, two on horseback, eight off to one side, and four brushing snow from their backsides, behind her. Her men, all, the two on horses from here, but the rest were those who had run as she flew.

Eyes on the men's faces, she asked, "Is it finished?" and felt relief sweep her when heads nodded. Lips pressed together, she nodded in return, exhaled a heavy breath, and looked to the men she'd knocked to the ground. "I'm sorry," she told them, and meant it. "I couldn't take time to look behind me." Heads bowed as the others hid smiles, but those with spots of snow still clinging to their clothes all met her eyes, and heads nodded as they accepted her words.

Even with earth strumming her veins, her legs shook from cold and exhaustion. Her face lifted toward the horsebound men. *Otuk*s. "I need to go back to Marco. Will one of you with a horse please give me a ride?" A big, black-haired soldier edged his horse toward her and she walked to meet him. Instead of taking her hand when she reached up, however, he met her eyes and nodded once to something behind her. When she turned, a hand offered a coat, which she took. She dropped her shield and pulled it over her back, threaded her arms into the sleeves, then took the soldier's outstretched hand. His foot lifted from the stirrup so she could use it, and from the ground, another hand, carefully placed, helped her find a seat behind him.

CHAPTER 24

A WALL OF FIRE STILL BURNED WHEN THE HORSE'S feet took them around the rock, and Kiera's breath caught. Why? Why would Marco leave a firewall burning after Vrishka had gone?

A quick check told her that his was the only magic, the only disruption to any flow as far as she could see. When the horse stopped she slid off one side and ran toward the shimmering half circle that cupped a hole between what she could now see were two large boulders. Her sight parted the air and fire as she passed inside, and what she saw stopped her heart.

There, in the bloody snow, lay Marco, eyes closed, Muukwa across his legs, wailing like a child. And two arrows nearly all the way through the right side of his chest.

Magic can't stop arrows, he had once told her.

Hadn't she taught him better than this?

Mouth dry, a scream wending its way inside her, she dropped to her knees next to his head and put a hand on his face, under his nose. Breath. Faint, but breath.

A healer. They needed a healer. "Muukwa!" she shouted. "Stop! You have to go find a healer! There are—are—two thous—tou soldiers out there! Go. Find. A. Healer!"

At her voice Marco's eyes fluttered, opened, and found hers. Pain—he was in so much pain. "Kiera," he mouthed, but no sound came.

Muukwa shot up. Her voice sounded hoarse, thick. "Will he live?"

A sob shook Kiera's shoulders, and another as she rubbed fingers across his forehead, down his cheek. "Marco, stop the storm," she whispered, "so Muukwa can go find a healer."

With a *whoomp* it fell, and Muukwa leapt to her feet, shifted, and flew.

The fingers on Marco's right hand flicked, and Kiera scooped them inside hers. Stared into the face she loved so much. Prayed that Muukwa would find a healer. Surely, surely, even one of these men knew how to heal?

A thump from behind sent Kiera to her feet, and she spun around, fire in her chest, and raised her hands, palms out.

An eagle. A giant, black-bodied eagle, easily thrice her size, with proud yellow eyes set in a white head. A wickedly sharp beak. Ten feet away. Another landed behind the first, beat closed enormous wings, then a third.

Adrenalin shot into Kiera's middle. What was this? What could they want?

Her mouth opened, but before she could speak, the closest, the largest, shifted.

The woman from the hills.

For a moment the two stared at each other, and Kiera could not begin to read the woman's face. The two behind the eagle woman shifted, both dark-skinned men, and one she recognized. That one stepped forward, around the woman, and inclined his head.

"Are you a healer?" Kiera blurted.

His eyes, as brilliantly gold as the woman's, were kind. "We are not. But we have come to offer recompense, Kiera Fire Mage."

Why now? Had they been watching her? *Why now?* "I need a healer," she told him, licked her lips, and gestured behind her with a shaking hand.

"Your mate?"

"My—my brother."

The woman spoke sharply, then stared over the man's shoulder at Kiera as he translated. "He is not your blood."

Tears rose. *How could this matter?* But when she spoke, she told the truth and prayed it shone through. In case it did matter—because she had an idea, and she sensed that the words she chose would dictate their answer. "He is the brother of my heart, and I could not love my own blood more than I love this man."

A pause, a long moment passed, but then the woman made a small movement, inclined her head.

Her throat convulsed when she swallowed, but she held the woman's eyes while she spoke. If they said no, she would beg. Offer anything. "Can you fly to Fairbanks? Take word that Marco—" she swept back her hand, "has been hurt?" Swallowed again. "And—and maybe fly someone back here? I've—uh—seen Yeil fly people, and I know you are very strong. Stronger than the Yeil." Hadn't Muukwa said that a Cha'ak had nearly taken her life? Her—a great bear? "If you will, I will owe you recompense, and will pay any price you ask, any but a life."

The woman spoke again, snorted, spat another word.

Kiera couldn't read the man's face when he translated. "It is but small."

"I don't understand," Kiera told him, heart sinking.

A corner of his mouth lifted, and she suddenly realized why they'd come now. A man she loved had been hurt, and yet, despite all her magical strength, she could do nothing to save him, to free him from what held his life, without help. Something like what had happened in the woods that turn past.

"You ask little," the man told her, but her eyes held the woman's. Filled, and overfilled.

"I ask everything," she whispered. "Please."

A nod, hers, then his. Knees bent, arms raised, and as they rose, giant wings brushed the ground, stirred a wind as the air lifted them.

Oh, God. "Wait!" Kiera shouted, and ran out, tried to follow. One stopped his ascent—she thought it was the man—and circled above her. "There will be soldiers with arrows!" she shouted. "To keep out the Yeil. Please don't fly over, or too close! Tell them Kiera sent you, and they will listen. Say that they need to come here as fast as they can, to bring a healer. Please, please tell them to hurry!"

Wings flapped as the eagle rose, higher and higher, until he disappeared.

Minutes passed. A quarter mark as Kiera held Marco's hand. Pain pinched his mouth, his eyes. Too much blood, too far away he drifted, too little breath. He was dying. No healer could get here in time. She knew that. Tears fell, but the dam in her chest stayed locked tight.

His eyes were so blue. Such a clear blue—

Chills shot up her back, and she yanked off her coat and threw it aside. Blue light. Green light. Marco. Laszlo. Water. Earth. "Marco!" she shouted, then made herself quiet her voice. "Listen to me. Listen!" She waited until his eyes opened, cleared enough to find hers. "Remember when you were little? You used to heal yourself?"

His mouth opened, probably to say this was beyond him, but she charged on.

"I know you can't, but I need you to show me." It was too frightening to consider what might happen if she poured fire and *earth*—some combination of which had healed her—into an air mage, and without his help, how would she know what to use to heal him?

Using one hand she tried to open his coat, but the ties and the arrows made it impossible. She made a frustrated noise through clenched teeth, then sent a sheet of fire, fire and air, and burned it—the coat and the above-skin shafts of the arrows—off his chest. It hurt, she knew it did, but she didn't have time to do this any other way. She reached across him, lifted his left hand and laid it on his bare chest.

"Wait until I squeeze your hand, Marco. Then do it as long as you can. Can you do that? *You have to show me!*"

Without waiting for a sign of agreement, she closed her eyes and sent her sight to his hand, into it, and squeezed.

Nothing. Earth flowed, air, weak circles turned.

"Marco!" she shouted, eyes closed, and clamped his fingers together. "Heal!"

Water. A four- or five-strand stream of water, earth wending it, and just the smallest stream of fire, flowing opposite the water, dribbled a rivulet inside his wrist and spilled into his chest.

"I love you, Marco," she breathed, and pulled all the earth from his body.

Her chest met his, covered the obscene holes, as she laid her head on the ribs below his far collarbone. Using her right hand she drew sigils for earth, fire, again, and mixed them in her chest. A deep breath, and she drew the mek. When it hit her she released the earth and mixed the heavy water in it.

Earth slowed, puddled, melted away.

Again she tried. Again. Teeth ground. Bitter sounds leaked from between her lips.

His heart stuttered. Started. A weak patter. Stuttered again.

"No!" she cried, and reached an arm across him. Water flowed from her eyes, washed his chest.

He had pulled it from inside him. He hadn't called it.

Eyes closed, she gritted her teeth and *pushed*. From her, everything. Skin to skin, elemental energy melted the space between them. It had to be mixed right inside her, didn't it? So she didn't try, didn't call more, just let it flow. Didn't try to send it anyplace but inside.

Time passed as Kiera pushed her living energy into the man who she could not bear to let die. The mark turned, water to fire. Five marks had passed since she'd stood on the hill with Muukwa. Since Laszlo had lived. Such a small space for so much loss, for so much grief to fill.

Her heart began to pound as her body weakened. Straining, she summoned what was left. Pushed. "Live, Marco," she breathed, and felt her hand slip down the smooth skin covering his ribs.

A scream, words, from behind her, but they didn't make sense. Her head felt so heavy.

"Kiera!"

Muukwa, she thought.

"You must rise! Vrishka comes!"

Breath came all at once and she strained, cried, pushed a hand into the bloody snow next to her hip. Heaved herself up to knees. A trembling finger drew a yar, another, another, called fire, filled herself with it.

And stood, breath still heavy, fingers drawing absent shapes. Murder blackened her thoughts, washed all else away as she stepped out, out of the lee, and into the space ahead of the two boulders.

A hundred foot wave of snow rose to the north, rolled forward, faster than a horse. Faster than she could fly. A dark spot rode it, arms akimbo. Commanded it.

The rocks covering the hill to her left, toward the north, hid all else but the wave, still a half mile away. Did her men wait out there? she wondered, and started to run. Slid on near-frozen feet, fell, but she pushed up and stumbled until her feet caught her, ran, calling earth.

Crimson thoughts came as fire filled her. Burning embers, hundreds, falling from the dying flames, blowing as they twisted in the wind, rising as fire caught and they joined to form a new flame, melted inside the cleansing fire. Hands rose, fingers traced patterns as she stopped to take in the clear field. As fire came, her mouth moved, spilled words, and a comet of fire exploded from her chest. Streamed through the air like a giant fist.

And exploded both up and down when it hit a wall of air and water.

"No!" Kiera screamed, and stumbled forward, started to run.

Tears streamed down her face. Xan, xan, xan. Feet slipped, and down she went into the icy snow. A yar, another, and she rose to her knees, but even with earth, what she had given Marco had weakened her too far.

Goddamn it, she knew it had been too easy. She needed time, time to draw earth and fire, to heal herself, but the sands had run. Her sight slipped, and she screamed, pounded a fist into the snow.

The ground. Down went her sight. Lightning fast through miles of rock and water. Found her final lava vein. *Come*, she urged the straining pool, fifty feet wide, and used earth to draw it through the rock. Up, up, to just under the field in front of her. Held it there, just below the surface.

Waited.

Someone shouted. Shouted again, but she refused to listen. Strength had leaked away, and she knew she had just minutes until even holding earth would be too hard.

The fingers of her right hand drew yar after yar after yar, but most of it burst and wafted away. The air had darkened—or maybe it was her eyes—but she waited, trusted her ears. A shushing sounded, snow on snow, told her the time had nearly come.

"Let. It. Go!"

Agni? *Agni?*

"Kiera! Listen to my words! Let go the earth! *Leave the fire in the ground!*"

The sound of running feet came forward, flowed all around her, as she knelt like a statue in the snow. Earth left her as she fell forward, but arms caught her.

Only then, as rage and fear leaked away, did she know whose.

"Kuruk," she breathed, and relaxed into his arms.

A hand rested on her shoulder, and strength flowed into her chest. Her eyes opened, blinked, flicked up, and found—

"*Saman?*"

"Be still," he commanded, face drawn.

"Marco!" she begged. "Please, Saman. He is back there. Dying. I did what I could, but please—"

A blur passed her eyes as Saman rose from a squat and disappeared behind her.

Kuruk barked a word, and after a moment someone handed him a coat. His hands shook as he wrapped her in it, then pulled her close and breathed hard breaths through his nose.

"Agni—"

"I am here, child."

"How—"

"I believe the spell of which we spoke was keyed to the man," she said brusquely, then stepped so Kiera could see her. Wild red hair rose like a halo above her head. And below her heavy coat she wore *pants*. "And now that he is gone, the spell has broken."

"The—the wave was *you?*"

A smile washed across Agni's face so quickly Kiera wasn't sure if she'd imagined it. "It was." Agni's gaze lifted, softened as Saman returned, and Kiera felt her brows raise.

"A crude job," Saman said a touch gruffly as he knelt down, as if her work had offended him. "But he is breathing well, and I have further strengthened his lungs. He will be fine, Lady Kiera."

Relief washed her in prickles that stung her skin. Eyes closed and lips parted as she sucked in the sweet air.

Kuruk's arms tightened around her. "Kiera, I must te—"

But Saman had not finished, and he talked right over Kuruk in a tone that opened Kiera's eyes. "*You*, however, have followed precisely none of the instructions I gave you, Lady Kiera."

"But—"

"No. From this moment, you will begin doing as I have told you. Foremost, that means that you will rest." His right hand reached under her coat and pressed into the soft flesh underneath. A tingle started where the pads of his fingers touched skin. Before she could exhale, he made a sound of annoyance and used his free hand to flip open the fabric covering the main of her body.

One side of his mouth twisted as his fingers brushed the pinked scabs below her ribs, then slid up to the one between her breasts, and Kiera found herself holding her breath as his magic slipped into her, seeking answers that she didn't know how to find on her own, and had been too busy, and too afraid, to think about.

It took long minutes before his eyes met hers, and when he did, he held them for a lengthy moment, perhaps to make his point, but then nodded, once, before turning his gaze to Kuruk's. "You will see that she rests, rests more than she stands, and will tell all that she must."

And though his words were meant for Kuruk, his eyes snapped back to hers. "And if she will not, you will not wait to tell me."

As if summoned by Saman's admonition, the headache rose. Wrenching agony tore through her skull, and her body arched, clenched as her stomach heaved.

"Alathic shite!" Saman swore disgustedly, and his hand on her face was the last thing she knew.

When her eyes opened, they found the canvas of a tent above her. Blankets wrapped her tightly, and she had to struggle to free an arm. The slit between the two cloth doors revealed that night had fallen.

Afraid to move further, Kiera waited for the headache, and wondered if someone had remembered her pack. How many packets did she have left? Not many. Maybe two. Enough to—

Oh yeah. Saman was here, and—

Her shoulders lifted, she cried out, as grief rose, breached the silver seal, and rushed to fill the space inside her. A heavy sob drew her back down and she flung out her arm, turned to one side, drew up her knees.

And something fell from her chest, where it had been laid, and hit the bare skin inside her elbow before sliding to the floor beside her.

Her breath caught. With trembling fingers she picked it up, but the light was too dim to be sure. Clasping it tightly in her hand, breathing hard, Kiera pushed up. "Hello?" she called, and feared that someone would answer, that someone wouldn't.

But no one did.

Using her free hand, Kiera unwrapped herself. Still naked, she rose and pulled a blanket from the floor. Walked out of the tent and into the moonlight, where she could see what her fingers held. Confirm that it was her comb. The one Laszlo had made her that turn. The one she'd left for him, and had left again at his feet.

The icy snow stung her feet almost unbearably, but a fire crackled and spit from a rocky nest a dozen yards away, set inside a small clearing, and she took careful steps to it.

"Hello?" she called again, but her bladder pressed hard, and she ducked behind the closest tree, lifted the blanket, and emptied it. When she finished she rewrapped herself and walked to the fire. Someone had pulled a stump close, and she sat on it. Whoever guarded her must be walking rounds, or—or something.

Who would have found this? Who would have known what it meant? Marco knew, but was he healed enough? Did Kuruk know? Heart sinking, her head nodded. Yes. He knew. He'd heard the words the men spoke when they gave it to her, and told her Laszlo was *gone*.

Her chin dropped to her chest as she let out her breath. For a moment, for just a moment, she'd thought, just maybe—

Sobs came, quietly at first, then harder. The fire sensed her grief, rose, lifted spinning fingers to her, offering what comfort it had to give. From under the blanket Kiera stretched her hand, let the fire wrap her arm once, twice, a dozen times before it whuffed out.

"My name is Laszlo of the Denaa."

Kiera shot to her feet and the blanket fell back, slid to the ground. Across the fire a figure stood, staring into the far trees. The flickering light silhouetted a large back from which a long black coat hung.

Her ears roared. "Wha—"

"I am a soldier. Once, I was a slave." He turned, and it was his face, his beautiful, glorious face. The face she loved more than any other.

Tears fell, streams of water bled down her cheeks. "Laszlo," she whispered, and took a step, but he raised a hand. *Wait.*

"You will listen to my words," he told her, and from here, from across the fire, she couldn't see his eyes, the set of his mouth. Her breath stuttered, and she stumbled back and sat down, hard, on the stump.

Was she dreaming? Had she died? What was this? Was this Laszlo? It couldn't be Laszlo!

"My name is Laszlo of the Denaa," he said again, softly this time, but his words stilled the torrent of her thoughts. In, she breathed, and out, and all the world fell away, all but one face, aglow from the fire. "And you will now listen to my words, Kiera."

He took the steps separating them and stood staring down at her, back

247

to the flames. Reached a hand to touch her face, and tears spilled anew, washed her cheeks and dropped like gems into her lap. "I have given near thirty cycles as a slave, a soldier in the army of Fairbanks. But then," he told her as he stood in the snow next to her knees, "the turn marking the turn of my fortieth cycle, I met a woman. A woman of unsurpassed courage, and compassion, and beauty.

"She freed me, Kiera. She helped me free my people. And then she took me to husband, with the city to witness. But soon an enemy attacked, and took me from her." He paused, clenched his jaw, and spoke slowly. "In the prison they held me I found my daughter, one I had thought lost for near twenty cycles. Her lord had used her, made her a whore for the pleasures of passing travelers."

For a moment Kiera couldn't breathe.

He stared overhead into the trees. "A spell held her, one that kept her locked inside the walls of the manse. As I searched to unlock it, I played her mate and fought to keep away the men who would have used her. But I did not betray my wife." His eyes found hers, his gaze almost too intense to hold. "My *wife*, and wife she remains, for no words can undo what was done, Kiera.

"She divined the truth in the lies the enemy told her. She stayed true to me, she searched tirelessly for me, and when she found me, she came in disguise and at very great risk to herself, and our people, and freed me again, even thinking I had abandoned the oaths I swore to her."

A hand lifted, but he dropped it. "I am not worthy of such love," he said quietly to the trees, but then his burning eyes again found hers, and she fell into them, helpless. "But I am a selfish man, Kiera, *a'kala*, beloved of my heart, and I will not release her. If she goes, I will follow her." He dropped to a knee, wrapped her hands in his. "On my oath, not even death will separate me from her, because I will follow her to the next life, and the next, or unto the seven hells should her heart ever stop."

There was nothing else in the world but that face, and even had she wanted to, Kiera could not have done more than breathe.

Arms swept her up, and she rested her head against his chest and let the tears fall. Inside the tent they lay for long minutes, fingers touching skin, then lips met, and bodies, and the wind whispered to the shining moon.

When their breath slowed, and strong arms locked away the fears of the world, memories rose. Even inside the peace of his arms, the grief she had thought stilled burst forth and drove spikes into her heart. Great rolling sobs racked her body, pulled down her shoulders and lifted her knees.

Laszlo lifted her—both of them—until he sat up and cradled her inside his arms, then pulled a blanket over them and rocked her back and forth. "*A'kala*, my heart, what is so wrong?"

It took long minutes for the worst to pass, for the anathemas that had burned holes through her eyes to drift back and blur into the soft black background. When her sobs melted into hiccups, the words fell like stones from her lips. "I saw you die."

His chest rose and fell. Fingers traced circles on her back, then lifted to brush her hair, smoothed it into the skin of his chest. "Oh, my heart." His voice sounded aggrieved. Grieving. And still he stroked her hair. "I did not die. I will not leave you."

"But—but—I saw black blood. He—his sword—it hit your heart."

He spoke softly. Carefully. "I do not know, *a'kala*. But when the harm is very great, the body must shut down to heal."

"How did he not know?"

Again, his chest lifted and fell as he sighed. "Arrogance, perhaps. I do not know."

It seemed incredulous that Vrishka would not understand this, but then neither had she. And even the remembrance of the grief, the despair that unknowing had wielded, forced closed her eyes. "I—thought I'd lost you, Laszlo. I—"

Fingers brushed her lips, as if he could not bear the darkness her words would spill. "I know, *a'kala*. My thoughts were the same when you lay before me on the ground. But I will not leave you."

"You can't help it if you die!"

The blanket slid up her back as he shifted her in his arms, and he used a hand to smooth it back. When he spoke, his voice sounded cold. Resolute. "Death will not keep me from you, Kiera."

She knew his words were meant to comfort her, to seal that chasm of horror and the ocean of grief it erupted, and she loved him for them. Her fingers found his wrist, pulled it until his arm wrapped her again. "It was my fault, Laszlo. I should never have put my own feelings ahead of the duty I owe Fairbanks. And you."

"No. The fault is mine, Kiera—"

"I *knew* you would blame yourself, Laszlo. But don't." She took a breath. "It's mine. Mine and Hunter's."

His arms eased her back down, down to the bed in which she woke, and they lay, side by side, eyes open, face to face, after he covered them against the cold.

"I want you to do something for me," she told him, then pressed lips to his. As she lifted her head, his eyes narrowed, filled with heat, sunlight that opened a bud of joy in her heart. "No. Not that. Not yet."

"Tell me what you wish," came his husky whisper.

Lips lifted, but she pressed a circle into his arm with a fingertip. "I want you to start talking to me. Telling me what you want, and what you think. And everything. I don't want to have to drag everything from you, Laszlo."

For a moment she wondered if she'd offended him. His face closed, but his eyes held hers as he considered her words. "Kiera," he finally said, and she couldn't quite read his tone. "Who would want the words of a slave? Who would care what he thought, or what he held dear?"

A breeze ruffled the tent flap, and moonlight spilled in and flowed like milk across the dark floor. "I would. *Me*. Your wife cares, and wants to know what you think. About everything! You're so smart, and *so many times* over these past turns I've learned things about you that I wish I'd known before. How insightful you are, how hard you work. How much respect you command. What a good man you are. Well, I knew that, but I didn't know everyone else did. How talented you are. How much you know about—about *everything*, and I need that knowledge, Laszlo, not just because I want to know what you want, and how to make you happy, but also because I need to know how to rule our deconn. You—*you!*— are the mortar that holds us, holds Fairbanks together."

The white of his smile flashed in the frail light, and Kiera lifted a hand and pressed it to his cheek. He deserved the praise, even more so because every word was true, but he also needed to understand why he had to try to unlearn the silence slavery had forced him to embrace, and to know that she had learned her lesson as well.

"When they took you, Laszlo, we nearly fell. Neither Marco nor I have a fraction of your—your talent, or knowledge, and without all you had done, for us, for the army, we would have. I have to know these things, and the only person who can teach me is you."

His hand rose, and he pressed a finger to her lips, outlined them, before he leaned in and kissed her, softly, and again. "I will do as you ask, Kiera." Another kiss, feather light. "Your words honor me, and I thank you for them."

In the near dark his eyes glittered like ink on an alabaster sculpture. "You can start," she smiled and pushed herself up on one elbow, "by telling me your daughter's name, and who her mother is. And how you freed her."

A flash of white, then gone before he flipped to his back, raised hands to cradle his head, and stared up at the canvas shield. "Her name is Lakti, *a'kala*," he told the stars above the roof. "Her mother is Naga, and yes, I know you will ask how she came to be sold to Talium. Naga did that as well, as many *ta'alak* children are sold." He slid a glance to her, clarified, "Those born to Skani, or by them. Those who carry our blood."

Kiera's eyes closed and she tried to focus on breathing. In and out.

Sorrow wound the sigh he blew through his nose. "Lakti was but a babe last I saw her, and Naga would not say where she had sent her."

The blanket beneath her pulled tight when he shifted, and she leaned closer, rested her head on his chest. Listened to his heart beat. Breathed out when his arm wrapped her back.

"As I told you, a spell tied her to the manse. To the rock, I now think. None of the whores could leave. I could not trace the spell, Kiera, though I could feel it. But when the house fell it severed the spell, and freed Lakti and the others."

A frisson of panic shot up Kiera's back and pulled her head from the warm cradle that held it. "You stayed inside that house when I brought it down, didn't you?"

"Yes."

A heaviness poured like sand into the space behind Kiera's ribs. "Laszlo, I—I nearly filled that house with lava. Let the volcano fill it. Oh Jesus," she breathed out and laid her head back down. "Sweet Jesus."

In long sweeps his hand brushed the hair away from her neck, then rested against it. "All is well, my heart." The lake-smooth calm in his voice coaxed her heart to slow its frantic pace. He took a breath before adding, "I understand the wanting, *a'kala*. Every mark the horrors turned stones in my guts. Made me long to rip the flesh from Nick's bones, to watch the life bleed from his eyes."

Her head raised, and she knew she looked shocked. Never, ever, had she heard him say such things. His answering smile, both open and surprisingly playful, stole her breath. "I am but spilling my thoughts, *a'kala*, as my wife has commanded me."

That startled a laugh, and she shook her head before laying it back down. "He will never have a manse, or pits, or slaves again," she told him. "That counts for something."

"No," Laszlo told her, satisfaction wending his voice, "he will not."

Up popped her head, brows raised in a question, but the look on his face spoke the answer.

His hand raised, traced a line down her face. Her mouth opened, but she closed it, because she didn't want to know. Not the details. Nick had deserved it, a hundred times over—a thousand—but Nick wasn't the only one she'd left lying there with a thoroughly pissed, recently freed Laszlo, though she hadn't actually thought about that until this very moment. "Did you kill Chanda?"

His hand stilled, but he didn't let it fall. No answer rose to his face.

"Laszlo, I—"

"Yes."

Her eyes closed. Had he deserved that? Her heart searched, found anger, disgust, even a slice of hatred. Chanda had betrayed the Alak of Fairbanks. Her. Laszlo. Marco. Brought such devastation to so many. But still. She just didn't know.

His fingers drew a circle and moved off her face. Slid down her shoulder and rested on the floor behind her. When he spoke, his voice was cold, as cold as the death for which she had longed when she thought him taken from her. "I offered mercy, Kiera, and he used it to press my wife's face into the ground. Bleed her heart with lies. He betrayed his oath, his deconn. But for what he did to you, Kiera, his life was mine to take." A breath slid out, and he moved to sit up. "I am sorry if that grieves you." He pushed back the blanket to uncover his legs. Spoke fiercely. "But I am not sorry I did it. *I died that day they told me you were dead*, you told me, and your grief crushed me. In that moment, his life was mine."

When she realized he meant to leave their bed, Kiera sat up, snaked out an arm and grabbed his wrist before he could rise. "Please. Stay with me. I'm not angry. I—I am just shocked. I don't know how to feel about that. But Laszlo. Don't leave me. Please."

The face he turned to her still had an edge of anger to it, but he swept her into his arms and pulled her across the space separating them. Crushed her against his chest. "I will never leave you," he whispered into her hair. "I am sorry I frightened you."

Air spilled from parted lips and her eyes closed. "Lie with me, Laszlo. I am so tired."

The blankets had tangled, so he yanked one, then the other, from under them and she helped him wrap them before they lay back. Even with the weight of his arm bracketing her shoulders, a knot still clenched Kiera's stomach, and so she slid a leg across his, skimmed a hand across the soft skin below his ribs, and rubbed her cheek against his shoulder before letting her eyes close. Would this need to touch him ease? she wondered. To remind herself that he was here? Real?

A thought rose, a terrible thought that pushed a spear into her gut. What if this was a dream after all? What if she woke and found herself alone, in her bed, or somewhere else, and all this had just been a fantasy, a dream her sleeping mind had woven to spare her, to deny that the man she loved more than life was dead?

Her fingers closed over smooth skin and pinched closed, and she felt him flinch. His chest moved as he laughed, and muscles flexed beneath her face as he raised his other arm and captured her offending hand.

Need washed her. Need for his touch, need to drown the devil tracing her thoughts. "Make love to me," she whispered.

Slowly, gently, his hands guided her hips across his body. Lifted her until their lips met. Breathed her breath, tasted her mouth as he eased himself inside her. Love urged every thrust, wound between them even as it tied them together, a gentle hand that led sorrowing hearts from the cold and the darkness. When light came, hers as his, stars danced across her sight, a stinging joy that stole her breath.

A lurking sleepiness chased away the stars, and she laid a weary head on his chest. His skin felt so good. So warm, and she made no move to get off him. Legs relaxed first, and then her shoulders. In the morning she would have to find something to wear. She couldn't ride, fly, or walk home in a blanket.

The morning. Oh God.

Her lips pulled back in a grimace. Best tell him now, because he would know in the morning anyway when the headache struck. "Laszlo, I have to tell you something."

His fingers rose and brushed her hair. "Tell me."

"I—I'm sick."

Gently, so gently, he lifted her face from his chest. "What do you mean?"

"Well, *sick* isn't quite the right word, though I am going to be sick, physically sick, for a while. Very sick."

His lips pressed together, but he waited for her to explain.

"It seems that we—you and I, I mean—have slightly different—um—bodies."

He nodded slowly.

"And well—uh—joining them, our making love, has caused—well—me to get pregnant." The words tumbled out. "I don't know how, Laszlo, because I—uh—I didn't think I could, but I am, and because we're different, just a little, it's causing my body to do some—uh—strange things."

His face grew taut. "What *things*, Kiera? And—"

She raised the fingers of one hand. "I'll be fine, Laszlo. Honestly." Well, that was very likely true. "It's just that I—I will need to rest a lot. And take some medicine. But. Well. I'm going to have a baby."

"A child?" he whispered. "You carry my child?"

The smallest of smiles lifted the corners of her mouth. "It will be born just before the cycle turns."

He crushed her to his chest, and his heart pounded beneath her.

"Does it make you happy?"

His chest shook when he laughed, a string of joy that wound the room like a yellow silk ribbon. With hands that trembled, he raised her face and kissed her mouth with smiling lips. "The gods, Kiera, have less than I."

For a time they lay together, quietly, until a thought rose and again pushed back against the night's waiting arms. "Laszlo, do we have side scouts, because if we don't—"

To be continued in
Rising Embers
Book Three of The Embers Series

GLOSSARY

A'kala: "My lover/my woman" in Denaali.

Agni, Lady: Skani noblewoman who lives in Fairbanks. Magic teacher. Has red hair and green eyes. *Sunwyr*, but of which element is not known.

Air: One of the four elements. Travels in large streams and does not require a mage to expend extra energy to summon. It feels like a painless buzzing when touched with a mage's sight. The opposite of, and can cancel, earth energy. This element's symbol/sigil is a vata.

Alak (ah-LUCK): The indigenous, shapeshifting peoples of Alaska, who are further denoted by tribe. Most have dark hair and eyes.

Alak'shin katmodit dis'Alak: "Honor others to earn honor in return" in Denaali.

Alaska: The country in which Kiera and Alex are transported. Geographically very similar to the 49th U.S. state, but the resemblances end there.

Alex: Kiera's nephew. Son of Julia, Kiera's deceased sister, and Hunter Daniels. Has dark brown hair and eyes. Age 6 in *Fallen Embers*.

Aliyah (Allie): Skani. Daughter of Lord Vriksha, Governor of Barrow. About 15. Blonde hair, blue eyes. *Awyr*.

Amba: Alak farming slave who lives in Fairbanks. Has dark brown hair and eyes.

Anchorage: A city/deconn in southern Alaska. Ruler is unknown.

Asana: Governor of Bethel.

Awyr (**AY-weer**): A Skani who was born under different, but complimentary, sunsigns and moonsigns. These mages can manipulate, and sometimes summon, one or two elements weakly. Not ennobled, but not enslaved, this very large group functions as a middle class of Skani. *Awyr* make up approximately thirty percent of the Skani. *See also* **sunsign** *and* **moonsign**.

Barrow: A city/deconn in northern Alaska. Ruled by Lord Vrishka, a water *sunwyr*.

Bethel: A city/deconn in western Alaska. Ruled by Lord Asana.

Call: Part one of a spell in which a mage sends out her sight, locates and then summons an element into herself.

Captain: The leader of a deconn's army. Always a slave, but this person holds more authority than mayors and answers only to the governor.

Cardinal marks: The hours in which elements flow most heavily and with the most force. Plusses: Mages can do very strong workings. Minuses: Can overwhelm user. Cardinal marks are: 12–1 A.M./P.M. (fire); 1–2 A.M./P.M. (earth); 2–3 A.M./P.M. (air); and 3–4 A.M./P.M. (water).

Chanda, Lord: Skani. Nephew of Lord Vayu and Lady Leith. Has dark hair and blue eyes. Air *sunwyr*.

Cycle: One complete solar year.

Dagna: Skani slave woman who works as a farmer and lives in Fairbanks. Has brown hair and blue eyes. *Nuwyr*.

Deconn (DEH-conn): The governed area surrounding one of four cities in Alaska, including Anchorage, Barrow, Bethel, and Fairbanks. A deconn's area extends approximately fifty miles in any direction from its city's center. Each deconn is ruled by a governor.

Denaa (de-NAH): "Big bear;" one of the Alak tribes in which the members can shapeshift into Kodiak bears. Laszlo is a member. Denaali tribal lands are located on an island in the southern Alaska nadeconn.

Earth: One of the four elements. Originates from all living things on the planet. Travels in very small streams, and mages must expend extra energy to pull it, although Alaks apparently do not. It is heavy and thick, and appears green. It is the opposite of, and can cancel, air energy. This element's symbol/sigil is a yar.

Element: One of the four types of energy that form the building blocks of everything in existence. They include air, water, earth and fire.

Emmy: Skani slave woman who works as Kiera's maid and Alex's nanny and lives in Fairbanks. Has dirty blonde hair and blue eyes. *Nuwyr.*

Fairbanks: A city/deconn in eastern Alaska. Ruled by Lord Vayu, an air *sunwyr.*

Fire: One of the four elements, fire originates from the sun and the stars. It travels in varying-sized streams and does not take energy to pull. It feels like a smooth jolt of electricity when touched with a mage's sight. Fire is the opposite of, and can cancel, water energy. This element's symbol/sigil is a xan.

Fixed marks: The hours in which the elements are the most balanced. They flow strongly, but not aggressively, and their flows are reliable. Plusses: Very stable magic. Not fancy, but reliable. During these marks, elements seem to seek stability and are more forgiving of mistakes. Minuses: Few. Fixed marks are: 4–5 A.M./P.M. (fire); 5–6 A.M./P.M. (earth); 6–7 A.M./P.M. (air); and 7–8 A.M./P.M. (water).

Gethor: Skani man who lives in Fairbanks. Friend of Valen. Has brown hair and blue eyes. Air *awyr.*

Governor: The ultimate ruler of a deconn, similar to a king or emperor. The governor owns all of the property, including slaves, in a deconn.

Helfarch (HEL-fark): *Sunwyr* Skani who have learned to use their magic to do very great workings. Very rare.

Hunter Daniels: Father of Alex, husband of (deceased) Julia, and brother-in-law to Kiera. Has brown hair and green eyes.

Hyhi eeido: "Beautiful, brave woman" in Denaali.

Julia: Deceased mother of Alex, sister of Kiera and wife of Hunter.

Kelktok: The fish camp/village in eastern Alaska where Kiera and Alex first landed.

Kiera: A woman who is transported to Alaska and learns that here she is a fire *sunwyr*. Has dark brown hair and eyes. Aunt of Alex, sister to Julia and sister-in-law to Hunter.

Kuruk of the Tungak: An otuk in the Fairbanks army, a Tungak shifter, and Kiera's personal bodyguard.

Laszlo of the Denaa: Alak slave captain of Lord Vayu's army. A huge, near-giant of a man with dark brown hair and eyes.

Laws, the two: (1) "All is power." Everything is made and operates by use of four types of power/energy, called elements, and elements are always flowing. Elements move and change because of the positions of the stars. (2) "Vessels of glass." Bodies are weak, so mages must not pull elements into themselves without having a reliable method by which they can deflect or send them back out.

Leith, Lady: Skani. Lord Vayu's—the governor of Fairbanks'—wife, mother of Valen and Marco. Has blonde hair and blue eyes. *Sunwyr*, but of which element is unknown.

Lorgda: Skani slave man who works as a farmer in the summer and lives in Fairbanks. Has blond hair and blue eyes. *Nuwyr*.

Manifest: Part three of a spell in which a mage causes an element to appear in the normal world in a certain, predesigned manner.

Marco: Skani. Lord Vayu's youngest son. Age 16 in *Fallen Embers*. Has blond hair and blue eyes. Air *sunwyr*.

Mark: One full hour.

Mayor: A subruler of a deconn. A mayor is allowed to own both property and slaves, although he must answer to the governor.

Mek: The sigil/symbol for the element of water. When written it resembles a point-side down triangle and is associated with the color blue.

Moon: One full month.

Moonsign: The word that denotes one of twenty-four periods of time during each day when the stars are in a particular alignment (but note that they are not otherwise named). Moonsigns are grouped into one of four categories by the element that dominates during the time they mark, including air, earth, fire and water. The first sign is fire, which commences at midnight. The second is earth. The third is air and the fourth is water. The fifth is fire, the sixth is earth, and so on. A mage's proclivity for magic is determined in part by the moonsign under which he or she is born. The other half of their magical ability is determined by their sunsign. If the two match—e.g., air sunsign and moonsign—the person will become a *sunwyr*. If the two compliment (fire and air or earth and water), the person will become an *awyr*. But if a person is born under opposite signs (fire and water or earth and air), the person will become a *nuwyr*.

Mosha: Skani. Slave member of the Fairbanks army. Has dirty blond hair and blue eyes. *Nuwyr*.

Mutable marks: The hours in which the elements are the most changeable and their flows fluctuate. Weakest magic, but flows fastest. Plusses: Easiest to blend elements with others. Minuses: Can produce weak, unreliable spells. Mutable marks are: 8–9 A.M./P.M. (fire); 9–10 A.M./P.M. (earth); 10–11 A.M./P.M. (air); and 11–12 A.M./P.M. (water).

Muukwa of the Denaa: A nadeconn (never enslaved) Denaa shifter, and Laszlo's cousin.

Nadeconn (NAH-deh-conn): The unincorporated area outside the deconns, which makes up most of the country. Peopled almost entirely by Alaks.

Naga: Skani. Lord Valen's paramour. Has strawberry blonde hair and blue eyes. *Awyr*.

Nakeetna: The abandoned city in eastern Alaska where Kiera first found Marco and Allie.

Nexturn: Tomorrow.

Nickinum (Nick), Mayor: Skani mayor of Talium, a Fairbanks possession, and Lord Vayu's spymaster. Has dark hair and icy blue eyes. Water *awyr*.

Nighttide: Midnight.

Noontide: Noon.

Nuwyr **(NEW-weer):** Skani born without magical ability, or possessing only very weak abilities. *Nuwyr* make up approximately two-thirds of the Skani. Always enslaved, usually during childhood. *See also* **sunsign** *and* **moonsign**.

Otuk: A squad leader in a Skani deconn's army, whose authority lies just below the captain's.

Pull: To seek out and summon, as in an element.

Saman, Lord: Skani healer who lives in Fairbanks. Mage, but rank and element are unknown.

Sen'ikcha a'kala achubruk: "Do not touch my woman" in Denaali.

Shatru: A group of invading people who persecuted and drove the Skani out of their home country approximately one hundred years ago.

Shima's tit: An exclamation.

Shunakah (shuh-NUH-kuh): "Snow dogs;" one of the Alak tribes in which the members can shapeshift into large dogs that resemble African wild dogs in both looks and temperament. Shunakah tribal lands are located around Bethel, which is in the southwest Alaska nadeconn.

Sigil: An element's symbol. Many types, broken down by cardinal, fixed, mutable and by working, used to invoke an element's energy. The four primary sigils are yar (earth), xan (fire), vata (air), and mek (water).

Sight: The manifestation of a person's magical ability. Mages seek out elemental energy using their sight.

Skani: A group of people who immigrated to Alaska approximately a hundred years ago to escape persecution in their former homeland by a people called the Shatru. Most are light haired and blue-eyed and many are mages of varying degrees, but none can shapeshift.

Slave: A person who is stripped of their legal personhood to become the property of another, generally including the governor of a deconn. In Alaska, slaves include (kidnapped) Alaks and *nuwyr* Skani, who may work on farms, as fishers, hunters, in the church, or in the armies. Slaves cannot marry, own property, choose their employment, or bring claims against any other person for any reason.

Spell: A three-part magical undertaking in which a mage uses her sight to call (or summon) an element, spin it inside her, and manifest it someplace else. Also called a working.

Spin: Part two of a spell. A mage first sends out his sight and summons an element to him, then pulls it into his physical body, where he shapes it inside his magical boundaries (called "spinning"), and finally he sends it out to the "real" world (called "manifesting").

Strand: The smallest unit of elemental energy that a mage can use, it resembles a piece of thread or string when a mage examines it with her sight. Each element flows in this manner, sometimes singularly and sometimes with many other strands of the same element. Different elements flow differently, in different places, and exhibit different properties.

Sunsign: The word that denotes one of twelve month-long periods of time during each year when the stars are in a particular alignment (but note that they are not otherwise named). Sunsigns are grouped into one of four categories by element that dominates during the time they mark, including air, earth, fire and water. The first sign is earth, which commences at winter solstice. The second is air. The third is water and the fourth is fire. The fifth is earth, sixth is air, and so on. A mage's proclivity for magic is determined in part by the sunsign under which he or she is born. The other half of their magical ability is determined by their moonsign. If the two match, e.g., air sunsign and moonsign, the person will become a *sunwyr*. If the two compliment (fire and air or earth and water), the person will become an *awyr*. But if a person is born under opposite signs (fire and water or earth and air), the person will become a *nuwyr*.

Sunwyr (**SUN-weer**): A Skani mage born under the same sunsign and moonsign. These most powerful mages can summon and manipulate their element, and often one to two other elements as well. Cannot usually sense their element's opposite, much less summon it. These rare mages are ennobled and constitute the ruling class of Skani. See also sunsign and moonsign.

Symbol: A drawn sigil, generally used to display under what element a mage is born (and often used to decorate). In Fairbanks, the Skani child's symbol is tattooed or branded inside the left wrist three days after birth.

Talium: Protectorate of Fairbanks, located inside the Fairbanks deconn. Mayor is Nickinum.

Thesin: Skani man who lives in Fairbanks, and Valen's friend. Has blond hair and blue eyes. Air *awyr*.

Thisturn: Today.

Tikaani (teh-KAH-nee): One of the Alak tribes in which the members can shapeshift into grey wolves. Many Fairbanks slaves are members. Tikaani tribal lands are located in the eastern Alaska nadeconn.

Tribe: The Alaks, or indigenous, shapeshifting peoples of Alaska, each belong to a group of shapeshifters called a tribe who all shift into the same animal. The known Alak tribes are Denaa (brown bear), Tikaani (wolf), and Shunakah (snow dog). There are others as well, including Nanuk (polar bear),Cha'ak (eagle), Aivik (sea lion), Yeil (raven), Tungak (black bear), Aabluk (orca whale), Kaviak (coyote), Gakut (lynx), and Kidjuk (goshawk).

Turn: One full day.

Valen, Lord: Skani. Oldest son of Lord Vayu and Lady Leith, and brother of Marco. Has white hair and blue eyes. Air *sunwyr*.

Vata: The sigil/symbol for the element of air. When written it resembles a point-side up triangle bisected by a horizontal line and is associated with the color yellow.

Vayu, Lord: Skani governor of Fairbanks. Has white hair and blue eyes. Married to Lady Leith. Air *sunwyr*.

Vriksha, Lord: Skani governor of Barrow. Water *sunwyr*.

Water: One of the four elements. Originates from the great bodies of water both above and under the ground. Travels in large streams, largely underground, and takes extra energy to pull. Water is temperature sensitive and feels soft and metallic when touched by a mage's sight. The opposite of, and can cancel, fire energy. This element's symbol/sigil is a mek.

Working: Another word for spell.

Xan: The sigil/symbol for the element of fire. When written it resembles a point-side up triangle and is associated with the color red.

Yar: The sigil/symbol for the element of earth. When written it resembles a square and is associated with the color green.

Yesturn: Yesterday.

ABOUT THE AUTHOR

L AURI OWEN IS A CIVIL RIGHTS LAWYER who grew up in Idaho's Treasure Valley. She started reading fantasy novels in the third grade, and
other than taking time out to sleep, never really stopped. The oldest
child of a homemaker and police officer, Lauri worked for more than a decade in law enforcement. But Lauri's not-so-secret passion is social justice,
and so in 2002 she decided to become a lawyer.

After completing U.C. Berkeley's law school Lauri moved to the Alaska
Bush, where she fell in love with the magic and majesty that exemplifies her
new home state. She was selected in 2006 for inclusion in the Who's Who
of American Women directory in part for her commitment to civil rights,
and she now lives in metro Alaska with her elementary school-aged son and
her many rescued cat companions.

ABOUT PEARLSONG PRESS

PEARLSONG PRESS IS AN INDEPENDENT publishing company dedicated to providing books and resources that entertain while expanding perspectives on the self and the world. The company was founded by Peggy Elam, Ph.D., a psychologist and journalist, in 2003.

Pearls are formed when a piece of sand or grit or other abrasive, annoying, or even dangerous substance enters an oyster and triggers its protective response. The substance is coated with shimmering opalescent nacre ("mother of pearl"), the coats eventually building up to produce a beautiful gem. The self-healing response of the oyster thus transforms suffering into a thing of beauty.

The pearl-creating process reflects our company's desire to move outside a pathological or "disease" based model of life, health and well-being into a more integrative and transcendent perspective. A move out of suffering into joy. And that, we think, is something to sing about.

PEARLSONG PRESS ENDORSES Health At Every Size, an approach to health and well-being that celebrates natural diversity in body size and encourages people to stop focusing on weight (or any external measurement) in favor of listening to and respecting natural appetites for food, drink, sleep, rest, movement, and recreation. While not every book we publish specifically promotes Health At Every Size (by, for instance, featuring fat heroines or educating readers on size acceptance), none of our books or other resources will contradict this holistic and body-positive perspective.

We encourage you to enjoy other Pearlsong Press books, which you can purchase at www.pearlsong.com or your favorite bookstore. Keep up with us through our blog at www.pearlsongpress.com.

FICTION:

The Season of Lost Children—a novel by Karen Blomain
The Fat Lady Sings—a young adult novel by Charlie Lovett
Syd Arthur—a novel by Ellen Frankel

Bride of the Living Dead—romantic comedy by Lynne Murray
Measure By Measure—a romantic romp with the fabulously fat by Rebecca
    Fox & William Sherman
FatLand—a visionary novel by Frannie Zellman
The Program—a suspense novel by Charlie Lovett
The Singing of Swans—a novel about the Divine Feminine
    by Mary Saracino

Romance novels and Short Stories Featuring
Big Beautiful Heroines:
    by Pat Ballard, the Queen of Rubenesque Romances:
            Dangerous Love | *The Best Man* | *Abigail's Revenge*
        Dangerous Curves Ahead: Short Stories | *Wanted: One Groom*
            Nobody's Perfect | *His Brother's Child* | *A Worthy Heir*
    by Rebecca Brock—*The Giving Season*
    & by Judy Bagshaw—*At Long Last, Love: A Collection*

Nonfiction:

Fat Poets Speak: Voices of the Fat Poets' Society—edited by Frannie Zellman
Ten Steps to Loving Your Body (No Matter What Size You Are) by Pat Ballard
Beyond Measure: A Memoir About Short Stature & Inner Growth by Ellen
    Frankel
Taking Up Space: How Eating Well & Exercising Regularly Changed My Life
    by Pattie Thomas, Ph.D. with Carl Wilkerson, M.B.A. (foreword by
    Paul Campos, author of The Obesity Myth)
*Off Kilter: A Woman's Journey to Peace with Scoliosis, Her Mother & Her
    Polish Heritage*—a memoir by Linda C. Wisniewski
Unconventional Means: The Dream Down Under—a spiritual travelogue by
    Anne Richardson Williams
Splendid Seniors: Great Lives, Great Deeds—inspirational biographies by
    Jack Adler